SONG OF SILVER, FLAME LIKE NIGHT

银曲夜焰

Also by Amélie Wen Zhao

Praise for *Song of Silver, Flame Like Night*

'Lyrical and richly imagined, *Song of Silver, Flame Like Night* brims with pure magic. Zhao has woven together a story of self-discovery, slow-burning romance, and heart-pounding revelations. I was swept away from the first page!'
Rebecca Ross, #1 *Sunday Times* and #1 *New York Times* bestselling author of *Divine Rivals*

'Devastatingly gorgeous. From the bustling, conquered port city to the mysterious school waiting in the mountains, each page of *Song of Silver, Flame Like Night* unfolds with a deliberate, skilled hand. Amélie Wen Zhao writes with a direct line to my heart'
Chloe Gong, #1 *New York Times* bestselling author of *These Violent Delights*

'A captivating epic fantasy set in a rich world steeped in culture and legend, filled with intricate magic and unforgettable characters, woven into the gripping plot. I can't wait for the sequel!'
Sue Lynn Tan, *Sunday Times* bestselling author of *Daughter of the Moon Goddess*

'Zhao serves the action, stunning visuals, and philosophical underpinnings of the xianxia genre in high style. Perfect for fans of *The Untamed*. I loved it!'
Shelley Parker-Chan, #1 *Sunday Times* bestselling author of *She Who Became the Sun*

'A thrilling quest, a wild and wondrous magic system, twists and turns aplenty—but the true jewel in *Song of Silver, Flame Like Night* is how Zhao expertly handles the heart-wrenching impact of generational inheritance. Prepare to stay up all night!'
Sara Raasch, *New York Times* bestselling author of the Snow Like Ashes series

AMÉLIE WEN ZHAO

SONG OF SILVER, FLAME LIKE NIGHT

银曲夜焰

HARPER

Voyager

HarperVoyager an imprint of
HarperCollinsPublishers Ltd
1 London Bridge Street
London SE1 9GF

www.harpercollins.co.uk

HarperCollinsPublishers
Macken House,
39/40 Mayor Street Upper,
Dublin 1
D01 C9W8
Ireland

First published by HarperCollinsPublishers Ltd 2023
This paperback edition published in 2024
2

献给爸爸妈妈，姥姥姥爷，爷爷奶奶

To my parents, my grandparents, and theirs

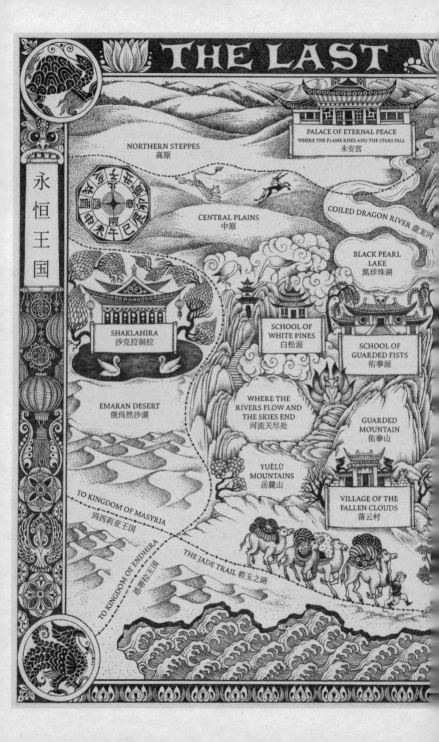

CHRONOLOGY

Warring Clans Era
~500 CYCLES

The Ninety-Nine Clans fight one another to defend their lands. Several dominant clans survive (most notably the Mansorian clan of the Northern Steppes and the Sòng clan of the Southern Valleys) to become powerful hegemons that take on other clans as vassals.

First Kingdom
CYCLE 0 — 591

The hegemon clans establish powerful courts, their rulers taking on the title of "king" in an attempt to consolidate power. Territorial disputes arise, yet the hegemon clans remain in a gridlock for most of this era.

Near the end of this era, General Zhào Jùng of the powerful Central Hin Kingdom begins a war to absorb the other hegemons into what he envisions as a single, standardized kingdom of Hin. The Mansorian clan—along with its vassals—puts up a fierce fight but takes heavy losses. The Sòng clan surrenders, and members become advisors to the Emperor. General Zhào becomes the First Emperor Jīn.

Middle Kingdom

CYCLE 591 — 1344

The unification of the once-fragmented hegemon clans ushers in an era of stability, in which the First Emperor Jīn and his ancestors implement policies to instigate the economic development of the newly formed Middle Kingdom. Most notably, they outline the Way of Practitioning to standardize all practitioning activity within the Middle Kingdom and as a way to limit the power of the conquered clans. Throughout this era, skirmishes and uprisings by rebel clans are swiftly quelled by the Imperial Army.

At the end of this era, Emperor Yán'lóng—the Dragon Emperor—grows paranoid about a potential Mansorian uprising. He believes that Emperor Jīn's policy of allowing the Ninety-Nine Clans to retain their own lands, cultures, and identities ensures there will be rebellion. Weak, greedy, and afraid of a decline of power, he binds the Crimson Phoenix, the Demon God that has lain dormant in his family's control, and begins his military campaign of the Ninety-Nine Heads Massacre.

The Mansorian general Xan Tolürigin, aligned with the Demon God the Black Tortoise of the North, leads the counterattack and is joined by former clan allies. They lose, and in a fit of rage, Xan Tolürigin flees north, destroying Hin cities and massacring civilians along the way. To this day, it is unclear where his spirit rests—or whether it rests at all.

Last Kingdom

CYCLE 1344 — 1424

The Ninety-Nine Clans are almost eradicated or dispersed and forced to assimilate into the Hin identity. The Last Kingdom survives for only eighty cycles. Then, on the thirty-second cycle of the Qīng Dynasty under the rule of the Luminous Dragon Emperor, Shuò'lóng, the Elantians invade.

Elantian Age

YEAR 1 (CYCLE 1424) — PRESENT DAY

Power is always borrowed, never created.

— Dào'zǐ, *Book of the Way*
(Classic of Virtues), 1.1

Elantian Age, Cycle 12
The Black Port, Haak'gong

The Last Kingdom had been brought to its knees, but the view was mighty fine from here.

Lan tipped her bamboo hat over her head, parting her lips in pleasure as the cool evening breeze combed through strands of her silky black hair. Sweat slicked her neck from the afternoon's work of hawking wares at the local evemarket, and her back ached with the beating she'd received from Madam Meng for stealing sugarplum candies from the kitchens at the Teahouse. But in rare moments like this, when the sun hung ripe and swollen as a mandarin over the glittering sea, there was still a shattered-glass beauty to be found in the remnants of a conquered land.

The city of Haak'gong unfurled before her in a patchwork of contradictions. Red lanterns were strung from curved temple eave to gray-shingled rooftop, weaving and wending between pagodas and courtyards wreathed in the halo of night bazaars and evening fairs. On the distant hills, the Elantians had settled on higher ground, building their strange architecture of stone, glass, and metal to watch over the Hin like gods. The skyline glowed a dusky auric from their alchemical lamplight that spilled through stained-glass windows and arched marble doorways.

Lan rolled her eyes and turned away. She knew the story of the gods—any gods—to be a big, steaming bowl of turd. Much as the Elantians wished to pretend otherwise, Lan knew they had come to the Last Kingdom for one thing: resources. Ships full of powdered spices and golden grains and verdant tea leaves, chests of silks and samites, jades and porcelains, left Haak'gong for the Elantian Empire, across the Sea of Heavenly Radiance, each day.

And whatever was left over trickled into the black markets of Haak'gong.

At this bell, the evemarket was in full bloom, merchants having filed in along the Jade Trail with jewels that gleamed like the light of the sun, spices tasting of lands Lan had never seen before, and fabrics that shimmered like the night sky itself. Haak'gong's heartbeat was the clink of coin, its lifeblood the flow of trade, its bones the wooden stalls of marketplaces. It was a place of survival.

Lan paused at the very end of the market. She took care to lower her dǒu'lì—her bamboo hat—over her face lest any Elantian officials prowled nearby. What she was about to do could very well earn her a spot on the gallows, along with other Hin who had broken Elantian laws.

With a surreptitious glance around, she crossed the street and made for the slums.

This was where the illusion of the Last Kingdom ended and the reality of a conquered land began. Here the cobblestone streets carefully constructed by the Elantians after the Conquest faded to dust; the elegantly renovated facades and shiny glass windows gave way to buildings crumbling from disrepair.

The trading house sat in a derelict corner, its cheap wooden doors chipped and faded with time, paper windows patched with grease yet sagging with the humidity of the south. A wooden bell tinkled somewhere overhead as Lan stepped inside.

She shut the doors, and the hubbub of the outside world fell silent.

The interior was dim, dust motes swirling in the late-afternoon sunlight that spilled onto cracked floorboards and shelves crammed with an assortment of scrolls, tomes, and trinkets. The entire shop looked like an old painting left to fade in the sun, smelling of ink and damp wood.

But this was Lan's favorite place in the world. It reminded her of a time long past, a world long gone.

A life wiped from the pages of the history books.

Old Wei's Pawn Shop dealt in odds and ends of goods left over from the evemarket after the Elantians had their pick, purchased by the shopkeeper at wholesale and sold to Hin buyers at a thin margin. The shop escaped the notice of government inspectors, for secondhand goods held no interest to the colonizers as long as they weren't made of metal.

This was why the shop had also become a hub for contraband. The wares Old Wei had on display were innocuous enough: reels of wool, hemp, and cotton, jars of star anise and bay leaves, scrolls of cheap paper made from pounded dried bark. But hidden somewhere inside the shop, Lan knew, was something for her.

Something that could cost her life.

"Old Wei," she called. "I got your message."

Silence for a moment, and then: "Thought I heard your silver-bells voice. Come to bring me mischief again?"

The old shopkeeper announced himself in a shuffle of feet and a hacking cough. Old Wei had once been a teacher in a northeastern coastal village, before his family was killed and he'd lost everything in the Elantian Conquest twelve cycles ago. He'd fled to Haak'gong and used his literacy to pivot into the trading business. Constant hunger had whittled him to a stick, and the damp air of Haak'gong had afflicted him with a permanent cough. That was the extent of what Lan knew of his life—not even his truename, banned under Elantian law and reduced to a monotonous single syllable.

Lan gave him her sweetest smile from beneath her dǒu'lì. "Mischief?" she repeated, matching his northern dialect, the tones harsher and rolling compared to the sweet, singsong southern tones she'd become used to. It was a rarity to speak either these days. "When have I ever brought you mischief, Old Wei?"

He grunted, casting her an appraising look. "Never brought me fortune either. And I still let you come back each time."

She poked her tongue out. "Must be my charm."

"Hah," he said, the word cracking through a thick layer of phlegm. "Any gods watching would know what lies beneath that charm."

"There are no gods watching."

It was a point she often liked to debate with Old Wei, who was a stout worshiper of the Hin's pantheon of gods—in particular, his favorite, the God of Riches. Old Wei liked to tell Lan he'd devoutly prayed to the God of Riches in his childhood. Lan liked to remind him that the God of Riches must have a twisted sense of humor to have rewarded him with a rundown contraband shop.

"There are," Old Wei replied. Lan raised her eyes heavenward and mouthed the words along with him—words she had heard a hundred times: "There are old gods and new gods, kind gods and fickle gods—and most powerful of them all are the Four Demon Gods."

Lan preferred not to believe that her fortunes lay in the hands of some invisible old farts in the skies—no matter how powerful they were meant to be. "Whatever you say, Old Wei," she replied, leaning over the counter and cupping her chin in her hands.

The old shopkeeper wheezed a few times, then asked, "Evemarket again? What, is the Teahouse not feeding you enough?"

They both knew the answer to that: Madam Meng ran the Teahouse like a glass menagerie, and her songgirls were her finest display. She fed them just enough to keep them dewy and ripe for the picking, but never enough so that their bellies grew full—gods forbid they become lazy or fat.

"I like it here," Lan said, and she did. Out here, hawking alongside other vendors and pocketing the coin she made into her *own* pockets, was where she felt some semblance of control over her life—a taste of freedom and free will, if only temporary. "Besides," she added sweetly, "I get to drop by to see you."

He cast her a shrewd look, then *tsk*ed and wagged a finger. "Don't try your honeyed words on me, yā'tou," he said, and bent to the cabinets beneath his counter.

Yā'tou. Girl. It was what he'd called her since he'd found her, a scrap of an orphan begging on the streets of Haak'gong. He'd taken her to the only place he'd known that would welcome a girl with no name and no reputation: Madam Meng's Teahouse. She'd signed a contract whose terms she'd barely been able to decipher, and whose length only seemed to swell and swell the harder she worked.

But at the end of the day, he'd saved her life. Gotten her a job, put a stable roof over her head. It was more kindness than one could ask for in these times.

She grinned at the sour old man. "I would never."

Old Wei's grunt turned into a bout of coughing, and Lan's smile slipped. The winters down in the south had none of the biting cold that she'd grown up with in the northeast. Instead, it encroached with a damp chill that sank into bones and joints and lungs and festered there.

She took in the state of the battered old shop, the shelves that stood fuller than usual. Tonight, on the eve of the big festivities for the Twelfth Cycle of the Elantian Conquest, security had been tightened around Haak'gong, and the first thing people tended to avoid in those circumstances was a shop trading in illicit goods. Lan couldn't afford to dally either: soon the streets would be crawling with Elantian patrols, and a lone songgirl in their midst was an invitation to trouble.

"Lungs acting up again, Old Wei?" she asked, running a finger over a small stained-glass dragon figurine on the counter—likely a prized trade from one of the Jade Trail nations across the great Emaran Desert. The Hin had not known glass until the era of the Middle Kingdom, under which Emperor Jīn—the Golden Emperor—established formal trade routes reaching all the way west to the fabled deserts of Masyria.

"Ah, yeah," the shopkeeper said with a wince. From the folds of his sleeve, he drew what must once have been a fine silken handkerchief and patted his mouth with it. The cloth was sodden and graying with grime. "Ginseng prices have shot up since the Elantian farts learned of its healing properties. But I've lived with these old bones all my life, and they haven't killed me yet. Nothing to worry about."

Lan drummed her fingers on the wooden counter, polished with the comings and goings of so many others before her. Here was the trick to surviving in a colonized land: you couldn't show that you cared. Every Hin you came across would have his share of sob stories: family slaughtered in the

Conquest, home pillaged and plundered, or worse. To care was to allow a chink in the armor of survival.

So Lan asked the question that had been brewing in her chest all day. "Well, what do you have for me?"

Old Wei gifted her a gap-toothed smile and bent beneath his counter. Lan's pulse began to race; instinctively she pressed fingers to the inside of her left wrist.

There, imprinted into flesh and sinew and blood, was a scar that only she could see: a perfect circle encompassing a character in the shape of a Hin word that she could not read, sweeping strokes blooming like an elegantly balanced flower—blossom, leaves, and stem.

Eighteen cycles she'd lived, and she had spent twelve of those searching for this character—the only clue to her past that her mother had left her before her death. To this day, she could feel the searing heat of her mother's fingers on her arms, the hole in Māma's chest bleeding red even as the world erupted in blinding white. The expensive lacquerwood furniture of their study darkened with blood, the air filled with the bitter scent of burnt metal . . . and something else. Something ancient; something impossible.

"Now, I think you'll like this one."

She blinked, the images dissipating as Old Wei emerged from the dusty shelves and placed a scroll on the counter between them. Lan held her breath as he unfurled it.

It was a worn piece of parchment, but even with one look, she could tell that it was different: the surface was smooth, unlike the cheap papers made of hemp or rags or fishnet common these days. This was true parchment—vellum, perhaps—singed black in the corners and smudged with age. She'd known the feel of it intimately, once a world ago.

Between the wear and tear, Lan could make out faded

traces of opulence. Her eyes raked over the sketches of the Four Demon Gods in the corners of the page, barely visible but present nevertheless: dragon, phoenix, tiger, and tortoise, all facing the center of the scroll, frozen in time. Swirls of painted clouds adorned the top and bottom margins. And then . . . *there,* in the very center, ensconced within a near-perfect circle: a single character, blooming with the delicate balance of a Hin character, yet with nothing recognizable. Her heart jumped into her throat as she leaned over it, barely breathing.

"I thought you'd be excited," Old Wei said. He watched her carefully, eyes glinting with the prospect of a sale. "Wait till you hear where I got it."

She barely heard him. Her pulse thundered in her ears as she traced the strokes of the character, following every line and comparing it to the character she'd memorized well enough to know in her dreams.

Her excitement faltered as her finger stuttered over a stroke. No . . . *no.* A line cut too short, a dot missing, a diagonal slightly off . . . Minute differences, but all the same—

Wrong.

She slumped, letting out a sigh. Sloppily, she rotated her wrist, finger tracing a loose circle to finish up the character.

That was when it happened.

The air in the shop shifted, and she felt as though something *inside her* had snapped into place—an invisible current that rushed from her fingertips into the shop. Like a static shock in winter.

It was gone in half a second, so quickly that she must have imagined it. When she blinked again, Old Wei was still watching her with pursed lips. "Well?" he asked eagerly, leaning forward over the counter.

He hadn't felt it, then. Lan touched the tip of her fingers to her temples. It hadn't been anything—a momentary lapse in focus, a trick of the nerves, brought on by hunger and exhaustion. "It's a bit different," she replied, ignoring the familiar disappointment that curdled in her stomach.

It had been so close . . . and yet it *wasn't*.

"Not what you're looking for, then," Old Wei said, clearing his throat, "but I think it's a start. See here—the syllabary seems to be composed in the same style as yours, with those curves and dashes . . . but the circle outside is really what caught my attention." He tapped two calloused fingers to the page. "Everything we've seen with a circle around the character has been there only for decoration. But see how these strokes bleed into the circle? They were written in a conjoined line—a clear beginning and end."

She let him drone on, but really, her mind reeled with a crumbling realization: that she might never understand what had happened the day her mother died and the Last Kingdom fell. That she might never know how it was possible that her mother had reached up, fingers trembling and slicked with red, and, with her bare skin, *burned* something into Lan's wrist. Something that had remained after all these cycles in the form of a mark visible only to Lan.

A memory that existed between dream and imagination— the faintest spark of hope for what *shouldn't* be possible.

". . . hear anything I just said?"

Lan blinked, the past swirling away like smoke.

Old Wei was giving her the stink eye. "I was *saying*," he said with the peevishness of a teacher who'd been ignored by his pupil, "that this came from an old temple bookhouse and was rumored to have originated at one of the Hundred Schools of Practitioning themselves. I do know that the practitioners of old wrote in a different type of script."

Her breath caught at the word. *Practitioner.*

Lan curved her lips into a smile and slid forward, propping

herself on one elbow on the counter. "I'm sure the practitioners wrote these, alongside the yāo'mó'guǐ'guài they bargained their souls to," she said, and Old Wei's face dropped.

" 'Speak of the demon and the demon comes!' " he hissed, glancing around as though one might jump out from behind his cabinet of dried goji berries. "Do not curse my shop with such portentous sayings!"

Lan rolled her eyes. In the villages where Old Wei was from, superstitions ran deeper than in the cities. Stories of ghouls haunting villages in forests of pine and bamboo, of demons eating the souls of babies in the night.

Such things might have sent shivers up Lan's spine once, given her second thoughts about walking in the shadows. But now she knew there were worse things to fear.

"It's all just folklore, Old Wei," she said.

Old Wei leaned forward, close enough that she could see the tea stains on his teeth. "The Dragon Emperor might have banned such topics when he founded the Last Kingdom, but I remember the tales from my grandfather's grandfathers. I have heard the stories of ancient orders of practitioners cultivating magic and martial arts, walking the rivers and lakes of the First and Middle Kingdoms, fighting evil and bringing justice to the world. Even when the emperors of the Middle Kingdom attempted to control practitioning, they couldn't hide the traces of evidence across our lands. Tomes written in characters that are indecipherable, temples and secret troves of treasures and artifacts with properties inexplicable—practitioning magic has always been ingrained in our history, yā'tou."

Old Wei was one of those ardent believers in the myths of folk heroes—practitioners—who had once walked on water and flown over mountains, wielding magic and slaying demons. And perhaps they once had—long, long ago.

"Then where are they now? Why haven't they come to save

us from . . . *this*?" Lan gestured at the door, at the dilapidated streets. At the old man's hesitation, her lips twisted. "Even if they did once exist, it was probably centuries and dynasties ago. Whatever folk heroes and practitioners of old you believe in are dead." Her voice softened. "There are no heroes left for us in this world, Old Wei."

Her friend gave her a penetrating look. "Is that what you *truly* believe?" he said. "Then tell me, why is it that you make your weekly visits down here, searching for a strange character on a scar only *you* can see?"

His words cut like a blade to Lan's heart, pinning the smallest flicker of a spark she hadn't dared utter—had never dared utter: that, in spite of all she told herself, what she had witnessed on the day of her mother's death . . . had been something like magic.

And the scar on her wrist held the clue—the only clue—to the truth of that day.

"Because it lets me hope that there's something else for me out there. Something other than this life." The dust motes before her swirled, stained red and orange by the setting sun, like the dying embers of a fire. Lan set her hand over the slip of parchment. Perhaps there was something to be learned in the inscrutable strokes of that character. It was the closest she'd gotten in the past twelve cycles, after all.

"I'll take it," she said. "I'll take the scroll."

The old shopkeeper blinked, clearly surprised at this development. "Ah." He tapped the scroll. "You be careful, eh, yā'tou? I've heard too many a tale of marks created by dark, demonic energies. Whatever's on your wrist inside that scar . . . well, let's just hope it was left by someone with a noble cause."

"Superstitions," Lan repeated.

"All superstitions must come from somewhere," the shopkeeper said ominously, then crooked his fingers. "Now, let's see the payment. Nothing comes for free. Got rent to pay, food to buy."

She hesitated only briefly. Then Lan leaned over the counter, brushing aside a small sack of herbal powders Old Wei had been weighing, and placed a ragged hemp pouch on its surface. It landed with a clink.

Old Wei's hands darted out, pawing through its contents. His eyes widened as he drew something out.

"Ten Hells, yā'tou," he whispered, and drew his old paper lamp closer. In the light of the flames, a sleek silver spoon glistened.

The sight of it brought a stab of longing to her heart. It had been her prize find, accidentally thrown out with the broken dishes in the back alleys of the Teahouse. She'd been counting on selling it to buy off a moon or two from her contract at the Teahouse. The thing would clearly fetch a small fortune, for metal—any type of metal—was a relic of the past. One of the first things the Elantians did when they took over was to monopolize the supply of metal from all over the Last Kingdom. Gold, silver, copper, iron, tin—even a small silver spoon was a rarity these days. The Elantians had stopped short of seizing all the metalware in the Last Kingdom; Lan surmised that a few spoons and some coins and prized jewelry were hardly enough to build weapons of resistance for a revolution.

Lan knew where all the metal was going: to the Elantian magicians. It was said they channeled magic through metal. *That* Lan could believe. She had seen, with her own eyes, the terrifying power they held. They had brought down the Last Kingdom with nothing but their bare hands.

They had killed Māma without even touching her.

"I couldn't sell that spoon," Lan lied. "No one's taking anything metal these days, and it's more trouble than it's worth if an Elantian officer catches me. Not to mention Madam Meng'll have my skin if she finds out I stole it. Just use it to get some ginseng for those old lungs, will you? It chafes my ears to have to listen to you cough like that."

"Right," Old Wei said slowly, still peering at the silver spoon as though it were made of jade. The remainder of her proffered payment—a sack of ten copper coins she'd earned from her day of sales—lay untouched. "Possessing any metal can be dangerous these days . . . best leave it with me . . ." His gaze sharpened suddenly, and he broke into a toothy smile. He leaned over to her and whispered, "I think I'll have something *really* good for you next time. Source of mine's introduced a Hin courtdog to me, and he's in the market for—"

The shopkeeper stopped and drew in a sharp breath, his gaze darting behind her to the paper screens he'd thrown open to let in the cool evening breeze. "Angels," he hissed, switching to the Elantian tongue.

The word sent terror spiking through her veins. *Angels* was short for White Angels, the colloquialism that Elantian soldiers used to refer to themselves.

Lan spun around. There, framed in the fretwork of Old Wei's shop windows, she caught sight of something that made bile rise to her throat. A flash of silver, the gleam of a white-gold emblem with a crown and wings, armor colored in winter's ice—

No time to think. She had to move.

Lan cast Old Wei a frightened look, but something in the old shopkeeper's expression had steeled, his mouth pressed into a resolute line. He caught her hand as she reached for the scroll. "Leave it with me, yā'tou—don't let them catch you with something like this on the eve of the Twelfth Cycle. Come back for it when it's safer. Now go!" In the blink of an eye, the scroll and silver spoon had vanished.

She tipped her dǒu'lì low over her head just as the bell over the entrance rang, a toll now sharp with menace.

The air thickened. Shadows fell over the floor, long and dark.

Lan made for the door, glad for her rough hemp duàn'dǎ, a loose, cheap garment that concealed most of her figure. She'd worked long enough at the Teahouse to know what Elantians could do to Hin girls.

"Four Gods preserve you," she heard Old Wei mumble to her. It was an old Hin saying based on the belief that the Four Demon Gods would watch over their motherland and their people.

But Lan knew, with cutting clarity, that there were no gods in this world.

Only monsters in the form of men.

There were two of them, burly Elantian soldiers dressed in full armor, their steps clunking as they passed her. Instinctively, Lan's gaze darted to their wrists—and it was then that she loosed a breath. Bare wrists—no glint of metal cuffs wound so tightly that they seemed fused to their flesh, no hands that could summon fire and blood with a flick of pale fingers.

Just soldiers, then.

One of them paused as she passed him, the door just paces away, a sliver of cool evening air already brushing her face. Her heart lurched like a rabbit's beneath an eagle's gaze.

The Angel's hand darted out, fingers closing over her wrist.

And that seed of fear in her stomach bloomed.

"Say, Maximillian," the soldier called. With his other hand, he flicked up the rim of her dǒu'lì. Lan stared into his eyes, the youthful green of a summer's day, and wondered how a man could make a color look so cruel. His face might have been cut of the marble statues of the winged guardians the Elantians erected over their doors and in their churches: handsome, and utterly inhuman. "Didn't think I'd find such a *fine* specimen of flea in this kind of a place."

She'd learned the Elantian tongue—she'd had to, to work at the Teahouse—and it never failed to strike ice into her veins. Their words were long and rolling, so different from the sharp-cut, dragonfly-touch characters of Hin speech. The Elantians spoke with the slow, unhurried slur of a people drunk on power.

Lan held very still, not even daring to breathe.

"Leave the thing be, Donnaron," his companion called, already halfway to the counter, where Old Wei bent at the waist and bobbed his head with an obsequious smile. "We're on duty. You can have your fun when you're done."

Donnaron's gaze roved over Lan's face, down her neck, and lower, and she felt violated with that single look. She wanted to scratch out those youthful green eyes.

The Angel shot her a wide grin. "That's too bad. Don't you worry, my pretty little flower. I'm not letting you go so easily."

The pressure on her wrist increased slightly—like a promise, a *threat*—and then he released her.

Lan stumbled forward. She had one foot out the door, hands pressed against the handle, when she hesitated.

She looked back.

Old Wei's silhouette was small between the hulking Elantians, a shadow in the setting sun. His rheumy old eyes flicked up to her—just for a single moment—and she caught the tilt of his nearly imperceptible nod. *Go, yā'tou.*

Lan pushed through the door and ran. She didn't stop until she was well clear of the stone parapets that marked the entrance to the evemarket. Ahead stretched an expanse of darkness that was the Bay of Southern Winds, glittering crimson as it caught shards of fading sunlight in its waves. Here the winds were sharp and briny, rattling over the wooden jetties and whistling over the old stone walls of Haak'gong as though they wished to raise the land itself.

To be so free, and to be so powerful—what might that taste like? Perhaps one day she would know; perhaps one day she would be able to do more than gift an old, ailing man a slim silver spoon and run when danger knocked on the door.

She tilted her face to the skies and breathed, massaging the part of her wrist where the soldier had grabbed her, wishing to scrub the feeling of his fingers from her mind. Tonight was the winter solstice, marking the Twelfth Cycle of the Elantian Conquest; with the highest Elantian officials in the land gathering for the festivities, it made sense that the government had increased surveillance and patrols across the largest Hin cities. Haak'gong was the Southern Elantian Outpost, the jewel of trade and commerce of Elantian colonies, second only to the Heavenly Capital, Tiān'jīng—or, as it was now meant to be known, King Alessandertown.

The Twelfth Cycle, Lan thought. *Gods, has it been that long?*

If she closed her eyes, she could remember exactly how her world had ended.

Snow, falling like ashes.

Wind, sighing through bamboo.

And the song of a woodlute weaving to the skies.

She'd had a name, once. Her mother had given it to her. *Lián'ér,* meaning "lotus": the flower that bloomed from nothing but mud, a light in the darkest of times.

They'd taken that from her.

She'd had a home, once. A great courtyard house, green weeping willows sweeping stained-glass lakes, cherry blossom petals coating fanstone paths, verandas yawning to the lushness of life.

They'd taken that from her.

And she'd had a mother who loved her, who had taught

her stories and sonnets and songs, who had nurtured her calligraphy stroke by stroke across soft parchment pages, fingers twined around hers and hands wrapped around her entire world.

They had taken her mother, too.

The long, booming tolls of the dusk bells echoed in the distance, cutting through her memories. Her eyes flew open, and there it was again, the empty sea looming so lonely before her, echoing with all that she had lost. Once upon a time, she might have stood here, at the precipice of her world, and tried to make meaning of it all—how it had all gone so wrong, how she had ended up here with nothing but broken memories and a strange scar only she could see.

But as the bells' sonorous tolls continued to sound across the skies, reality washed over her. She was hungry, she was tired, and she was late for the evening's performance at the Teahouse.

The scroll *had* been promising, though. . . . She brushed a hand over her left wrist again, each stroke of the strange, indecipherable character burned indelibly into her mind.

Next time, she told herself, just as she had for the past eleven cycles. *Next time I'll find the message you left me, Māma.*

For now, though, Lan tipped her dǒu'lì over her head and dusted off her sleeves.

She had a Teahouse to return to.

She had a contract to pay off.

She had Elantians to serve.

In a conquered land, the only way to win was to survive.

Without another glance back, she turned to face the colorful streets of Haak'gong and began making her way up the hills.

2

In life, qì blazes and moves as yáng; in death,
qì cools and stills as yīn. A body with a restless
qì is indicative of a restless soul.

— Chó Yún, Imperial Spirit Summoner,
Classic of Death

The shop was in ruins, and the night air stung with the acrid
scent of metal magic.

Zen stood in the shadows of the dilapidated houses down
this alleyway of Haak'gong, wrestling with his shock at the
scale of destruction mere steps from him. Though it had been
neither unexpected nor uncommon throughout the earliest
cycles of conquest, he hadn't prepared for such a brash display of violence and dominance in the supposed crown jewel
of Elantian power. The reminder rang almost personal: that
the Elantians loved to make examples out of Hin traitors and
rebels, to send their message in blood and bones that there
was no hope, there was no point in resisting.

Zen had almost believed them.

He hesitated only a moment before removing his gloves.
The air was cool and crisp against his fingers, the flow of
wind and humidity brushing against his skin. He could sense
fire, too, in the candles that burned low in this district—the
people too poor to afford the alchemical light supplied by the

Elantians—and the ground, holding steady beneath his two feet. The metal and wood, in the housing structures along the street.

No other disturbances in the flow of energy—the qì—around him.

Zen straightened and stepped out onto the road. In three brisk strides, he was at the shop door, the frail frame of old, rotting wood smashed easily through. The dusk bells had just ceased their tolling, which meant that the Twelfth Cycle celebrations were to begin imminently. The highest-ranking officials of the Elantian government's southern stronghold would be gathered in the cushiest district of Haak'gong while foot soldiers prowled the streets.

Not that Zen had anything to fear from them; in his long black peacoat, flat cap, and those horrible patent leather dress boots, he was effectively disguised as a Hin merchant under Elantian employ.

The only government officials Zen needed to avoid were the magicians.

He glanced up and down the street and, seeing and sensing nothing, stepped inside the small store.

The place was drenched in blood. He sensed it as soon as the currents of qì enveloped him—water and metals constituting the makeup of blood, all tinted in yīn: the side of qì that represented cold, darkness, wrath, and death. The counter to yáng, comprising warmth, light, joy, and life.

Yīn and yáng: two halves of all qì, two sides of a coin constantly shifting, one into the other in a continuous cycle of balance. Warmth to cold, light to dark . . . and life to death.

It was when the balance was thrown off that there was a problem.

He picked his way across the wreckage: splinters of wood from overturned shelves, shreds of floorboards torn away to reveal patches of foundation beneath. He caught sight of objects amidst the ruin: a horsetail brush with the handle snapped, a dragon figurine split in half, a folding fan bent like a broken wing. Objects that had significance for the Hin, yet that the Elantians destroyed without a second thought.

Zen drew a deep, stilling breath and turned to the figure on the floor. He took in the sight of the corpse, limbs jutting at awkward angles, mouth parted in surprise or a helpless plea. The shopkeeper had been an elder: liver spots dotted his forehead, white hair gleamed in the moonlight. Zen could sense an unnatural wetness to the man's lungs—a disease, perhaps, as a result of the eternal damp of the southern atmosphere.

Pushing down the fury that roiled up to his chest, Zen cleared his mind and called on his master's teachings. *Calm the storm of your emotions. A restless ocean is not one to sail upon.* He needed to treat the body as naught more than evidence, a puzzle waiting to be pulled apart and put back together.

Old Wei, he thought, eyes taking in details of the dead man with clinical precision. *What happened?*

The shopkeeper was a contact Zen had procured after moons of searching. It was said that the man dealt in contraband: items the Elantians had banned and knowledge strictly classified by the government.

Zen was here for one thing: the trading ledger of metals purchased by the government, key to understanding Elantian troop movements. The past twelve cycles had seen the conquerors ignore the Central Plains—a vast, untamed region of the Last Kingdom—in favor of establishing their foothold in the major trading ports and cities down the eastern and southern coastlines.

Something had changed in the last few moons: sightings of the trademark Elantian metal armor deeper in the bamboo forests than ever before, rumblings of troops gathering in the Southern Elantian Outpost. All this had led Zen here to investigate.

And now his contact was dead.

He clenched his jaw against embers of anger and disappointment. So much travel and time lost for nothing. The Elantians had not just removed a valuable tipoff that would set him and his school back a step, but they had also committed the ultimate crime in Hin eyes: the murder of an elder.

It slowly occurred to him that there was something off about the smell of the place. Elantian magic smelled of burnt metal from the way magicians harnessed the alchemical power within metals to craft their spells, but the shop held the faint—almost undetectable—aroma of something different. Something almost familiar.

Zen reached into the black silk pouch he carried at his hip at all times and drew out two sticks of incense. He inhaled, lowered his index finger toward the tips of the joss sticks, then began to trace the Seal for heat in the air. His finger was quick, practiced, and precise, sweeping in the way a calligrapher might have—only he traced a character an ordinary calligrapher would never have understood.

As soon as one end of the circular stroke met the other, he sensed a shift in the qì around him: a concentration of fire swirling into the glowing Seal before him, sparking to life on the tips of the incense, which flared red for a moment before curling to gray smoke.

All this took place in the blink of an eye.

Zen raised the incense sticks to the corpse, holding it above the old man's heart.

For a moment, there was nothing. And then, in the silver fluorescence of the moon pouring through the torn paper windows, the smoke began to turn. Instead of a steady spiral upward, it wafted toward Zen, shrinking away from the corpse as though it were . . . fleeing from it.

Zen leaned forward and took a short, precise inhale. The smoke was warm, carrying the fragrance of sandalwood and the faint tinge of ground bamboo. Yet beneath it all, like shadows clinging to light, hung a peculiar scent. A bitter smell that he'd mistaken for Elantian magic.

But . . . no, this wasn't a trail left by Elantian Royal Magicians.

Zen exhaled slowly, looking down at the corpse with faint alarm. The Hin burned incense for their dead, yet the roots of this custom had long been forgotten, wiped from the pages of history. Long before the era of the Last Kingdom, when the Dragon Emperor had limited practitioning to the confines of his court and eradicated the rest, practitioners had used incense to parse between yīn and yáng energies. Yáng, the energy of sun, of heat, of light and life, attracted smoke. Yīn, the energy of the moon, of cold, of darkness and death, repelled smoke.

Most corpses held a neutrality to the makeup of their qì— yet Old Wei's body held the lingering stench of yīn.

Though village folktales whispered otherwise, there was nothing inherently wrong with yīn energy. It was a necessity, the other side of the coin constituting qì.

It was when yīn energy was left unbalanced that the issues arose.

For yīn was also the energy of the supernatural.

Mó was Zen's first thought. *Demon.* A soul that held insurmountable wrath or hatred—an excess of yīn energy—coupled with the strength of an unfinished will would not dissipate into the natural qì in the world in death. Instead, it would fester into something evil. Something demonic.

Zen's stomach tightened as he reached for the hilt of the dagger strapped to the inside of his boot. He missed the length of his jiàn, but it was simply too risky to carry a long-sword with him into Elantian territory, especially now that the Twelfth Cycle festivities had brought in a slew of patrols. Besides, this dagger—That Which Cuts Stars—was created to fight demons.

The thought of a soul warping into a demon or a ghoul of sorts here, in the midst of the Southern Elantian Outpost, felt incongruous, almost laughable, to Zen. It would be irony enough to spin into a tale should a horde of demons descend upon the elite military generals of the empire.

Yet much as the Hin had begun to fade from their own lands after the Conquest, so, too, had the spirits.

No, assuming that the old man's soul would corrode into something demonic did not feel right. A demon's core—the concentration of qì that gave it vitality—took cycles, if not decades or centuries, to form. Besides, focusing on the flow of energies all around, he found a slight distinction: the yīn he felt did not come from the corpse itself but, rather, hung over parts of it like clouds of perfume. And now that he expanded his senses, he found traces of it lingering in the air, on the floor, by the door, all around the shop.

Zen's eyes flew open. His knuckles whitened over the hilt of his dagger. The answer to this mystery was something far more intriguing and ominous.

Someone *else* had left the trail of yīn energies here. And in a world where only trained practitioners could manipulate qì, Zen could think of just one type of practitioner who would wield qì consisting largely of yīn: a demonic practitioner. One who used the forbidden branch of practitioning that drew on the energies of a demon bound to their soul.

Impossible.

Restrictions over demonic practitioning had tightened throughout the nearly eight-hundred-cycle era of the Middle Kingdom, yet it wasn't until the end of the era that this branch was eradicated. Emperor Yán'lóng, the Dragon Emperor, had massacred the rebel Mansorian clan's last demonic practitioners, transitioning the former Middle Kingdom into the Last Kingdom: an era of peace, without the tumult and tension between the Ninety-Nine Clans and the Hin imperial government. The surviving clans had surrendered, pledging allegiance to the Imperial Court; those that didn't had spent the majority of the era being hunted to extinction.

This had lasted just eighty cycles before the Elantians invaded.

Zen drew back as though burned, breaking his Seal with a slash of his finger. The tips of the incense extinguished with a hiss, leaving the pounding of his heart to seep into the silence that followed.

His attention shifted from worrying about the ledger he'd come for to scouring the area for more traces of this qì.

He found another concentration of it: a scroll of paper that lay flattened beneath one of Old Wei's hands. He pried the scroll loose and unfurled it, dusting debris and splinters of wood from its surface. His pulse quickened.

On the scroll was an incantation Seal, likely copied from a practitioning tome. He felt a jolt of surprise as he studied it—structurally balanced, a combination of straight strokes and curved sweeps that mimicked Hin characters yet were arranged completely differently, all enclosed in a circle—and realized that, for all his cycles of study, he didn't recognize it. He flipped it over and, finding nothing on the back, examined the markings in the margins of the page, of the Four Demon Gods perched upon swirls of painted clouds.

The page hadn't come from a tome he'd seen before, but the question was: What was it doing here? The thin scroll resting in his hands seemed to swell, representing a great impossibility: something that had slipped through the cracks of time and the waters and fires of history against all odds. After the Dragon Emperor's defeat of the Mansorian clan and the capitulation of the remaining clans, practitioning had become limited to serving the court by imperial decree; anything outside of that was to be obliterated. The Dragon Emperor's Burning of the Hundred Schools was an event wiped from the pages of history books but quietly passed along through word of mouth by practitioners who still remembered.

By the tail end of the Last Kingdom, the knowledge of practitioners and the Hundred Schools had faded from the minds of common folk, thought of as no more than old folktales.

Then the Elantians had come and burned the remaining Hin temples to the ground, razing through the practitioners serving the Imperial Court so that the Hin would never again rise. The few remaining schools of practitioning quietly endorsed by the emperor had fallen within days of the Conquest.

All but one.

Gently, as though the scroll were embellished with gold and lapis lazuli, Zen rolled it up and tucked it into his black silk pouch. His trade with Wei was forfeit. The old shopkeeper had put out a call on the Hin black market for any surviving tomes from the Hundred Schools; Zen, seeing the man's profession, had put in a request for the Elantian government trade ledger for metals.

Specifically, precious metals.

Metals that were being hoarded and used by Elantian Royal Magicians to channel their magic.

Zen hadn't actually planned to give a real practitioning

tome to the old man. Whatever surviving relics had been salvaged from the ruins of the Hundred Schools were worth more than the finest jade.

Why? he thought now as he considered the elder's corpse, the incense smoke swirling around it like shadows. *Why did you want a practitioning tome?*

More important, to *whom* had the shopkeeper planned to sell it?

Zen had a guess: the same person who had left a trace of yīn energies in the air.

Zen brushed a hand over his black silk pouch, the scroll stored safely inside. If only he could speak with the old man.

Zen knew practitioners much more proficient at spiritual summonings than he, and performing one could possibly drain him of his strength. But even if it didn't, creating anything more than the smallest of disturbances in the energies would have the Royal Magicians on him faster than ants on honeyed dates. Performing a spiritual summoning would be akin to shooting a barrel of firepowder into the night sky.

And for Zen, a surviving Hin practitioner, to fall into the hands of Elantian Royal Magicians would bring a fate worse than death . . . and expose the existence of the last-standing school of practitioning from the Last Kingdom.

He twisted the sticks of incense between his fingers, running through his options. The incense did not lie: there was a rogue practitioner loose somewhere in this corrupt city. The game had changed, and it was now crucial for Zen to be the first to find them. Not only to keep them and their skills from the hands of the Elantians but also to find out what business they'd had with his contact, to interrogate their allegiance . . . and to find the answers to the trail of yīn energies they had left here.

The Seal on that scroll would be key to his search.

Zen leaned forward. In the darkness, the old man's eyes were still open, his face frozen in fear. The moonlight blanched his skin white, the Hin color of mourning.

Zen slipped his gloves back on and, with two fingers, pulled the shopkeeper's eyes shut. "Peace be upon your soul," he murmured, "and may you find the Path home."

Then he stood, drew his black peacoat tightly around him, and stepped out of the ravaged shop. Within moments, the shadows had swallowed him, and he was no more than a silhouette in the night.

3

To know the future,
one must first understand the past.

—*Kontencian Analects*
(Classic of Society), 3:9

Lan remembered the exact words her mother had said to her about her future: *You will succeed me as Imperial Advisor,* she'd said as she stood, framed in the rosewood fretwork of their study window, watching Lan trace her calligraphy. Her mother's hair was a sweep of black ink, her silken páo robes pale and fluttering in the breeze of the spring solstice. *The kingdom will be your duty. You will protect the weak and find the balance in the world.*

It had all seemed possible, once.

She wondered what her mother would think if she saw Lan now.

The dusk bells had long finished tolling by the time she arrived at the Teahouse. Known in Hin as the Méi'tíng Chá'guǎn, and directly translated into Elantian as the Rose Pavilion Teahouse, it sat below King's Hills, the richest area of Haak'gong, where the Elantians had established themselves.

From where she stood, Lan could see the foreign houses rising on the mountains cupping the eastern border of the city:

sharp, multilayered metal-and-marble buildings that stood like pale sentries, standing watch over the conquered lands from the highest points in the city. King's Hills overlooked King Alessander's Road, once known as the Four Gods' Road: the most prosperous stretch of Haak'gong, packed to bursting with restaurants, shops, and services alight with the burning gold of alchemical lamps from dusk to dawn.

Meanwhile, the rest of Haak'gong, which stretched below the evemarket to the Bay of Southern Winds, continued to fall into ruin, its people reduced to starving in trash-packed slums.

But, oh, how the Elantians had adored Hin culture: enough to preserve the most beautiful portions of it and capture it for their own use.

There was no better example than the Rose Pavilion Teahouse.

Lan stumbled down the back alley of the Teahouse, where the gutters were streaked with grease and runoff from the kitchens. She turned down a familiar corner and pried open a thin bamboo door.

Immediately she was accosted by the smells of sizzling food, the hot rush of steam billowing from vats of boiling water. Several kitchen girls in gray linen smocks knelt, scrubbing dishes by the door; they called out to her as she barreled past. "'Scuse me—sorry, Cook—running late—"

"Did you girls spit in my pots again?" bellowed Li the cook, emerging red-faced and sweaty from a cloud of steam.

"No!" Lan yelled back, but this reminded her: she needed to think of what to do with all the winnings she'd scraped together from flattening the other songgirls at spit-in-the-pot. Rich women played spit with fancy decks of gold-lined cards and bejeweled fingers; penniless waifs played spit with stolen pots and quick-working mouths.

She heard Li yell something back at her, and she caught the

scallion pie he flung at her head and tore off a chunk. "Thanks, Uncle Li!" she called, her voice muffled as she ducked through the partition to the stairs to the basement. This back corridor was hidden from sight from the main dining room of the Teahouse by a wall of paper screens; through it she could hear the chatter of patrons and the clinking of cutlery. The corridor smelled of roses, the signature perfume of the Teahouse and the national flower of the Elantians. Madam Meng might be ruthless and amoral, but one had to admit she was an excellent businesswoman.

Lan flew down the staircase and burst into the dressing room, stumbling straight through the cluster of her fellow songgirls and eliciting a wave of protests in her path. Ignoring them, she shoved through to the very front and began to undress, peeling off her now-sticky hemp shift and lathering soap and cold water from a stone basin sink. A few glares and *hmphs*, and within moments the other songgirls were back to chattering about the big show tonight, their variety of dialects weaving together like birdsong.

"Lanlan, where in the Ten Hells have you been?"

A girl's reflection was outlined in the mirror beneath the yellow lantern light, a collection of features that was everything Lan was not: soft rosy cheeks, gentle doe eyes, cherry lips, currently pursed in a look of concern.

If there was one person Lan hated to worry, it was Yīng'huā—Ying, in the new age. Ying was the only person in this world who knew Lan's truename—the one she'd had before the Elantians came and required the Hin to identify by a monosyllabic moniker. Apparently, three syllables was too long for the hypocrites, who themselves held godsawful-sounding names like Nicholass and Jonasson and Alessander. Lan often fell asleep murmuring the names of high-ranking Elantian officials to herself, twisting her tongue around the strange syllables so they would come smoother and faster and she could use the names to her advantage (which currently meant working them into bawdy songs as she did chores at the Teahouse).

"The Madam decided to have a last-minute rehearsal earlier this afternoon," Ying continued to chide as she began attacking Lan's hair with a brush. "Apparently there are some high-ranking Elantian officials attending tonight. *Royal Magicians.*" This last part was spoken in half-fear, half-awe. "We were looking for you everywhere."

"Really?" Ice spread through Lan's veins at the thought of having missed one of the Madam's orders. "Did the Madam say anything?"

"She just asked if we knew where you were. I covered for you." Ying's gaze grew sharp as Lan loosed a breath. "Where *were* you?"

"Sorry," Lan said to her friend, splashing her face with water again and toweling off with her own hemp shift. "Was just down at the evemarket."

Ying sucked in her cheeks, eyes brimming with disapproval. Without another word, she snatched the evening's performance outfit from the drawer that belonged to Lan and began to dress her. "I don't get why you always want to go there," she fussed, pulling on a silk sleeve. "Songgirls from the Teahouse mustn't be seen mingling in that area, or we'll get in trouble. Besides, it's so . . . dirty. And you'll get tanned—even more than you are now. You'll look like someone from an ancient clan!"

Lan refrained from rolling her eyes. Ying loved the soft comforts and small luxuries the Teahouse offered, but Lan was far too restless. Still, she thought as she tilted her head to swipe rouge over her cheeks and lips, she'd learned that sometimes kind lies were better than hard truths. She could never tell Ying why she had been at Old Wei's in the first place; why it was there that she disappeared to a few times a moon.

She studied her face in the looking glass, a few shades darker than Madam Meng would prefer. The Elantian standards of Hin beauty meant snow-pale faces, willowy figures—but Lan couldn't help how she'd been born. If anything, she'd decided she would rather stick out like a thorn in the White Angels' eyes.

"Nothing wrong with that," she replied, poking out her tongue. "Besides, aren't we all meant to be descended from the clans somewhat?" Even post-Conquest, it was regarded as somewhat of a taboo among Hin to speak of the clans—the Ninety-Nine Clans, they were once called. All Lan knew was that they had threatened the peace and stability of the Middle Kingdom and had been defeated by Emperor Yán'lóng, establishing the peace and prosperity that had been the era of the Last Kingdom. The clans had quickly disbanded or faded into obscurity, taking on the mainstream Hin identity to avoid imperial persecution.

More likely than not, most Hin these days had one or two clan ancestors unbeknownst to them.

"Help me with the liner?" Lan asked.

Ying's lips curved into a smile as she took the kohl pencil from Lan. Her fingers were warm, soft and careful, as she traced the line of Lan's lashes. Lan continued to dab rouge onto her lips, humming as she did so.

"What *is* that song you're always singing?" Ying asked, bemused.

Lan shrugged. She couldn't place the melody—she sometimes felt as though she'd caught it from a dream one night. It was one she'd known as long as she could remember. "Probably an old lullaby," she replied.

"Hmm." Ying leaned back, pursing her lips to survey her

work on Lan's eyes. She beamed. "One day you're going to find a rich nobleman and marry yourself off."

Lan snorted, earning herself a firm pinch from Ying. "Ai'yo, that hurts! Marrying a handsome nobleman is *your* dream, Yingying."

"Can you stop squirming for just five seconds? And yes, it is." There was a hint of tightness to Ying's voice as she fixed some flyaway strands of Lan's hair. "Nothing wrong with making the best of a bad situation. I know you dread the possibility, but I dream of going to the Peach Blossom Room one day."

A coil tightened inside Lan. The Peach Blossom Room had been the source of numerous arguments between herself and Ying. Nicknamed the Room of Delight in the Teahouse, it was in an area of the second floor that was sectioned into closed-off quarters and strictly off-limits at all times. Word was, it cost a hundred gold ingots to book a single night, and if an Elantian official or nobleman requested a songgirl there, it wasn't the room they were paying for. If the songgirl was lucky, her contract was also transferred to the buyer and she would be taken away under his ownership.

If she wasn't, she would be taken for a single night and then cast out by the Madam. No one wanted a tainted flower.

But, Lan thought as she studied her face in the mirror, the still-wet strands of her hair and the powders and blushes coating her skin, in the entirety of this process, there was never a time when the songgirls were given a choice.

Work at the Teahouse or starve in the streets.

Please an Elantian or die at his hands.

Lan touched a finger to the little hemp pouch of crushed dried lily petals she kept on her at all times. Refusing to smell like roses, the Elantian national flower, was one small act of rebellion.

"No changes to the show for tonight, right?" she asked,

switching subjects. The rest of the songgirls were already in costume, shimmering flowers to be put on display night after night after night. "We're still doing 'Ballad of the Last Kingdom'?"

Ying opened her mouth to answer, but at that moment, a cold voice cut through their conversation with the precision of a scalpel. "You would know this had you attended the rehearsal."

At once the cheerful hubbub of the songgirls' conversation died. The temperature in the room seemed to plummet as a shadow swept over the door.

Madam Meng's steps fell, soft and sinuous, across the wooden floor, her silken robes slithering behind her. While the saying generally went that beauty faded with time, the madam of the Rose Pavilion Teahouse had aged like fine plumwine. Black hair fell in smoky plumes across her shoulders before sweeping into a traditional Hin updo, her face framed like a portrait by black-rimmed eyes and a blood-red mouth. As she lifted the hem of her robes, her metal nailguards—made in the same style as those of ancient Hin concubines—glittered, long and sharp as claws.

Like Haak'gong, Madam Meng and her Teahouse had survived the Conquest and even gone on to thrive as the other restaurants and taverns around the area had been cleansed, replaced with adaptations more palatable to the Elantians' tastes. The Madam had used her beauty as a weapon and abandoned the pride, values, and morality of a fallen kingdom, running straight into her conquerors' arms.

The people who might have judged her—well, they were all dead.

Now she stalked across the floor like an empress in her own halls, songgirls falling into line with murmurs of "Madam" as she passed by.

"Well, well, look who decided to show up," Madam Meng said. Her voice was delicate, a near-whisper, but Lan flinched as though she'd just shouted.

"Forgiveness, Madam, I—"

The Madam's hands darted out, curved nailguards digging into Lan's upper arms. Lan swallowed a gasp of pain; her heart fluttered like a bird in a cage as she drew her gaze to meet the Madam's. They were a terrifying obsidian black.

"Need I remind you," Madam Meng murmured, "what happens to songgirls who grow too *comfortable* here?"

The nails pinched, but Lan knew the Madam wouldn't draw blood—not on the night of her greatest show of the cycle.

Lan lowered her eyes. "No, Madam. It won't happen again."

In a sudden motion, the Madam lifted her hand as though to strike. Lan flinched, shutting her eyes—but the next moment, those sharp nailguards came to rest on her cheeks. Madam Mei never hit her songgirls where the marks could be seen.

"I expect nothing less than your best performance tonight," she crooned, tracing a finger down the length of Lan's cheek. Gently she dabbed at a spot on Lan's face, drawing away a thin sprinkling of powder. "There. Now you look as perfect as a doll. No man will look at you and suspect the wily fox–spirited girl inside."

It was remarkable how the Madam could deliver a compliment and make it sound like a threat. She turned and disappeared through the doors, leaving a cloud of rose-scented terror in her wake.

Somewhere upstairs, a gong rang out. The songgirls straightened; costumes shook into place and silk slippers skidded over wooden floors as the girls lined up at the door.

Lan cast one last glance at her reflection. As always, she was in her white silk qípáo, plain and flat compared to the other girls' luxurious dresses, and just as she liked it. Better to stay hidden as a plain dove than stand out as a peacock in these times. She was the lead—and only—singer for the Teahouse shows, eternally playing the part of the Teller of Tales. The Madam had taken one look at her scrawny appearance ten cycles ago and declared that she wouldn't be wasting any fine cloth on "a curbside fox."

But there was something Lan had that the other girls didn't, and that was a voice purer than the finest jade. Even when, as a child, she sang from behind screens, her song seemed to mesmerize patrons; soon the performances at the Rose Pavilion Teahouse caught the attention of Elantian generals, and business began to boom. And when Lan's lips and chest filled out, the Madam noticed that she'd grown up not half-bad: a slim waif with looks more sharp than beautiful, but one more doll to add to the Teahouse's collection nevertheless.

Lan scurried to the back of the line of songgirls as they trailed upstairs at the second sound of the gong. Beyond the cherrywood screen that led to the kitchens and the dormitories, she could already hear the hubbub of voices in the Teahouse. A packed show, then—fitting for the eve of the Twelfth Cycle of Elantian rule.

A third gong sounded, and Madam Meng's high-pitched voice rang out: "My noble patrons, I thank you for choosing the Rose Pavilion Teahouse on this very special night. I can promise you it is one you will not forget. Tonight, to honor the Twelfth Cycle of Elantian enlightenment, I introduce to you the 'Ballad of the Last Kingdom.' Please welcome our beloved songgirls!"

In the cracks between the folding screen, Lan watched as the girls twirled onstage in a whirl of gossamer and gauze, each outfit representing a different Hin folklore creature tailored to

Elantian tastes. There were the Four Demon Gods, the green serpent in shimmering emeralds and jade, the colorful qí'lín with its headband of stag horns, the moonrabbit in a soft fall of fur, and so on. Ying was, as always, dressed as the magical lotus flower in a beautiful blush of pinks and fuchsias.

"The Teller of Tales!"

Lan took her cue and glided onstage as she had been trained to do. She wove through to center stage, scanning the patrons here tonight. A blur of pale faces with hair ranging from wheat to copper to sand-brown, dressed in the white winter livery of the Elantian military, flashing with silver collars and cuffs.

Lan dipped into a curtsy, hands on her hips, head bobbing. As she did so, she caught sight of a patron sitting alone at a table in the very first row.

At first she felt a flash of surprise, for no other reason than that the man was Hin. The first row held the most expensive tables, as it offered the closest view of the stage and was typically reserved for high-ranking Elantian generals. This man leaned back against the rosewood chair, chin posed jauntily on one black-gloved hand with the air of someone accustomed to exceptional treatment—someone with authority.

He was the most startlingly beautiful man Lan had ever set eyes on. A tangle of midnight hair, cropped short in the Elantian style, spilled over a slim, chiseled face like ink on porcelain. Eyes the gray of smoke, framed by straight black brows, tilted with the slightest edge of insolence—a portrait completed by an insouciant curve of a mouth, corners currently sloping downward in boredom. He was dressed like an Elantian merchant, perhaps even a plainclothes court official: smooth white shirt and black trench coat and pants, not a spot of color on him.

A Hin courtdog, Lan thought; a Hin who had turned traitor

to work for the Elantian government. Her stomach did a small flip.

He was looking straight at her.

She forced her heart to still as she rose from her curtsy and went to her spot at the edge of the stage. With each step, she could feel his gaze trailing her. Yet his eyes . . . they weren't hungry or sleazy, like those of the Elantian soldiers who watched the songgirls as if they were prey. Instead, there was something . . . assessing about them.

Lan shifted her attention to the other girls, already gathered at the edge: Wen, her bamboo pipe raised to her lips; Ning, her five-stringed zither perched on her lap; and Rui, pear-shaped pipa lute leaning against her shoulder.

As the first note of the song struck, though, the rest of the world—the smells of tea, the bright pops of peonies on the tables, the shimmering gold-and-bamboo screens on the walls, the waiting patrons squirming in their seats—faded.

Lan began to sing.

The melody was warm on her lips, flowing smoothly from her as though in a dream. An image found her, bright and sharp, as the room around her fell away. Tonight she saw a dusk sky, the tangerine sun lingering at the edge of the world, its light gilding a forest of golden larches beyond eggshell-white walls. A woman leaned against a moon gate arch, fingers dancing over the strings of her woodlute and spilling song into the world.

Māma.

Each time Lan sang, it felt as though her mother were alive again, an echo of her spirit stirring inside Lan's heart, guiding her.

The "Ballad of the Last Kingdom" told the tale of the Four Demon Gods who had fallen from the sky into the world of mortals. There they governed with their great and terrible powers, worshiped and feared by the Hin . . . and once in a dynasty, it was said they lent their power to great warriors to change the tides of fate.

Then, nearly a hundred cycles ago, they had disappeared.

The ballad itself had been written thousands of cycles ago, some said by the ancient shaman poets. The scattered verse, a traditional prose style, was beautiful in Hin; even translated to Elantian, Lan found it palatable.

> *Long ago, the Heavens split*
> *Like teardrops, its fragments fell to the ground*
> *A piece of the sun bloomed into the Crimson Phoenix*
> *A slice of the moon turned into the Silver Dragon*
> *A shard of the stars gathered into the Azure Tiger*
> *A splinter of the night became the Black Tortoise*

And so the tale went, a sorrowful folktale of a fallen land forsaken by its gods. It was a tale the Elantians were familiar with—a beautiful reminder, in their eyes, that the fate of the Last Kingdom belonged to them.

Songgirls spun onstage, blending in a flurry of silks and jewels flashing beneath the lantern light, weaving the tale of their land, the fate of their people.

Lan opened her eyes only when the last quavering note of the ballad had melted like snow. The soft red light of the lanterns held the Teahouse in a muted silence, the patrons as still as statues even as the songgirls crouched into the final positions of their dance.

Lan wet her lips, letting the silence steep for several more moments before she prepared for the curtsy.

And then something extremely strange happened.

From the quiet offstage came the jarring, unmistakable sound of clapping.

Just as a master did not clap for a prized trick dog, Elantians never clapped after shows at the Teahouse. A murmur rose up among the patrons as they looked to the source of the noise. The songgirls stirred, saccharine smiles yielding to surprise.

A man in one of the front rows was standing, bringing his hands together over and over again in a slow clap.

Lan looked at him. Their gazes met, and her blood froze.

Summer-green eyes, marble-cut face, a grin that was widening by the moment as he caught her expression.

It was the Elantian soldier from Old Wei's shop.

"Brava!" he called. Coming from his mouth, it sounded like mockery. "I'll take one of those, yes, ma'am!"

Two of his fellow soldiers wrestled him back down. A titter of laughter spread through the Teahouse among the Elantian customers as they turned back to face the stage. A Hin might have been beheaded for such effrontery, but an Elantian soldier's drunken debaucheries on a night of celebration only served to improve spirits.

Lan's pulse began to race. She could hear the Angel calling after her as she turned and followed the other songgirls off-stage, and she knew with utter certainty that he hadn't been jesting. The world grew muted, the conversation of the girls a distant blur as her mind blanked with panic.

The kitchens were awhirl with motion, and the songgirls picked up trays of tea and snacks that had been laid out for them to serve their customers. Lan shoveled sunflower seeds and dried jujubes onto her tray, barely noticing what she was doing. The kitchens around her shifted, and suddenly, she was back in Old Wei's shop, shelves and cabinets locking her in place, the press of hard fingers against her skin. Grass-green eyes that roamed her body as though they owned her, hot breath against her cheeks as the soldier thrust his marble-cut face into hers.

Don't you worry, my pretty little flower. I'm not letting you go so easily.

Nausea roiled in her stomach as she thought of her earlier conversation with Ying, of the Peach Blossom Room. Soldiers were not known to be rich, and the price to buy out a song-girl's contract would be out of their range.

The most they could afford was a single night.

That meant—

Her hands trembled so violently that she dropped the butterknife she was holding.

"Lanlan! Are you all right?" She could barely speak as Ying bent to pick up the knife, placing it by the plate of scones, butter, and jam Lan had picked out. The girl took one look at Lan's face and her smile dropped. "Lanlan?"

Lan looked into her friend's face. Was it just a bell ago that they had been teasing each other about suitors and the future?

Now Lan looked to the future and thought only of the press of pale fingers against her wrists, the gleam of green eyes too close to her face.

Help me, she wanted to say, but the words wouldn't come. What could Ying do for her, even if she asked? Her friend's heart was as soft and as fragile as a peony; to tell her the truth—that Lan might be a breath away from being sold out like cattle and then cast onto the streets—would break her heart.

Māma had once told Lan that one day she would grow up to protect those who needed her.

Lan forced herself to smile. "I'm fine." The words tasted like broken porcelain.

Ying's eyes lingered on Lan's face for a moment more, her lips parted, and for the cycles to come, Lan would wonder what she might have said.

At that moment, Li the cook popped out from behind a cabinet. "What are you two still chitchatting about here?" he demanded, dumping lotus seed cakes onto a tray. "It's our busiest night and you have patrons to serve. Go on, get out! Out!"

Ying snatched up her tray, shot Lan a helpless look, and scurried out.

The tray felt leaden in Lan's hands. As she stepped out into the front of the Teahouse, the sounds of conversation, laughter, and clinking plates and cups washed over her. The low light of the lanterns seemed to paint the room in a mist of blood.

Through the fog of her thoughts, a realization cut clear as a blade. If she was going to be thrown out after tonight, she might as well make a run for it now. Why wait for an Elantian soldier to have his way with her? Why wait for Madam Meng to beat her and cast her out into some ditch like the curbside fox she'd been since the very start?

Her heart pounded like battle drums as the reality of her choice set in. She'd done it once before, when her home had been conquered and her world had fallen apart. She'd survived.

She could do it again.

The Teahouse seemed to settle around her again, the noise and scents and sights flooding back. She saw the other songgirls weaving through expensive lacquered tables. She spotted Ying, standing demurely to one side as a group of Elantian noblemen roared with laughter, precious stones flashing on their fingers and coats. Her friend hovered uncertainly, one man's arm slung around her waist as she attempted to serve him tea.

A knot rose in Lan's throat. It wasn't fair—it wasn't fair that this was the last look she might have of Ying, someone she loved, someone she had spent cycles of her life with. That they might never see each other again, and their last words to each other—what had they even been?

"Four Gods watch over you," Lan whispered. Turning

away from the only person she had left in this world who felt like family, she could now do nothing more than to pray that somehow, somewhere, by some impossible chance, the gods existed and they were watching.

She turned and began to make her way toward the doors, smiling at patrons and dodging their wandering hands. *Calm,* she thought to herself. It would all be over in ten seconds. Less.

The Teahouse doors were in sight; night spilled in like a bowl of fresh-ground ink. Hope drummed to the beat of her heart—hope, fear, and a thrill of adrenaline at the knowledge that, for the first time in a long time, she was making a choice utterly on her own.

Then she caught sight of two figures standing before the filigreed screens.

Madam Meng was wearing her most charming smile, which displayed all the pearly teeth in her mouth—the ones she'd bought from the blood and sweat and tears of her songgirls. She laughed, and those teeth were *dazzling,* and Lan wanted to rip them from her mouth.

Across from the Madam, grin stretching like that of a predator, was the green-gazed Elantian Angel. Donnaron. Even as they spoke, those poisonous spring eyes shifted to Lan like the flick of a snake's tongue.

He straightened slightly. Raised a hand, and pointed.

Right at her.

Lan's plan fell apart at the seams.

Panic spilled over. She turned sharply, her ears filled with a buzzing sound, her vision blurring, unaware of what she was doing or where she was going except *away* from him.

She only had time to catch sight of someone tall, someone dark, before she crashed headfirst into that someone.

4

Peace be upon your soul,
and may you find the Path home.

—Hin funerary rites

"Forgiveness." A black-gloved hand darted to her waist to steady her, the other catching the edge of her tray before it tipped and the contents went crashing to the floor. "I didn't mean to startle you."

A voice, lovely and deep as velvet midnight, speaking to her in near-perfect Elantian.

Lan blinked as she was set back on her feet, the tray returned to her hands. Her rescuer stepped back quickly, lightly, like a retreating shadow, and it was then that she caught sight of his face.

It was the Hin man from earlier—the one she had noticed. Who had been looking at her. He stood a courteous two paces away from her, looking utterly discordant among the gleaming lacquerwood panels and red screens decorating the Teahouse walls. Up close, she realized that he was young, all smooth skin and black hair, perhaps only a cycle or two older than her. A boy so beautiful, he looked as though he belonged in a painting.

"I—" She shifted her stance, glancing behind her, too agitated to bother with subtleties. Madam Meng was tipping her head back and laughing, her fingers pinching the air in the way that Lan had learned to recognize meant she was talking about money. It would only be a matter of minutes. "Sorry, I—excuse me—"

"One moment. Please." His hand snagged on her right wrist, light, loose, tracing what might have been a question mark. Nothing like the grip of the Elantian soldier from earlier. "I'd like to talk to you."

Ordinarily she would have been extremely flattered; none of the Elantians would have even entertained the notion of *asking* a Hin girl to talk to them. It was always an order. One expected to be obeyed.

Fate would have sent him to her on the precise night her path would take a turn.

"I'm sorry," Lan said distractedly, "but I'm in the middle of—"

And then the Hin reached into the folds of his coat and drew out a torn, dusty, and utterly familiar piece of parchment.

The rest of the world peeled away as she caught sight of the Demon Gods at the corners of the scroll, the top of the curved character she'd studied just a few bells ago. She blinked, then looked to him. He had her full attention now.

His face was careful, impassive, but his eyes—they seemed to pierce her mind, slowly unraveling each of her thoughts. Beneath it all, though, there was a hint of surprise mingled with confusion, as though he had found something unexpected in her. "What do you know of this scroll?"

She was out of time, out of patience for courtesies and games. "Where did you get that?"

He was still watching her with those unsettling eyes. In response, Lan felt something stirring in her belly, something deep and ancient . . . and then a sudden tingling on her left wrist, right where her scar lay.

"Who are you?" he asked. His question was so broad, so unexpected, that Lan felt a startled laugh bubbling up in her throat. She glanced at the door. Madam Meng was still talking, but she was looking straight at Lan. Those crimson lips curled into a smile, yet those eyes were cold as she lifted a hand and crooked a sharp gold nail.

Come.

Lan whirled back to the Hin boy, her brain working fast. In half a second, a new plan formed. "I can tell you everything," she said, flipping her voice into a sweet, ingratiating tone. "You just need to tell the Madam that you wish to buy my time tonight."

The boy's cheeks flushed with a spot of color. The edges of his eyes tightened, almost as though in disdain. "I have no intention of doing such a disreputable thing," he said.

Lan barely felt the sting of his words. "Please, mister."

"Mister?" He raised an eyebrow.

"Gē'ge. Older brother." She summoned her most sugary smile. "You have money. You could pay out my contract. I promise you, I'll tell you everything I know about that scroll." Not that she knew much, but, well, Lan wasn't about to admit that.

The edge to the Hin's expression softened slightly. He opened his mouth, and for a moment, Lan thought he might agree.

Then he said, "Forgiveness, but I haven't the means to do such a thing." He tapped the scroll. "If you please—tell me what business you had with Wei."

"Old Wei?" The name fell from her lips in surprise. "I . . . he's someone I know."

She glanced to the door again. Madam Meng's smile had

dropped; her mouth looked sharp enough to cut as she began to supplement her dainty gestures with more aggression.

The Hin boy was watching Lan. "I was meant to meet with him," he said at last, and in the midst of the growing panic in her mind, Lan suddenly remembered. *I think I'll have something* really *good for you next time,* Old Wei had told her in confidence, grinning with his mouth full of missing teeth. *Source of mine's introduced a Hin courtdog to me, and he's in the market—*

This . . . was the Hin courtdog Old Wei had spoken of?

His next words hit her like a punch in the gut. "He's dead."

She exhaled sharply, as though the blow had been physical. "He's—" She couldn't bring herself to say it.

"His shop was ransacked and much of what was left inside was destroyed. He was dead by the time I got there." The boy's eyes were steady as a blade. "If you were involved, be truthful. I will get to the bottom of it all."

She barely heard him; her mind was still spinning around the fact that Old Wei was . . . was . . .

Her thoughts landed on the silver spoon, and just like that, the dots connected. The White Angels who had come barging into Old Wei's shop. The spoon was the one thing that might have provoked their attention. In this day and age, the Hin knew well the ramifications of being caught in possession of any substantial amount of metal—especially one so precious as silver.

Old Wei. She closed her eyes, throat tightening to the point that she could barely breathe. He'd died because . . . because she'd thought giving him a stupid silver spoon would help him ease some of his troubles. Buy him enough ginseng to heal that cough of his.

The Hin courtdog leaned in, his gaze pinning her. "If you know anything, I'd advise you to tell me *now.*"

Across the room, Madam Meng was moving toward them.

She cut through the tables like an impending storm, wrath billowing in the wake of her beautiful silken qípáo. By the fili-greed screens, Donnaron caught Lan's eye, winked, and made a slow, obscene gesture.

Lan turned to the Hin courtdog. If this man worked for the Elantians, confessing that she'd been anywhere near Old Wei would only bring her closer to a noose. They could find out that *she* had been in possession of the silver spoon—worse, they might know *she* had been searching for the scroll.

Swallowing, she met his gaze—and in spite of the little she knew about him, she had the strangest, instinctive feeling that he wasn't here to hurt her.

Help me, she wanted to beg him.

Lan opened her mouth.

"*There* you are, my little singer." Madam Meng's voice sounded by her ear, and suddenly Lan's shoulders were caught in a viselike grip. The Madam stepped to Lan's side and ran her eyes up and down the Hin courtdog's body in a glance that would determine whether or not he was worthy of her atten-tion. Evidently he was. "Heavens, Lan, you're so popular! Is she keeping you entertained, my lord?"

Something resembling disgust crossed the courtdog's face. It was gone in a moment, and he inclined his head at Madam Meng. The scroll had vanished. "She is a delight, Madam."

"*Wonderful.*" The Madam spun Lan to her, eyes glinting with the look of a freshly minted sale. "I have some *excellent* news for you, my dear. Come, come."

Without waiting for Lan's response, she began to steer her away, nails digging into her flesh.

Lan glanced back.

The Hin courtdog stood rooted to the floor, watching her. Their eyes met, and she felt something stretch taut between them. His brows furrowed, his lips parted, the space between them widening with what he might have said.

Then he turned away.

Lan kept silent as she turned back. She couldn't make a scene, not in front of these Elantians, who might decide she'd ruined their night of celebration and have her killed for treason against the Elantian Empire. She let the Madam take her all the way up the flight of stairs to the second-floor landing.

Here it was quiet, empty.

She waited until they had turned down a corridor and then wrenched herself from the Madam's grip. The items on her tray clattered, sliding unsteadily.

Lan lifted her gaze to the Madam's and drew a breath. "I'm not going."

The Madam was no longer smiling. "Excuse me?" Her voice was the softest Lan had ever heard it.

"I said I'm not—"

CRACK.

The world blanked for a moment in a searing streak of heat across her cheek. Lan reeled, just managing to keep her balance. Her face tingled; she felt a trickle of warmth dribble down her chin, tasted copper in her mouth.

The Madam's fingers wrapped around her chin so tightly that it hurt. "You think you have a gods-damned *choice*?" she hissed, the cloying scent of her rose perfume choking down Lan's throat. "The Angel bought your contract for the night. You belong to him now. If he says kneel, you kneel. If he says crawl, you crawl. *Got it?*"

Lan was vaguely aware of the Madam sliding open a pair of wooden doors and pushing her into a room. Of the Madam whipping out a silken handkerchief and wiping the blood from Lan's chin.

"There," she murmured, straightening and trailing a cold finger down Lan's chin. "Can't have you looking like a broken doll. Now you'll wait here while I go fetch him. And if you try anything . . . well." A cold smirk. "I shall leave it to the Angel to decide what to do."

She plucked the tray from Lan's hands, set it on the small tea table by the wall, and exited. The wooden doors slid shut with a final *thump*, trapping Lan inside.

In her many cycles at the Teahouse, she had never entered the rooms upstairs except to clean. She remembered every detail of the smooth sandalwood floors, the sleek lacquered panels on the walls featuring paintings of blossom trees. The pink petals sprinkled like rain over a pair of lovers crouched by a lake.

She'd hated scrubbing those panels, digging into the grooves and etchings of every one of those accursed petals.

A glint of light near the doors caught her eye. It came from the tray the Madam had deposited on the little round tea table. The tea had gone cold now, but Lan was looking at something else.

At the edge of the tray, near the plate of scones, was the glass butterknife she'd nearly cut her hand on. The one Ying had picked up and put back on the tray. It winked at her from beneath the low-burning alchemical lantern.

Footsteps sounded down the hall: slow and heavy, with the *thud-thud-thud* that was the trademark of the thick leather boots of Elantian make.

She'd crossed the room before she could think. The knife was cold and sleek in her hand, made to cut only butter and other soft things, but it didn't matter. Better than nothing.

Her gaze darted around the room, assessing every nook and cranny—the scarlet loveseat, the altar table, the locked glass windows overlooking a black, sightless night.

In the end, she positioned herself in the center of the room, knife hidden in her sleeve. Whatever came, she would face it head-on.

The footsteps paused right outside the wooden doors, and then they slid open. The soldier stood grinning at her. He'd shed his bulky metal armor from earlier in the day and now wore a silver doublet hemmed with fine blue stitching that culminated in the emblem of crown and wings on his front and back.

The angels in the Elantian churches and places of worship were all depicted as pure, as kind; according to the stories peddled by Elantian preachers, the angels were meant to have saved the poor and vanquished evil. Lan tried to imagine the distant Elantian Empire, across the Sea of Heavenly Radiance. If the angels truly existed, Lan thought, would they be horrified that a man who wore one of their faces could distort it so much, turn their beauty into something so cruel and so corrupt? Or had their beauty been born of cruelty in the first place?

"Well, my love," Donnaron said, the Elantian language rolling oleaginously from his tongue, "I did promise you I'd find you again, didn't I?"

Lan's heart was a bird trapped in a cage. Sweat slicked the handle of her butter knife.

"Donnaron J. Tarley," the soldier continued with a mock bow. "*General* Donnaron J. Tarley. I must say, I do appreciate the hunt you took me on. I don't like women who make it too easy."

"Bet you don't like it when women say no either." The words somehow slipped out of Lan's mouth, smooth and sharp, if not accented. This was it, this was one of the moments that would come to define her life, and she would no longer beg or cower.

The Angel barked a delighted laugh. "Oh, but that makes it so much more *exciting,*" he said, and lunged for her.

Lan ducked; she'd been waiting for this. She spun, stumbling across the floor; whirled back, whipped her arm out, the knife gleaming—

One of the soldier's meaty hands came up and wrapped around her wrist, then twisted. A flash of blinding pain streaked across her forearm; her fingers spasmed, and the knife fell, slowly, steadily, tumbling through the air.

It clattered at her feet.

Donnaron's hands clasped over her throat; he lifted her bodily so that her toes scraped the floor. A strand of his wheat-gold hair had fallen into his eyes.

She couldn't breathe.

He was laughing. "I can't wait to tell this to the lads. A *butterknife*! I've half a mind to keep you after all, with the spirit you've got."

He slammed her into the wall, and Lan saw stars. Dimly, she felt the press of his hips against hers, his hands roaming from her neck to her collarbone and continuing to trace lower. There was an ache building in the space between her forehead and her teeth, a strange kind of energy that felt different from any other headache she'd ever had. A hum in the air . . . that she'd felt only once before.

Then Donnaron's right hand crushed her left forearm, and the pain exploded.

It was excruciating: a searing white burn that encompassed her entire world, expanding like the light of stars, a pale-jade moon. Out of that whiteness rose a great shadow, serpentine in the ways it twisted and coiled. Something rushed out from her and filled her at the same time, and Lan's consciousness drifted.

She'd known this kind of pain only once in her life.

It was the day her mother had died.

The day her world had ended.

It was the winter solstice of the thirty-second cycle of the Qīng Dynasty—the Age of Purity, it was called, before it all came crashing down. The Luminous Dragon Emperor, Shuò'lóng, sat on the throne eighty cycles after the Clan Rebellion, when his ancestor Emperor Yán'lóng defeated the dissenting clans and established peace upon the land, transitioning the Middle Kingdom to the Last Kingdom. The Hin had lived in a period of luxury with the success of the Jade Trail, and their fattening bellies had distracted them from the changes their new emperor made to their history. A history that many would begin to forget as time wore on.

Lan was six cycles old, bright-eyed and with her entire future ahead of her. Her mother had been away for the past two moons on a trip north, to the Heavenly Capital of Tiān'jīng— some squabble with foreign traders over ships and territory, apparently. The Last Kingdom sat comfortably among its neighbors, the linchpin to the foreign powers along the Jade Trail: the Kingdom of Masyria, which traded in glass; the great Achaemman Empire, across a sprawling stretch of desert; and so on. But contact with a nation across the Sea of Heavenly Radiance, once believed to lead to the edge of the world, was new. Māma had come back with stories of people with faces the color of snow and hair that looked to be spun of gold and copper. They had appeared over the skyline, ships of gleaming metal borne impossibly by ocean waves. *Yī'lán'shā rén*, Māma had called them. Elantian people. They had been interested in all the natural resources the great sprawl of the Last Kingdom had to offer, in the Hin civilization that had spanned thousands of cycles. They asked to establish trade relations with the Last Kingdom and learn from Hin culture at the Imperial Court in exchange for their strange metal inventions. And the Luminous Emperor, so confident in the greatness of his kingdom, had entertained them.

Lan remembered the exact moment she'd looked up from her sonnets, remembered the way the window of her study had framed a perfect portrait of her courtyard house: the larches and willows frozen in sheaths of white snow, the lakes still beneath a surface of ice so blue it reflected the sky, the gray-tiled roofs of her home jutting out and curving to the Heavens. A figure on horseback cut through the plumes of snow that fell like goose feathers, páo flashing in alternating black and red as she rode hard and fast. Lan thought of the heroes in her storybooks: the immortals and practitioners who crossed the lakes and rivers of the Last Kingdom and communed with the gods of old.

Yet today, the prophecy would not be a good one.

Her mother had ridden back on the tides of the end of their world as they knew it.

Later, Lan had hidden in the hot water vents beneath her study floor, trembling with fear. The snow outside had bloomed red, bodies of the household staff strewn like poppies in a field. Foreign soldiers in ice-blue armor pressed against the gates, spilling into the courtyard, thick leather boots trampling the snow, breastplates glinting with wings of white gold that encircled a crown. She heard them shout in a foreign language. Heard the sounds of swords slicing from scabbards.

She hadn't known it at the time, but this had been the beginning of the Elantian Conquest.

Bile had coated her throat; fear pressed against her chest. She looked through the cracks in the floorboards and took in her mother's stance—as straight-backed and proud as that of any man serving in the Imperial Palace. In that moment, she expected her mother to do the impossible, the astonishing, like whip out a sword and slay these strange men who'd barged into their home.

What Lan *didn't* expect her mother to do was calmly pick up her woodlute and begin playing.

The first thrum of strings quavered through the air, and time seemed to freeze. The notes were an overture, lingering like a promise: this was only the beginning of the song.

A chill settled all around.

Three more notes. *Do-do-sol.* The last twisted artfully a half-note up, a tick of tension. For all the years that her mother had sat by her bedside and played her to sleep, Lan had never heard this melody before. The notes were staccato, wavering in the air with a twang that faded like the edge of a blade. There was something different to this song; it rippled through the air like an invisible wave, stirring something inside Lan that had lain dormant until now.

The foreign soldiers growled something. There was the silver arc of a sword.

Her mother's song picked up in a sudden strum. The air broke like waters over a cliff, waves cutting and dancing in a frenzy beneath a storm-tossed sky. Lan could *see* the notes, knife-sharp and curved like scythes, slicing through the air.

And the most peculiar thing happened.

A soldier's metal breastplate split. Blood spurted from the center of the crown insignia, the wings curling red.

The soldier stumbled back, and the floorboards obscured Lan's vision so that all she could see was her mother as she riffed another chord.

This time, something hit the floor with a *thud*.

Another soldier yelled and charged, a blur of silver between the cracks in the floorboard. Music thrummed. Red splattered against the lines of the floorboards like music notes.

Lan was frozen in time, her reality fractured between what she could and couldn't see. Her mother, sitting there, playing the lute. And blood, crimson as cinnabar, splashing like notes of a red, red song on the wall.

Then a shadow fell. The tides of the battle shifted.

Lan had felt it in a force that rippled through the soldiers. They parted like the waves of the ocean. A man walked through, and she immediately knew that this one was different. His eyes were a winter's blue, his skin the noncolor of ice. He carried no weapons, but when he lifted his hand, there was the glint of silver across his wrists.

"Give it to me."

She hadn't understood his words, then—only the sounds falling from his mouth, echoing perfect and pristine in her memory throughout the long nights in the coming cycles. She'd held on to them until she'd understood the Elantian language enough to decipher the last words her mother's killer had said.

Māma's words, though, Lan had known with a sense of dread. *"Never."*

Lan would never forget the smile frozen on the Elantian soldier's face as he brought his fingers together.

Click.

The strings of her mother's woodlute snapped. It was the sound of a bone breaking.

Click.

Just like that, her mother reeled back. When Lan blinked, the man's hands were red. Clutched between his fingers, like some nightmarish prized gem, was a still-beating heart.

Cycles later, she'd regret that blink. In the space of one flutter of her eyelids, the Elantian man had done the impossible. Perhaps if she hadn't blinked, her mother would still be alive.

A magician, Lan thought numbly. *A magician who has brought winter with him.*

Her mother crashed onto the floor right above her. Lan tasted her blood on her lips. Warm, copper-scented, and so undeniably human. The heroes in her stories had never bled.

She opened her mouth to scream, but her mother made a sudden motion—a gesture with one of her hands—and suddenly Lan had found her throat clamped shut, the cry buried in her chest. Her mother's eyes, wide and gaping, moved to meet hers.

Whether it was magic or simply the strength of a woman with unfinished will, her mother had taken a long, long time to die that day. By the time Lan had crawled out of the vent, the Winter Magician and the soldiers were gone, leaving only a trail of screams and scarlet in their wake. There, lingering in the air had been the unmistakable scent of burnt metal.

There was a growing, thrumming pressure in her forehead, as though something inside were trapped, waiting to be let out. Tears tracing the curve of her cheeks, Lan crawled across the wooden floor to where her mother lay dying. She took Lan's hands between her shaking fingers, holding on to her entire world with the last of her strength.

At that moment, her mother had turned to her, eyes brighter than all the silver stars in the night. Eyes that had been *glowing.*

And then she'd pressed a finger to the inside of Lan's left wrist, and Lan's world had exploded in a blinding burn of white light.

Slowly the light receded. The world filtered back again, the lacquered panels of the Teahouse, the scarlet loveseat, the faint thrum of noise from outside the windows. The dull ache pounding through her head, the buzz of something in her ears and the taste of bile and something like metal on her tongue.

There, sprawled on the clean sandalwood floor between her and the loveseat, was the corpse of General Donnaron J. Tarley.

5

Kind lies can kill kingdoms.

—General Yeshin Noro Surgen
of the Jorshen Steel clan, *Classic of War*

A scream was working its way from her chest to her throat, she was sure, but Lan only stared at the body. Watching it as though it would move again if she looked at it hard enough.

Just as her mother might not have died had she not blinked.

But as the dull pounding of her heart echoed in her ears and a sharp bout of laughter from Madam Meng rose between the floorboards, the reality of her situation filtered back. She looked at the corpse then, truly *looked*, taking in the unnatural bend of its neck, eyes still open and mouth still curved in that grin. There was only the slightest hint of surprise, a shadow if she tilted her head and observed. But to a bystander it might have seemed that he had simply fallen to his death—an unlucky accident, perhaps, resulting from a frivolous bedmate.

Don't be stupid. An Elantian Angel found dead in the company of a Hin had only one possible outcome. Would it be the gallows for her? A public execution? Or a painful, torturous death at the hands of one of the magicians?

The torrent of morbid thoughts was interrupted as footsteps sounded down the hall, soft as wind creaking against the old walls of the Teahouse.

Breaking through the fugue of her shock, she snatched the butterknife, which lay at her feet, where Donnaron J. Tarley had knocked it from her hands seconds before he'd died. The footsteps were approaching. It was too late to hide the body—she had to—she had to—

Her eyes landed on the scarlet loveseat several paces away. Lan dove for the corpse, dragging it like a sack of rice and stuffing limbs, head, and floppy appendages beneath with zero decorum. She gave an outstretched arm a good kick and straightened.

By the time the wooden doors slid open, she was ready.

"Unless you intend to surprise me with pastries, you can put down that butterknife."

She froze. She recognized that voice—rich and dark, with all the makings of a smoky night sky.

The Hin official from earlier in the night stepped inside with two neat clacks of his patent leather boots, and slid the doors shut again. She immediately noticed that one of his black gloves was off. She'd expected the skin on his hands to be smooth as polished wood, a sure sign of aristocratic upbringing—only it was marked by dozens of pale, crisscrossing lines that puckered on the flesh.

"Well? Don't just stand there. Where is he?" In the silence of the room, his voice held absolute command. It was beautiful—imperial, almost.

It took her another moment to realize: he was now speaking to her in *Hin:* perfect, Imperial Court standard Hin, spoken by her mother and her tutors, without any influence of the myriad dialects found across the vast kingdom.

It was the norm now for Hin to converse with each other

in Elantian in public; those who dared, and still cared, could try to speak Hin in the privacy of nooks and crannies and behind closed doors. The Elantians had enforced this as law "to promote greater unity in the Great Elantian Empire," but Lan knew better. They were trying to eliminate the Hin tongue completely, to prevent uprisings and secret political movements—because, well, how did you destroy a people? You began by cutting off their roots.

But . . . what was an official of the Elantian government doing speaking to her in *Hin*?

Lan licked her lips. That didn't matter—neither the man's language nor his voice. The *only* thing she should be thinking about pertaining to either was how to stick this butterknife through those husky vocal cords.

The young man strode across the room. Lan watched with increasing despondency as he rounded the back of the loveseat and crouched to examine the corpse, stuffed hastily like a doll, arms and legs all twisted, head crooked against the floor and eyes still open.

The boy turned to her, and his brows were stitched together in a way that did not mean good news. "What have you done?" His voice was low. "Who are you?"

They stared at each other, the words stretching out between them.

What *had* she done?

Lan opened her mouth.

It was at this unfortunate moment that her stomach decided to give way.

Lan turned and vomited right onto the carefully polished lacquerwood screens. *Madam Meng's going to kill me* was her first thought when she straightened, followed by: *Four Gods. I'm losing it.*

"Have some water," she heard the Hin courtdog say. There

was the sound of porcelain clinking, of liquid being poured. "You're in shock. It's all right."

A cup was offered to her; without thinking, she took it and drained it to wash out the putrid taste in her mouth. When she lowered it, the edge of the cup where her lips had been were stained copper.

Blood.

The Hin official had taken a step back and now surveyed her with a look of such intensity, it burned. "Can you tell me what happened?" he asked.

Looking down at the porcelain teacup between her fingers and the butterknife in her other hand, Lan finally gathered the dregs of her thoughts.

One: she had just—*somehow*—killed a high-ranking Elantian White Angel.

Two: she was being interrogated by a Hin courtdog.

You need to run, she told herself. *Now.*

Lan studied the teacup in her hands, the white glaze and blue patterns of prancing rabbits amidst willow trees. Her gaze trailed up, all the way to the tray on the table, where the teapot sat, filled with tea gone cold. She remembered how heavy she'd found it when she'd first arrived at the Teahouse, a slip of a girl barely past her eighth cycle. Madam Meng had beaten them whenever their hands shook as they poured tea. It was because of this teapot that Lan had made herself strong so that she would never be hit again.

She knew what she had to do.

Lan looked up. The Hin boy had moved closer to the windows, peering through the glass. In the lowlight of the alchemical lantern, the streets were in full view. He glanced down, and then back up at her. Face open, waiting.

Lan slipped the butterknife into a seam at her waist—one she'd used to pocket nuts and dried jujubes, the occasional sesame candy. She pitched her voice high, breathless as she began to move toward the tea table. "I . . . I'm trying to recall." She needed to paint a pretty picture of compliance, of submission, that might be expected of a Hin girl. "He was . . . well, we were . . . near the wall, I suppose . . ." Lan held the cup he'd offered her with one hand. With the other, reached for the teapot as though to pour herself a cup of tea. "And he—he . . ."

She sank to her knees with a well-timed gasp.

The Hin courtdog moved as though to help her. He crossed the room remarkably quickly, a shadow outlined against the red lantern. "Are you—"

He never finished his sentence. Lan gripped the handle of the teapot and, with all her strength, swung it into his face.

In the split second before contact, she felt something in the air shift.

The teapot shattered in an explosion of noise, porcelain, and cold tea. Instantly there came the pressure of warm fingers, tight across her wrist. Looking down, she saw shards of the teapot strewn everywhere, liquid dripping across Madam Meng's beautiful rosewood floors.

Lan looked back up. The boy's face was utterly unmarred, not even a splash of tea on those smooth cheekbones.

Impossible, she thought, taking in the wreckage all around their feet. She hadn't even seen him move.

The courtdog's expression was not amused. His mouth was pressed into a thin line as he held her arm. "You'll have to try a lot harder than that if you want to run."

"Got it," Lan said, and with her other hand, smashed her teacup into his face.

She didn't wait to see what happened; the pressure on her wrist loosened, and by the time she registered the sharp pain that seared across her palm, she was already at the sliding wooden doors, ripping them open. The hallway was empty;

she careened past gauze screens and lacquerwood doors. Any second now and the courtdog might come after her—she needed to get as far away from this Teahouse as possible—

Blood splashed onto the floor, dotting the white canvas of her dress like red blossoms in the snow. A steady trickle was winding its way down her arm. Lan tucked her injured hand into her sleeve as she swerved onto the staircase. The Teahouse unfolded beneath her, a blend of Elantian blue-and-silver, ebony-colored tables, and fluttering songgirls. She was three steps down the stairs when movement at the doors caught her attention.

There, through the filigreed screens erected between the entrance and the main dining room, an Elantian man stepped in—and all of Lan's blood rushed from her head. He was dressed in pale armor from head to toe; the only spots of color on him were the blue of his cloak as it caught an evening breeze and the winter's-ice color of his eyes.

No. No, this couldn't be. She was dreaming—she *had* to be.

Then the man shifted and she caught the glint of something on his wrists. As his cloak slid back, Lan saw a series of metal cuffs lining his forearms in different shades of gray, gold, and rust-red. Different types of *metal*.

Everything inside her froze. A single word snaked into her mind, the cut of silver across a snow-tinted landscape.

Magician.

Madam Meng was making her way to him, lips already peeled back in a dazzling smile, eyes bright with the promise of gold from the pockets of an Elantian Royal Magician.

That was before the magician twisted his fingers and split her torso right down the middle.

Time seemed to slow in that moment, and Lan felt as though she were trapped in a memory of twelve cycles past, watching blood spill down her mother's robes, trying to reconcile the image of the magician holding a live, beating heart with the hole in her mother's chest.

It was him.

It was the monster of her nightmares.

The Winter Magician, who had slaughtered her mother twelve cycles ago, was standing right here, in her Teahouse. His eyes, with the accuracy of an arrow sailing across a battlefield, fixed on her, and reality snapped back in a rush.

Madam Meng fell.

Someone screamed.

And pandemonium erupted.

Lan clung to the balustrade. Her brain screamed at her to do one thing but her heart another. The magician was cutting a warpath straight for the stairs, straight for *her*, and yet she trailed her gaze across the dining room floor, searching for a girl in a blush-pink páo.

Ying . . . Ying, where are you?

She spotted her best friend crouched by a screen, a shattered tray by her side. Ying's gaze followed the magician, sweeping along his route until she found Lan.

Their gazes met. It took Ying a moment to connect the dots.

Then she sprang up and ran for the magician.

Lan's mother had once told her that she was destined for greatness; that the kingdom would be her duty, and that she would protect her people.

Lan threw up her hands and shouted, "No! Ying, stay back!"

It was the moment that cost her.

The Royal Magician raised his arms, those metal cuffs gleaming, and Lan screamed. She had the sensation that something had speared through her veins and frozen her from the inside out. The feeling was so foreign, so agonizingly violating. She was burning. She was freezing. She was cracking like a porcelain vase, and there was a searing white light emanating from the fissures between all the shattered pieces of *her*.

Then, with painful abruptness, it stopped.

Breath in, breath out. Ribs grinding, lungs swelling, rosewood beneath her bloodied fingers. The unbearable heat of a fire flickering out, leaving her insides raw and red.

A voice rang out, clear as a spring, cutting through the mist of her pain.

"Stop!"

Later Lan would recall lying on the floor, blood filling her mouth, the world flipped upside down so that the alchemical lights and lanterns hanging from the ceiling looked as though they would fall onto the familiar face that appeared over the threshold of the stairs. A face gentle in its beauty and fierce in its love, blazing from round black eyes.

Lan had felt fear like this only once before in her life.

Ying stepped forward. She had nothing; she shivered in her scanty performance outfit of silks and gauze, hair unbound like skeins of black silk. She spoke in a trembling voice, the Elantian language clumsy on her tongue. "Please, my lord . . . please leave her alone!"

The Winter Magician's gaze was flat as he beheld the girl. He lifted his hand. The next sequence of actions happened slowly, very slowly.

Lan sensed a tremor in the air—an invisible energy, almost like the whistle of a whip, extending toward Ying.

A red gash appeared on Ying's body, neck to belly. Red began to weep from her, spilling down her gown and pooling at her feet. The girl's lips parted in surprise.

Slowly, like the last petal on a blossom tree, she fell.

The Winter Magician turned back to Lan.

There was a sudden rush of wind, bone-cold. A shadow fell over her.

Someone stepped over where she lay, his coat whipping behind him like night incarnate. Midnight eyes, harder than obsidian.

He lifted a hand.

Plucked off his black glove.

And light exploded from the tips of his fingers.

It was him—it was the Hin courtdog. The one she'd smashed with a teacup.

A drastic change seemed to have overcome him. Whereas earlier his moves had been subtle, smooth as a song, they were now bladed, burning, sharp as a sword.

The Hin swiped his hands across the air. The move resembled a martial arts pose. She blinked; time seemed to jump again as her mind struggled to catch up, and the next moment flames erupted from the Hin's hands, sweeping over the landing and obscuring everything: the Royal Magician, the pandemonium of the Teahouse, and Ying, Ying's lifeless body—

The Hin turned to Lan, and she caught a glimpse of his face: beautiful, terrible, furious as a storm-tossed night. A trickle of blood wound down the side of his face. He was saying something to her, his lips moving quickly, urgently, but the words slurred in Lan's brain. She was looking at something else.

Glowing in midair before them was a foreign character that almost—*almost*—resembled a Hin word, but not. And around it, blazing like a trail of fire, was a sealed circle. The wall of flames seemed to pour from it like molten lava, licking across the floor and growing from nothing.

The sight brought forth memories of snow falling like ashes, a red beating heart bleeding to the tune of a broken lute. An impossibility.

He scooped her up, his hands looping around her waist and supporting her elbows, and then she was half-stumbling, half being dragged down the corridor, the Hin boy at her side, the world slipping as though she'd downed one too many cups of whitefire liquor.

They burst into the Peach Blossom Room. The Hin boy slowed and turned his palm to the windows. This time Lan did not blink.

His finger traced fluid strokes in the air. The motion was elegant and eerily similar to how her mother had written calligraphy. The air over the window, too, began to ripple and shimmer; with each stroke of his hand, those blazing trails of light appeared, and this time they appeared written into the glass. A different character, if Lan's memory served, from the last one.

She watched, taking in the final stroke: an uninterrupted circle encompassing the unknown character. As soon as the end met the beginning, a shockwave seemed to pulse through the room.

The glass shattered, shards arcing through the air and falling around them like rain.

He turned to look at her then, and his eyes held command of her world in that moment.

"If you wish to live," he said quietly, "you will come with me."

If you wish to live. So obvious the choice seemed until, all of a sudden, it wasn't. Lan thought of the crumpled body of her best friend, torn open from the inside out. Heard the screams coming from somewhere down the hallway, the songgirls dragged into this carnage, flowers swept into a winter storm—

Did she wish to live? How many lives was hers worth?

"M-my friends—" Her voice was small and pathetic.

Māma had told her once that she would grow up to protect the ones she loved.

She had let them all die instead.

The boy's eyes were hard, unyielding, his grip on her waist unrelenting. "There is nothing more you can do for them," he continued in that even, clipped voice. "They are dead."

Footsteps pounding down the hallway.

The boy lifted his gaze to the door behind them. "We've run out of time," he said, and with a decisive leap, swung onto the ledge of the window. They teetered on the sill, the streets below a distant current of auric lights and shadowed movement.

"Hold on." The boy drew her close to him. His arm fell to her waist, his hand clasping her wrist, careful to avoid the wounds from the porcelain shards of the teacup. Lan stiffened against the memory of Teahouse patrons reaching for her with their wandering fingers.

The boy's touch was light, courteous, his fingers warm against her skin.

Out of the corner of her eye, Lan saw a figure appear by the sliding doors of the Peach Blossom Room.

She twisted her head to look back. The last that she saw was the winter gaze of the Elantian Royal Magician piercing her with a promise.

He would find her.

And he would do to her what he'd done to everyone she'd loved.

The world tilted beneath her, and then they were falling.

6

Practitioners suspected of utilizing demonic powers in
any shape or form by the banned practice of demonic
practitioning shall be subject to interrogation,
punishment, and death by the Imperial Court.

—Emperor Jīn, "Second Imperial Decree on
Practitioning," era of the Middle Kingdom

Zen was not prepared for this.

Practitioning had begun as the gentle commune between the natural world, the spirits, and the ancient shamans
of the Ninety-Nine Clans, each to their own. The myriad practices had grown and flourished with the union of the clans
into the First Kingdom and its relative period of peace and
economic prosperity; education had blossomed, and with it,
the Hundred Schools of Practitioning had risen. The arts of
practitioning had been taught to any born with talent to control qì, the natural flow of energies in the world that existed
ubiquitously yet could be harnessed only by a select few to be
wielded.

But throughout the Hundred Schools, with their wildly
diverse branches of practitioning arts from all across the
kingdom, one common thread had united its teachers and disciples: a practitioner was meant to work in tune with the flow
of worldly energies around them and call upon them in times
of need. Balance and harmony were key principles to the Way.

Practitioning was not meant to be used to harm.

Even as the Middle Kingdom sought to rein in the arts of practitioning under imperial control, even with the Last Kingdom's eradication of the Ninety-Nine Clans and removal of practitioning from history, this way of thought had persistently shaped Hin culture. Perhaps that was why the remaining practitioners who served the Imperial Court and the emperor's Dragon Army had lost so terribly and so easily to the Elantian Royal Magicians during the Conquest.

Zen considered himself a devout disciple of the arts of practitioning, but falling out of three-story buildings was not something one did on a regular basis, and it required improvisation.

Unfortunately Zen was someone who went very much by the book. He was not one for improvisation.

Air screamed past his ears, the girl was screaming *in* his ear, and the sky and stars tumbled in a jumble over his head. He flung out a hand and pulled on the threads of Seal art ingrained in his mind from years of study and practice, weaving strokes into a Seal. This one tethered their bodies to the wood of the balcony above, and pushed against the earth rising to meet them below.

They slowed as soon as he closed the Seal. The ground rose to meet them; the landing was unkind but not deadly.

Zen stumbled and righted himself. Next to him, the girl lay sprawled on the street. Her skimpy performance robe was spread across the road, drawing looks from passersby. She lay still, as though she had lost the will to stand again.

Ordinarily Zen would never have risked revealing his identity for a songgirl indentured at some high-class bordello in an Elantian stronghold.

But common songgirls did not kill Elantian soldiers in the blink of an eye. Zen had felt it from downstairs: the shockwave of qì that had ripped through the Teahouse, detectable only by trained practitioners. It had been a qì full of shadows and darkness, of *yīn* energies without balance.

It had been the qì he'd been following from Old Wei's shop—the one that had become too faint for him to track in the crowded space of the Teahouse.

The problem was, he wasn't the only one who'd sensed it.

Movement from above; a shadow appeared in the broken window, lantern light staining his pale armor red. The silhouette raised a hand, and the air around him began to tingle. The scent of burning metal choked down Zen's throat.

Magic. Elantian metalwork magic.

Whereas Hin practitioners borrowed the energies of qì from all elements of the natural world, Elantian magicians harnessed the power of metals to create their magic. Each type of metal, as far as Zen knew, yielded different strengths and weaknesses, and each magician was born with a connection to one, which they wore around their forearm.

Very few, Zen had surmised, had the ability to work *multiple* metals.

The man hunting them was a rare class of magician known as an Alloy. The more metal cuffs an Alloy wore, the more metals they could control, and the more powerful they were.

This man's forearm was a rainbow of ores. Zen had no wish to face him in combat, especially with a deadweight by his side. One who had smashed porcelain into his head.

Zen traced a series of strokes. A whirl of shadows exploded from his Seal like black flames, clouding the area around and hiding them from view—a trick he'd learned from a master who'd served as an imperial assassin.

He turned and hauled the girl up by her armpits.

Questions remained: her allegiance, for one. The only surviving Hin practitioners, as far as Zen knew, were hidden away with him at his school. But he could interrogate her on that later. Right now it was imperative that he kept her out of Elantian hands before she became another weapon they could use to gain access to Hin practitioning.

Zen ran a thumb over the scars on his hands—a motion that had grown habitual over the cycles. The girl would be better off dead than having to go through the things they would do to her.

"We have to leave," he said. Around them, people were screaming as his black smoke rolled over them; it wouldn't be two minutes before the patrols would be upon them. "Please. *Move—*"

He heard the whistle of metal behind him too late.

Zen turned, but the glint of a blade flashed past him, followed by a searing pain in his side. He let out a sharp exhale, his knees buckling with surprise. When he put a hand to his midriff, it was warm and wet with blood.

He knew immediately that the blade had been poisoned, coated with some Elantian metalwork spell that began to seep wickedly through his veins. Essence of mercury, perhaps, or arsenic or antimony.

His mind blurred.

Small, firm hands wrapped around his waist. He felt his arm slung over a bony shoulder, silken hair brush against his chin. Smelled, amidst the aroma of burning metal and bitter blood, the perfume of lilies.

With some difficulty, he focused his vision. The girl was dragging him forward along King Alessander's Road. The auric lights were blurring; sweat slicked down his cheeks as the world thudded with the pounding of his steps. All that kept him anchored was the feel of the girl's arms around his waist, the scent of lilies drifting in the fog smothering his mind.

Gradually, the crowds thinned, the stalls grew sparser, and the roads darkened as lantern light faded.

They swung into a narrow side street, shoes splashing on grime. The pungent odor of kitchen waste and sewage permeated the air . . . mixed with the briny tang of ocean water.

The girl slowed at last. Zen was grateful as she propped him against a wall. The burning in his side had faded somewhat with the distance they'd put between themselves and the magician. The longer the distance, the weaker the magic's hold—or the more powerful its wielder had to be. That, at least, was one principle Hin practitioning had in common with Elantian magic. It was frightening how little the handful of surviving Hin practitioners had learned of Elantian metalwork in twelve long cycles.

Zen raised a shaking hand to wipe the sweat from his forehead. It came away mixed with blood. He blinked for a moment, stumped by where that might have come from—and then nearly laughed when he remembered.

The girl had smashed a teacup on his face.

"Are you all right, mister?"

Her voice was like song: sweet as silverbells, clear as a halcyon sky. He looked up to see her peering at him, moonlight draping her pale outfit like a pure spill of milk. Her chin-length hair was slick with sweat, but she was lovely. He'd noticed back at the Teahouse—he hadn't been able to help himself. Lips bowed over a sharp chin, dark lashes sweeping over smile-curved eyes that were currently studying him just as he studied her.

Zen averted his gaze. "Yes," he said, his voice rough. "Thank you."

She loosed a breath and stepped back. "So you're not a Hin courtdog."

Zen blinked at her wearily. "Do I look like I work for the Elantian government?"

She lifted her eyebrows and gave him a slow, sweeping

once-over from the tips of his patent leather boots to his Elantian-style merchant's coat.

Heat rushed to Zen's face. Right. He had dressed *exactly* like a Hin courtdog. A traitor.

"How did you do it?" The girl's tone had changed. She watched him intently, face half-shadowed. "Those cheap tricks with the lights and the fire and the glass window breaking—"

"They're not cheap tricks," Zen said. The girl's eyes glimmered, but she said nothing more. "And I have questions of my own for *you,*" he shot back, "such as how a songgirl at a teahouse managed to kill a high-ranking Elantian Angel." *With so much yīn in the energies you use.*

His scrutiny focused on her at the thought. He took in her outline, small and balled up tight like an animal prepared to strike. No matter how he searched, though, he could no longer find any trace of the yīn energies he had sensed in Old Wei's shop and permeating the Peach Blossom Room, clinging to the corpse of that Elantian Angel.

It made no sense. If she *were* a demonic practitioner, or even a regular practitioner, why could he sense no traces of *any* form of qì emanating from her person?

The girl's gall turned to defensiveness. "None of your business."

"It is now."

"I never asked for your help."

It was Zen's turn to raise his eyebrows. "Oh? Do I misremember the offer you made me back at the Teahouse?"

Without batting an eyelash, she closed the gap between them and held out a hand, palm upturned. "Show me the coin, then, O Not-Courtdog Mister of Magic."

Zen's breath caught as he flattened himself as much as physically possible against the brick wall. Unabashed little ingrate, using her cheap songgirl's ways against him. His school would have had her expelled for such effrontery.

He was better than that. Trying to steady his pulse, he ignored her and glanced around them, taking in the narrow alleyways, the uneven street, the darkness that felt more comfortable than the superficial auric lights the Elantians used. "Where are we right now?"

"The slums." The girl tipped her head to look in the direction of the main road. She still stood disconcertingly close. The scent of lilies was jarringly at odds with the rose-scented perfume that had choked the Teahouse. As though hearing his thoughts, her gaze snapped back to him, bright and bold. "I know it's not exactly your cup of tea, mister, but the patrols never look here."

Mister. He ignored the insult. "They might now," Zen said, straightening slightly. The magician's spell had faded enough so that the pain across his wound was bearable. It was still bleeding, but he had neither the time nor the materials to treat it right now. "We must get out of the city."

The words had no sooner fallen from his lips than a faraway sound drifted to them: a rhythmic litany that clanged deep into the night.

The girl sucked in a breath. "The bells," she whispered, and then her eyes snapped to him. "The dawn and dusk bells."

Zen was not sure what to make of this. He had not grown up in a conventional Hin city, had barely spent any time in the Last Kingdom before it had been ripped from him. The Elantians had invaded, and the cities had become death traps for people like him. What he *did* know was that the distant capital of Tiān'jīng—a city his family had staunchly avoided—held a pair of bells that rang at dawn and dusk each day without fail. He was not sure why their song would drive such anxiety into the girl.

She was still staring at him as though he were mad. "Four

Gods, did you grow up in a nunnery? The city—it's going into a lockdown."

Ah. Zen tipped his head in the direction of the bells, eyes narrowed. Keeping a hand on his side, he pushed off from the wall and was relieved to find his legs steady. The world was no longer spinning. "Make for the city gates," he said. "No time to lose."

She shook her head. "That's the first place they'll check. The gates will be closed and swarming with Angels."

"The city walls, then."

"Impossible to scale. There are patrols that'll kill us on sight."

He hesitated. If they did not get out of Haak'gong soon, it would be crawling with Elantian soldiers and—worse—government magicians. The Elantian military stronghold would have been alerted by now, he thought, and soon he and this girl would be smoked out like ants in a trap.

If it really came down to it . . .

Zen made a split-second decision. "As long as you can lead us there, I can get us through."

Her eyes shone like dark pebbles as she glanced in the direction of the Teahouse, a dozen or so streets back. Emotions shifted across her face like clouds across a night sky: hesitation, guilt, and raw sorrow.

It struck a chord.

The edge to his voice softened. "First time you've seen a massacre?"

"No."

Her answer surprised him, and that single bladed word held a thousand more. Her gaze might have been the unread pages of a book, a story burning within.

One Zen suspected he would be achingly familiar with.

His jaw hardened. "Then you know there is nothing we can do but survive."

The girl blinked, and the raw emotion on her face vanished. She stepped forward, and her gait was steady, grounded, as though she were a performer back at the Teahouse switching from one act to another.

"Keep up," she said, and slipped into the shadows.

The bells tolled across the city of Haak'gong.

The crowds had been sent into a frenzy, and the Elantian city guard was out in full, marshaling people like fish into nets. The girl led Zen through back alleys, keeping to grime-slicked streets and narrow, crumpling walls that bled misery. She darted before him like a phantom, surefooted as a mountain goat.

Haak'gong was a port city, one side open to the sea and the other three surrounded by tall walls—built thousands of cycles ago to keep out Mansorian invaders, reinforced in the era of fear instilled by the now-infamous demonic practitioner the Nightslayer toward the end of the Middle Kingdom. Now the Elantians used them as a means to control the workings of the city and keep its people in. The walls were high, nigh impossible to scale, and, as Zen saw now, patrolled by archers.

Zen and the girl crouched in the borrowed darkness of a chipped clay roof, surrounded by spavined houses. They'd reached the edge of the slums, which huddled beneath the shadows of the western walls. Torchlight flickered by the watchtowers, providing a lick of light against the night. Zen could see White Angels patrolling, their pale armor winking between crenellations like a macabre game of hide and seek.

He'd have to time it well. Get to the highest vantage point possible, seek the darkness between watchtowers, the space between one Angel and another . . . and then they'd take their chances.

Zen turned to the girl. "We have to get up to the roof."

"What, you're going to do one of your tricks again?" She waved a hand erratically, and it took him a moment to realize she was mimicking his practitioning.

"No," he said, trying not to feel insulted. "They—the magicians—will sense it."

She stared at him a moment longer, and it occurred to him that she wouldn't understand anything he spoke of in terms of practitioning. After all, the common folk thought practitioners were just beings of lore and legend.

The Imperial Court had made sure of that.

The girl waggled her eyebrows at him in an expression that might have been cheeky—one that *definitely* would not have been tolerated by certain masters at his school—before turning away. With a light hop, she was on a window ledge; another little shimmy, and she'd hauled herself over the protruding terra-cotta eaves.

It was almost humiliating how much longer it took him to get up without using any practitioning. By the time Zen had scrabbled over the roof, he was sweating profusely, his side aching with sharp, stabbing pains that did nothing to improve his mood.

The girl was crouched low, her eyes trained on the walls. She glanced at him, pressed a finger to her lips. "Magicians," she murmured, and pointed.

Blinking the haze from his eyes, Zen squinted. Past the roofs of the slums to the main roads of Haak'gong, he saw something that chilled his blood. Winding through the streets was an entire unit of Elantian Royal Magicians, recognizable by their cloaks, which fluttered like torn pieces of blue sky. Even from here, he could see glints of metal on their forearms.

He and the girl needed to get out, *now*.

Zen touched a hand to the wound in his side. It was still

bleeding freely, but he'd see to it once they were outside the walls. He was aware of how shallow and labored his breathing had become, how his vision slanted and slipped out of focus.

With tremendous effort, he stood and held out a hand. "You will need to hold on tightly to me."

There it was again, that shadow of fear that flitted across her face at the prospect of touch. Zen understood—and he related more than she might ever know.

The Elantians had left their marks on both of them, in ways both visible and invisible.

The girl cocked an eyebrow. "Shouldn't we be focused on running away instead of embracing?"

In spite of the rising urgency he felt, heat rushed to his cheeks. "We *are*," Zen said. The dizziness was now gripping his stomach. Soon he would not have the strength left to carry both of them out. "I will get us over the wall."

"How?"

Zen gritted his teeth. "Just . . . *watch*. I cannot possibly explain in the span of a few seconds what I am about to do."

She gave him a skeptical look, but then half-shrugged and took a step closer. She placed her palm gently over his. It hovered a hairsbreadth away, a question hanging between. "Why are you helping me?" There was no jest in her tone this time. "Your contact is dead, and I've nothing more to offer you."

Zen parted his lips to answer when his gaze caught on something. A pale pattern peeking out from beneath the sleeve of her left wrist like a curved crescent moon. A breath of wind stirred between them at that moment, lifting the gauze of her sleeve further, and he saw it then: a puckered scar across her skin, the strokes arranged in likeness to a Hin character, encircled by a smooth, uninterrupted arc.

A Seal.

One he had never come across before.

His mouth fell open, and when he looked up at her again, it was as though he'd been looking at her through a smoke-screen that had finally cleared.

The yīn energies he'd sensed in Old Wei's shop.

The way she'd killed the Elantian soldier in an explosion of qì.

The reason the Royal Magicians were after her.

This girl had a Seal *on* her person, which yielded only one possibility: a practitioner had left it on her, and with it, sealed away inside this girl whatever secrets they'd carried. A secret, perhaps, that explained the yīn energies she exuded.

Had she any idea?

She was still waiting for his answer.

Whatever false reply he had been about to give dissipated on his tongue. Instinct was calling on him, and this time it told him to improvise. He flipped her wrist over and peeled back her sleeve with his other thumb, careful not to touch her skin. "Because you have this," he said.

"You see it," she whispered, and the fear on her face gave way to wonder.

Zen was mentally preparing himself for more needling questions when she let out a breath. In a sudden, unexpected move, she closed the gap between them and slipped her arms around his waist. Her head bumped against his shoulder. There was nothing romantic to the gesture; it was a moment that sent a strange ache through Zen's chest, a motion drenched in desperation. A little girl clinging to the last piece of refuge in a dying world.

Gently, Zen let his arms fall around the small of her back. Her hair tickled his chin, the scent of lilies wrapping around him. Calming him. Exhaustion dragged at him, and in a way, she, too, was an anchor in the storm, her presence steady and solid.

The worst, though, was yet to come.

"Hold on," he said, and let qì flow through him.

The Light Arts was a branch of practitioning that channeled qì in a precise way through focal points in the body to achieve extraordinary movement—often exaggerated in stories and tales of practitioners flying or dancing on water that made their way to the common folk. Yet to get over those walls would take the skills of an extremely advanced practitioner . . . and impeccable timing.

Zen harnessed qì flowing from all around, letting its currents pour into him and trapping it all within. Ordinary people had qì inside them, too—it flowed everywhere, was the makeup behind everything in this world—yet it was the ability to draw in and control qì that gave practitioners their powers. Practitioners spent cycles cultivating and expanding the amount of qì they could hold within their cores. At this moment, Zen knew he was lighting up like a beacon, the pull of energies signaling his location to the Elantian magicians in the vicinity. Within moments, they would be on him.

The girl's arms were tight around him, as though she'd sensed the stir of qì around them. In the distance, he heard shouts, saw flashes of metal, smelled the acrid singe of Elantian magic.

Just a little more . . .

The soles of his feet were tingling, the flow of qì surging within him and filling him with a sense of vitality, an intoxicating rush of power. The colors around him became sharper, the sounds clearer, as though the world had spilled into fragments of painted crystals, blade-sharp and diamond-bright. At the same time, something in him stirred: a great beast inhaling, rumbling to wake with the influx of energy.

Zen clamped it down.

The flashes of silver armor winked between the crenellations in a rhythmic beat, the patrols still unaware of what was happening below. Zen counted down in his head, the energies at his feet burning.

And then he kicked off.

The world opened to him in a thrilling rush of light and darkness, yīn and yáng: the alleyways zigzagging between crumbling roofs of dilapidated houses, strings of fluttering laundry trailing outside windows like pale souls, a flickering candle here and there whispering yellow through paper windows. He could sense it all, elements of the world constituting the flow of qì: the sodden earth weeping beneath streets coated in waste and grime, the stale air hanging over hunched residences. The small pools of water choked with sewage, the coal fires lending little warmth in the autumn chill.

You could do something, a voice whispered in the recesses of his mind. *You could end the suffering of your people. All this power, all yours to command.*

If you would only break free.

The girl gave a muffled squeak in his arms. Zen stiffened. The air was suddenly asphyxiating, the scent of burnt metal smothering his throat, pressure building around his ears—

An iron whip descended upon them out of nowhere.

Out of instinct, Zen curled his body, flipping the girl beneath him.

He felt it the moment the lash struck his back, hard enough for him to see stars. Pain—excruciating pain—spread through his veins like wildfire. He couldn't breathe, couldn't move, couldn't think.

He lost his focus. The qì that had been propelling him upward scattered. The sky began to pull away from him, and the ground beneath rushed up.

Darkness closed in.

7

Practitioners of the Way engage in equivalent
exchange, for there is no give without take.
Borrowed power must be returned,
and power itself requires payment.

—Dào'zǐ, *Book of the Way*
(Classic of Virtues), 1.4

The boy had lost consciousness.

Something—a metal whip, perhaps wielded by an Elantian magician—had lashed at him out of nowhere, breaking their trajectory and sending them spiraling.

Lan screamed at him as they fell, fists gripping his waist as the lapels of his coat flapped in her face like the wings of a broken bird. The wind shrieked in her ears, snatching away her voice and tugging at the black ribbons of the boy's hair.

The ground rose up to meet them, hard and fast. No, not the ground—the crenellations of the wall, torchlight licking at them like the teeth and tongue of a great beast as it opened its maw. Lan saw the glint of silver and metal beneath—patrols who'd be on them within seconds.

She shouted again and, with extreme difficulty, pried back a hand and slapped the boy's cheek.

His eyes snapped open.

Lan's blood froze.

It felt as though she were staring into an inhuman face; so

glacial was his expression that it might have belonged to one of those Elantian marble statues of gods and angels. The careful, courteous boy she'd spoken to earlier was gone.

And his eyes—they were completely, utterly black.

Something swirled in that darkness: a glint of light, faraway stars in an ink-black night. She felt his hands shift against her back, felt a rush of something inexplicable—energy? power? wind?—around them.

The air thickened like rice syrup. Something brushed against Lan's back. As though cradled by a giant hand, Lan and the boy slowed, drifted down, and landed on the stone ramparts.

He sprawled on top of her, eyelids fluttering, head drooping. With a soft exhale, he fell unconscious again, pinning her under his weight.

Boots thundered against the ground nearby. Pressure on her arms. The world righted itself as she was jerked to her knees. Gloved hands grasped her chin so tight that it would bruise, twisted her arms behind her at an angle. She glanced up and found herself held by several Elantian wall patrols.

"What in the Hell?" The Elantian language rolled over her like a shock of cold water. "Did you see?"

"You think they jumped from somewhere? Was too dark to make out."

If Lan hadn't just literally *felt* the boy leaping through the air—almost flying—from the houses below to the wall up high, she wouldn't have believed it either. How? She thought of the way flames had seemed to pour out of his fingers. The way he'd traced that strange character in the air, and a window several paces away had shattered.

Her conversation with Old Wei earlier in the afternoon came back to her.

Whatever folk heroes and practitioners of old you believe in are dead. There are no heroes left for us in this world, Old Wei.

Is that what you truly believe?

A rough thumb across her cheek. Her thoughts scattered. "Pretty thing," one of the Elantian Angels crooned. "Shame to let her off."

Lan struggled against their grip, reaching inside her and into her memories for a scrap of whatever miraculous power had saved her from Donnaron J. Tarley.

This time, nothing happened.

She bit back a scream as the Angels shoved her against the rough-hewn stone. She tasted blood, warm and metallic, felt hard, cold armor brush against her back as the seams of her flimsy performance páo were ripped open as easily as rice paper.

Was this how it would all end? At the hands of a few Angels, freedom just several steps away on the other side of the wall?

"Leave her."

The voice broke through her haze like the thunder of a winter's storm. At once the pressure on her back loosened, and she was hauled to her feet.

Blinking the tears from her eyes, she looked up into the frosted blue gaze of the newcomer.

The Winter Magician strode toward them. Torchlight bled crimson into his livery of silvers and blues; his hair was a shock of ice white. She'd always remembered it as red, red like the blood from her mother's heart the day she'd seen him.

Except this time he saw her, too. A gleaming whip trailed behind him like a snake; even as she watched, it coiled up his arms, dissolving into one of the metal cuffs he wore.

"You," he said quietly. "I thought I recognized the magic from twelve cycles ago: the very one I told myself I would never forget." He knelt, his blue-gloved fingers wrapping around her jaw so tightly she let out a gasp as he jerked her face toward his. His eyes narrowed in triumph. "If you hadn't murdered General Tarley, you would have continued to dance under my very nose without my realizing it."

He recognized her. Worse . . . he'd been searching for her.

For her *magic*.

What magic? Lan thought desperately, but the knowledge burned through her mind in a series of images: General Tarley dead before her from that mysterious flash of white light; her mother, hair and páo adrift as though caught in an invisible wind, fingers dancing on her lute, then clutched over Lan's own wrist, leaving Lan with a scar only she could see, written in a language no one had understood.

No one—until tonight.

The magician lifted a hand and plucked off the glove. The sight of his fingers—long and spindly and sickly-white—sent a wave of revulsion through her. "It's time to finish what I started."

She'd sworn to herself that the next time they met, she wouldn't be the frightened, trembling child lying helpless in the hot water vents. That she'd have grown powerful. That she would fight back.

Yet as Lan met his gaze, she found her voice drying up in her throat. Fear overtook her—so violent that she shuddered in its grasp.

"This time," the Royal Magician whispered, "you'll give it to me."

She couldn't tear her eyes from his winter's gaze. Couldn't wrench her mind from the words that had haunted her for twelve cycles.

Give it to me, he'd said to Māma.

Never, she'd replied.

Time seemed to slow as the magician pressed his bare hand to her left wrist. The metal on one of his cuffs began to writhe. It sharpened to a needle point and punctured her skin.

Pain erupted, shooting from her arm to her chest and consuming her entire body. It was as though he were tracing a white-hot knife across her bones, carving out a space in her flesh. This time, when the memory of her mother's death found her again, there was something different to it—something *more*.

This time, Lan saw a serpentine shape uncoiling from her mother's shadow, writhing as Māma had grasped Lan's wrist, burning the invisible scar into her flesh.

Lan screamed. The Winter Magician's face was aglow in white light, lancing like fissures across his cheeks. A white light that, she realized, came from her own wrist.

Her scar was aglow, the character and circle blazing like white gold. The fire zigzagged through her veins, cracks appearing in her skin as though she were splitting from the inside out. There was a high-pitched shrieking in her ears as the world around her undulated and morphed.

With a cry, the Winter Magician let go. Lan dropped to her knees, clutching her left arm. Something had broken loose inside her, something growing in pressure in her head and howling in her ears.

A shadow sliced through the chaos. Cool hands wrapped around her shoulders, pushing her back. The sky tumbled, stars reeling and suddenly brighter than crystals, so close she could almost taste them.

Then they disappeared altogether.

Cool wind, grass-scented. Wetness on her cheeks.

Lan awoke to the soft pitter-patter of rain. Above her, the sky was slatted with bamboo leaves, the moon no more than a silver whisper behind storm clouds. She did not recognize her surroundings. She appeared to be in the midst of a bamboo forest. No Elantians, no city gates, no fear or pain. Here, there was only the soft susurrus of water winding down mossy stalks, dripping into the slumbering earth.

Lan turned her head, ignoring the sharp streaks of pain that shot through her teeth. Next to her, half a cheek in the mud, black hair spilling like streaks of ink over his face, was the boy.

He was utterly still but for the shallow rise and fall of his back. Blood trickled gently from his temple and from his nose; his skin was ashen. His coat pooled around him like a puddle of dark water.

They were alive.

Yet there was something different, something *clearer* about the world, as though she'd held a cracked-glass view of it her entire life and the fall had jolted everything into alignment. She could *feel* each raindrop spiraling from the sky, the dampness soaking into the earth beneath her, the cold currents of wind brushing between bamboo leaves that were now somehow, impossibly, *alive*. A strange hum of energies from the forest, the water, the clouds that came together into the purest harmony of a song.

It was as though the world had finally awakened . . . or perhaps *she* had been the one asleep all along.

Lan closed her eyes, pressing her fingers to her temple. She must have hit her head hard.

She pushed herself into a sitting position, her bones protesting. With some difficulty, she turned the boy over onto his back.

It was when she grabbed a portion of her sleeve to clean his wounds that she caught sight of her left arm. The world slipped from her, and she had to grasp her midriff to keep from throwing up.

It looked as though someone had injected molten silver into her veins and her scar: it puckered from her flesh, gray and glinting beneath a thin layer of skin, bleeding out into the rest of her arm like the roots of a sick, twisted tree. Rain slicking her hair and streaking down her face, she sat staring at her mangled arm until a shadow stirred by her side.

The boy had awoken and sat up. He wiped mud and rainwater from his face and blinked blearily at her. His gaze sharpened. "Four Gods," he whispered. "Your qì . . ."

"What?" she croaked.

He stared at her a few moments more, then his gaze caught on her arm.

"Let me see that." His voice was husky from exhaustion, yet still carefully controlled. Giving away nothing.

Lan swallowed and held her arm out to him. She tried not to flinch as his fingers brushed her skin.

The boy's eyes flicked up to hers. Without a word, he drew his hands back and let them rest in his lap. He leaned over her arm, staring at it for a very long time. When he spoke, his expression was inscrutable. "I believe the Elantian magician injected a metalwork spell into your veins in an attempt to break the Seal on your arm. If not treated, it will seep into your blood and eventually kill you."

The words fell dully against her ears. Lan squeezed her eyes shut briefly, but that did not stop the flashes of images that ran through her mind: Ying, her body splitting beneath the Winter Magician's magic. The White Angel's hands all over her, tearing into the fabric of her dress.

Her mother, bleeding to death on the rosewood floor of their home.

After twelve cycles of her running and hiding, the Elantians had, once again, destroyed a small piece of refuge she'd found in the storm. They'd killed the only people left in this world she cared for. Her clothes hung like rags over her, bare shoulders and back exposed, her body having come within a hairsbreadth of being violated.

If she lived, that was the kind of life that awaited her: splintered fragments of a half existence in a pillaged land, at the mercy of the Elantian conquerors like rats in a cage.

The rain on her cheeks warmed. "I don't"—she choked—"I don't want this life . . ."

Something heavy draped over her shoulders. The boy crouched before her; he'd wrapped his cloak around her. With one sleeve, he began to dab at her face, pausing every now and then to gauge her reaction. She let him, let the rain wash over her and numb her as he wiped away the blood from her cheeks and her split lip. He was gentle, careful, and efficient, each swipe of fabric cleansing away the memory of Elantian hands.

When he finished, the boy drew back and folded his fingers together. "I know how it feels," he said quietly. "I know how it feels to have everything taken from you. And I know how difficult it is . . . to continue to live."

She looked up at him then, arms wrapped tightly around herself. There was nothing of the foreign, ancient blackness to his eyes as he gazed back, face marshaled and restrained. There was no kindness either, only a hard, bladed empathy.

"But you must remember that, should you choose to live, you do not live only for yourself." He made a gesture as though to touch his heart. "You live for those you have lost. You carry their legacies inside you. You see, the Elantians destroyed everything that made the roots of our kingdom: our culture, our education, our families and principles. They wish to take us out on our knees, to subdue us so that we will never lift our heads again.

"But what they do not know is that, so long as we live on,

we carry inside us all that they have destroyed. And that is our triumph; that is our rebellion." Rain clung to his lashes as neither of them broke their gaze. "Do not let them win today."

She closed her eyes, and he let her cry in silence, the rain muffling any sound she might have made. When her shoulders stilled and her ragged breaths grew calm, Lan lifted her head again. She drew the cloak tighter over her shoulders and glanced at the boy, suddenly aware that he was sitting in nothing but a thin white shirt in the rain. The broadcloth was soaked and semi-transparent, outlining the lean, corded muscles of his torso like a charcoal sketch. One side was torn; blood had spread across it like an ugly inkblot.

"Can you fix my arm?" Her voice was barely a whisper.

His gaze snapped back to her, and she saw thoughts of his own dissipating like smoke from his eyes. "I cannot. But if you trust me, I can put a temporary Seal on the metal—and your qì."

"My . . . qì?"

His expression was shrewd. "You really do not know?"

She stared at him. An inkling of understanding stirred inside her.

"You truly are no practitioner, then," he asserted after several moments of silence. His brows stitched together in calculation, but whatever he'd thought to say, he shook away. "You have a strong connection to qì. I had sensed a faint trace of it in Old Wei's shop earlier and in the chamber at the Teahouse, but nothing else . . . until now. It seems the Elantian magician unlocked your power when he penetrated the Seal on your wrist. You are *aglow* with qì."

Seal. Qì.

Words she had only read of in storybooks, heard of in old legends.

Lan touched a finger to her forehead. The thrum of energies she'd felt after they'd landed in the forest . . . the way the world had hummed to life in the purest, most incredible harmony she'd experienced. Was it possible . . . ?

The boy tilted his head. The rain was running in rivulets down his black hair, but he looked at her with a spark of weary earnestness. "I know the practitioners of old are spoken of as no more than legends and lore these days. But we exist. We always have. And you . . ." He made as if to reach for her left arm, then thought better of it and pointed, instead, at her scar. "If you are not one of us, then you have been in contact with one of us. It is a great undertaking for a practitioner to imbue a Seal unto someone."

Her heart—she had never felt it beat so hard before. Staring at the boy, she had the sudden urge to hold on to him, to make sure he didn't melt away into the darkness like smoke, like shadows.

Like Māma.

The boy sighed at her silence. "Let me show you," he said. "Give me your arm. I promise, it will hurt less than what he did to you earlier."

In spite of everything, she liked the way he spoke: bluntly, honestly, presenting the truth to her no matter how difficult it was to hear. She'd had enough of lies, of things left unsaid.

Lan hesitated. "What will you do?"

He looked tired. "I will place a Containment Seal on the metalwork embedded in your flesh and veins to slow the spread of the silver. I will need to combine it with a Filtering Seal to allow the flow of blood while the metal remains trapped so your arm does not die. Then . . . I will apply a numbing balm for the pain."

Slowly, she held out her arm. She forced herself to hold still as his hands came to wrap around her skin, but he was gentle, the barest tips of his fingers grazing her wrist to steady her.

With his other hand, he pressed his index and middle fingers to her flesh.

Lan drew a sharp breath. The air seemed to shimmer—not visibly, but in a way that resonated in her soul, like the missing chords to a harmony. She *felt* something flow from his fingertips into the flesh of her arm, seeping through blood and bone.

She spoke into the silence. "What did you mean when you said the magician unlocked my power when he . . . when he penetrated my Seal?"

Surprise flickered on the boy's face. "Do you know nothing of this Seal on your arm, and why the Elantian magicians might be after you? Specifically, a high general?"

"High general?" Lan repeated, stunned.

"That man reported directly to the Elantian governor of this kingdom. I believe he holds command over all other Elantian magicians. Did you not see his badges?"

"I was too busy looking at his metallic murder-arms."

The boy frowned. "You are evading my question."

She wasn't; she simply hadn't known how to respond. She thought of the Winter Magician, his eyes piercing her like ice. *I thought I recognized the magic from twelve cycles ago: the very one I told myself I would never forget.* Then he'd spoken the very words he'd uttered to her mother twelve cycles ago—now Lan understood him.

This time, you'll give it to me.

Give what to him? A new question formed in her mind, hardening and sharpening until it felt like she'd swallowed a stone. He'd wanted something from Māma, something that Māma had sworn to never give to him. Something she had *died* to protect.

The last thing she'd done before her death was to burn that scar—that Seal—into Lan's wrist.

And now the Winter Magician was after her.

The boy watched her, waiting for her response. Lan had never trusted anyone in her life with this information—not even Old Wei, not even Ying.

She did not even know this boy's name.

"I don't know," Lan lied. "The magician must have been after me because I killed his general."

The boy's eyes might have narrowed a fraction, but he did not press. "You possess a latent connection to qì that the magician released earlier tonight when he pierced your arm with his metalwork magic." He leaned forward just slightly, curiosity flickering on his face as he studied her arm with the interest of a scholar. "This Seal is remarkably complex, holding many layers . . . yet I now see that one of those layers was to suppress your natural connection to qì. I believe there are other layers of functionalities woven into this Seal that were not broken through, but regardless . . . you hold the mark of an extremely skilled practitioner on you."

Relief rushed through her, so strong she thought she might weep. For twelve cycles, she'd thought of her last memory with her mother as a hallucination born out of the trauma of that day.

It hadn't been. Everything she'd thought of as impossibility was true. That her mother was—had something to do with—the practitioners of old. That she had died to protect a secret, to lock it inside Lan . . . and to suppress Lan's connection to qì so the Elantian magicians would not find her.

And that the practitioners of old—those who had walked the lakes and rivers of the Last Kingdom in lore and legend—were still very much, impossibly, alive.

Lan leaned forward. "Can you tell me more about my Seal?" she asked.

"I cannot read it." Gently, the boy lifted his fingers from her arm. The scar—Seal—on her wrist was still a dull sheen of silver, but the bleeding stopped near her elbow. There, among the twisted metallic protrusions of her veins, rested a new Seal: ink-black and wreathed with strands of cinnabarred. It glowed faintly, and when she removed her gaze from it, it seemed to disappear. "The Seal I have placed on your arm will last approximately one moon. The silver will not progress farther into your bloodstream, and the necrosis of your arm will slow."

"Necrosis?" she repeated.

"Yes. Without treatment, your arm will die."

And with it, she thought, her Seal. Whatever was hidden in it.

The thing the Winter Magician had sought for twelve long cycles. That her mother had died for.

Lan opened her mouth, but her torrent of questions faded on the tip of her tongue when she caught sight of the practitioner. He'd leaned gingerly against a stalk of bamboo, and she suddenly saw how weary he was. Blood had clotted on the side of his head, and the stain on his shirt was still spreading. He closed his eyes. He was breathing hard.

He had saved her life. And he was the closest link she had to finding out more about all this—the Seal her mother had left her, the reason the Winter Magician was after her.

Lan ripped the fabric of her torn sleeve, separating it into long, thin strips, and knelt by the boy; he flicked a glance up at her in dull surprise.

I wish to live, she thought, and then in conjunction: *I need you.*

Lan had learned that nothing in life came without a price. This stranger had helped her this far, and it was likely he would not continue without something in exchange.

"Take me with you," she said. "I can be of use to you. I can cook, I can sing, and I'm good with chores."

The practitioner looked to the strips of cloth in her hands. Understanding shifted his features as she reached forward to pull his blood-soaked shirt from his black trousers, makeshift bandages in hand.

The knife wound in his side was raw and red; in spite of the cool winter rain, his skin was hot, as though he burned with a fire she could not see. His muscles tensed as she began to wrap the strips of cloth around his midriff.

The boy's hand caught on her wrist. Lan froze.

"I do not require anything from you," he said. "I am neither enemy nor trickster, nor a merchant well versed in the language of trades. But"—he drew a shuddering breath and released her—"in this moment, I would be infinitely grateful for your help."

Something eased in her chest. She hoisted him straighter against the thick stalk of bamboo, and they were quiet as she dressed his wound, then dabbed the cut on his temple. She let her fingers rest on his skin for moments longer here and there to warm her numb hands, and in the silence and soft fall of rain against bamboo leaves, a new connection might have been forged between them.

Trust.

The practitioner spoke after a little while. "I seem to have forsaken my manners when we first met." His eyes were still fogged with exhaustion, but his voice was pleasant again, imperial and commanding, as when they had first met back at the Teahouse. "My name is Zen."

Zen. It was a monosyllabic moniker as ordained by the new Elantian laws—but it was something. A half-name, a half-truth . . . yet it would do for now.

Lan pulled her lips into the ghost of a smile. "I'm Lan."

8

Meditation is the practice of complete
detachment from the physical world, becoming
one with the external and internal flow of qì
and the constant harmony of yīn and yáng.

—*The Way of the Practitioner,*
Section Two: "On Meditation"

*L*ián'ér. Sòng Lián. It means "lotus," Māma had once ex-plained. She'd always had a voice like song bells.

A flower? Lián'ér poked out her tongue. She had seen the lotuses in bloom in their courtyard home. How easily they were picked, snapped at the stem without a second thought, leaving nothing but a scattering of petals in the wake of their short lives.

Māma had taken her hand. *Yes, flowers. I, too, am named after a flower—méi, a plum blossom. Did you know, they are stronger than they look?*

Lián'ér let her mother lead her outside, down the fanstone steps and over the small bridge that arced over the pond. The spring solstice had just breathed life into bloom, and winter's colorless screen of snow had yielded to a shy blush of greens. On the jade-smooth pond rested a single lotus.

See how they bloom each and every cycle, without fail, her mother said. *See how they can grow out of nothing but mud, how their resilience brings light and hope.*

Plum blossoms, too, Māma had said, were symbols of courage and persistence, for the way they bloomed through the thickest winter snows.

That had been a lie. Winter was here again. Yet Māma was gone.

Lan jolted awake. She lay very still for a moment, trying to hold on to the dream slipping from her grasp. To her mother's voice, which she hadn't heard in twelve long cycles; to the name she'd had a lifetime ago.

The dream was dissipating like mist in the sun, but something remained: a song she'd heard in the space between sleep and wakefulness. The melody had beckoned to her like a phantom in the dark. As though someone were calling out to her.

Wind brushed her cheeks, grass tickled her feet, and the chirps of cicadas and hum of forest life surrounded her. The air was damp with the chill of morning dew and rain-soaked earth.

Overhead, bamboo leaves framed a sliver of sky caught in the liminal space between night and dawn, dark and light—a scene she struggled to place for several moments. She'd always awakened at sunrise to the low slatted ceiling of the Teahouse, the soft breaths of Ying by her side, the warmth of twenty or so other bodies clustered around.

Like a string snapping, the harmony of the forest broke. Memories of last night rushed back.

The Winter Magician, eyes as vivid as she remembered them from twelve cycles ago.

Madam Meng's silhouette against the gauze screen, falling amidst embroidered patterns of flowers and mountains and laughing songgirls.

And Ying—

Lan sat up abruptly, her throat making a sharp noise as she drew in breath. The pain of the thought had her clap a hand to her breast—and she caught sight of the mangled flesh on her wrist beneath the torn sleeves of her páo. Her scar—her *Seal*—a pale slash of puckered flesh against the streaks of silver coating her veins. And then, atop it, a new Seal of black wreathed in crimson, the strokes rippling like fire.

The practitioner.

Zen.

The clearing was empty. Lan scrambled to her feet, her heart slamming against her chest as she looked around for any signs that he'd been here. That she hadn't imagined what had happened last night. It felt too good to be true.

Lan wrapped her arms around herself. The fabric her fingers gathered was unfamiliar.

She looked down and realized she was still in his black coat, the sleeves hanging long from her shoulders. The practitioner had given it to her because the Angels had ripped her páo down the back seam.

She drew the coat tighter around her, thumbing the fine material—jǐn, a refined silk once used by Hin nobility. The make was Elantian, with a high collar and a pinched waist with loops that might have fit a sleek samite belt. She hesitated before dipping her head and touching her nose to the collar. Beneath the smells of grass and bamboo were hints of acrid smoke and incense . . . and an undoubtedly masculine scent.

"Good morning."

Lan jumped. Zen stepped out from between the stalks of bamboo. He looked well rested and impossibly *clean*, hair wet and combed into some semblance of style, skin scrubbed of sweat and dirt and as shiny as pale jade. Even without his long coat, he was a regal sight in a white shirt tucked into black breeches. He'd removed his boots, and his bare feet made no sound as he approached.

"Breakfast," he said, holding out two orange persimmons as he approached. "We should move. My Gate Seal transported us to the Jade Forest. It's a distance from Haak'gong, but I don't want to risk Elantian scouts picking up our trail."

Lan took one of the fruits. "Where will we go?" she asked. In the predawn light, the persimmon suddenly looked too bright, too *normal,* next to the mangled mess of her arm. How was it that such beautiful, ordinary things could continue to exist at a time when her entire world had been upended?

Zen paused, his eyes flicking over her as though in assessment. "Northwest," he said at last, "toward the Central Plains, where the Elantians' grasp is weakest."

The Central Plains. Lan had heard stories of the vast, sprawling lands constituting most of the Last Kingdom. The Elantians had easily conquered the more populated coastal regions; the central area remained a mystery for them and for most of the Hin, too. The Central Plains, along with the Shŭ Basinlands and the Northern Steppes, were described in the stories and myths as territories that the clans had once occupied—including the legendary Nightslayer's Mansorian clan.

"Isn't it haunted?" she blurted. Old Wei had spoken often of how supposedly, after the Ninety-Nine Clan Massacre, vast swathes of land had become haunted with the spirits of clan practitioners, from empty deserts that howled like mourning widows to fir forests where ghosts roamed.

Old Wei.

Another piercing pain spasmed through her chest. Lan squeezed her eyes shut for a moment. *Focus. Focus on the task at hand.*

Surviving.

"Indeed," Zen said distractedly. He was strapping on his boots, and Lan caught the glimmer of a blade tucked into bindings on his shin. "Nothing I cannot deal with."

She stared at him. "Is there anywhere else we can go? Is the cure for my arm *only* to be found . . . out . . . out there in the Central Plains?"

"Correct." He looked up, and she caught a glint of mirth in that ever-serious face. "Surely you do not believe the village folktales?"

"I didn't," Lan said, "but then *you* turned out to be real, didn't you?" The practitioner gave her a flat look. "I've heard of the hauntings and demonic affairs that happen in villages out there. *Some* of them have to be true."

He considered her for several moments. "You wish to know the truth of this world? To see the world of practitioning in lore and legend?"

She watched him, her hand instinctively drifting toward her left wrist. The answer was at the tip of her tongue. One so grand, so obvious, and so certain that she was afraid to speak it. Yet it had been given to her long ago, a door left open a crack with her mother's dying breath.

A door to the questions Māma had left her.

Something flickered in Zen's eyes. "If you want the truth . . . if you set out on this path, you must know that there is no way back."

There never had been, not since the path to the future and the life she'd planned had been ripped from her twelve cycles ago. Since then, she'd walked a different path, carved out by a Seal-shaped scar on her wrist.

By a magician with the gelid eyes of winter.

By death and destruction.

She thought of Ying. Night had passed, and the nightmare

that was no nightmare remained with her, a bloodstain that could not be washed away by the light of day nor the passage of time. The pain came so suddenly that she held her breath and twisted her hands behind her back, digging her fingers into her palm.

What use are tears? Ying had murmured to her once, back when they had just crossed their twelfth cycle of life and the wounds of Lan's losses still cut deep every night. *The dead will neither feel them nor be called by them. Grief is for the survivors, and I think that, rather than living my life in pain, I would live it in laughter and love. To the fullest.*

Lan lifted her face to Zen. He was watching her with that inscrutable look.

"Yes," Lan said. "I want the answers. All of them."

"Very well," he said, with the slightest bow of his head. "In that case, I have decided: I would like to bring you to the School of the White Pines, the last of the Hundred Schools of Practitioning, to understand the Seal a former practitioner marked on your wrist."

The words hung between them for several moments as the first rays of the sun cracked over the horizon, spilling a brilliant, fiery red over the land.

"Take your time to consider my request." Zen stood, holding out a hand. Without thinking, Lan took it. He had slipped on his black gloves; his grip was tight as he steadied her by the elbows, drawing her close. Those eyes snapped across her like black lightning. "But I must warn you now that, should you refuse, I would have no choice but to kill you."

The statement was so dramatic that Lan let out a laugh.

The practitioner frowned. "I do not jest," he said.

"I did not take it as a jest," she replied, all traces of mirth vanishing as she met his gaze. "You think I am afraid of death? I have died many times over already, watching the Elantians take those I love one by one, knowing that I have no power to save any of them."

How long had she spent as a caged bird in the Teahouse under Madam Meng's thumb, forced to spin and smile and sing pretty songs? How many nights had she lain awake by Ying's side, holding her best friend's soft fingers and dreaming of a time when they would not be hungry or cold or afraid? How often had she stood at the edge of Haak'gong by the crashing waves, the seam between land and sea and sky, and wondered what else her life might amount to?

She had not been able to protect Māma. Nor Old Wei. Nor Ying—nor any of the others at the Teahouse. Yet fate had come knocking at her door and presented her with this chance.

She would take it.

She would no longer be the flower.

She would be the blade.

Lan pressed her palm against the practitioner's. "I would cross the River of Forgotten Death itself if I could bring them back," she said. "I have but one request for you. Teach me the art of practitioning. Teach me to be powerful, so that I will not have to watch another person I love fall to the Elantian regime."

She saw it again, that flicker of darkness in his eyes—a wall of black flames. The dawn's light was blood-red across his face, carving him into sharp angles and shadows. His hand tightened on hers briefly, then loosened, his grip fading to a light touch.

"Eat," he said, "and let us be on our way. If you are to attend the School of the White Pines, it would do no harm to begin your instruction today."

"Why must we travel on foot? I thought practitioners could fly."

"We cannot *fly*. We can direct concentrated bursts of qì

into our heels, propelling us to leap higher and farther than normally possible. That is a method of practitioning called the Light Arts."

"Well, why can't you just spirit us to the School of the White Pines the way you transported us from Haak'gong to the Jade Forest?"

They had been walking for several hours, and Lan was exhausted. Her silk slippers were made for the polished lacquered-wood floors of the Teahouse, not for unsteady mud paths. Her páo was too long and tripped her every so often, and the practitioner's ill-fitting cloak kept slipping from her shoulders.

"It was a Gate Seal. I didn't 'spirit us,'" Zen replied. He sounded not even remotely out of breath and showed no sign of physical exertion aside from his flushed cheeks—which made him look even more attractive, Lan noted irritably as she wiped the sweat from her forehead. "And it is exceedingly difficult to perform, even for short distances. Practitioners must be measured in the way we channel qì. Overuse may lead to accidents."

Lan thought of the moment in the air when his eyes had been completely black—from the whites to his pupils—and wondered whether that had anything to do with it. For some reason, that moment had seemed private, so she did not ask.

"But you said there are some more talented at using qì than others? Could a stronger practitioner do it?" Needling him was the only thing keeping her from falling asleep. Besides, it was fun to watch his face tighten and his jaw clench.

He shot her a sidelong look, evidently deciding to ignore her jab. "Everyone is born with qì inside them and all around them—qì is the makeup of this world. It is the flow of water, the gusting of wind, the roar of fire, and the steadiness of earth. It is day; it is night. It is sun and moon and life and death. Some people have an affinity for channeling qì and weaving different strands of it into Seals. With training, they can cultivate their ability and become practitioners. Think of it as how most people can hear music but only a few can become talented musicians."

Lan grinned. "I happen to be an *excellent* musician. What was it that you said? That I was *aglow* with qì?"

Zen closed his eyes, as though praying for patience. "Certain individuals," he said, "are able to hold *more* qì within them to channel. This makes them more powerful. Yet this ability—we call it the *core* of a practitioner—must be cultivated over time and through training. Without cultivation, even the gifted can perform only as many tricks as a mountainside monkey. And lest you wish to end up like that, you'd best return to your meditation."

Lan scowled. She'd anticipated that Zen would begin showing her the hand gestures to create Seals. Or at the very least, some beginner's martial arts training for how to channel qì, as she'd read in the storybooks.

Instead, he had instructed her to close her eyes and *breathe*.

"The circumstances aren't ideal," he'd said. "Meditation is best achieved while sitting and shedding one's awareness of the physical world around us. However, it seems we will not have that luxury for a while."

It was exceedingly difficult to *shed one's awareness of the physical world* while fleeing pursuit from a legion of soldiers. The forest floor was a maze of roots and uneven ground that threatened to trip her. Lan had tried at first, she really had—but as the sun climbed in the sky and the temperature warmed, sweat began to prick uncomfortably at her temples and beneath her clothes, and exhaustion and hunger began to sap her strength. The final straw came when she face-planted onto a mound of dirt.

"I'm not doing this," she said, rubbing at her face with her dirtied sleeves. "What kind of a ratfart instructor asks his student to close her eyes while *running through a forest*?"

"'Ratfart instructor'?" the accused ratfart instructor repeated, his eyebrows raised.

Indignantly, Lan pushed herself to her feet. "What, never heard a village girl talk?"

The sun had begun to dip in the sky; hardly a day had passed, yet she was already tired of putting on airs for the boy. He was refined where she was rough-cut; he was a scholar and she a songgirl; he spoke in riddles that befuddled her uneducated mind.

"I suppose not," Zen said with a sincerity that made it impossible for her to be angry at him. "Your tripping and falling indicates that you are not connected to the flow of qì. You must *feel* the grooves of the earth, the rising root of a pine, the movement to a puddle of water."

"Oh, I do," Lan grumbled. "I *feel* it all on my face when I fall onto it."

He ignored her. "Take heed. No matter how abundant your latent talent is, you will achieve nothing without training and discipline. Until you can move by feeling the qì around you, you cannot progress to the next stage."

The next stage: Seals, Lan thought, her gaze drifting greedily to his black-gloved hands. She had never been the most inclined to hard work or studying back at the Teahouse, and the thought of enduring days of face-planting into bamboo roots was unbearable in this moment.

She pushed a dramatic sigh through her nose and clutched her belly. "I've tried my hardest today, O Esteemed Practitioner."

Zen's brows shot up. "Now I'm 'Esteemed Practitioner'?"

"*Mister* Esteemed Practitioner."

"We appear to be about the same age. I am not a 'mister' to you."

"Well, you certainly act like one," she retorted. At the irritated look he gave her, she pouted. "I'm not feeling well. I'm on my moon's blood. Can't we . . . can't we eat and find a place for me to meditate, and learn some Seals?"

Two spots of pink appeared on Zen's cheeks; they spread, flushing down his neck and coloring his face a shade of mortification. "I—you—moon's—" he spluttered, taking a step back. "Yes. You rest—here—I'll go—food—"

He turned and all but fled into the trees.

With a snort of laughter, Lan flung herself down against a stalk of bamboo. Was that all it took? She should've thought of it earlier. She'd heard stories of how devout disciples—whether of monasteries or religions or practitioning—were sworn to a life of chastity and pledged to leave behind all worldly possessions and desires. It would be a shame, she thought, closing her eyes and wriggling into a comfortable position, for one with a face as pretty as that boy's.

When she woke from her nap, dusk was fading, pursued by the full dark of night. Yet something else about the air had changed, Lan thought, straightening and pulling the practitioner's black coat tighter around her. It wasn't the scent of the air, nor the temperature (colder, now that it was evening) . . . no, there was a distinct feeling all around her that she couldn't place. Something that spread cold through her veins, stirred a responding echo somewhere in her heart.

A crack of branches and dried leaves—she started as a figure peeled from the copse of trees. Starlight draped him: tall and hard-cut, moving with the precision of a blade.

"Apologies that I was gone for so long," Zen said, stopping several feet from her. "I've brought sustenance."

Indeed, he'd strung two fish and a slew of berries across his belt. He handed her the drinking gourd, filled with fresh spring water. She guzzled it as he settled across from her and pulled out a strip of corn-yellow paper inscribed with red sigils. With a tap of his finger, the paper burst into flame.

"What was that?" Lan asked as the fire spread into a ring on the ground that was too neat and even to be natural.

Zen glanced up at her as he speared the two fish on sticks. "Fú. A written Seal," he replied. Holding the two fish with one hand, he reached for something at his waist. It was a black silk pouch, slightly old and faded with time, but sewn with a crest of crimson flames. Lan had seen enough fine things at the Teahouse to know the look of expensive silk and sophisticated stitching techniques.

From within this pouch, the practitioner drew another slip of yellow paper. "There are several ways for practitioners to channel qì, the most basic of which is through written Seals," he said, handing the strip to her. She moved her thumb across it, noting from the texture that the paper was made of bamboo. He continued: "This is when practitioners write Seals with certain functions on fú paper, to be activated with a touch during battle. It's quick and convenient."

"But during battle," Lan said, recalling the sweeping strokes he'd painted across the air, "you . . ." She wriggled her fingers in a few circular strokes in the air, attempting to mimic his movements.

His lip twitched, the expression caught somewhere between indignation and amusement. "I *performed* Seals," he supplied. "The functions I needed were not in any of my pre-written Seals."

"Then why not write them all?"

"There are thousands, if not tens of thousands, of Seals—and those are only the ones that have been created by masters of Seal art. Even a single stroke in a slightly different direction might result in a completely different Seal. It would be impossible to write them all down." He turned the fish roasting on the fire. "Practitioners typically use fú to carry the most basic of Seals, such as the one I used to light this fire. The advantage of fú is their speed and accessibility; the disadvantage is the limit to their functions. Performing Seals takes more time, but the possibilities are almost endless."

The innocuous-seeming fú in her hand suddenly felt more dangerous. "What's this one for?" Lan asked carefully.

"If you worry that you'll activate it by accident, don't," Zen replied, and shifted closer to her. "I inscribe all my fú in my blood, meaning it carries my qì within and will respond only to me for activation."

"How morbid."

He ignored her as he shed his black glove, and she was again startled by the appearance of his flesh: pale skin marred by dozens of tiny, eerily uniform scars that shone white in the moonlight. She'd seen it the night before, back in Haak'gong, for a brief few moments.

Lan focused on the fú instead.

"This stroke," Zen said, pointing, "calls upon wood, then twists it through all these characters for metal and earth into a solid grid structure. And here, the strokes for defense arching over the grid structure . . . this is a Seal for a protective shield. One of many."

"Can you write me some?" she asked.

He cast her a shrewd look. "Perhaps I will, after you are adept enough at focusing on the flow of qì as we worked on in our exercises this afternoon." He took the fú back from her, swapping it for a stick of fish. "Here, eat."

As she tore into the roasted fish, Zen sat by her side, all the fú from his black silk pouch laid out neatly on the ground. With infinite patience, he broke down all the intertwined Seal strokes and characters on each fú, then summarized their functionality. For the first time in her life, Lan barely noticed her food. The fire was warm, chasing away the chill she had felt around her and in her soul; light lanced across Zen's features, limning his face and hair in red like the caress of a fine horsetail brush. Her entire life, she had had to barter and trade and sometimes even beg for scraps of information, from the newsboys and innkeepers in Haak'gong or even from Old Wei. To sit beside a boy whose status and education were to Lan's as Heaven was to earth and have him teach her without a flicker of intolerance or judgment was a new feeling.

It was a good feeling.

"Hand me the gourd," Zen said once they had finished eating. From a pocket in his pants, he fished out a handful of red fruits and dropped them into the gourd. Then, without a word, he quickly traced several strokes in the air and encircled them into a Seal. When he handed the gourd back to her, it was warm.

A familiar scent wafted from it. "Jujubes!" Lan exclaimed. "We used to steal—I mean, hoard—them from our kitchens. They were expensive, and the Madam was stingy."

Something softened in Zen's face. "Drink it," he said. "Our Master of Medicine advises boiled jujubes for . . . for girls . . . at certain . . . certain times." In the firelight, his cheeks had reddened, and he averted his gaze from hers, suddenly busying himself with gathering the fú and tucking them back into his silk pouch.

Lan smothered a smile. She hadn't known enough boys to understand their embarrassment over the female body, but she found Zen's reaction hilarious, even endearing. "Thank you," she said sweetly, lifting the gourd to her lips. The hot drink filled her with warmth from the tips of her toes to her nose.

"We will resume meditation," the practitioner said. "*Proper* meditation."

Whatever gratitude Lan had felt toward him dissipated. She was full and warm and beginning to grow drowsy, and the last thing she wanted to do was to focus on nothingness. "I don't know if I can," she said quickly. "My moon's blood—"

"You were the epitome of alertness just moments ago when I explained all the fú to you," Zen retorted without pause. "Would you like me to write you some or not?"

At this, Lan straightened and brushed the dirt from her sleeves, then crafted her face into what she hoped was the expression of a pliant student.

The fire from the fú had extinguished, leaving them in a faint dusting of light from the crescent moon. Zen sat cross-legged opposite her, perfectly still without effort. Lan did her best to mirror his pose.

"Qì, remember, is the flow of energy around us and within us," Zen began. "It comprises all the natural elements of this world—threads of energy that form the basis of practitioning and of life. These different forms of energy are then bifurcated into two halves that make a whole: yīn and yáng. They are constantly shifting, constantly changing, and one cannot exist without the other. Take water, for example: the crest of a wave is made of yáng energy, the trough of yīn energy. A pounding waterfall is yáng, whereas a still pond is yīn." His voice was pleasant, velvet as the darkness around them, blending into the gentle whisper of wind and chorus of cicadas that had begun to arise in the forest night. "Close your eyes and tune in to the harmony of qì around you and inside you."

Lan did as she was bid, concentrating on the elements

around her: the wetness of the grass, the snaps of wood and other forest sounds, the remnants of warmth from Zen's fire wafting toward her. It was pleasant, and dark, and she was exhausted . . . the susurrus of bamboo leaves and the chatter of bugs began to shift into some semblance of a distant melody . . . Was that the melody she had tried to chase in her dream? She imagined her mother's woodlute, her fingers strumming the notes. The melody twisted ahead of her, a ghostly brush of silver as she chased it, trying to catch its song . . .

"Lan?"

Lan jolted. Her eyes snapped open. She wasn't sure how much time had passed. Around her, the air had cooled. Clouds swept over the stars. The bamboo forest seemed to have quieted. The song—where was the song? "Yes?" she said and was horrified to hear her words slur with sleep.

"You fell asleep," Zen said in disbelief.

"I—" She swallowed and decided to own it. "Sorry."

"Do you understand that rules and customs are one of the first aspects you will learn at the school?" The practitioner was indignant. "There is a literal *book* of them, named *the Classic of Society*—otherwise known as *Kontencian Analects*. And each school has its own principles engraved in stone, to which you *must* adhere. Any effrontery will be punished by the ferule."

Lan had no idea what a ferule was, but she imagined being spanked by a stern-looking version of Madam Meng. "Well, we're not at your school yet," she muttered.

This seemed to incense the practitioner further. "Do or don't, there are no excuses, and no shortcuts to the Way. If my instruction has the effect of putting you to sleep, then let us—"

"No!" Lan said quickly.

She'd never been the most studious or the most hardworking back at the Teahouse; she'd been known for cutting corners on her chores and learning songs and performances at the last minute. Ying had only sighed at her antics. *You talk your way out of everything, with your fast wit and silver tongue,* she'd said. *Those of us born with slower minds must work harder to survive.*

The memory fell through her mind like ashes, twisting her heart with guilt. Here she was, alive when others were not, with a gods-sent chance to learn *practitioning,* and already she was thinking of shortcuts and making light of her situation.

Selfish.

Coward.

"Please, Zen," she said, quieter this time. "Let me try again."

The practitioner regarded her, eyes narrowed. He sighed. "If you can manage it, search for the feeling of . . . of that Peach Blossom Room," he said. "Was that the first time your connection to qì fully manifested?"

No. "Yes." She shrank back from his gaze, which had intensified with curiosity.

"Interesting," he said. "See if you can find it."

Lan nodded. This time, when she closed her eyes, she loosed a breath—and instead of reaching outside, she reached inward.

To the memory of Ying, bright-eyed and red-cheeked, stumbling into the Teahouse with a batch of freshly picked lychees from the fruit vendor's son down King Alessander's Road. Ying, carmine-painted lips curving into a smile as she twirled in her soft camellia dress.

Ying, red spilling like petals from the gash down her middle. *Please . . . please leave her alone!*

The burning in Lan's eyes had spread to her forehead, snaking to her temples and down, down to her heart. Her heart pounded as emotions she'd locked away roared to life again. The world fell away from her, the grass, the wind, the ground disappearing in the tides of her grief.

The memory shifted, and she stood in a white-ash world, snow weeping from the skies. Ahead, a figure in a long páo trailing rivers of tears . . . and a song. It drifted to Lan, faint as the notion of spring in the dead of winter, stirring the strings of her soul.

The figure turned, and it was at once her mother and not: a rendition of what Māma had looked like, wreathed in ice and shadows. Its eyes were infinitely sad, and the fingers that plucked the woodlute played a song both familiar and forgotten.

You have finally awoken, the illusion of her mother said quietly, *Sòng Lián.*

Māma, Lan whispered.

Our kingdom has fallen; our final lines of defense have been breached. I place my last hopes in you. Hidden away behind a Boundary Seal at Guarded Mountain is something that you, and only you, can find. The illusion raised a hand, and there, from the sweep of her long sleeves, fell a character Lan had carved into her memory: the Seal on her arm.

Guarded Mountain? I don't understand, Lan cried. *How do I find it?*

Follow my song to Guarded Mountain. The voice grew faint; the snow, the sky—the dream was beginning to break, darkness pouring in through the edges. *Follow my song, and you will find me . . .*

The vision shattered with a streak of blinding white light. When Lan opened her eyes again, she and Zen were no longer alone.

9

The fox spirit yāo crept into the village at
night in human form, beguiling the hearts of
men and luring them into its cave, where
it consumed their souls.

—"The Fox Spirit,"
Hin Village Folktales: A Collection

The girl had summoned a spirit.

Zen had felt it: the subtle shift in the energies around
them as Lan sank deeper into meditation—then the great
pulse of qì from her core. His eyes had snapped open when
he'd felt a responding pulse from somewhere deep within the
forest.

A pulse that stank of demonic energy.

"What's that?" Lan's frightened voice came from behind
him.

Zen saw it, too: a shadow cut darker than dark, moving flu-
idly through the copse of conifers across the clearing. The energies around him began to shudder as a sudden wind picked
up, rattling the bamboo leaves and scraping dead branches
against the forest floor.

The creature stepped out into a net of moonlight. Her—
its—skin was the color of dead flesh, black hair trailing on the
ground like snakes. It approached with the awkward, lurching
movements of a newborn infant, arms dangling by its sides

and head lolling. Most disturbing, though, were its eyes: iris and sclera a lightless expanse of black.

"Do not be afraid," Zen said. "That is a yāo."

"*A yāo?*" she repeated. She'd scooted close to him, her face pale and drawn as she stared at the creature. "An evil spirit? The kind that haunt villages and eat people's souls?"

Zen suppressed a sigh. Common folklore conflated the four types of supernatural creatures. In the days of old, practitioners had been hired to investigate hauntings, murders, and other bloody affairs in remote villages that had been ascribed to the stalkings of the supernatural. Now these undertakings were reduced to fodder for folktales, spoken of in hushed whispers and half belief by villagers and townsfolk.

"I suppose now would be an opportune time to begin your first lesson on supernatural spirits," Zen said bemusedly.

"*Lesson?*" The girl's voice was unnaturally high. The yāo had come to a stop halfway through the clearing, its face slack, those black eyes unblinking as it watched them. "What's there to learn besides the fact that they're going to eat me?"

His lip quirked against his will—again, that tickling sensation in his stomach he'd almost forgotten. "They will not *eat* you," he said, then clarified: "Well, it depends on which type you encounter. Supernatural spirits are formed entirely of yīn energies. They hold within them a core of qì that has gained some form of awakening. Their goal—at the basic level— will be to continue to consume yīn energies to prolong their strength and existence, but that is where the similarities end. In all the books you've read, yāo, mó, guǐ, and guài are likely grouped together as *monsters*. At the schools of practitioning, we have separated them into four classifications, with distinct differences."

"What does it matter? If I see any one of them, I'm going to run."

Zen closed his eyes against a rising laugh. "It matters because knowing which classification it belongs to will clue you in as to how to defeat it. Now, the one across from us, a yāo, the first classification of the four, is merely a spirit—"

"It moved," Lan exclaimed, dragging Zen back a step. "It just moved again—I think it's coming for us—"

"—typically associated with guài, another classification. Both are born of animals and plants that have cultivated a spiritual awakening by absorbing qì, the difference being that yāo take on the forms of humans, whereas guài take on the form of monsters. They are the supernatural creatures you'll encounter most often in our travels." He watched the yāo, its features blank, its perfectly inhuman human face regarding them without an ounce of terror or fear. "This is likely a bamboo spirit. Relatively benign, unless it senses something inside you it wishes to consume to strengthen its existence."

As the wind around them calmed, another sound became apparent: the hollow, wending echo of music. It drifted from across the clearing, threading through the sigh of leaves and branches, spinning into a delicate, haunting melody.

Behind him, Lan froze. The grip of her hand on his arm relaxed and she stepped forward. "That song." Her voice was filled with wonder as she turned to him, and it was a look he would never forget: her expression was open with curiosity, eyes bright like a star-strewn night. "I know it. It's . . . it's my mother's. I was just thinking about it."

Zen watched her carefully. Since those two instances back in Haak'gong, he hadn't felt anything nearing yīn energies coming from the girl. Even after the Elantian magician had unlocked her Seal, the yīn and yáng of her qì had been balanced. He'd scrutinized her keenly all day as she'd staggered around the bamboo forest meditating.

Was it possible he'd been mistaken? That the yīn energies he'd sensed . . . had belonged to someone—or something—else? It seemed highly unlikely that a girl who'd thought of practitioners as nonexistent folktales would know to obfuscate the makeup of her qì.

"You awakened the yāo," he said slowly. "You sent out a pulse of qì earlier, and this creature responded."

"Is that . . . common?"

"It used to be." Before them, the yāo swayed, and he caught glimpses of its true form—a stalk, leaves, buried beneath the human skin it had acquired. "Most yāo and guài seek qì to maintain their human forms in our world—it serves as sustenance to them. Prior to the Elantian invasion, the Last Kingdom was filled with cesspools of qì that had gathered in plants and animals in remote locations over long periods of time. Sometimes, they awakened." He paused before adding: "Much like our coexistence with plants and animals in our world, their existence was . . . natural. A part of life."

Lan looked back to the yāo. "I don't think it means us harm," she said. "I can feel it, in its song. It just wants to . . . be alive." She tipped her head up to Zen. "All the stories I've read depicted them as malicious creatures. Why is that?"

He knew the answer—the full answer, the *true* answer—to that question. He knew it all too well, having carved it into his bones and inked it into his blood.

No. The truth hurt, so much that he'd decided to look the other way twelve cycles ago.

He would give her the answer written into the imperial records—the correct, accepted answer. "In the era of the Middle Kingdom, when Hin civilization rose to prosperity, supernatural spirits ravaged our lands. First Emperor Jīn classified all forms of spiritual energy as 'demonic' and ordered practitioners to destroy them on sight. Then he sought to set limits on the arts of practitioning across the kingdom."

Zen raised both hands to the yāo. It had not moved; it continued to watch them, that melancholy song spilling from its being. "Yīn and yáng, evil and good, black and white: such is the way of our world." His hands began to move, qì flowing through the veins in his arms as his fingers traced strokes in the air. "What is dead must remain dead, and what does not belong under the path of practitioning must be annihilated. Such is the Way."

His Seal exploded, appearing in the air as a wreath of glimmering, ink-colored strokes that rippled like fire. Qì shot out from the center of the Seal, enveloping the yāo in a circle of black flames. Its shriek echoed, a long, drawn-out wail of misery exuding yīn energies.

Lan's face was tight, her eyes dark pools as she watched. "It sounds like it's in pain," she said quietly.

Zen steeled his expression. "It knows no pain. Do not let its human form or its pitiful cries fool you, Lan. It is a *demonic* thing, and I am giving it what it deserves."

As though to drive his point home, he funneled more qì into his Seal, the energies spilling from the angriest, darkest place within him. The air cleaved open, shadows opening in the ground.

He heard the girl speaking as though from very far away: ". . . it's gone, Zen."

The storm broke. His qì cooled. The Seal dissipated. When Zen blinked again, he and Lan were alone in the clearing.

He drew a stilling breath. "Are you all right?" he found himself asking.

"I am." Her tone was uncertain as she looked to the copse of trees where the yāo had stood.

Zen made his way over. His ring of black flame had left

behind no marks. In the place where the spirit had been was a single stalk of bamboo. He could sense the swirl of demonic qì dissipating from around it.

"The bamboo spirit," Lan said softly, coming to kneel by Zen's side.

He nodded. "My Seal broke its existence and released the core of qì that gave it life. Now it returns to its true form: a stalk of bamboo."

She gave it a long look. "In the storybooks . . . there were tales of practitioners who bound demonic spirits to them."

"Oh?" The question fell dull against his tongue.

She nodded. Her voice was low. "There're lots of tales the villagers and townsfolk used to tell. I guess the most popular one is the one of the Mansorian clan general that the Dragon Emperor defeated at the end of the Middle Kingdom. I know that's the history of how the Last Kingdom was founded, but . . . well, urban legends say the Mansorian general lost control of his demon toward the end, and that that was why he went on a killing spree after he lost." Zen could feel her sliding a look toward him. "That can't be . . . can't be true, can it?"

He knew the tales. Knew how the commoners had always whispered of *demons* and *dark magic* with horror, as though it were an illness that could seep into their bones.

"It is true." His voice scraped. "The story of the Nightslayer—whatever you have heard—bears truth. Upon losing the final battle against Emperor Yán'lóng, the Mansorian clan general and practitioner Xan Tolürigin lost control and massacred thousands of innocent Hin civilians by channeling the power of the Black Tortoise."

He heard her intake of breath. "The Black Tortoise?" She spoke softly, with awe and fear. "The Demon God? I thought they were simply. . . . lore."

Zen looked straight ahead. "Long ago, the clans practiced

spiritual shamanism: manipulating spiritual energies in harmony with natural qì. One branch of spiritual shamanism became notorious for the dangers it posed: demonic practitioning. When a practitioner invites a demon into his core of qì—of power—he runs the risk of losing control. Of succumbing to the demon's will.

"The most infamous examples you might have heard of in your stories are those of the legendary Demon Gods. A demon is a creature that gains awareness and desires through a festering pool of yīn. The Four Demon Gods are beings that formed at the beginning of time, cultivating power and consciousness over thousands of cycles and hundreds of dynasties and blurring the lines between *demons* and *gods*. Many wars were fought over possession of the Four. Countless deaths, insurmountable bloodshed . . . over their power. The Hin emperors recognized the threat these Demon Gods could pose to the peace and unity of his kingdom and therefore sought to outlaw demonic practitioning altogether in the era of the Middle Kingdom. A sword's purpose may be determined by its wielder, but take the weapon away entirely, and neither the merciful nor the cruel may draw blood with it."

Her eyes were wide, reflecting the ink bowl of stars overhead.

Zen stood abruptly. The night had chilled, and a lone wind swept past the fabric of his clothing, sinking into his skin. "That is why demonic practitioning is a taboo against the Way," he finished.

"Was what I did . . . summoning that bamboo spirit . . . was that . . ." Lan swallowed. "Was that demonic practitioning?"

He hesitated. Demonic qì was composed solely of yīn, yet not all yīn energy was demonic. It was outlandish to think that a girl who believed practitioning to be the stuff of legends could in any way partake in demonic practitioning.

If anything, the abundance of yīn in her energies had something to do with whatever the Seal on her wrist hid.

"It was not," Zen replied, and she let out a breath of palpable relief. "Demonic practitioning is only possible if you have made a bargain with a demon to borrow its power. When channeling a demon's power, the energies you use, the type of Seals you would conjure—all those would be solely yīn, rooted in the power of a demon."

"Well, I haven't made any bargains," Lan said. "Unfortunately, demons were in rather short supply back at the Teahouse."

He did not smile. "You would do well to steer clear of such topics when we arrive at the school. And do not try to channel any more qì without my guidance. There is only one Way of practitioning, and anything that deviates from it is strictly taboo. The masters would not like to see what you just did—and neither would most people."

"Why not?"

Zen turned and began to walk away. "There is no 'why.' Do not question why things are the way they are, Lan. It will only bring you misery."

"Wait," she called out. Zen tensed, preparing himself for another question on demonic practitioning. Instead, the girl said softly, "Do you know a place called Guarded Mountain?"

Zen turned to her. "Guarded Mountain," he repeated. He'd not heard or spoken that name for many long cycles. "I do."

Her eyes lit up. "I know this is going to sound strange, but . . . I had a dream during my meditation that I'll find answers there. About . . . about this." She held her left hand up, her Seal pale against the horrendous metallic streaks the Elantian magician had injected into her skin.

Zen frowned. "You had a dream?"

"Sort of. I think it was a vision. My mother was in it, and

she told me—" The girl sucked in a breath, giving him a frightened look—a look of one who had said something she wasn't meant to. "I think I'll find out what's in this scar—this Seal."

He was silent for several moments, taking her in: torn páo and mussed hair, hands callused and swollen from a life's work at the Teahouse, speech tinted with the accent of the working class. She'd told him nothing of her background, of where she'd come from and who she was.

A question surfaced again—one he had pondered since he'd picked up on that trail of qì in the old man's broken shop. What was a girl with a practitioner's Seal and a powerful latent connection to qì doing as a songgirl in a lowly teahouse?

Zen straightened slightly and inclined his head. "I do know a Guarded Mountain. It was once home to the prestigious School of Guarded Fists." *And one of the last strongholds of the Ninety-Nine Clans,* he thought, but he did not say it. "Fortunately, it happens to be about two days' travel from our destination. I can take you."

He tried to ignore the look of gratitude she gave him. Hearing mysterious songs in the night, being chased by an Elantian Alloy, and now a vision directing her to one of the schools that had been run by members of the clans of old . . . If taking her there would bring him one step closer to understanding it all, Zen would do it.

The winters down south were different from those in his homeland up north, yet as they made their way northwest, the facade of summer fell into a semblance of autumn as bamboo yielded to the crisp scent of golden larches and frost pines. One morning, Zen woke to mist threading around them, a hint of frost fading as sunlight filtered through the canopy in watery drips.

They had taken care to avoid roads, but here, where the trees grew thick and the shadows stretched long, there were no large human settlements. Whereas Haak'gong, at the southern tip of the Last Kingdom, was a sprawl of rolling hills and soft beaches, the central and northern regions were underdeveloped and sparsely populated compared to the east coast, in part due to the mountainous landscapes, which yielded little land for farming. Aside from the Jade Trail, few roads had been excavated in this area. The landscape was rugged, and the trees grew together too closely, making progress difficult. The Elantians, too, had been stalled by the indomitable terrain. The central region of the Last Kingdom—known to the Hin as the Central Plains—was one of the areas they had not managed to conquer. Conspicuously missing were the strongholds and flat cement roads that marked the sprawl of Elantian trade routes throughout the land.

Zen loved it out here. There was a grand, untamed beauty to this kingdom that no poem or epic could do justice. Mountains plunged into the silver skies above, mists coiled around them like sleeping dragons. Rivers grew wide and plentiful, spilling into lakes that might have been oceans. One morning, he woke to a flock of white herons taking flight, their majestic wingbeats echoing long after they were barely stitches against a silken blue sky. Here was a land unsullied by Elantian rule. A land he could still fight for.

The girl kept up a pliant demeanor, following in his steps without complaint, duly carrying out the meditation exercises he assigned her. Much as Zen watched for them, he caught no more traces of yīn energies from her. She was pleasing; laughter came to her quickly, sparking across her face like wind brushing against chimes. Where he had always found conversation a chore, it seemed to delight her—a talent he attributed to her cycles of working at the Teahouse. Once or twice, he thought he caught a glimpse of the stubborn girl who'd unflinchingly smashed a teacup into his head, but otherwise she seemed determined to get along with him, or at least try.

She took care not to mention the incident with the yāo or anything related to demonic practitioning. She listened carefully as he lectured her on principles of the Way. Each night, she sat by his side and held out her arm as he examined it, testing his Seal to ensure that it remained strong enough to hold the metal at bay. The magician's metalwork—silver—was sinking deeper and deeper into her flesh and bone. The longer they left it, the more difficult it would be to root out without damaging her ability to channel qì. Most worrisome was that the parts of her arm impacted by the spell were beginning to turn purple.

"You're certain Guarded Mountain is a destination you wish to visit?" Zen asked her a week into their travels. They had found a burbling stream where they could wash and made camp for the night there. He'd built a fire to keep them warm as they dried. Her left arm rested on his knees as his fingers paused to prod acupuncture points with small bursts of qì. He supposed it shouldn't, but the fact that she had stopped flinching or shying away when he touched her arm inexplicably pleased him.

She looked up, chin in hand, eyes bleary with sleep. "You said it was on the way, didn't you?"

"I did." He pressed another nerve. "But if it is indeed protected by a Boundary Seal, as you mentioned, it may take us time to find it."

She smiled drowsily at him. "I'm sure you can do it."

Zen focused on her arm. It was these moments when she regarded him with complete trust that he found most difficult to guard against.

"You use your practitioning so sparingly." She'd shut her

eyes, her voice drifting quietly to him. "If I were as powerful as you, I'd use my practitioning *all* the time."

He pressed his lips together. " 'Power must be used sparingly, at the discretion of the user. It must never be abused.' Classic of Virtues, Chapter One, Verse Five."

One of her eyes popped open, peeking at him. "You *do* have the entire book memorized."

"Yes."

She shifted slightly. Her next words came in a murmur. "My mother told me that it is the duty of those with power to protect those without."

He had no idea what to say to that—it wasn't in any of the classics he'd memorized, or in any of the supplementary texts he'd come across.

Instead, he prodded a nerve point. "Does this hurt?"

A shake of her head.

"Hmm." He frowned.

"Should it hurt?" She perked up slightly at his tone, eyes opening. "Is something wrong?"

"I am afraid that the longer we leave your arm like this, the worse the repercussions."

Lan sat up, fully alert now. "Didn't you say your Seal would protect it temporarily?"

"Right, but . . ." He thought for a moment on how to best explain it to her. "How long it will last is only an approximation. And the condition will continue to worsen at an unpredictable pace depending on the strength of the magician's spell—and the power of my own Seal."

She smiled in a way that made him quickly avert his gaze. "Well, Mighty Master Zen. You'll keep me safe."

Unsure how to respond, Zen let her sleeve down and pulled on his black gloves. "We arrive at the Village of the Fallen Clouds tomorrow by sunset. It is at the base of Guarded

Mountain, so we should have time for a hot meal and some rest before we proceed with our search."

Lan leapt to her feet, stretching. "A hot *meal,*" she groaned. "Will there be a real *bed*?"

His lips curled at the corners. "I do believe that is the function of an inn."

"And unlimited pork buns? They're my favorite! Madam Meng was so stingy with them because pork was expensive."

"All the pork buns in the world."

She whooped and spun, then that devious look sparked in her eyes as she leaned toward him. "Tell me your favorite song," she said. "Because I'm in such good spirits, I'll sing it for you."

Zen hesitated. "You would not know it."

"I will," she insisted.

He looked into the fire. "Back home, it snowed a lot. We used to wake up to a different type of silence, a knowing that the world was spun anew and that winter had arrived. The song comes from there: 'The Sound of Snow Falling.' "

"You're right," Lan said. "I don't know it." Her face lit in a devious smile as she scooted closer to him, propping her elbows in her lap and cupping her chin with her hands. "Which means you must teach me."

"No. I'm terrible at singing."

"I'll more than make up for it."

"You mock me," he said, but the girl was relentless. "All right. Fine. Just once." And he hummed, closing his eyes as memories swelled in his mind. Grasslands stretching from one horizon to another. Skies so blue and vast, he had the impression he could reach up and touch them. And snow, flakes as fat as goose feathers, that covered the great earth in an undisturbed blanket. When he finished, he opened his eyes to find her watching him, the firelight flickering across her face.

"It's beautiful," she said, and stood. Her páo unfurled in a fall of white, and though she held his jacket carefully to cover the torn parts of the bodice, she was nonetheless graceful as she began to dance.

The song that spun from her lips was the most beautiful that Zen had ever heard: a soft, masterful rendition of his. The pale light of the moon dusted her silhouette, catching the edges of her smile. And Zen let himself drink in the sight of her as he had back at the Teahouse, the night around them disappearing as he fell into her spell of snow and silver, and a homeland he now knew only from memory.

10

No matter how luxurious a life the caged bird
leads, it remains at the mercy of its master.

—Collection of apocryphal and banned
texts, unknown origin

She stood in a room bordered by spirit screens, lit by the dim
glow of alchemical lamps. Beyond the screens, she could
see movement. Silvery voices drifted over: girls laughing, teasing each other, the words of their conversation indiscernible.
A shadow stirred behind one screen, a long-haired girl with
delicate features, and then that girl began to sing.

Ying. It was Ying.

Lan lunged forward, relief flooding her—only she wasn't
sure why.

I've missed you, she tried to say. Her lips moved, but no
sound came out. There was something she had to tell Ying,
something important, something that could change the course
of their lives . . . only she couldn't remember what.

She reached out to pull the screen back, but it seemed
to draw farther away from her. The room, the warmth, the
glow—it was all fading, and then she was looking at her friend
through a wall of ice. The songgirls giggled within, clustered
beneath a lush plum blossom tree.

A cold wind cut into Lan's bones. It rattled the tree, and its petals began to fall.

When they hit the floor, they turned to blood.

Behind the wall of ice, the songgirls began to scream. Lan was reaching for them, running as fast as she could, yet the air had turned thick as congee, and she felt as though she were sprinting underwater, the currents buffeting her back—

In the distance, a figure was approaching, silhouette outlined clearly behind the ice. It was only when he was ten paces away that Lan realized he was not behind the ice.

He was *in* the ice.

The Winter Magician stepped out from the wall of ice, his silver armor and rippling blue cloak unmarred. He was smiling, his expression unmoved as the songgirls behind him dissipated into mist, their screams echoing.

Hello, my little singer, he crooned in his language. *I see you. Now you'll give it to me.*

Terror froze her in place as he reached out a hand, spindly fingers reaching for her throat.

Found you, he said, and the ice all around them shattered.

Lan woke to the sensation of her arm being cut open by a hot knife. She opened her mouth to cry out—and tasted copper warmth against her tongue. Dawn was but a whisper in the gray-slatted sky beyond the canopy, and the ground was covered in a dusting of frost. Over the tufts of grass, she could see the top of Zen's head; he slept a strict six paces from her, yet as they'd progressed farther north and the nights had grown colder, she'd been quietly closing the distance between them long after his breathing evened out, huddling behind him for warmth.

She tried to speak his name again—and instead doubled over in a fit of coughing. Blood dribbled down her chin.

Zen stirred. He rolled over to face her, and as his eyes found her, all fog of sleep cleared from them.

"Lan? Lan." He was on his knees in an instant, gloves off, hands on her pulse. His fingers were like ice against her skin; she jerked away.

"The magician," she gasped. The words sounded garbled. "The Winter Magician—he said he found me—"

"Lan, calm down." Zen's grip tightened on her arms as she thrashed. "You had a bad dream."

A dream—it had only been a dream.

So why had it felt so real?

Zen took her left arm and flipped it over. Lan saw a horrifying sight: her flesh had turned green, the metal within her veins running a sickly dark gray.

"It's infected," she heard Zen say. There was confusion in his tone, the way his brows stitched together as he examined his Seal. "I don't understand. It has only been one week since I Sealed it. The Elantian's spell seems to have gotten stronger—"

Lan bit back a scream as pain sliced through her arm, stabbing into her bone. Sweat was beading on her forehead; she felt it roll down her temple. "You can . . . fix it . . . right?" Her breathing was ragged.

"I—" For the first time, a shadow of panic flitted across his face. "I cannot, not for long. We must get you to the school. There are practitioners of medicine there who can help—"

Even through the mist of pain, an image seized her, a purpose twined tightly around her heart, refusing to let go. Snow, a woman in white robes, the song of a woodlute.

"Guarded Mountain," Lan croaked. "I have to go there—"

"There is no *time*—"

"Please!" Her cry pierced the calm of his demeanor; he looked taken aback. She felt tears tracking down her cheeks, cool against her skin; felt, once again, the claw of powerlessness dragging her back, back from what she'd been searching for her entire life when she was so, *so* close. "It's the last thing my mother left me—my last chance to understand why she died. I *have* to find it. I *need to.*"

Her vision was blurring, whether from tears or from a slipping consciousness, she could not tell. Lan blinked, forcing herself to focus, and found the practitioner's face looming very close to hers. Somehow, she'd clawed a fistful of his shirt, drawing him down. Locks of his hair were plastered to his forehead, and his eyes darted between hers. Searching. There was a storm in those eyes, a swirl of fire and smoke, of a war raging deep inside him.

Then his expression cleared. His hand gently closed over hers. "I will take you to Guarded Mountain," Zen said. "But right now, I must bring you to my school so that the magician's festering metalwork in your arm may be neutralized."

She did not let go—of his shirt or his gaze. "You promise?"

"I vow it."

She let go then, her energy spent. She sensed the practitioner lean forward, his sleeves brushing against her as he lifted her left wrist. His fingers tapped over her Seal, sending numb sparks shooting down her arm, and she felt her consciousness slipping.

When Lan opened her eyes again, the sky had brightened. Her arm still ached, but the pain had dulled compared with the bright-hot agony from earlier. When she turned her head, she found a new Seal on her wrist. This time, she recognized the signature ripples of black that resembled flames.

Looking up, she found the practitioner slumped against the trunk of an evergreen. Even in the shadows, his face was drawn and pale.

Lan pushed herself into a sitting position. "Zen?"

His eyes fluttered; he regarded her through his lashes. "Are you all right?"

She nodded. "Are you?"

He shut his eyes again. "Countering Elantian metalwork . . . takes energy. Allow me a little time to replenish my qì."

She did not like seeing him like this: lips parched and cracked, sweat drenching his face and clothing. Lan reached for the gourd among their belongings. It was empty. "I'm going to get some water," she said.

Zen didn't answer. A look of peace had descended upon his features, which she'd come to learn meant he'd sunk deep into meditation. He'd taken off his gloves and boots, planting both feet in the soil—a method for restoring his qì by grounding as much of his body in the elements as possible, she'd learned.

Lan rose and headed for the stream nearby. Her body was still warm, yet nowhere near as feverish as earlier, and the fog of lightheadedness was beginning to clear from her mind. A morning mist had risen, threading between the golden larches, rendering their pine leaves a feather gray. She heard the burble of the brook before she found it nestled between mossy banks.

Lan squatted by the stream and dipped the water gourd beneath its surface, letting the currents cool her hand. The forest was unusually quiet at this time of the morning, devoid of the whistles of brown thrushes and the scurryings of grouses and other small animals through the brush. In fact, Lan thought, pausing as she lifted the gourd to drink from it, there was a tension to the silence like the air before a storm. As though the forest itself held its breath.

She took a swig of water—and froze.

First, she noticed the thick, oppressive feel of metal in the qì.

Then, she saw them.

Across the stream, between the ghostly silhouettes of the golden larches, were flashes of movement. Not shadows, but *light*—the gray of the sky reflecting against silver. Slivers of pure blue, winking in and out of sight. A sigil of a crown with wings.

Ice cracked up her veins.

Elantians.

Impossible.

How could they be *here*? Zen had told her the central region of the Last Kingdom was safe, that the Elantians had not yet managed to conquer this vast, wild piece of land. Here, where the pines grew gnarled and sprawling and free, there were no flat concrete roads tearing up the land. Here, where the mountains reigned beneath the unbroken sky, there were no Elantian strongholds of metal and marble.

Here was *their* land, the Hin's, the last of it.

And now the Elantians had found it, too.

At once, the memories of the past week traveling under the protection of the bamboo and pine forests and learning about the ancient arts of her kingdom fell away like a distant dream. Her limbs numbed; the gourd in her hand slipped. Lan caught it by its neck and ducked behind a bush. She watched as one of the soldiers peeled away from the formation, pausing to scour the bank of the stream where she hid. When she was certain he'd looked away, Lan began to back up slowly.

She had almost reached the safety of the treeline when it happened.

A rabbit shot out from the underbrush, ramming into her heel. Lan stifled a cry, but too late: she fell forward onto her hands, the gourd cracking beneath her.

Across the stream, the Elantian soldiers looked up. Their eyes pinned her like a butterfly to a corkboard.

As shouts rose, Lan abandoned all caution. She turned and ran.

Her pulse thundered in her ears, the crisp wintry air cutting her lungs like shards of glass. Elantians—there were Elantians here, deep in the safety of the forest, in the Central Plains. Yet again, they had found her; yet again, they had invaded this land of her ancestors, a private space in the kingdom that had only moments ago belonged to only her, Zen, and her people.

Something whistled past her ear. An arrow lodged in the trunk of the larch before her, shaft juddering to a stop. It was made completely of metal, polished and smooth and unnatural, so unlike the pinewood shafts and goosefeather fletching of arrows of the Hin army. The metal gleamed as she darted past it, the tip buried in the flesh of the larch.

To think she'd started to feel that danger was but a distant memory. She should have known better—that as long as the Elantians existed, danger was the shadow they cast over her entire world.

Her hands fisted as she ran, tears of fear turning to tears of fury, choking up her throat and spilling over.

When would she be completely free, completely safe?

She knew the answer.

When I am powerful.

Lan burst into the clearing where she'd left Zen. He looked up, startled. Lan sank to her knees, pain erupting again in her arm and her sides, breath burning in her lungs. She gasped out one word.

"Elantians."

11

Yīn and yáng, evil and good, black and white,
demons and humans—such is the Way the
world is divided. What does not belong on the
Way of practitioning must be annihilated.

—Emperor Jīn, "First Imperial Decree
on Practitioning," era of the Middle
Kingdom

"Impossible."

Zen lurched to his feet, grasping the trunk of the tree behind him to steady himself. Combating Elantian metalwork always took tremendous effort. There was something to their magic that felt unnatural to the way practitioners wielded qì: as though they had taken one of the natural elements and twisted it somehow, made it into something all-consuming, all-powerful . . . and utterly monstrous.

Lan was on her hands and knees, her eyes squeezed shut. "I saw them. They've found us."

In all his years post-Conquest, Zen had never run across Elantian forces beyond the outposts and the largest Hin cities.

What were the chances that a legion had ventured this far into the Central Plains and found the girl they'd been searching for—the girl with strange yīn energies and a mysterious Seal, who'd been the target of a high-ranking Elantian Alloy?

And yet . . . as he spread his awareness to the currents of qì weaving and wending all around them, he sensed it at last: the heavy, overwhelming presence of metal.

They had minutes, perhaps not even, before they were found. Zen looked to the girl, to the abhorrent metalwork in her left arm, to his own Seal he'd just performed to keep the poison back and rejuvenate her qì. Even so, she was trembling.

They would not make it far; there was no chance under the Heavens they could outrun the Elantians. If they moved at their current pace, they would risk leading the Elantians toward the location of the school. The School of the White Pines had remained hidden for centuries beneath a powerful Boundary Seal; as other schools had fallen to dust around it, it had outlasted the turn of dynasties, the rise and fall of emperors, and even the Elantian invasion.

Zen would rather die than reveal its location.

There was only one solution: a Gate Seal.

A Gate Seal had only two principles the practitioner had to remember. First, it had to lead to a location he knew existed, one that he could easily visualize and draw up from his memories. Second, the distance of transportation correlated directly with the amount of qì required.

Zen had never used the Gate Seal for anything farther than a hundred lǐ, approximately a day's travel. By his calculations, they were still five days out from the school.

In his current state, attempting that distance would be near-fatal.

It doesn't have to be this way. A dormant voice rose in a whisper in his mind, dust scattering before wind. *You know it doesn't.*

Lan stirred. She pushed herself to her knees and, with her right hand, reached to her waist. From an inner pocket, she palmed something. It took Zen a moment to recognize it.

It was the butterknife from the Teahouse—the one she'd held when he'd first found her in the Peach Blossom Room, a dead Angel on the floor. She'd raised it with full conviction on her face, as though her entire life were staked upon the little piece of glass.

It was with the same expression that she turned to face the direction of the approaching Elantians—only he saw the full truth of it now: not the courage of a warrior who would go down fighting, but the desperation of a girl with nowhere to run, nowhere to hide.

He thought of the first morning after they'd met, the dawn light carving her face in fierce strokes of red and gold. *Teach me to be powerful, so that I will not have to watch another person I love fall to the Elantian regime.*

In three strides, Zen crossed to her. He took her right wrist, spun her to face him.

Her expression flickered into bewilderment. "What—"

"I will use a Gate Seal to take us out of here," he said.

She blinked, those clever eyes darting between his. He could see her combing through all that he had taught her in the past week and drawing a conclusion. "You can't," she blurted. "You're not fully recovered yet—"

"I have strength enough," Zen said gently. "What use is power if I cannot protect those without it?"

Her face shifted with recognition at her mother's words, paraphrased. For the past few nights, he'd lain awake, staring at the stars, pondering the meaning of those few simple words.

"The place we are about to enter is called Where the Rivers Flow and the Skies End," Zen continued. "The School of the White Pines rests there, hidden within a powerful Boundary Seal. My Gate Seal cannot breach the Boundary Seal, but it will bring us very close. If I am unconscious—"

"Zen!"

"—I need you to leave me, and walk up the mountain to get help. No matter what you see or hear, do not stop, do not

listen." His grip tightened against her wrist. "Do you understand?"

Her eyes roved his face, burning, her chest rising and falling with rapid breaths. "I was right," she whispered. "You *are*
mad."

"At one point, you will trigger the Boundary Seal. You will
not be able to cross it, but it should summon disciples of the
school to you. Tell them you are with me, and they will help
you."

Another nod. The energies around them rippled, weighing
heavier with the stench of metal with each passing moment.
Nearby, he heard the snapping of twigs, the even press of boots
against the ground as the Elantian army neared.

He swallowed. "Hold me tightly."

Her arms were small yet strong as they cinched around his
waist. He felt her press her cheek to his chest, her ear resting
against his heart.

Zen drew a deep breath, lifted his other hand, and began
to trace. The Seal came to him from rote memorization, each
stroke and its function glowing brightly in his mind as his qì
flowed out from the tip of his index finger. The strokes for
earth and earth, facing each other from the farthest points of
the circle, separated by lines of distance. A swirl here, a dot
there, designating departure, then destination.

Footsteps drummed against the forest floor; the sound of
sword metal rang out beyond the clearing. Eyes closed, Zen
swept his arm in a full circle. Ending met beginning, yīn met
yáng, and the Seal opened to him in a blaze of black fire. As
it took effect, Zen focused on Skies' End. It rose from his
memory, mountains undulating as far as the eye could see,
wreathed in cloud and mist and laced with rivers of white,
verdant with life and beauty. He saw it more closely: the temples nestled within, all shell-white walls and gray-tiled roofs

curving toward the sky. To the unblemished boulder standing at the top of the mountain steps, announcing the area's name in flowing strokes of calligraphy:

Where the Rivers Flow and the Skies End

A straight stroke, connecting departure and destination. And then a sweep of a circle to close.

Energy flowed from him and into his Seal—the principle of equivalent exchange per the laws of practitioning. His Seal drank and drank, blooming into life from his qì, and Zen—Zen gave and gave, feeling his limbs numb and his lungs shrivel. He was sinking underwater, drowning, the light above him dimming—and still the Seal continued to take.

Spots bloomed before his eyes; he sagged against the girl and felt her respond, hands tightening around his waist. *It's too much. It was too much, from the very start.*

His heart slowed. His consciousness spiraled. Down, down, to the edge of the darkness, the abyss opening up to swallow him whole.

And then, from within, a voice rose up to envelop him.

I am here.

Black flame erupted in his vision, encircling his arms and legs, propelling him forward. Somewhere deep in the recesses of his mind, something stirred to life: a deep, rumbling echo followed by a rush of power. Qì flooded him like a gasp of fresh air. The Gate Seal was suddenly so small, so insignificant, and Zen could not recall a time when performing it might have been difficult.

This is but a taste. He and that voice spoke, their thoughts blending into one. *Unleash me, and you could have all the power in the world.*

No, *no,* he could not, he *would not.* This thing inside him was an abomination, a monstrosity, an erroneous blight to the Way that his master had somehow tolerated for all these cycles. What did not belong under the path of practitioning must be annihilated.

With all the strength he could muster, Zen pulled back and away from that black abyss. When his eyes cleared, the flames of his Seal had wrapped around them. An illusion shimmered before him: green mountains, pale mist, a line of herons making their way across the sky like a sweep of a brush in a painting. A familiar sight, a safe place.

Home.

Zen closed his eyes, held tight to Lan. She shuddered against him, pressing into his chest with a small whimper.

Together, they tumbled forward.

Zen landed on soft grass, wet mud. It took him a moment to orient himself. The air was suddenly thinner, the cold sinking into his bones with a damp chill. From all around came the song of birds, the chirp of insects, the brush of wind through leaves.

Ahead, a mountain rose, with no discernible path and no distinguishable markings but for an old, gnarled pine that leaned toward him, branches jagged and extending like outstretched arms, as though to welcome him home.

Zen loosed a long breath. This was the Most Hospitable Pine, a marker that the first grandmaster of the school had set. Only those who had learned the true location of the school would know that to walk beneath it was to trigger the Boundary Seal: an ancient and commonly used Seal that marked the borders of a certain territory. Criteria for passage varied. In this case, the Seal was drawn to allow entry for those who wished to enter Skies' End with no intention of harm. It was a clever Seal: those who stumbled unwittingly into the area would simply meet rising fog and a mountain path that disappeared the farther in they forged. And those who entered with the intention to harm the School of the White Pines and its occupants would be met with the wrath of practitioners long dead and buried in this earth, their spirits forever tethered to protecting the sanctity of the school.

Even successfully passing through the Boundary Seal meant a climb of nearly a thousand stone steps before one reached the school's gates. Most disciples bypassed this by using the Light Arts, propelling themselves ten, twenty steps upward at once, but Zen had barely the strength to stand.

In his current state, he would need help.

"Lan," he mumbled, but that was when he felt sticky warmth against his hand and realized that she had gone unusually still in his arms. They were lying at the foot of the mountain in a tangle, her páo against his pants, her arms still around his waist. Blood drenched the grass beneath them, a discordant pool of red in the gently woven landscape of greens and grays.

Panic cut through his fog of exhaustion when he found the source: a metal arrow protruding from her side. He recalled the way she'd twitched in his arms right before the Gate Seal had swallowed them—the sound she'd made. It hadn't been out of fear; it had been out of pain.

Lan coughed, a wet, hacking sound. Blood dribbled from her lips, winding a crimson path down her chin. He took in the curves of her cheeks, the dark crescents of her lashes, that wide, fast-talking mouth, so quick to smile beyond pain. Without help, she would die.

My mother told me that it is the duty of those with power to protect those without.

He could barely summon the energy to move, let alone

perform a Seal. But Zen knew that if he clawed into that abyss deep inside him, he would find power brewing like a storm.

He closed his eyes. Reached.

The world grew dark as qì flowed into him with the roar of an ocean upturned. He was at once drowning and coming to life.

When Zen opened his eyes again, there was someone—some*thing*—else with him, seeing with his eyes and breathing with his mouth and moving his arms and legs.

He bent and picked up the girl before him, cradling her to his chest. She was so oddly light, her head lolling against the crook of his neck like that of a rag doll. He noted the blood leaking from her wound with a strange, clinical detachment.

He blinked. Sweat pricked at his forehead. *I am Zen,* he thought. *I am in control. You answer to me.*

The presence in his mind drew back. His vision cleared. The Boundary Seal wavered before him, the innocuous-looking pine tree seeming to watch as he approached.

Zen held his breath and stepped through.

He felt a resistance of qì for a moment, swirling over him like a thick fog. In that fog were whispers of souls lost to time, the breath of ghosts unforgotten against the nape of his neck, invisible claws reaching into the depths of his heart to test him. For a moment, he was afraid of what the Seal might find there—the monster he'd been when his grandmaster had carried him up this mountain eleven cycles ago, perhaps. Or the things his nightmares were made of: knives made of metals that burned and the conquerors who wielded them against people like him. And then, earlier still: distant screams, the smell of grass burning, blood seeping into his shoes. The ripple of a golden pennant beneath an unbroken blue sky.

Lan's breathing hitched against him, rooting him back to

the present. Her cheek rested against his chest, the soft parts of her throat exposed. He could see the dark vein winding up her neck, the semblance of a heartbeat pulsing against it.

I can be of use to you, she'd said to him the first night they'd met. Rain-darkened lashes, eyes like pebbles beneath water, lips trembling.

Beneath it all, there had been fire. He'd sensed it. Any ordinary person might have given up, but the girl—she'd looked straight at him and asked him for an equivalent exchange.

Zen drew her closer, anchoring himself against the maelstrom in his mind.

The fog, the whispers, the claws retreated in a collective sigh. The storm cleared. As the Boundary Seal yielded to let him pass, a path opened between the pines, the clouds yielding to a spill of crisp sunshine with the diamond-cut quality of winter.

Zen climbed.

The presence—the power—in him was fading, retreating into the chasm in which it resided. Each step demanded more of him. In his arms, Lan grew heavier.

Nine hundred ninety-nine steps to the top. The first lesson of practitioning, wrought in the entryway to the school itself: There were no shortcuts to the Way.

Whether it was out of sheer will or desperation to live, Zen made it. The air grew misty and cold as he ascended, the steps wet with condensation, leaves and branches rustling in harmony with the sound of running water nearby. At last, the stone steps gave way to a flat expanse of ground; the bamboo and evergreens cleared, revealing a zigzag of temples nestled into the mountain, a pái'fāng made of two stone pillars, and a large polished boulder that seemed to have sprung from the ground itself.

Before it all stood a man with robes that spilled like snow.

As Zen fell to his knees, the grandmaster of the School of the White Pines spoke, his voice as clear as a drop of ink unfurling in water. "Ah, just in time, Zen. The snow camellias have bloomed."

12

The nobleman is indiscriminately kind toward
both his equals and his inferiors.

—*Kontencian Analects*
(Classic of Society), 6:4

She came to slowly, pulling herself from the threads of sleep. The scene before her unfolded as though from a dream. Sunlight spilled onto her skin, soft and warm. A fresh breeze kissed her cheek, bringing with it the scent of rain and pine trees. High overhead rose a ceiling slatted with redwood, cornices adorned with carvings of mythical creatures and gods of the Hin pantheon. By her side: a folding screen, painted with figures of Hin scholars bent over scrolls amidst jagged mountains and winding rivers. It might have belonged to a study from her old courtyard house. In her state between wakefulness and slumber, she almost expected her chambermaid to come bustling through the wooden doors with a tray of steaming congee laden with nuts and jujubes.

Lan turned her head and immediately regretted it. Her left arm was bare, and protruding from her flesh were about a dozen long needles thinner than wisps of hair. Biting back a scream, she sat up, seized a fistful of the needles, and pulled.

The wound in her side pulsed with pain. Lan gritted her

teeth, flung the needles to the floor, and ripped out another batch.

There was movement beyond the screen as she threw the last handful of needles to the floor. "Miss?" came an unfamiliar voice. A light tenor, soft and unimposing. "Are you awake?"

A young man appeared, dressed in a nondescript white páo cinched at the waist with a crisp blue sash. His complexion was as clear as spring water: a slim, gentle face framed by a fall of long hair that curled at his pale, slender neck. His upper lip broke at the center—a cleft lip, Lan realized, or what the village folk crudely called *rabbit lips*.

Those lips parted in surprise as he beheld the scene before him: Lan, panting and swaying where she sat, the bandages on her side splitting, needles scattered over the floor.

"Oh no," the newcomer said.

"What," Lan panted, "is that? Who are you?"

The young man suddenly looked rather bashful. "Forgiveness—I seem to have left my mind and manners in my studies, as my shī'fù would say. My name is Shàn'jūn, disciple of Medicine. I was . . . I was attempting to heal your arm through acupuncture."

Shī'fù—master. Disciple of Medicine. Lan looked around her again. Beyond the screen, she could make out wooden shelves that lined the opposite wall—only instead of books, they were filled with boxes, drawers, and crates.

"This is the Chamber of a Hundred Healings," the boy— Shàn'jūn—continued. "I'm not sure if you know . . . but you are at the School of the White Pines."

Her head cleared. Lan studied her surroundings again with a sharper eye. The chamber was dim, lit only by the glow of paper lamps. Sunlight spilled softly through the open doorway. She had the distinct feeling that she'd been unconscious for at least several hours.

Her hand went to her side. Someone had changed her out of her torn páo from the Teahouse into a clean set of robes, too large for her frame but comfortable. Bandages wound neatly around her midriff.

The arrow. The Elantians—

"Zen," Lan blurted. "Where is Zen?"

"He is with our grandmaster" was all the disciple said as he bent to scoop up the acupuncture needles. "Forgiveness, if I startled you. These needles serve to balance out the qì in your body. In your case, you have an excess of yīn stemming from your left arm; I tipped the needles in yáng to draw it out." He held one up; the metal seemed to have darkened slightly. "Our traditional Hin medicine might not be as effective against Elantian metalwork, but it will at least help."

Lan examined her left arm again. The veins remained a dark gray, the flesh around them mottled with purple and green, as though the metal within was beginning to rust. The infected patch had spread as far as her elbow; over it, Zen's Seal was beginning to fade. Her scar, however, shone pale, a circle unmarred by the Winter Magician's metalwork.

Scar. Seal.

Guarded Mountain.

She needed to get to Guarded Mountain.

She flicked an assessing glance at the disciple of Medicine. "Can you fix my arm?" she asked.

"Traditional Hin medicine is a slow process, and your arm requires immediate attention. Fortunately, there is a master well-versed in the language of metals here at the School of the White Pines who should be able to help. With our combined efforts, you will be back to normal in no time." He gave her an encouraging smile. "You must be starving—it is past the hour of the sheep. Let me bring you something to eat."

Hour of the sheep. Lan hadn't heard Hin timekeeping

expressions since she was a child—most of Haak'gong had converted to the Elantian clocks, chiming hourly. A Hin bell was roughly equal to two Elantian hours, each slot assigned an animal of the twelve zodiac signs based on ridiculous reasoning that Lan had found a headache to memorize as a child. The hour of the sheep began the first bell after noon.

This place—with its traditional Hin infrastructure, clothing, and customs—felt like the past preserved in a bottle. Something that had impossibly, miraculously survived the passing of time and the mark of Elantian hands.

She followed the Medicine disciple past the folding screen, but he'd already disappeared into the back room. From within came clattering sounds and wafts of something pungent.

Footsteps sounded from across the chamber: sharp, loud, and almost militaristic in their might. The next moment, the light from the open doorway dimmed as a tall figure strode in.

The newcomer was dressed in a páo with plated battle armor padding shoulders, chest, and thighs. Her thick black hair was parted down the middle and coiled into two tight buns behind her head. Her face, long and angular, broke with the bold red slash of a mouth. One eye was covered by a black patch; the remaining eye was the gray of swordmetal and storms. It narrowed as they swept the chamber and came to a stop on Lan.

"So you're the one causing all the stir," she said. In spite of her height, she appeared to be a girl perhaps around Lan's age. The way she spoke reeked of condescension.

Lan resisted the urge to roll her eyes. "Seems quite peaceful around here," she said.

The other girl's jaw tightened. She pointed. "I'm here to examine the Elantian metalwork."

Lan tipped her head. "You mean my arm?"

"The metalwork *in* your arm."

"Normally, I'd agree," Lan said, "but your dogfart attitude changed my mind. Come back when you've fixed it."

For a moment, the other girl was stunned into silence. She recovered quickly, her features twisting into righteous anger. "Who raised you, you mannerless dog whelp?" she snapped. "That metalwork in your arm must be destroyed. I can sense its corrosive stench from here, even under that Seal Zen attempted to hide it with."

"Where is Zen?" Lan demanded.

The girl's lips curled. "You have the audacity to speak his name? After all, it was *you* who forced him to nearly go Wayward—" She cut herself off.

Wayward. It was Lan's first time hearing the word, but somehow, she thought of Haak'gong, of when Zen's eyes had gone all black and his face cold, as though something had taken control of his body. That had been right before he'd used his Gate Seal to transport them to the Jade Forest.

He'd used it again to get them to the school—a much farther distance.

"Dilaya shī'jiě?" Shàn'jūn had emerged from the kitchens, his tone pleasant as he referred to her with the honorific title indicating that she was a senior disciple. He held a steaming porcelain bowl he'd been in the process of stirring and blowing on to cool it down. His eyes flicked between the girls, then crinkled. "Have you been introduced yet? If not, allow me to do the honors. Miss Lan, this is Yeshin Noro Dilaya, disciple of Swords. Dilaya shī'jiě, this is—"

"I need no introduction to an Elantian whore with a single-character name," Dilaya snarled.

"Me neither," Lan said. "Only that whore has a three-part name."

It was almost worth the trouble it might have brought her to see Shàn'jūn nearly drop the bowl he held.

Two spots of bright red flushed Dilaya's cheeks. "Out of my way," she all but spat at Shàn'jūn. "Have you not heard of the rumors all day? The Elantians want her, and that cretin Zen led them right to our gates!"

"Dilaya shī'jiě tends to speak with exaggeration," Shàn'jūn said, turning to Lan. "I'm sure it's all just a big misunderstanding. Now, I'm no cook, but would you like a bowl of—"

"What do you mean, 'Zen led them right to our gates'?" Lan asked Dilaya. "The reason we decided to use that Gate Seal was so that they would not be able to follow."

"They are closer than they have been for the past twelve cycles, since they destroyed all the schools in the vicinity," Dilaya snarled. "It cannot be a coincidence that a girl bearing their mark on her arm shows up within our Boundary Seal. Such disgusting Elantian metalwork should never have crossed through. And now I'm going to destroy it, no matter what it takes."

"Dilaya shī'jiě, please," Shàn'jūn said quickly. "I need the Master of Medicine to examine her arm and assess whether there will be any long-term impacts of removing the metalwork. As far as I can see, the spell has embedded itself quite deeply; removing it without proper information may prove dangerous."

Lan clutched her left arm. The Elantian metalwork had wound through her Seal; Zen said it had unlocked her qì. What if removing it meant damaging her mother's Seal—or worse?

She could not risk that. Not before she could find out what it meant. Not before she understood why the Elantian magician had spent twelve cycles searching for the mark her mother had left on her—and why he had killed Māma for it.

Not before she could get to Guarded Mountain.

"Don't touch me or my arm," Lan said to Dilaya.

Dilaya bared her teeth. Metal rang as she drew a long,

curved blade, palming the dāo as though it were an extension of her. At this moment Lan realized that, under the girl's armor, she had only one arm. The sleeve of her right arm fluttered loose.

"We'll see about that," Dilaya retorted, and sprang.

Lan reached into herself, leaning into memories, just as she had on the night she'd awakened the yāo. She recalled Zen's voice, teaching her to open her senses to the flow of qì outside and within; the stir of an ancient calling at her core each time he performed a Seal; and the soft echoes of song that seeped through the cracks of her mind, bleeding silver. Haunting her. It was a tune she knew instinctively, drawn from her very blood and bone and soul, filling her like rising ocean water.

The song spilled over, and there came a responding pulse from her left wrist. The scar—the *Seal*—against her flesh had begun to glow, and even as Lan looked, the brightness grew blinding.

A streak of white light shot skyward before her, cleaving the chamber in monochrome. Lan gasped and flung her hands before her eyes; she heard porcelain shatter, someone hiss, and harried footsteps approaching—

Black flames rose to wreathe the silver light.

13

The blade itself is naught but a piece of cold
steel; it is the wielder who draws blood.

—General Yeshin Noro Surgen of the
Jorshen Steel clan, *Classic of War*

Eleven cycles later, the School of the White Pines looked
exactly as it had when Zen first set foot within, unchanging and unyielding to the tides of time. Nestled into the lush,
green mountains and veiled by thick plumes of mist that rose
from rivers, the school might have been part of a different
world—one unaffected by the lives and deaths of emperors,
the rise and fall of dynasties, the eternal spin of sun and stars
overhead.

Zen had woken on a kàng platform bed, in what he recognized as the back room to the Chamber of Waterfall Thoughts,
the main hall of the School of the White Pines and the favored
meditation chamber of the grandmaster. Fretwork ran beneath the eaves of the roof; the chamber was utterly open to
the elements but for bamboo blinds drifting gently in the wind
between rosewood pillars. From outside came the sound of
running water and birdsong. It was afternoon, sunlight falling
across the landscape in golden drops.

Someone had stabilized his qì; his head was clear, and the

horrifying experience of the yīn energy, the echoing voice in his head, seemed like a dream from a distant time. He was still weak—it would take at least a day of rest and meditation for him to recover—but he could function. Zen had bathed and changed into the flowing páo and clean boots set out for him by the bed, then gone in search of the grandmaster.

He'd found him walking the paths of the school, white robes swaying to the tune of his steps, face tilted to the serenity of their surroundings. In eleven cycles, Dé'zǐ, too, seemed to have avoided the corrosive power of time. Zen did not know his age but had the impression that he was somewhere in his forties, old enough to be a father figure. His once-jet-black hair was now peppered with gray, yet there was a calming pleasantness to his face that might have been described as handsome.

If Zen thought of himself as fire, then Dé'zǐ was water: smooth-flowing and gentle yet capable of surging storms, clear on the surface yet with depths unseen. After eleven cycles, Zen had yet to see to the bottom of his master.

Now Dé'zǐ cut through the air with the fluidity of a blade, carrying that same, inscrutable half smile. The sash at his waist bore the sigil of the school—a white jagged Hin pine against a black circle—and conferred his status as grandmaster.

"Ah," he said. "Zen."

Zen pressed a fist to his palm and inclined his head in a salute. "Shī'fù." There was so much he needed to relay—the girl, Haak'gong, the magician, and the Elantians in the Central Plains—but Zen kept silent, waiting, as was customary, for his master to speak. There was no telling where Dé'zǐ would take the conversation.

The grandmaster was silent for a while, studying a bush of snow camellias. Zen tamped down his impatience. He had the impression that the world could be ending and he would still find his master strolling through the vegetation of Skies' End with a cup of fermented pǔ'ěr tea.

"You have the look of a lover in mourning."

Zen started. "Sh-shī'fù?"

Dé'zǐ gave him a sly look. "The girl will be well," he said. "Shàn'jūn is as fine a medicine man as they come."

Zen's face heated. At the core of his worries was Lan—naturally, as recent events had seemed to follow in her wake—but he'd given no indication of that to his master. And he certainly was no *"lover in mourning."*

"You mistake me, shī'fù," Zen replied stonily. "I do not worry for the girl. There is much we must discuss, including troublesome new findings on the Elantian front."

Dé'zǐ peered into his pupil's face. "Oh? Do you care nothing for whether the girl lives or dies? You risked a great deal, bringing her here."

Sometimes his master truly tested him. "Forgiveness, shī'fù," Zen said stiffly. "Of course, I wish her well. I merely meant she was not a priority, in the grand scheme of things."

"Hmm. We may all very well be surprised," Dé'zǐ said, and turned to face Zen properly. "You speak of 'forgiveness'—that is another matter."

Something inside Zen drew taut. What he had risked to use the Gate Seal and transport him and Lan here . . . how he had lost control twice in the past week . . . if the other masters of the school heard, there would be an uproar. It was only by Dé'zǐ's grace that Zen remained at Skies' End at all. A monster. An abomination. A reminder of what happened when one strayed from the Way.

Zen bowed his head. "I erred, shī'fù. I broke a fundamental rule of the Way. I will take the ferule."

His master's brows furrowed at the mention of the great

plank used to dole out punishments—a Hin tradition that had once been favored in schools and courts alike.

"Zen," his master said, "you and I both know I did not agree when the other masters voted to keep such an outdated method of punishment. The ferule is effective only as long as you hold its lessons in here." He tapped a finger to his chest. "It is not just our bodies and flesh that must complement the Way—but our minds as well. The Seal I placed upon your heart is only as strong as your will."

"I had no choice, shī'fù." The words pushed through his teeth at last. "The Elantians would have caught us—we might have died."

"You and I both know that there are worse things than death that await us in this world," Dé'zǐ said quietly.

Zen flinched. He knew they shared a memory: of him prior to his arrival at Skies' End, of how the grandmaster had found him, barely a shell of a human, beaten, bloody, and broken inside and out.

"The very first practitioners, who established the Hundred Schools and wrote the classics—before the Imperial Court repurposed them—intended for practitioning to be a path to balance," Dé'zǐ continued. "All qì has the potential for great power and immense danger. It simply depends on who wields it. Humans are greedy things. We set ourselves promises we cannot keep, boundaries we break. That is what the classics advise against: not how we practition but *why*."

Zen lowered his eyes. "That is blasphemous, shī'fù."

Dé'zǐ laughed. "And who will come and strike me down? The souls of the dead emperors who failed this kingdom and the last?"

Sometimes Zen thought the grandmaster of the School of the White Pines defined the fine line between brilliance and madness.

"Natural qì, demonic qì, whatever the Imperial Court wishes to force us to believe changes nothing of its nature," the grandmaster continued. "All qì is but a tool to be used at our discretion. Unfortunately, too many before us have been seduced by the aspect of power and lost their way." Dé'zǐ regarded Zen through half-lidded eyes. "I have told you this many a time. Wayward, under my instruction, refers not to the type of qì you use—but whether you control your power, or whether you allow it to control you. Whether you are able to hold its balance. You hold within you a great power, Zen. You must remember to never let it control you."

Under his master's piercing scrutiny, it was all Zen could do to remain still. He thought of the voice locked inside him, the fountain of qì that had come spilling from him at the slightest summoning. He bowed his head again. "Yes, shī'fù."

"Now." Dé'zǐ bent his face to the fragrance of the snow camellia bush again. "Let us finish admiring this beautiful winter bloom and head to the Chamber of a Hundred Healings to visit our new friend. In the meantime, why don't you update me on your adventures over the past moons?"

Zen began to tell his master of his pursuit of the metals trading ledger, of how the trail had gone cold with Old Wei's death in Haak'gong and, instead, he'd happened upon the girl. Of the Alloy who'd pursued them and the Elantian forces who'd followed them deep into the forests at the heart of the kingdom.

He didn't, however, tell his master of Lan's vision, of his promise to take her to Guarded Mountain. Of the strange qì he had—or thought he had—sensed within her. After the conversation they'd just had on demonic qì, he had no wish to bring up any further taboo subjects.

"These events yielded the opportunity to observe the Alloy

up close through hand-to-hand combat," Zen said. "The El-antian magicians continue to draw their power from metals and wielding their properties, conducting lightning and raising fires and forging swords out of thin air."

Dé'zǐ hummed, nodding to himself. They had wound through the stone paths nestled into the mountain, passing schoolhouses half hidden by lush evergreens. Gray-brick eaves curved skyward, adorned with motifs of flora and fauna and the gods. Once in a while, the tinkle of a windchime rang out in the early evening breeze. At this hour, the day bells would have rung and disciples would be rotating to their next classes. The Chamber of a Hundred Healings, where the Master of Medicine taught his craft, sat on a flat stretch of fertile ground on which all sorts of herbs were tended to by his disciples. A quiet pond with an arced stone bridge cut through it, growing an assortment of water plants.

"A pity Master Nóng is away on a procurement trip," the grandmaster said. "I would have liked his help in treating the young lady's injuries. We may have to wait . . . yet on the bright side, Master Ulara has just returned. With her clan's knowledge of metals, she will have valuable insights on the El-antian metalwork in the girl's arm—I have asked for her presence shortly. It seems there is much to discuss."

A sudden pulse of energy cut through their conversation—one that felt distinctly familiar. One consisting solely of yīn.

Dé'zǐ and Zen spun as a streak of white qì flashed over the Chamber of a Hundred Healings like lightning. And then Zen felt it: his qì being drawn by the activation of the Seal he had inked on Lan's arm.

He was already running, boots pounding against stone, his páo offering more flexibility than the stiff Elantian merchant's outfit he'd worn while traveling. The medicinal garden drew closer; he sprinted past the stone bridge and carp pond, past the assortment of herbal plants, and hurtled up the front steps of the chamber.

The interior was dim: the chamber was more tightly sealed than most schoolhouses in Skies' End to preserve the dried herbs. In the center, the black flames of his Seal encircled a pillar of white light in an attempt to marshal it.

It lasted only a moment. A third pulse of qì bifurcated the two, smothering them like fire. Zen recognized the steady earth-gold light it emitted.

Dé'zǐ had interfered.

The scene before them cleared. The Medicine disciple, Shàn'jūn, was straightening amidst a cluster of smashed porcelain. Stew seeped across the wooden floorboards between the other two figures in the chamber.

The first was someone Zen would not have wished to offend at any cost: Yeshin Noro Dilaya. A disciple of Swords, she had a temper like a blade and was not afraid to use it. Her mother's noble lineage as last matriarch of the Jorshen Steel clan and position as a master of this school firmly cemented Dilaya's position of privilege.

And the other figure . . . Something stretched taut inside Zen as he beheld her. Lan had changed into disciple's robes that were large for her small songgirl's frame. She held both hands before her in defense. A sliver of bandages showed on her midriff; as she lowered her arms, she winced, one hand going to her wound from the Elantian arrow. Her face was pale and drawn, but a spark of fire ignited in her gaze as she turned to Dilaya.

"Don't touch me, you horse-faced fox spirit," she spat.

Zen fought back the ridiculous urge to laugh.

Yeshin Noro Dilaya straightened from her crouch. Her

face was contorted in fury as she drew her sword. "Wayward practitioner." The words were soft but laced with poison. "The likes of you were never meant to grace the doorstep of the School of the White Pines."

Zen stepped between them.

"Move," Dilaya snapped at Zen. Her sword glistened orange in the light of the setting sun.

"Dilaya." Zen inclined his head, keeping his tone even. As always, he could not bring himself to look at her face, to meet one gray eye and the dark eye patch, the mark of his mistake that haunted him to this day. "This girl has been my charge. Any crimes she has committed, any taboos against the school, are mine to bear. Though I do request that you think before accusing anyone of anything egregious."

He sensed when Lan looked up sharply at him.

"What, did my accusation touch a nerve?" Dilaya sneered. "Is this bringing back memories of what transpired in this very chamber not ten cycles past? Perhaps you should bear your *own* taboos before you go shouldering anybody else's, *Zen*."

Zen felt his entire body freeze over. There it was, the stain to his name that could never be erased. The proof that the scholars and emperors of the Middle Kingdom had been right to fear demonic power.

"She cannot yet control her qì to adhere to the Way," he said at last. "Be not hasty, Dilaya."

Dilaya's lips curled. "Surely you also sense the yīn energies she emits? I would have thought you'd know precisely what that might mean—or is that the reason you are shielding her?" At Zen's silence, she continued: "That girl nearly exposed us to the Elantian army. I can sense the wrongness to the metal in her arm. It must be destroyed. Now, for the last time, *get out of my way, or I will make you.*"

"I do believe that fights, duels, and all forms of physical altercations are against the Code of Conduct within the boundaries of this school," came a mild voice.

Instantly, Dilaya's face drained of color.

Dé'zǐ strode in, taking care to step over the raised wooden threshold of the door. His words had been temperate, but the effect was worse than if he had shouted.

Yeshin Noro Dilaya was hotheaded, but she was first and foremost a disciple to one of the Hundred Schools of Practitioning, and an heir of a former great clan. It was nearly comical how quickly she shifted tack, the ire on her face disappearing as she dropped to her knees before the grandmaster. "Forgiveness, shī'zǔ. Grandmaster."

"You might remember," Dé'zǐ said, "that I sent you here to examine the metalwork and to report upon it, not to take it upon yourself to destroy it. Such a heavy decision should not have been made without discussion first."

"Forgiveness, shī'zǔ," Dilaya repeated. "But I sensed the danger from the Elantian metalwork. I don't believe it should ever have entered our Boundary Seal—"

"My, my, what a ruckus on such a pleasant evening," came a voice.

Zen tensed as a sixth person strode into the Chamber of a Hundred Healings.

The passage of time had wrought the matriarch of the Jorshen Steel clan, like refined metal, into something far sharper, crueler, and more beautiful than her daughter. Master Yeshin Noro Ulara's hair was also done in the classic two-bun fashion of her clan, yet instead of Dilaya's verdant black, Ulara's was grayed with experience.

"Ah," Ulara said as her gaze fell on Zen. "Of course." She tipped her head back, mouth curling with disdain as she beheld him. For a moment, they watched each other, and Zen felt something in his blood turn, echoes of an age-old enmity stirring inside. Members of the school, though united by the common mission against the Elantians, were embroiled in historical feuds and tussles for power often born into their bloodlines.

By familial obligation, Yeshin Noro Ulara despised Zen.

He swallowed and wrested his face into a semblance of courtesy, then inclined his head. "Ulara."

It was the most overt disrespect he could direct at her without breaching societal customs. Zen had long held a privileged position within the School of the White Pines. Handpicked by Dé'zǐ, he'd been accepted as a disciple of the grandmaster of the school, a ranking no other disciple held. This meant that Ulara had never formally been his master, and Zen had no obligation to address her as such other than out of respect.

From the way she'd treated him since his arrival at the school, Zen had no such inclination.

"Dilaya," the Master of Swords said. "Come here."

Any trace of rebelliousness had drained from Dilaya's gaze. She stood and walked to her mother's side like a scolded dog. "É'niáng," she said respectfully. "Mother."

Yeshin Noro Ulara raised her hand and struck her daughter squarely across the face.

The crack reverberated through the space of the chamber. Zen looked to Dé'zǐ. The grandmaster's face betrayed no expression. The Classic of Customs had parsed Hin society into five different relationships: ruler and subject, master and student, husband and wife, elder and younger, and parent and child. Interfering with any of the relationships was taboo.

In the ensuing silence, Yeshin Noro Ulara dusted off her palm. "Perhaps this will teach you to remember your place," she said. "The ways of this school are not for you to bend, and the instructions of the grandmaster are not for you to disobey."

Dilaya clutched her cheek, face turned away. She said nothing.

"Master Ulara." Dé'zĭ spoke calmly. "I assure you that no harm was done. Dilaya merely acted out of her loyalty to the school. Now, let us all take a seat and have a civil discussion. Tea, anyone? Shàn'jūn, might I trouble you to bring up a pot of your finest pŭ'ĕr?"

As the Medicine disciple bowed out, Dé'zĭ took a seat on the floor. Zen followed suit; he was aware of Lan sinking to her knees by his side.

"First, on the subject of reported Elantian forces approaching our location," Dé'zĭ began, "our Boundary Seal masks all practitioning and qì-related activity, keeping this school hidden after thousands of cycles. Vigilance is necessary, yet an abundance of it becomes paranoia and will detract from our course."

"Grandmaster." It was Ulara who spoke. "I suggest we strike preemptively. Be rid of those imbeciles before they have a chance of approaching this school."

"Fighting fire with fire will only cause more harm, Ulara. You know this. Do not let your anger impair your judgment. Let us, instead, fight fire with water—by adjusting to the situation and being best prepared for when the opportune time comes. Currently, we are severely outmatched in both manpower and strategy. Patience is key. A battle is not won without knowing oneself and one's opponent."

"My people—what was left of us—*died* at the hands of the Elantians," Ulara said, and it was the first time Zen heard a tremor of emotion in the woman's voice. "Forgive me if I have less *patience*."

Zen looked away. Once a long time ago, he had argued the same points with his master.

Dé'zĭ looked unperturbed by Ulara's outburst. "Your clan

famously wrote the *Classic of War*: 'He who rushes into battle unprepared is already accepting a loss.' I am prepared to follow the guidance of your ancestors, Master Ulara."

Ulara pressed her lips together, and Zen marveled at his master's tact. By invoking the words of Ulara's ancestors, Dé'zǐ was humbling himself by paying respect to her name and, at the same time, reminding her that the reasoning behind his choice was rooted in the wisdom of her clan and her elders.

Shàn'jūn reentered the chamber with a tray of tea, breaking the silence. Dé'zǐ took the first cup; everyone followed suit except Ulara. Suddenly pointing in Zen's direction, she said, "Then what of *her*?"

By Zen's side, Lan made a small move, as though to grasp the sleeve covering her left wrist.

Dé'zǐ's face broke into a crinkled smile. "Ah, our new friend. Lan, is it?"

Zen sent a prayer to his ancestors that the girl's next words would not break the taboos of the school and get her expelled before she even started. But all that she said, voice high and clear as bells, was "Yes."

Dé'zǐ held out a hand. "Might I see that arm of yours, which I believe has been the source of all this commotion?"

"All right," Lan said, scooting forward. She gingerly held out her left wrist to the grandmaster.

Dé'zǐ gently placed a finger over the inside of her forearm and closed his eyes. He hummed and nodded, and several times, his eyebrows twitched. Zen had always found it both endearing and embarrassing how the most powerful practitioner in the Last Kingdom had many of the habits of an aged uncle.

At last, Dé'zǐ leaned back. "Would you mind so terribly," he said to Lan, "if I had Master Ulara take a look?"

Something in his tone tightened a thread of caution inside

Zen. As Lan murmured her consent, Yeshin Noro Ulara crossed over in two brisk strides. Roughly, she grabbed Lan's arm and pressed two fingers to it. Moments passed; Zen watched emotions flit across the Master of Swords' face like clouds across a sky.

Her eyes narrowed and she let go, stepping back to look at the grandmaster. They exchanged something in a glance—an agreement of sorts.

"What is it?" Lan asked.

"There is a tracking spell in that metalwork in your arm," Dé'zǐ said gently. "Fear not, for its effects have been temporarily negated by the Boundary Seal—but should you step foot outside Skies' End, I believe whoever put that spell in you will be able to track you."

Everything clicked into place. The Elantians deep in the pine forest—*that* was how they had found her.

"We must be rid of the metalwork immediately," Ulara supplied, folding her arms. She spoke only to Dé'zǐ. "Given how much the spell has progressed, extracting the metalwork could come at the cost of the girl's life."

The words hit Zen like a physical blow, knocking the wind from him. *Her life.* He thought of Lan, rain-soaked with a torn páo, kneeling before him and bleeding tears. It felt as though he had just snatched her from the jaws of death at Elantian hands; now she faced death once again.

I did everything I could.

Did you? that whispering voice inside him hissed. *You could have taken the Gate Seal directly to the School of the White Pines from Haak'gong. All you had to do was choose to let me free.*

No. He knew well enough that that was not an option to consider. He knew the risks, and the consequences of what he had done ten cycles ago sat across from him in this very chamber.

"Master Nóng will return from his journey within the next fortnight," Dé'zǐ replied. "We will require the oversight of the Master of Medicine during this difficult operation."

"I'll wait," Lan blurted. Zen's head snapped in her direction. "In the meantime . . . please, let me stay here. I want to learn practitioning."

Ulara made a furious noise, but Dé'zǐ looked intrigued. He leaned forward, cup of tea forgotten in his hands. "You wish to join the School of the White Pines and study practitioning and the principles of the Way?"

"I do."

The steel in her expression cast Zen back to the morning after they had met, the sun breaking fierce over her face. He had known this girl for her joviality, her quick wit and words, yet there had been no hint of a jest on her face at that time. *Teach me to be powerful, so that I will not have to watch another person I love fall to the Elantian regime.*

"Shī'fù." Zen's voice rasped, yet he could not stop himself. "I would vouch for her. Allow me to train her here, as a disciple."

In a sudden move, Lan pressed her arms and forehead to the floor in prostration. "Please, Grandmaster."

Dé'zǐ looked between the two of them. Finally, he took a sip of tea and sighed. "Master Ulara, kindly perform a new Seal on the metalwork to restrict the tracking spell and slow the metalwork's spread. Lan, I will ask that you rest tonight and regain your strength in the more-than-adequate care of Disciple Shàn'jūn."

Shàn'jūn blushed. Ulara scowled. Zen held his breath. Behind them all, Dilaya's gaze promised murder.

"And tomorrow, you will begin classes." Dé'zǐ raised his cup of tea. "Welcome to Where the Rivers Flow and the Skies End."

14

Caterpillar fungus (also known as yartsa gunbu
or winter-worm, summer-grass) is part animal,
part vegetable, and contains an excellent balance
of yīn and yáng with myriad healing effects.

—Medicine Master Zur'mkhar Rdo'rje,
Instructions on Ten Thousand
Healing Herbs

Lan remembered little of the rest of that afternoon. Shàn'jūn gave her a cup of numbing draft and had her lie down on the kàng. The warm liquid filled her stomach; the sheets were warm and soft against her skin. The sun hung low on the horizon, the color of a ripe mandarin, when Yeshin Noro Ulara was finally ready to perform the Seal.

"This will hurt," the Master of Swords said, and without further ceremony pressed her fingers to Lan's forearm.

Lan felt a dull, throbbing pain before she gave herself over to the effects of the numbing draft. It fogged her brain and blurred her senses until time seemed to skip and skid. The sun's shifting light slipped across her like a fast-flowing stream, voices rushing all around her as though she were underwater. She saw phantoms in that blur of consciousness, saw the ghostly shape of Ying turn into the silhouette of her mother in that snowfall twelve cycles ago, before darkness swallowed them all. And in that darkness came a shadow, writhing gray, rearing its head to watch her.

Find me, Sòng Lián.

The shadow turned into a colorless light, bright and searing, until it tore across her entire world.

When she came to, sunlight slanted gold across the windowsill. A late-afternoon breeze stirred across her cheeks, bringing with it the distant chimes of bells and the sound of laughter. For a moment, she might have been back at the Teahouse, rousing from an evening nap, the chattering of songgirls at their chores drifting upstairs to her.

"Ah, you're awake." A distinctly non-songgirl voice, though gentle and unimposing.

Lan turned to see Shàn'jūn seated on a stool near the back room, a tome splayed open in his lap. He closed it carefully, set it aside, then stood and disappeared into the back room for several moments. When he reappeared, he held a steaming bowl. The porcelain spoon he used to stir made little clinking sounds against the rim.

"My arm," Lan croaked, looking down. Her left forearm was an ugly mottled map of greens and purples where the flesh had bruised, and swollen reds where the Winter Magician's metalwork had spread through her veins. Now, in the center of her forearm was a small, concentrated blot of metal, darkened to near-black. Over it, she could sense the strokes of a Seal, holding in magic that seemed to ooze from the metalwork.

Most important, the scar on her wrist stood out, pale and gleaming amidst the carnage.

"They contained the metalwork where it was spreading through your blood," Shàn'jūn explained. "It's now concentrated in one area, where the spell is still active yet restricted by Master Ulara's Seal. Do you mind if I . . . ?" He gestured at the edge of the kàng.

"Go ahead," she said, pushing herself up and trying not to stare at the strange new sight that was her arm.

Shàn'jūn sat. He scooped out a spoonful of whatever was in the bowl and blew on it. "I admit, I'm no cook, but I promise you'll feel better if you drink this." He raised the spoon and bowl toward her, lifting an eyebrow and curling the edges of his mouth, as though to entice her.

Lan obliged. She regretted it instantly. It was the worst soup she had ever tasted, as though someone had made the bitterest medicine and attempted to mask it with salts and sugars and stirred in some soft, chewy chunks of . . . was that *garlic?*

She spluttered, dripping the abomination of a concoction all over the clean sheets.

"Oh," Shàn'jūn said in dismay. "That was the last of our caterpillar fungus."

"You fed me *caterpillar?*" Lan choked.

"Caterpillar fungus," Shàn'jūn corrected with a hint of pride. "It's one of the rarest materials in Hin medicine. The caterpillars burrow into the soil of a specific climate and turn into fungus in the winter. They're so hard to get—one of the younger disciples swears he almost froze off a finger digging them up."

Lan gagged. "I thought this was supposed to make me feel better!"

"It is! But I never said it would taste good." The boy looked so doleful that Lan took pity on him. She grabbed the spoon and, bracing herself, took another mouthful of the stew.

"So," she said, wishing to turn the subject to something other than deadly Elantian spells and noxious-tasting caterpillar stews, " 'Shàn'jūn.' 'Kind, Noble One'?"

He smiled and lowered his gaze in a gesture that rendered him unfairly pretty, soft black hair framing his slim face, eyes that curved with the flutter of long, dark lashes. Her eyes, however, faltered again at the cleft in his upper lip. She remembered hearing the other songgirls speak of harelipped babies in the villages, how they were cursed and brought bad fortune to their parents. How they were products of demonic bargains.

Now that Lan had learned of the four classifications of supernatural spirits, she knew it was all a load of horseshit.

"Grandmaster Dé'zǐ named me, after he found me crying in a forest by a village one night." Shàn'jūn looked thoughtful for a moment. "I think he hoped it would change my fate—that the circumstances of how I came into this world would not hamper who I would become."

Lan shivered. "The Elantians came to your village?"

"No." He touched his lip. "My parents discarded me."

It seemed like a deeper betrayal, to find out that it was Hin who had chosen to leave him for dead. With the Elantian Conquest, it had become almost instinctual to think of them as the only perpetrators of cruelty.

"Well, they must regret doing so now," she said.

Shàn'jūn smiled. "I don't know if I can say I've lived up to the Grandmaster's name for me . . . but I try. I'm not in the best of health, so I tend toward more scholarly activities. My friend jokes that I have read the entire bookhouse."

"Bookhouse?" Lan asked. "There's a bookhouse here." She shouldn't have been surprised—it was a *school,* a real school with Hin students and masters and life and laughter.

"Of course." Shàn'jūn laughed, a sound as clear as river waters. "It's my favorite place in the world. Once you're situated with your classes, I'll take you."

Lan found herself smiling. It was so easy to slip into the carefree warmth of the safety and security the school offered. But like shadows seeping in came memories of Haak'gong, of the metal-clad Angels who had stormed the thin wooden doors of the Teahouse, the screams that had echoed in rooms once filled with song and laughter.

Of Ying, picking up a kohl pencil, her lips pursed and brows furrowed as she traced perfect lines across Lan's eyes.

Lan drew her knees to her chest and pushed the memories away before the lump in her throat became anything else. She needed to do something—she wasn't sure what, but *something*—and the only thing that came to mind was finding Zen, finding Guarded Mountain, and discovering whatever it was that her mother had Sealed into her.

". . . help but notice the Seal on your wrist." Shàn'jūn's voice tugged her from the whirlpool of her thoughts, jerking her back to the present.

Instinctively, she moved to cover it, but the disciple's next words gave her pause.

"It looks like nothing I have ever seen before. Master Ulara seemed quite taken by it. She had Master Gyasho, the Master of Seals, look at it while you were asleep." Shàn'jūn shook his head. "It stumped even him. I do not think he has ever before come across a Seal he could not decipher."

"They all could see it?" Lan blurted. It made sense: Zen had, which likely meant that the Seal was visible only to practitioners. Yet it somehow felt intrusive, as though the masters had peered into an intimate part of her. Now that she combed back through her memories, she did remember a pair of storm-gray eyes, a blood-red mouth parting in consternation.

What is this? Ulara's voice drifted to her as though from a dream. *What in the Ten Hells is this?*

"Master Ulara seemed in a fuss over it," Shàn'jūn said, and added lightly, "but she's always in a fuss. She nearly lost someone to demonic practitioning, so her paranoia isn't unfounded." Shàn'jūn poked the bowl in her face again. "More soup?"

"I feel fine now," Lan said hastily, pushing the bowl back toward him. "Are you *sure* this stuff's healthy for you?"

"You are in good hands," came a voice.

Zen stood in the doorway, practitioner's páo falling in an elegant sweep. The setting sun gilded him as he stepped over the threshold, black boots thudding across the wooden floor. He inclined his head. "Apologies for the interruption."

Shàn'jūn stood. His posture was suddenly stiff and tight, the easy smile that sparked on his face like sunlight against water dimming. He bowed. "It is no interruption. You are always welcome in the Chamber of a Hundred Healings."

There was softness to his voice, different from any tone he had used with Lan.

"Thank you," Zen said. His gaze drifted to Lan. "I've come to check on Lan."

Lan leapt to her feet. "I feel great," she said brightly. "In fact, I think I'm ready to leave the medicinal chamber."

Zen cast her an appraising look, and her hopes withered. Why had she thought the stiff-backed stickler of a practitioner would help her in any way?

Confirming her suspicions, he said, "You'll remain in the Chamber of a Hundred Healings for tonight. In your condition, you need experienced care."

Lan shot Shàn'jūn a furtive glance. She would have to scheme to avoid that accursed soup for one more night. "Fine."

"Shàn'jūn," Zen continued steadily, "will you see to it that Lan takes classes tomorrow? Have her attend the morning meditations with you, then see the Master of Texts."

Shàn'jūn dipped his head. "Of course."

Zen turned to address Lan. "Take a walk with me, please."

There was a new caution to the way Zen moved around her that made Lan feel as though she were a barrel of firepowder that might explode at any time. Zen had led her to a natural courtyard, framed by outgrowths of rock and stone. The blood of sunset was fading, chased by a watery gray aftermath followed by ink-black night. Birdsong had been replaced by the steady chirp of cicadas through the brush. The entirety of Skies' End was so beautiful Lan felt as though she'd sunk into a dream. A miracle. An impossibility.

She was aware of Zen watching her closely. When she turned to look at him, he quickly dipped his gaze down to her arm. "How do you feel?" he asked. "Nothing unstable or off?"

She tapped a finger of her good hand to her chin. "Well, now that you mention it . . ."

Alarm flared in Zen's expression. "What?"

"I feel something inside me. A voice, whispering to me . . . telling me it hungers . . ."

Zen leaned closer. "Hungers for what?"

". . . for steamed pork buns," Lan finished.

The practitioner drew back, giving her a flat look. "You mock me."

"I wouldn't dare."

"There are some topics you must not jest about."

"What, so I can become as fun as you?" Lan poked her tongue out.

Zen frowned. "Now that you mention it, I meant to ask: What were you thinking, channeling qì in front of *Yeshin Noro Dilaya*, of all people? After I specifically told you *not* to wield it without my guidance?"

"Because that horse-faced fox spirit was going to cut off my arm! And I didn't do anything wrong. I just did the same thing as the night I accidentally summoned the yāo."

"It isn't about doing anything *wrong*," Zen said. "It's about how they view you. An orphaned songgirl with a Seal that no one can decode shows up here pursued by an Elantian Alloy and an army . . . once people see how you use your qì, they will ask questions."

"What's wrong with my qì?"

"It is . . . unbalanced," Zen said at last. But he wouldn't meet her eyes. "I think there's something in that Seal on your wrist impacting the makeup of your qì. Sometimes . . . well, only three times, to be exact, I sensed an overwhelming amount of yīn to it."

Yīn: the energy that common folk associated with demons, darkness, and death. Dark magic.

"So? What does that mean?" she asked, and when he wouldn't answer, she continued: "Well, it worked for me when I needed to defend myself from that Elantian pig who thought of my body as his plaything." Zen's expression softened, and she pushed on: "And I'd do it again. You've never had the need. You don't know what it's like, to suffer at the hands of the Elantians."

"And if I did?" His gaze was sharp as a black blade.

They were close, so close that she felt tension drawing tight between them like a bowstring. There was something so intimate to his words, so private to the way he regarded her, eyes flaming with a mix of anger and vulnerability at once.

She held her ground. "Then you would know that the desperate have no *choice* as to the type of power they use. What does it matter whether my qì is balanced or unbalanced if the end result is the same?"

The anger swept from Zen's face, leaving only a sorrow so profound that, for a moment, his eyes seemed to be drowning in it, a lake beneath a starless night. He turned from her, tilting his face to the darkening sky. A lock of hair fell over his forehead. Lan had the sudden, strange urge to brush it back.

"Lan," he said, and somehow her name coming from his mouth unsteadied her into silence. "When I first arrived here, the masters did everything they could to get rid of me. Trust me when I say that you do not wish to stray from the teachings of the Way. Practitioning has been heavily scaled back and regulated by the Imperial Court since the beginning of the Middle Kingdom, and this scrutiny intensified after the defeat of the Ninety-Nine Clans and the establishment of the Last Kingdom. The paranoia of using qì in ways that fall outside the rules of the Way as defined by our emperors has long been instilled into practitioners—the ones who have survived to this day, at least. Those who defied it . . . were killed."

She had never heard this part of her kingdom's history before. The last rays of sun had ebbed from the world. Like a tipping scale, the moon rose on the other side of the sky, its fluorescence carving the boy before her into black and white, parts known and hidden. Lan thought of the way his eyes had turned black, of the scars on his hands, of the storms in his eyes, and suddenly felt ashamed of her own lightheartedness on the subject matter.

"All right," she said, lowering her gaze. "I won't do it again."

He watched her for a moment. "But . . . ?"

Her head snapped up again. "But you have to take me to Guarded Mountain."

"Ah," Zen said slowly. Lan knew that look. It was the one that came before a denial.

"You promised," she pressed. "I thought you were a man of honor."

The practitioner gave her a look of wearied resignation. "The tracking spell Ulara discovered in your arm complicates things. The moment we step beyond the Boundary Seal of Skies' End, we will be vulnerable."

"I have to go before they attempt to extract the metalwork from me," Lan said. "I can't die not knowing why my mother left behind this Seal."

"Your mother."

She hesitated. If she was going to ask for his help, then she would need to tell him enough of the story so that he was convinced.

Lan drew a breath and nodded. "I think whatever's in this Seal . . . whatever is at Guarded Mountain . . . has to do with why the Elantian magician was after me. Why he's been searching for me all these cycles. That night in Haak'gong, he asked me to give something to him. That's the same thing he said to my mother before he killed her."

Zen's eyes blazed. "Your mother gave you that Seal." He asked the question flatly.

A knot formed in her chest. "Yes."

"That Elantian magician killed her in an attempt to take something from her."

She nodded.

"And you think"—Zen's eyes found her left wrist—"you think the clues to whatever he wanted . . . whatever it is that he has spent cycles tracking down . . . is in your Seal."

"Yes—clues that lead to Guarded Mountain," Lan said quietly. "Whatever we find there, we may also understand why you sensed so much yīn to my qì."

Zen was silent for a long time. "We will need to be quick," he said. "We must return before the Elantians can locate us with the tracking spell—for though Ulara's Seal is strong, the spell is still embedded in your arm. Stepping outside the Boundary Seal removes another layer of protection."

Her heart lifted. She wanted to throw her arms around him. "When can we go?"

"Within the next fortnight. Before the Master of Medicine returns to operate on your arm."

Her blood roared in her ears. *Within the next fortnight.* Twelve cycles of searching, and the answer to her question was only days away.

"But before we go, you must focus on training," Zen said. "No more near-death experiences until you can hold your own against me and know enough practitioning to not be a deadweight."

Her intense joy dissipated, replaced by a fiery determination.

Lan drew back and folded her arms. "Fine. In that case, you'd better sleep with an eye open and a knife in your hands, Mister Practitioner."

"Stop calling me 'mister.' I am not so much older than you."

"Then stop acting like it."

"I have a better idea." He leaned forward and gave her a look so searing, she had the sudden impression that his propriety had all been an act. "How about I teach you, personally?"

Lan met his eyes, and for the first time in a while, she felt a smile come to her from the inside out, warming her. She lowered her gaze. "I know I gave off the wrong impression when I met you, with the butterknife—"

"The teapot," he supplied. "*And* the teacup."

"*You* were the one who told me to try harder. I had to think fast." She grinned. "I know I shall make for an excellent student under your—"

Whatever she had been about to say vanished from her mind, for at that moment, Zen smiled. It was slow, and small, a slight curving of his mouth that crinkled his eyes and dimpled his cheeks, cracking the facade of stern rigidity to his features and giving a glimpse of a boy who might have been. A night of black clouds, parting to reveal a bright moon.

"If I train you and take you to Guarded Mountain," he said, "you promise you'll study hard and stay away from channeling qì irresponsibly?"

Lan pressed a fist to her palm in a salute. "I swear it on all the pork buns in the Last Kingdom."

"Well, now." His eyes held playfulness like a dusting of stars. "That is a very serious vow."

15

In a journey with three disciples,
I am bound to find a master.

—*Kontencian Analects*
(Classic of Society), 2:3

In typical Lan fashion, she woke up late for her first day of class. The morning bells were already halfway through their chiming as she washed with clear spring water from the bucket the disciples filled each night. Then, she flung on her new practitioner's páo and followed the stream of white-robed disciples down the footpaths to the school halls.

The disciples began their day with morning chores. These rotated each day so that more favorable tasks (such as organizing tomes in the bookhouse) and less favorable tasks (cleaning the latrines) were equally distributed among all. Then, with the sound of the bell, the disciples raced to the refectory for a breakfast of congee, vegetable stew, and some tofu dishes. Lan managed to chat up the cook, a cheerful, plump-faced woman named Taub, whose son, Chue, was a disciple. They'd fled the Elantian Conquest in their southwestern village together and crossed paths with the Master of Iron Fists, who'd subsequently brought them to safety in Skies' End, Taub told Lan between extra scoops of tofu and red bean soup.

Lan found the classes as fascinating as the masters who taught them. There was Nur, the Master of Light Arts, a kindly, slight man who moved like the shifting waters of a river. For Lan's first lesson, he had her practice channeling qì to specific parts of her body while she watched the other disciples leap from impossibly high places and scale walls. Cáo, the Master of Archery, handed Lan a basket of jujubes and had her toss one into the air. Faster than she could blink, the master had sent an arrow cleaving through the heart of the jujube.

And he'd done it with his eyes closed.

Ip'fong, the Master of Iron Fists, was a ruddy man with a torso harder than boulders. Iron Fists, Lan learned, was a specific style of martial arts. He had taught at the School of Eternal Spring, which specialized in all types of martial arts; of his fellow masters and their disciples, he was the sole survivor. For Lan's first class, he set her a variety of strength-training exercises. Sweating profusely as she attempted to do a push-up balancing on two fingers, Lan watched her fellow disciples practice sparring and neatly lop heads off wooden dummies with flying kicks.

Yeshin Noro Ulara, Master of Swords, was relentless. Lan suspected she'd been chomping at the bit to punish Lan for her transgressions on that first day in the Chamber of a Hundred Healings. For Lan's first lesson, the master had her spar with Dilaya with wooden sticks, without any instruction or guidance. Dilaya did not bother to hide her vindictive pleasure with every blow she landed on Lan.

Lan did not even manage to touch Dilaya.

"That's bad luck," Shàn'jūn said, grimacing sympathetically when she plopped down next to him at the refectory, covered in fresh bruises. He reached into the hemp satchel he always carried with him. Lan heard clinking sounds inside. "Good thing I always come prepared. Hold still."

"Everyone knows Yeshin Noro Dilaya would do anything to win her mother's favor," Chue chimed in over his hearty bowl of tofu stew. "She wants to earn Ulara's sword."

"Why?" Lan asked, holding out her arm as Shàn'jūn began to apply acrid-smelling creams to her bruises.

"Because it's Falcon's Claw," Chue said dreamily. "Every disciple of Swords knows it: it's the legendary dāo of the Jorshen Steel clan. The handle's made of ivory, and it comes with a thumb ring Jorshen hunters used to wear to hunt. The lore says that every generation, the leader of the Jorshen Steel clan would select an heir from one of the eight Jorshen noble houses."

This piqued Lan's interest. *"Clan?"* she repeated, setting down her bowl of congee. "As in the Ninety-Nine Clans?"

"Yeah. Why?"

Like most Hin, Lan had grown up thinking of the clans as a cross between ancient history and myth—not as real, live, flesh-and-blood people who walked and talked and had prickly dispositions. "Are there many other clan members here?"

"I'm descended from a clan," Chue said cheerfully. "The Muong clan."

"The presence of the clans began to fade in the late Middle Kingdom," Shàn'jūn supplied, drawing back to examine his work on her arm. "In a bid to appease the Imperial Court's growing unease over their presence, many of the smaller clans spread out to try to assimilate into the mainstream Hin culture. Most of the Hin are descended from clans, though with the rise of the Last Kingdom, families began to keep any association with a clan a secret."

"Think of the Hin as a huge clan, too," Chue chimed in. "Only, they expanded so rapidly, they became synonymous with the people and the culture of the kingdom. Most dynasties—all but a handful—have been founded by Hin emperors."

"And the other clans rebelled against the Hin Imperial Court?" Lan filled in.

She seemed to have said the wrong thing. Shàn'jūn's expression was still, a pond without a ripple, but Chue—his face fell. "Not all," he said, sounding hurt. "The Muong people only ever wanted to keep to our own culture and customs."

"Many clans were known to have developed their own special branches of practitioning," Shàn'jūn said. He rolled down her sleeve and began tucking his vials and balms back into his hemp satchel, but Lan had the distinct impression that he was intentionally avoiding meeting her gaze. "These arts are passed down through their bloodlines. Some grew exceptionally powerful, and the Imperial Court became afraid. So they sought to limit both practitioning and the presence of the clans. But the Ninety-Nine Clans were still around . . . until the end of the Middle Kingdom." He said this with his eyes downcast. Chue's head was lowered as he made a great show of slurping his congee.

For the first time in her life, Lan had nothing to say. She had learned the broad strokes of her kingdom's history with her tutors as a child, and then she'd picked up scraps of stories from the elders and the villagers, the townsfolk and the dishwashers.

Now it felt as though she were learning a part of history that had somehow disappeared from the books, been scrubbed from the collective memories of the Hin.

She was quiet for the rest of the meal.

Lan excelled at Seals, taught by the monk Gyasho in the Chamber of Waterfall Thoughts. The master wore a silk blindfold over his eyes, which Lan had heard other disciples say were white as snow: a mark of clan descent. It was rumored that whichever clan he'd belonged to had the custom of training with blindfolds from an early age to elevate their awareness to the world of qì.

While the other disciples practiced their Seals in the pavilion outside, Gyasho drew Lan into the chamber, which was more of an open-air hallway than a chamber. Translucent gauze veils fluttered between stone pillars, a cool breeze threading through them that stirred Lan's hair and the master's golden robes. The lotus lamps spaced across smooth stone floors flickered gently; behind them, from the end of the hallway, came the susurration of a waterfall. Gyasho had Lan practice distinguishing between different strands of qì. Lan was a quick study, for she had learned the concepts with Zen during their journey. There was qì in absolutely everything: water, air, light, stone, soil, grass, skin, blood, and even, Gyasho said, the metaphysical: emotions, thoughts, and the soul.

By the end of the hour, once the incense used to keep time had burned to its end, Lan was attempting to summon the different types of qì.

"Very good," the master said encouragingly when she saluted him to the next ring of bells. "Remember to think of each combination of qì as a musical note. You cannot make music without knowing all the notes like each one of your fingers." He gave her an enigmatic smile. "I look forward to meeting you for our next session."

When she recounted Master Gyasho's words to Chue, who met her outside the chamber after class, the disciple appeared excited. "Maybe he'll take you as a disciple to his art," Chue suggested.

"A disciple to his art?" Lan asked.

"Every disciple typically chooses an art of practitioning to specialize in, just like how mine is Archery. And when you're good enough, you're initiated as a xiá—a practitioner. That's what Zen and Dilaya are. Only practitioners have the chance to learn the Final Art and become a master of their school."

"And what is the Final Art?"

"It's a secret technique to practitioning that differentiates each school." Chue's eyes grew dreamy. "Here, I've heard, the grandmaster comes and selects you, and he takes you to the Chamber of Forgotten Practices."

"Where's that?" Lan asked. "And what *is* this school's Final Art?"

"Well, nobody knows! If they did, we'd all be learning it and graduating to become masters. Even Zen and Dilaya haven't been selected yet." Chue winked. "I think you have a good chance with Seals. Master Gyasho's nice, but he's not *that* complimentary."

Lan thought of what Zen had said about her qì—that she was *aglow* with it—and said nothing.

Her good spirits, however, took a turn during her final class of the day: Texts. The Master of Texts, a difficult old man named Master Nán, looked horrified to find out that Lan had not memorized the eighty-eight rules of the school's Code of Conduct by heart. He sent her running up and down the mountain steps balancing a rock on her head while reading the list of Codes, telling her to return only when she could recite all the rules by heart.

But Lan had not grown up in a Teahouse for nothing. She'd racked up the most punishments from Madam Meng and had spent her solitary hours reciting poems or texts she'd learned as a child out of sheer boredom. When she returned to the Chamber of Waterfall Thoughts in the late afternoon and rattled off the eighty-eight rules without pause or hesitation, the master's displeasure only seemed to deepen.

"Then recite the first chapter of the Book of the Way," the Master of Texts demanded peevishly.

Lan bit back a string of colorful insults. In her sweetest voice, she said, "Shī'fù, I'm new here, and I haven't had time—"

"Insolence!" the master barked. " 'It is not the place of the student to question the master!' How can you call yourself a student of this school if you do not know even the first Kontencian Analect regarding the relationship between student and master?" He pointed at a heaping pile of tomes by his seat. "You'll take the Four Classics and copy them as many times as it takes for them to get through that slippery skull of yours. You'll not leave this hall until you have copied them all, word for word."

Lan stared at the stack. "There must be thousands of pages in those!"

"And still you waste your breath pointing out the obvious," Master Nán said nastily.

Stomach growling and fresh practitioner's robes already stained with sweat and dust from her morning's punishment, Lan sat in a back corner of the Chamber of Waterfall Thoughts to begin. Each classic was thicker than her wrist span, not to mention that the pages were made of xuān paper, an especially thin type of rice paper efficient at absorbing ink.

This would take her forever.

Rubbing her eyes, she glanced at the brush pot, upon which leaned a half-ground inkstick and a slender horsetail brush. A lump rose in her throat.

The last time she had held one had been in Māma's study.

Lan shook her head and grasped the brush firmly, banishing the memories. She had four thousand-page tomes to copy.

The sun continued to sink; when it hung just above the horizon, the supper bell tolled throughout Skies' End. Lan shifted her aching shoulders, clamping a hand over her stomach as it emitted another loud growl in protest. Beyond the jagged pines, she could make out the darting white of practitioners' robes as the other disciples headed for the refectory.

If she just snuck out now . . . grabbed a bite to eat . . . Master Nán would be none the wiser . . .

He could also sentence her to *more* punishment. She was sure of it. Massaging her sore wrists, Lan scowled and leaned back, wriggling as she stretched. The sweat on her skin had dried to salt, crusting her practitioner's robes and making them uncomfortably hard and prickly. And she was so, so thirsty . . .

A new sound filtered into her awareness: the sound of rushing water.

Lan stood and made her way to the back terrace. The hall was situated before a sharp incline in the mountain. From the ledges above plunged a waterfall, tumbling down before being swallowed by a pool. Mists plumed over the crystal-clear water, which sparkled in the late evening sun.

Lan glanced around at the empty mountain. If she couldn't risk going to the refectory, at least she could take a quick bath and have a drink.

The wooden floorboards gave way to slick stone as she approached the pool. Lan kicked off her sandals, flung her robes over her head, and jumped in with the grace of a sinking rock.

The water was so cold that she almost let out a curse (which would breach Code of Conduct rule number fifty-seven). She emerged gasping and sputtering, pawing the hair from her eyes and blinking the water from her lashes. Teeth chattering, she quickly scrubbed her arms, composing a neat little ditty as she did so.

> "Rat fart, dog soul, pig-brained fool
> Is how I'd describe Nán shī'fù.
> Horse arse, turtle egg, blown cow stick,
> The Master of Texts has a tiny—"

"*What the—*"

Lan spun at the voice, her hands darting to cover her breasts. Standing on the back terrace of the Chamber of Waterfall Thoughts, frozen in equal parts disbelief and outrage, was none other than Zen. The sound of the waterfall had masked his footsteps.

It was almost comical how wide his eyes and mouth stretched, the tips of his ears flaming red—whether from fury or embarrassment, Lan couldn't tell. Pointing a shaking finger at her and covering his eyes with his other hand, he spluttered, "You—that's—sacred—out—*out!*"

Lan scrambled, her feet slipping on the wet rocks as she pulled her robes over her head. She made it to the wooden patio, dripping water, wet splotches already blooming on her pale robes.

Zen turned to her, one hand lingering over his eyes. Between the cracks of his fingers, he squinted at her, then, seeing that she was properly covered, straightened. He swallowed and closed his eyes briefly, as though praying to his ancestors for patience.

"That," he said, "is the Spring of Crystal Cold."

No wonder it was freezing, Lan thought, but she dipped her head and said, "Sorry."

"It is a sacred spring that is said to flow from the tears of the moon, representing the heart of yīn energies on this mountain. For thousands of cycles, masters and worshippers have held their prayers by its waters, hoping to unlock the balance in their energies . . . and you have just *bathed* in it."

Lan was mortified by an urge to laugh, so she thought the most appropriate course of action was to remain silent.

Zen brushed a hand over his face and sighed into it. His flush was fading. Finally, he cleared his throat and turned to fully face her. "Master Nán informed me of your tardiness and insolence."

"I wasn't!" Lan said, then paused. "Well, I *was* tardy, but I wasn't insolent."

Zen cast her a skeptical look. " 'A student is not meant to question his master,' " he said. "*Classic of Society*—otherwise known as *Kontencian Analects*—Chapter Two, Principle One."

"But what if his master is wrong?" she argued.

He sighed, rubbing a hand over his mouth as he looked at her with an expression so weary, she could practically hear *What am I to do with you?* echoing in his mind.

Then Zen drew himself straighter and cleared his throat. "I have an idea. Why don't you learn the classics before questioning them?" He held up a bamboo basket. "Come, I'm here to help—and I brought steamed buns."

The buns were delicious. Lan wished everything in this world could bring her a joy as simple as that of eating steamed buns. Granted, these were vegetable buns, not pork (" 'There shall be no lives taken within the Boundary Seal of Skies' End,' Code of Conduct rule number seventeen," Zen reminded her), but to her empty stomach, anything was a relief.

"The Four Classics," Zen said, and his voice echoed in the empty hall. Gauze curtains stirred in the gentle evening wind; moonlight drifted through them to silver the floor. Zen had lit the lotus lamps swinging from the eaves of the roof, cocooning him and Lan in a warm glow. "Did Master Nán at least go through the basics of each with you?"

Lan shook her head. She hadn't cared to digest the contents—she'd merely flipped open one of them and begun copying the characters as quickly as she could.

"Well." Zen knelt with perfect posture and reached for the tomes. He held the books up one by one, with great care. Each was bound by silk stitching in plain, thick paper and inscribed with stern black characters too complicated for Lan to read. "First: the *Classic of Virtues*, otherwise known as *Book of the Way*. Second: the *Classic of Society*, otherwise known as the *Kontencian Analects*. Third: the *Classic of War*. Fourth: the *Classic of Death*. Each is a foundational pillar from which the Hundred Schools of Practitioning have sprung; each contains historical records and interpretations that the people of the Last Kingdom have followed for thousands of cycles."

He picked up one of Lan's pages, and she suddenly felt a rush of shame at her unruly scrawls, at the places where she'd gotten frustrated or lazy and the characters had become barely legible.

Zen set the page down. "It isn't physically possible to copy all four tomes tonight," he said. "I will speak to Master Nán. For now, let us do our best. I see you began with the *Classic of Society*—this won't make sense until you've gone through the first classic, the Book of the Way." He picked up a brush and dipped it in ink, raising it over a clean scroll of parchment. "Go on. I'll write with you."

Zen's calligraphy was perfect, effortless, each sweep of his brush bearing the precision of a scalpel and the grace of art. Lan felt her cheeks heating as she did her best—but her education had stopped at the age of six, and until this afternoon, it had been twelve cycles since she'd picked up a brush.

"You're holding it too tightly," Zen said. Lan sensed him assessing her page, her characters jutting out like overgrown clumps of weeds.

The heat spread down to her neck, jumbling her mind even further. She'd always prided herself in her quick wit and silver words and her propensity for getting out of trouble—but in this moment, with Zen watching her, she would have given anything to have been a proper, educated noblewoman.

"Try to loosen your grasp and let the brush flow like an extension of your hand," Zen said. "It'll take time, but—here." He closed his cool fingers over hers, and the heat in her face had nothing to do with shame anymore.

She felt his breath against her neck as he leaned over her to reposition her fingers in the correct grip. Her heart tumbled in her chest; he quietly spoke to her on methods to balance the brush, but all that she could focus on was the sensation of his touch.

He no longer wore the black gloves he'd had on for most of their journey. The candlelight outlined the ridges of scars on his hands, too evenly cut to be from an accident.

"Your scars," she found herself saying in a stretch of silence. "How did you get them?"

Zen paused, tipping his head to her. A streak of black hair spilled over his face. This close, she could make out the individual lashes of his eyes, see her face reflected in the midnight of his irises.

He looked down, and she felt a small thrill that he did not pull back. "An accident," he said, and then, to her surprise, he lifted a part of his sleeve. There, carving up his forearm, were pale white marks like the crude slashes of a blade. "These the Elantians gave me."

The spark of thrill turned to horror.

"They captured me during the Conquest. Held me for one entire cycle." His voice was flat; his gaze was shuttered. She recognized that look. It was the look of someone doing his best to shut out memories.

Lan had heard stories—rumors spread among fearful villagers—of Hin captured by the Elantians after the Conquest and dragged off as experimentation subjects. Most died, their bodies cast into the Coiled Dragon River; the corpses found by fishermen had been distorted to horrifying degrees, with eyeballs and fingernails plucked out, flesh split open and embedded with all sorts of metallic objects.

"You were an experimental subject," she whispered.

He closed his eyes. "Yes."

If a songgirl had told her this, Lan would have gathered her into her arms and held her until the sun rose. But it was Zen, elegant, beautiful, distant Zen, and she could think of nothing more to do than sit here with her knuckles white against her brush, his hand still draped loosely over hers as though he'd forgotten all about it.

Instead, a thought came to her.

I want to be powerful.

She hadn't been able to protect her mother.

She hadn't been able to protect Ying. The songgirls. The Teahouse. Even Madam Meng. Their names trailed her like weights—their laughter, then their tears and their endings.

"Zen," she said softly.

He gave a slow blink, gaze clearing as it found her from a torrent of memories. "Hmm?"

"Thank you," Lan said. "For everything. I'm going to work hard."

The drowsy, distant look of his face had gone, replaced by a steely expression. As though by instinct, his thumb swept a stroke over the back of her hand, sending shivers up her arm.

"Good," he said, and stood. "It's time we begin our second training for the night."

He led her down some rocky footpaths to a flat stretch of mountain that ended in plunging cliffs. The Last Kingdom opened before her beneath a waning moon: a sky like a bowl of black ink flecked with silver dust, mountains forming the jagged edges. The breeze here was cool, carrying a bite of winter rarely felt in the southern regions.

Zen turned to her. "I have a gift for you," he said. He palmed a soft leather scabbard and slid out its contents: a dagger that winked silver. Holding the flat of the blade between his fingers, he took her hand in his and rested the hilt in her palm. It was cool to the touch. The handle was ringed with engravings of stars dancing amidst flames, along with elegant, curling characters she did not recognize. "It is better to begin practicing with the weapon you will use in combat, for each weapon has a different length and weight and trick to balance."

"It's so small." Lan eyed the jiàn strapped to Zen's waist, which extended down to his calf. "Can't I have one like yours?"

"Judge not the potency of a blade by its length," Zen said. "Look closer at your dagger."

Lan did, flipping it over in her palm. Its blade caught the glint of moonlight, and this time she noticed a steady trickle of qì shimmering in the metal, wrought into the semblance of Hin characters. "There is a Seal on this," she said at last, looking up.

The edges of Zen's lips lifted slightly. "There is qì in this," he corrected. "Stories often say practitioners' swords are imbued with souls. That isn't quite true; what *is* true is that we fill our chosen weapons with our qì to better protect us. The name of this dagger is That Which Cuts Stars. This blade pierces not only human flesh but supernatural as well. Its purpose is to sever demonic qì to stop a demon's attack. It will not destroy a demon, but it will do what ordinary swords cannot: maim one, though only temporarily."

Chills erupted down Lan's spine at the word *supernatural*. The little blade in her hand would protect her against demons. "How would one pierce a demon's flesh?"

"Like this." Zen drew her hand toward him until the tip of That Which Cuts Stars pointed against his chest. His smile was faint, his fingers warm and steady against hers. "No difference from a human. You aim for the demon's core of qì—the equivalent to our hearts." His gaze flickered, drifting over her face. "Then you pierce."

For some reason, her heart tumbled and her breath came fast. "I'll remember that," Lan said.

"Try not to miss. A demon will not be inclined to give you a second chance."

Her blade pressed against the fabric of his black páo. "I won't miss."

His thumb tapped involuntarily against her skin. "I imagine this will be an upgrade from your previous weapon of choice, teacups," Zen said.

The joke came lightly, but she suddenly wondered whether he'd remembered what she yearned for the most: a way to protect herself and her loved ones. The dagger he had gifted her, though small, held a world of weight.

Lan stepped back. "Thank you."

A slice of metal, and Zen faced her with his jiàn: a long, straight sword with a blade of dark steel. The handle was black, inscribed with what resembled red flames—the same sigil, Lan realized, that she had seen on the silk pouch Zen had carried.

"Lan, meet Nightfire," Zen said, holding the blade straight out before him. "Your task will be to get past its defenses by the end of the moon."

For the rest of the evening, Zen trained with her. He had her practice set moves, watching and stepping in to correct her posture where he saw fit.

"Think of the blade as an extension of your body," he said. "Channel your qì into the tip when you pierce. Into the edges when you slash. Into the hilt when you withdraw. This is the reason people believe the jiàn holds parts of its practitioner's soul: because we fight not only with technique but with our qì."

She paused, sweat wetting her páo in spite of the cool evening breeze. "Zen, when exactly will we go to Guarded Mountain? A fortnight is long."

"Not for at least another week," came the answer. "Currently, the entirety of Skies' End is abuzz with your arrival. Give the masters some time to shift their attention away. Especially Ulara and Dilaya." A sigh. "Leaving here would be against their judgment, so I would not wish to draw any attention to our excursion."

One more week. The thought both excited and terrified her. "Will I be good enough to fight by your side then?"

Zen gave her a half smile. "In one week? It takes cycles for practitioners to merely gain control of their qì." Gently, his hand came to rest against the handle of her little blade, his fingers cool against hers. "When you are able to pierce my heart with this dagger," Zen said, "you will be good enough to stand as my equal in practitioning."

16

In death, a soul may leave an imprint on this
world, whether on an object or on a living being.
That soul will pass into the next world
incomplete and never find rest.

—Chó Yún, Imperial Spirit Summoner,
Classic of Death

On the sixth day at Skies' End, Lan received a summons from the grandmaster.

She had arrived at her last class of the day by the Chamber of Waterfall Thoughts and was told by a sullen Master Nán that the grandmaster of the school had summoned her and that she was to meet him at the Peak of Heavenly Discussion.

"Why?" she attempted to ask the Master of Texts, who merely glowered at her and snapped, "Remind me again what is Principal One, Chapter Two of the Kontencian Analects?"

"If you can't recall it then you shouldn't be teaching," Lan replied, and ran for her life.

The mists curled around her feet as she made her way up the worn stone steps that led to the summit of Skies' End, where the Peak of Heavenly Discussion was located. The stone path grew narrower the higher she climbed; the mists seemed to thicken until Lan could barely see five steps ahead of her. The edge of the steps ended in what seemed like a precarious fall, shrouded by fog at the moment; a mass of gray so still and silent that it was like looking into a dead sea.

And then, on the last step, the clouds disappeared as suddenly as if she'd emerged from under the ocean.

She stood at the peak of Skies' End. Cliffs on every side plunged sharply into the mist below, but up here, the air was clear. The sky was an endless stretch of pale gray, broken by the undulating shadows of the Yuèlù Mountains. As the sun rose, light and color seeped into the world like ink, blotting fiery reds and golds across the clouds and dotting the landscape emerald with the Last Kingdom's famous pines.

"Beautiful, is it not?"

Lan started. Dé'zǐ had appeared at the top of the steps as silently as a ghost. He walked to Lan's side and stood there, his robes and hair fluttering in the breeze, his face set in a mask of utter serenity. The grandmasters in the stories she'd grown up with had all been old and wizened, perhaps somewhat resembling Master Nán's wrinkled, white-bearded countenance— but Dé'zǐ's hair was still ink black with a few streaks of gray, and he was lithe and strong. More of a father's age than a grandfather's age.

In his hands, he held a cup of steaming tea.

"Yes, it is," Lan managed. She spoke less rather than more, for her insides fluttered with nervousness at being alone with the grandmaster. There was something so calming, almost *familiar*, about Dé'zǐ's presence that made her want to trust him and relax. "Grandmaster," she added, wishing to make a good impression.

"It is at this peak that the first master of the White Pines achieved his enlightenment with the gods and founded this school—hence, the Peak of Heavenly Discussion." Dé'zǐ gave her an enigmatic smile. "I see you are well settled into your classes. Master Ip'fong is adequately fond of you, Master Ulara thinks you of little talent, and Master Nán claims you have tofu for brains."

She might have shown cheek to the other masters, but for some reason, Dé'zǐ's presence evoked in her a wish to impress him. "I'm but a peasant songgirl, Grandmaster, with little education and talent. Give me some time—"

"Master Gyasho seems to find in you an extremely promising pupil," the grandmaster interrupted, and she blushed. "Besides, between you and me, I could not care less how ugly Master Nán claims your calligraphy to be. Now I'd like you to show me the most important thing you have learned in these past few days."

That was easy. She thought to the Chamber of Waterfall Thoughts, to Master Gyasho's kindly smile, his face lifted skyward and his lips parted as he sensed the parts of her Seal coming together.

Lan closed her eyes and opened her senses to the flow of qì around them. She traced the strokes liberally: a thick arc of earth structured by ramparts of wood, the fortifying weave of stone, and since they were high on a mountain, the mighty gusting of wind. Picking out the strands of qì, she thought, was akin to finding notes from the strings of a zither or a lute, creating the Seal equivalent to composing song.

She closed the circle, and her Defensive Seal sprung from the ground: a solid shield made of the elements around them, curving between her and Dé'zǐ.

"Not bad," the grandmaster said, yet she had the impression she had somehow failed a test. "Tell me why this is the most important thing you have learned."

Lan cut through her Seal, and her protective wall collapsed in a cloud of dust and rock. "Because I wished to use my power to protect those I loved," she said quietly.

The grandmaster was silent for a while, studying her face. She fidgeted under his scrutiny. "You bring up exactly what I wished to discuss today," he said at last. "*Power.* Is that not the reason most who are able would pursue the arts of practitioning?"

She thought of the songgirls, the Teahouse, the silent vow she had made, and nodded.

"Everything you learn here, Lan, will be focused on training your power. Making you stronger, better, and more invincible. Archery, Swords, Fists, the Light Arts, Seals, and all forms of knowledge. Yet none of it matters if you do not know *to what end* you are using that power."

"I do know. I would use it so that no one need ever be hurt again when they are vulnerable."

"And what would you give in exchange for this power?"

The answer came to her from the morning her world had ended, from watching her mother's life bleed out before her eyes. "Everything," Lan whispered.

"And that," Dé'zǐ said, "is the first desire that puts one in the danger of falling Wayward."

The words hit like a gut punch. Lan had come to understand Wayward as bad, as somehow associated with yīn and demonic practitioners and the evils in the world. Not something as innocent as seeking power for protection. She spluttered, "I don't—I wouldn't—"

"Wayward," the grandmaster said, "has less to do with the type of qì one wields . . . and everything to do with how and why one wields it."

Lan hesitated, Master Nán's furious drillings of the *Classic of Society* warring with her desire to express herself. "But, Grandmaster," she said, "I was under the impression that Wayward had to do with, well, demonic qì."

The grandmaster hummed thoughtfully. Then, instead of

answering her, he said, "Tell me what you have learned of the Way."

She was immensely grateful for the hours Zen had spent by her side, copying the classics. "I continue to study the classics, Grandmaster," she said quickly, afraid she had offended him. "If you wish, I can recite—"

Dé'zǐ waved a hand. "My ancestors would turn over in their graves, but I have always had little patience for the Hin methods of rote education and strict customs. All surface-level nonsense stipulated by some boring old farts hundreds of cycles ago and still carried out by boring young farts at our school to this day."

"*Grandmaster,*" she exclaimed, unable to hold back a startled laugh.

Dé'zǐ gave her a conspiratorial grin, then tapped at his chest. "I want to know what you think of the Way in here."

Lan thought through all the principles she had studied in the past few days. "I think the Way speaks of balance," she said carefully, "and control. There is always a give and take—an equivalent exchange. Especially as practitioners, the more power we wield, the more restraint we must have."

The grandmaster looked pleased. "Precisely," he said, and she felt a warm glow in her stomach. "The Way is naught more than a path of balance. It is written into everything we study, into the blood and bones of this very world." He tipped his cup, and liquid fell in a thin stream, darkening the surface of the rock.

With the tea, Dé'zǐ drew a circle, using the liquid to color half of it but for a small dot. The other side remained untouched but for a small drop diagonally across from the first pale dot.

Lan knew the symbol; it was a common motif used in decor.

"Yīn," the grandmaster said, pointing to the wet, darkened half. "And yáng." A gesture to the dry, lighter side. "The fundamental principle that governs not only qì but our world. Our Way."

Lan asked a question that had been at the front of her mind all these days. "Isn't yīn bad? I heard . . . well, I heard it was the only type of energy that demons feed on."

"Ah," Dé'zǐ said with a crooked smile. "You've been listening to Zen and the fishwives. You are correct, that all types of supernatural qì are classified within and composed solely of yīn, because such creatures belong in death, not life. Of course, that includes demonic qì. But does that make yīn bad?" A tip of his head, a slight lift to his brows. "Yīn is as bad as shadows are bad. Or darkness, or cold, or death. Such concepts are normally dreaded or given negative connotations compared to light and warmth and life . . . and yet, can you think of a world without them?"

Lan could not.

"The fundamental concept of the Way is balance. See the two dots in the midst of each half. One cannot be without the other. The world is constantly shifting, yīn changing to yáng, yáng changing to yīn, in a perpetual cycle of *balance*. Life results in death, and death gives way to life; day turns to night, and night will always yield to day. Sun and moon, summer and winter—both are eternally present in this world.

"Wayward, then, points to the opposite: when something falls out of balance, and out of control. Take the creation of a demon, for example: when a cesspool of yīn remains unbalanced for too long. Similarly, the danger for demonic practitioners lies not in the nature of their art but in their loss of control."

"Forgiveness, Grandmaster," she said, "but I do not understand why the pursuit of power is Wayward."

"Ah. There is a balance to power, too. Too much, and one is corrupted. Too little, and one is vanquished. To be willing to give everything in exchange for power . . . well, that is dangerous. I assume you are familiar with the tragic tale of the last high general of the Mansorian clan—commonly known now as the Nightslayer. A man with good intentions, drowning in power. In the end, he no longer controlled the Demon God he summoned; it was the Demon God who controlled him."

Lan nodded solemnly. The grandmaster had a faraway look on his face, the light of the setting sun haloing his profile in red and gold.

"So, for one to adhere to the Way, one would need only steer clear of demons." Lan grinned. "Doesn't sound too hard."

"Oh, you would be surprised," the grandmaster replied, blinking as though he had just woken from a long dream. He squinted at the sunset. "Now I profess to you my gratitude for taking time out of your day to entertain me, but I would not wish to deny Master Nán the opportunity to critique your handwriting any longer. We will meet again, Lan."

That evening, Lan made her way to the Chamber of a Hundred Healings as she had for the past week. The only reprieve she'd found from her schedule was when she met with Shàn'jūn by the carp pond near the chamber. The Medicine disciple would listen with a faint smile as she recounted the day's happenings, sometimes helping him with the herbs he tended to. After, with That Which Cuts Stars strapped to her waist, she would set off to meet Zen at their training grounds.

Tonight, however, she found the Chamber of a Hundred Healings deserted but for another young Medicine disciple watching over the vats of stewing broths. Shàn'jūn, apparently, had left for the bookhouse.

The night was clear, the moon brightening the stone paths to a polished silver as Lan set out to find him. She climbed the steps, following the young disciple's instructions, winding through Skies' End to a section near the back of the mountain, a little way up from the other school halls. At last, turning into a copse of conifers, she found a gently sloping hill with orchids in full bloom, fluttering in the evening breeze.

In their midst rose one of the most elegant buildings Lan had seen, mist coiling gently around it so that it almost appeared to be drifting among clouds. Open terraces gazed out at plunging waterfalls on either side, while full moon–shaped windows were half covered by bamboo curtains. The building rose two stories high, gray-tiled roofs curving to the skies. Unlike the other halls, its eaves were sleek and bare, unembellished by the usual carvings of flora and fauna and gods.

SCHOOL OF THE WHITE PINES BOOKHOUSE, a wooden sign above the slatted cherrywood doors announced. The doors were closed; the bell hung from the eaves, silent after the day's classes were done.

Lan entered through the sliding doors.

While the Teahouse had boasted opulence, this hall was imbued with modest refinement. The walls were a soft eggshell color, outlined by bold rosewood pillars and eaves. Separated by openwork partitions were shelves packed with tomes, their white silk bindings shimmering. Windows were interspersed throughout the hall, moonlight spilling through the sheer gauze attached to delicate fretwork and drenching the entire hall in a pearly sheen.

Lan wondered if the young Medicine disciple had made a mistake in sending her here. The bookhouse was deserted, all disciples having returned to their living quarters to rest so they could wake with the sun. Her straw sandals were quiet as she padded down the rosewood aisles. An air of reverence permeated the place, suffused with the musty scents of parchment and ink. The rooms to either side of the hallway were partitioned by spirit screen doors made of the same gauzy material and rosewood fretwork to allow in light and circulation yet minimize damage to the books.

The swaying gauze and the pale gray light filled the place with phantom shapes, and Lan felt almost as though she walked among ghosts. She had the strangest feeling that if she turned a corner, she would find a familiar study with a circular window framing a courtyard of snow, woodlute music flowing through the air.

One that now existed only in her memory.

Voices drifted to her through a set of sliding doors. Beyond, an open veranda overlooked a line of willow trees that dipped into a softly flowing river. A figure sat on the pinewood terrace; from the gap in the half-closed door, Lan thought she recognized Shàn'jūn's slim build. She opened her mouth to call out, but that was when she caught Shàn'jūn's words.

". . . any trace of it?"

Someone was with him, and for some reason, the way her friend spoke made the conversation seem private. Intimate.

Lan bit her lip, caught between wanting to leave Shàn'jūn to his privacy and wishing to linger so she could tease him about it tomorrow. Courtship at the School of White Pines was strictly frowned upon for being distracting from learning. Shàn'jūn had struck her as an obedient goody-two-shoes; this new discovery was one that pleased Lan to no end.

The presumed lover spoke, voice deep and masculine. "No. No." The speaker spoke slowly, as though it took time for him to gather his thoughts and formulate them into words. "The Nightslayer. He is dead. His soul long gone. His Demon God— the Black Tortoise—vanished."

Lan froze, the words echoing in her head: Nightslayer. Black Tortoise.

"I have often wondered why the grandmaster is adamant about sending you on these missions. It takes you away from here for too long." There was a gentle wistfulness to Shàn'jūn's voice. "He thinks you may remember something from your days at the Imperial Court twelve cycles ago."

The words fisted around Lan's chest. An image found her: Māma, dressed in a court hàn'fú, all gold-stitched silks and samites instead of the long-flowing páo she normally wore.

Lan leaned forward, her heart pounding.

"He believes," the other man scoffed. "I do not remember. I was but a child when it fell. I have been at Skies' End since."

"But you must know more than any of us commoners." There was a light, teasing edge to Shàn'jūn's tone. "Come, Tài'gē, if you tell me you learned nothing growing up in the Imperial Court, then I am afraid—"

"I learned. I *learned*." His companion bit down on those words. "We who were descended of the clans learned discipline at the Imperial Court. Utter obedience to the emperor. To use our arts of practitioning solely in service to the emperor. To forget the atrocities they committed against our ancestors and elders . . . and to know the history of the clans as *they* would have it written."

Out on the veranda, a shadow shifted as Shàn'jūn leaned his head against the other boy's shoulder. "And did you catch any hints as to who in the imperial family might have made the bargain with the Crimson Phoenix while you were at court?"

"The prince. I think."

Lan's jaw dropped. The Crimson Phoenix was one of the Four Demon Gods—said to have been lost for at least a hundred cycles. But Shàn'jūn and the other boy spoke of it as though it still existed. As though they might *know* where it was.

A pause, the rustling of silk. Shàn'jūn's voice was somber when he spoke again. "I do not believe that the grandmaster thinks the clans will rise again. Is he, then, trying to understand more of the history? Is there something even you do not know?"

"So much. *So much.*" The other boy spoke vehemently. "The history of this kingdom has been rewritten. The Imperial Court determined the narrative. The Elantians destroyed it. The grandmaster wishes me to recover it. By interrogating one ghost at a time."

"Do you think he searches for something? I have long wondered about the grandmaster's goals and his deviation from the standard Hin beliefs. He sheltered me, a harelipped orphan. He took you and countless other clan members in. And he raised Zen—"

Shàn'jūn stopped speaking abruptly. Lan caught a sudden movement, and then the door slid open.

Too late, she scrambled back.

Outlined in the backlight of the moon was one of the most attractive men Lan had ever seen. If Zen held an imperial and commanding beauty, this man bore a feral type of charm: all sharp, rectangular angles and hard planes of muscles. His hair was cut short, like Zen's, but with untamed, windswept curls. Most arresting, however, were his eyes: gray irises ringed with pale gold, shadowed beneath strong black brows.

That face was currently arranged in a scowl that somehow seemed to befit it better than any smile.

"You," the young man said. "I have not seen you here before. How much. How much have you heard?"

"Heard? I just got here," Lan said quickly, but the boy took a threatening step toward her.

"You lie," he growled, and then his gaze raked over her, searching. It landed on her left arm. "I heard. I heard the sound of your soul."

Either this was some new practitioning term she had yet to learn, or he was barking mad. "Well, consider your ears blessed," Lan said.

"Lan'mèi." Shàn'jūn stepped through the open door.

The air of jaunty insolence Lan had put up vanished. "There you are, Shàn'jūn," she said lightly. "I went to find you at the Chamber of a Hundred Healings, and the disciple told me you were here." She dropped her gaze, opening herself to his rebuke or even anger at her eavesdropping.

Shàn'jūn's eyes curved in a smile. "And here I am. Ah, but where are my manners?" He stepped back, rubbing his head. "Tài'gē, this is Lan'mèi, a new disciple." The other boy's eyes narrowed again at Shàn'jūn's use of -mèi after Lan's name: a word that meant "little sister," and a shorthand for endearment—much as Shàn'jūn referred to the boy as gē: "older brother." "And Lan'mèi, this is Chó Tài—"

"That's 'Tai' to you," the boy said, the Elantian shorthand a clear insult to Lan.

"—disciple of Texts," Shàn'jūn persisted. "We were just discussing Tài'gē's mission, from which he has returned. Pray tell, what did you hear?"

She should ask about the Demon Gods—who in their right mind wouldn't?—but as Lan glanced at the other boy, she found a different question taking hold of her tongue. "You were a part of the Imperial Court?"

Tai looked furious, but Shàn'jūn closed the gap between him and Lan. "Lan'mèi is my good friend," the Medicine disciple said. "We can trust her to keep secrets."

The other boy looked at Lan as if she were the last person he would trust with his secrets.

"When did you work at the court?" Lan probed again.

"In the None of Your Business Dynasty," Tai growled.

Perhaps she should have tried harder to charm him. Cover blown, Lan rolled her eyes at Tai, but he was frowning at her, gaze fixed on her left arm. "You," he said suddenly, in a very different tone. "You bear the will of the dead."

The way he spoke those words sent a chill through Lan. She collected herself and crossed her arms. "What are you talking about?"

"There," the boy replied. He stretched out a large hand and pointed to her left wrist. "Something is there. I feel a tethered will."

"Tài'gē is a Spirit Summoner, Lan'mèi," Shàn'jūn said. "He senses spiritual qì—the qì of the dead, a type of yīn energy."

"What in the Ten Hells is that?" Lan asked, her eyes never straying from the other boy's.

"My clan's specialty," Tai explained with a glare, "is finding and summoning ghosts."

"We ordinary practitioners can sometimes sense qì of the spirits, seeing as they are all subsets of yīn energies," Shàn'jūn said patiently, and Lan thought suddenly of the yāo, the ghostly apparition she had seen in the bamboo forest. "But Tài'gē's clan has an affinity with the imprints ghosts and spirits of the dead have left in this world. Think of it as a branch of practitioning—an art—taught in this school . . . only his runs in his blood."

"And you can sense a ghost . . . on my arm?" Lan asked Tai.

"Not ghost. *Imprint,*" the Spirit Summoner emphasized. "Souls unconsciously leave imprints in many different forms: A memory. A thought. An emotion. A footprint of sorts indicating they have walked or existed somewhere in this world. It is how we Spirit Summoners track down the paths of ghosts.

Imprints are unintentional—a tangle of thoughts or a stream of consciousness left during moments of heightened emotion. Some are faint. Some are easy to catch. Some are louder. And yours . . ." He paused. "Yours screams."

Lan realized her nails were digging into her wrist. She fought against a shiver as a cold wind stirred the gauze curtains, pale moonlight making the shadows dance. "What is it saying?" she whispered.

Tai held out a hand. "I would need to listen."

Her heartbeat roared in her ears. Slowly, she held out her left wrist.

From a gray silk pouch at his waist—similar to the one Zen had, only with a different sigil—Tai drew out three sticks of incense. With a wave of his long fingers, he lit the tips. They sparked a jarring red in the silvery light of the moon, mountain, and water around them.

With his other hand, he drew a white bell from his sleeve. Carefully, he held it over her arm, then shook it.

The bell rang once—a pure, high note that seemed to ripple all around them . . . and *within* them, too. Its jingle echoed in a space that did not seem to exist, an in-between. It grew cold, the light and veranda and water fading as though she were slowly disappearing from this world.

The Seal on Lan's wrist was the only thing that brightened. Over it, a pale handprint formed. Lan recalled staring at those bloodied fingers clasped over her wrist as her mother lay dying.

In the darkness of the space in-between, a familiar voice rang out: *"Gods watch over my daughter, if there is any mercy left in this world."*

It was Māma—Māma's voice. Every nerve in Lan's body stretched taut. Her throat tightened, and an ache built in her chest. Her vision blurred.

"I wish I had the time to tell her everything," Sòng Méi's voice continued weakly. She seemed lost in her own thoughts, speaking to no one but herself. And she was, Lan realized. These were words her mother had wanted to speak but couldn't, accidentally captured in the form of an imprint, a stream of consciousness. *"Of the underground rebellion her father and I led, of the true history of this kingdom. May she find it in her to forgive me someday, that I must hand her the keys to shaping the destiny of our people for her to bear alone."*

Her words grew faint, beginning to slur. The handprint over Lan's wrist started to fade.

Lan knew what was coming—knew when this imprint had been formed.

In her mother's final moments.

"No, Māma," Lan choked. "No, wait—"

"Gods guide her to hear the song of the ocarina," her mother murmured, seeming to grow lost in her own thoughts, *"and follow its power to protect those who need it. To save our kingdom."* The voice swept away like wind, the handprint dissipated, the shadows and darkness unraveled, and then Lan was alone again, kneeling on the smooth pinewood of the open terrace, her cheeks warm and her body shaking. She was aware of a gentle voice in her ear, a steady arm over her shoulders, as Shàn'jūn consoled her.

"That . . ." Even Tai looked shaken. "That was an unintentional stream of thoughts. Your mother . . . she must have entrusted you with something important, for this imprint of her consciousness to have remained with you."

"And we'll soon find out what that is," came a sharp, familiar voice.

Lan looked up. Through the blur of her tears, she saw a tall figure striding toward them. A curved dāo glinted at her side.

"Thought I'd have to try harder to find out," Yeshin Noro Dilaya said, her vivid red lips curling. She drew her sword and pointed it at Lan's neck. "Shall I take your life now to save you the trouble, or would you prefer to explain yourself before the Council of Masters?"

The grief in the pit of Lan's stomach hardened.

"Bitch," she whispered. "How much did you hear?"

Dilaya smirked. "Enough. I know you seek some instrument of power, something your mother left you. I always knew there was something off about you."

Anger made Lan's arms tremble—anger that Dilaya had heard her dead mother and that she had the cruelty to use that against Lan. The girl seemed to have heard only the end of the imprint's stream of thoughts—but that was something Lan's mother had left *her* and her alone. Lan did not want Dilaya to have heard *any* part of it.

A strange energy burned inside Lan. All of Master Gyasho's lessons over the past few days had given her a stronger awareness of qì, including the qì she held inside her at her core. And in this moment, she had never wanted to hurt anyone more.

Satisfaction and curiosity lit up Dilaya's eyes, and Lan realized that the girl *wanted* her to summon her qì—unbalanced qì, qì that the masters would question. Qì that Zen had warned her against using.

The turbulence of her emotions calmed. The churning qì within her fell still.

Lan focused on Yeshin Noro Dilaya with cutting clarity. "I have no idea what you're talking about," she said, taking care to enunciate each word, "you horse-faced bitch."

Dilaya didn't flinch at the insult. "Oh? Then explain to me what that voice was."

"I'm sure Tai can answer your question," Lan said with

forced brightness. "I have no idea what he did, but he *has* just returned from a mission for the grandmaster." She touched a finger to her lip, pretending to come to a realization. "Unless you'd rather ask the grandmaster directly what business he has with Tai?"

Dilaya's lips thinned. "You conniving little fox spirit," she said, her grip tightening on her dāo. "I'll—"

"You'll apologize," came a cold voice, "for breaking Code of Conduct rules seven and twelve within the matter of a half minute: 'Thou shalt not engage in violence' and 'Thou shalt treat thy practitioner brothers and sisters with respect.' "

From the darkness of the bookhouse hallway, Zen stepped out. He was empty-handed, Nightfire sheathed at his waist, yet as he and Dilaya beheld each other, it was as though he held the sword. They were almost the same height, but where Yeshin Noro Dilaya's fury was feral and unfettered as a wild-fire, Zen's was a blade forged in the blue heart of flame.

"Well?" Zen pressed, and the tone of his voice might have cut. "Will you ask forgiveness of Lan, or will you wait for me to recite the other rules you have breached tonight, Yeshin Noro Dilaya? Perhaps I should take this to the grandmaster. He would be intrigued to understand why you question his decisions—"

"Don't pretend you hold the Code of Conduct in the high-est esteem, Wayward practitioner," Dilaya spat.

The atmosphere instantly shifted. Shàn'jūn, who had been watching in silence, flinched; by his side, Tai's jaw dropped.

Zen blanched. The rage in his eyes shifted into something Lan couldn't read. Something like guilt.

Dilaya's mouth curled in triumph. "That's right, *Zen*. Think carefully before you choose to lecture me on my trans-gressions against the Way." She took a step back and sheathed her sword, her loose sleeve fluttering with the motion. "One day, the grandmaster will no longer be here to protect you. And then it'll be too late for him to regret what he should have done at the very start: left you in that Elantian laboratory to die."

Without another look back, she shoved past them and disappeared down the halls of the bookhouse.

17

Dove trees flower at the spring and summer
solstices. Also known as ghost trees for the
white color of their flowers, each of which is
said to represent a lingering soul.

—"The Ghost Trees,"
Hin Village Folktales: A Collection

"Lan." She flinched at Zen's tone. He had not moved. "Let's go."

His face had been wiped clean as a slate: beautiful yet terrible to behold, like a night without stars. That expression—it reminded her of the time his eyes had turned completely black at the walls of Haak'gong. As Zen turned to leave, he paused and looked directly at the Medicine disciple.

Shàn'jūn dropped his gaze. Behind him, Tai tensed. His eyes trailed Zen as the latter strode past him and back down the halls of the bookhouse.

Without another word, Lan followed.

The night had become smothered in clouds, the orchids outside darkened and moving in a fury as a wind picked up. Zen walked briskly, not waiting for Lan.

She hurried to catch up to him. Forcing cheer into her tone, she said, "Dilaya seems popular around here. Hey—I have an idea: maybe we should name those wooden dummies after her for our training tonight—"

"We are not training," Zen said abruptly. "We are going to Guarded Mountain."

Her steps faltered. She realized they had taken a different path than the one that led to their training site. Zen was making his way in the direction of the school halls and the entrance to Skies' End.

She hurried to catch up. "Does this mean I've graduated? Am I good enough to fight with you now?"

"No. We are going tonight because Master Nóng returns on the morrow, and he will want to treat your arm. I promised to take you before that, and I intend to keep my promise." A pause. "And now that Yeshin Noro Dilaya has ideas about whatever it is your mother left you, matters may become complicated. We must take our chances before she confides in her mother and possibly in shī'fù."

Shī'fù. Master. Zen was the only one to call the grandmaster that. Lan thought of Dilaya's words. "Zen," she said. "If taking me to Guarded Mountain poses any risk to your status or reputation here, then—"

Zen stopped and turned to her so abruptly that she bumped into him. He caught her by the shoulder and held her as he spoke. "Nothing I do will affect my reputation at this school anymore, nor change any of the masters' minds about me." His eyes burned. "If you have any questions for me from whatever rumors you may have heard in the past few days, then by all means, ask away."

Something caught in her throat as she searched his face. She thought of the scars covering his hands, the ones lacing his arms, hidden to the world. *One day, the grandmaster will no longer be here to protect you. And then it'll be too late for him to regret what he should have done at the very start: left you in that Elantian laboratory to die.*

Lan did not break his gaze as she shook her head. "No

questions," she said softly. "Thank you for taking me to Guarded Mountain. Thank you for finding me and saving me back in Haak'gong. And thank you for training me. Thank you, Zen."

The fire in his eyes cooled.

Zen stepped back. "Follow closely" was all he said to her.

She had been unconscious when he'd brought her up the mountain, yet now Lan could sense how truly alive it was, imbued, it seemed, with a sense of vitality that transcended this world. Several times, she thought she sensed a ripple in the energies, saw a shadow at the corners of her vision, felt a breath down the back of her neck. Zen had warned her of the nine-hundred-ninety-nine step climb down the mountain ("There are no shortcuts to the Way"), and she'd professed her dread. Now she kept silent, following the practitioner and counting the steps.

After what felt like hours, the stone stairs ended, giving way to a patch of mossy grass and pine forest.

"This is the end of the Boundary Seal." Zen's voice was a low thrum, his figure a half shadow cast by the moon's shifting light. "It is marked by this tree, called the Most Hospitable Pine. You will feel a moment of resistance upon crossing the Seal."

He stepped through, his silhouette rippling and then settling as though he'd walked through a wall of water.

Lan couldn't help throwing a glance back. In the deep night, the mountain was a swath of shadows, smelling of wet soil and pines and filled with the sleepy chirp of critters in the brush.

A part of her wanted to stay: extract the metalwork from her arm, destroy the tracking spell, and stay at Skies' End, where, in the past moon, she had begun to find a semblance of a home.

But she had spent enough of her life hiding. Twelve long cycles, most of it spent looking away from the truth of her kingdom, casting her gaze down and bowing before the Elantians even as her friends and loved ones and other people around her continued to die.

It was time to stop running. It was time to face the truth of whatever her mother had entrusted to her.

Heart in her throat, Lan followed.

Passing the Boundary Seal felt like walking through a thickened patch of air. Qì swirled in shades of white, blanketing her world for a breath. In the distance before her, in the whorl of wind, the shape of a woman stood in the fall of snow, no more than a ghost. In the silence, the haunting echoes of a song. There were figures moving all around Lan—figures that vanished when she tried to look at them directly. People were talking, just out of earshot, voices familiar and unfamiliar, twining around a thread of music . . . if she could just walk deeper into the snow . . . she might be able to reach them . . .

Something latched onto her wrist, and she found herself jerked forward. All at once, the snow, the voices, the song, vanished.

She stepped out on the other side of the barrier. Zen's hand was steady over her bare wrist, the touch of his skin both grounding her and unsettling her. "I think . . ." Lan swallowed. "I think I saw my mother."

Zen's mouth tightened; he did not let go. She did not want him to. "The Boundary Seal reaches into the very depths of your heart to understand your intentions toward this school," he explained. "It is held together by the spirits of masters and grandmasters who served the school in life and now protect it in their eternal deaths. So long as you bear no ill intentions toward the school, the Seal will allow you to enter."

Lan glanced back. The stone steps had vanished, replaced by an outcropping of rock covered by mossy ferns. There was no trace of the school.

"Now come," Zen continued. "We are short on time."

The Gate Seal he was to perform would lead to a location he had passed by before, one that was close to where Guarded Mountain sat. At about a day's travel from Skies' End, the distance, he'd assured her, would not require excess qì.

It felt almost natural to wrap her arms around his waist and gently press her cheek to his chest. She felt his fingers fall gently against her back. Then he raised his other hand. The energies around them surged as they rose to his calling.

"Zen," she said, tipping her head up to look at him. "What do you see when you pass through the Boundary Seal?"

The Gate Seal glowed against the night, black flames rimmed silver. Zen's hand tightened around her waist as he drew the finishing stroke.

"Pork buns," he replied, and they tipped forward. The scenery around them blurred, trees lifting and soil shifting and sky churning in the space of a drawn breath.

When it all settled again and the flare of energies died, they stood on a dirt path in the midst of an evergreen forest.

Zen shot Lan a look. "Here we are," he said, taking in their surroundings. "I passed by here once, cycles ago. Do you know where to go, or what you're looking for here?"

Slowly, Lan shook her head. She had no idea where to even begin.

Zen tipped his head and began to walk. "I have never gone up to Guarded Mountain myself, but I do know that a village sits at its base. That might be a good place to start; it should be this way."

The trees grew sparse, and a dirt path appeared beneath their feet. Through the canopy, they could make out the jagged silhouettes of mountains in a shade darker than night.

The pái'fāng appeared suddenly in the midst of the forest, the stone pillars of the gateway bone white in the moonlight. They might once have borne characters, but the surfaces had been worn smooth by the relentless beat of weather, their messages stolen by the erosion of time. Only a sign at the very top of the path was still legible: *Village of the Fallen Clouds.*

A cold wind rose, scattering husks of leaves as they stepped through the pái'fāng and into a street of clay-walled houses with ridged roofs, eaves curving downward so that rainwater flowed off them during the wet season. The farther they walked, the more evident it became that the village had been abandoned. Windows gaped, some with slashed screens; a few doors stood open, the wreckage within gleaming like exposed ribs.

Lan shivered. Something festered here—something rotten that permeated the air and energies.

Zen turned to her, evidently sensing her unease. "The yīn energy is strong here."

She wrapped her arms around herself. "What does that indicate? More spirits?"

"Not necessarily. Do you remember we went over the makeup of qì?" Zen brought his two hands together, one curving over the other. "All around us, the natural elements are constantly in motion, being created and consumed in an endless cycle. Water grows wood, wood sustains fire, fire births earth, and so on. It is the same on the spectrum of yīn and yáng: both are perpetually shifting, one into the other.

"It is at a location where either of the energies linger in excess that problems arise. Here there has been much death— death that was unnatural, that was wrought with pain, and fear, and agony. This has resulted in an accumulation of yīn. Do you feel it?"

The clouds shifted overhead, shedding a cold white light upon the scene. To the side, something glinted.

"I do. I think I know why," she said, and pointed.

The cuff of silver lay half buried in dirt. Zen dusted it off, revealing an engraving of a crown with wings. A breeze stirred locks of his hair, twining through the fabric of his páo, as he studied it.

"Elantians," he said quietly.

But Lan's attention was drawn by something else. Something so faint, she'd first thought it to be wind.

It was music.

Gods guide her to hear the song of the ocarina, her mother's imprint had prayed.

She turned sharply, cold spreading through her veins. The sign she'd been searching for. "Someone is playing a song," she said. The melody was not one she recalled, yet she felt as though she had heard it before, like a half-forgotten dream. "Do you hear that?"

Zen stood, frowning, the silver band dangling from one hand. "No," he said.

"Listen!" She grasped the fabric of his sleeve, leaning her head in the direction of the song. "That's an ocarina. Have you heard one before? It sounds like . . . it sounds like a flute. Not quite." She closed her eyes and began to tap out the rhythm on Zen's arm.

She felt his fingers on hers and opened her eyes to meet his. He watched her with a slight crease in his brows. "I do not think I can hear it," he said slowly.

She shivered. A song only she could hear . . . The words of the vision she'd had back in the Jade Forest came to her. *Hidden away behind a Boundary Seal at Guarded Mountain is something that you, and only you, can find.*

"I know where to go," she said.

She started walking, following the music through the deserted streets, houses once full of light and laughter now silent and abandoned to either side of her. An entire village wiped from existence, like so many others across the Last Kingdom. Zen kept close to her, his hand on Nightfire's hilt.

The disembodied song grew louder, and Lan had the feeling she was somehow finding her way home. The notes struck a responding chord in her heart.

"Look."

She started as Zen's voice broke through the trancelike lure of the music. Ahead of them stood a row of silhouettes: pale and tall, arms spread as they swayed in the wind.

Her heart leapt into her throat.

"Those are dove trees, Lan," Zen said, and she realized she'd grasped a fistful of his sleeve in her sudden fright. As they approached, the illusion of tall white ghosts yielded to the shape of trees in bloom, pale limbs and hair morphing into branches. Bell-shaped white flowers hung from the branches.

Zen paused in front of one of the trees and touched a finger to a flower petal. "Colloquially, they're also called 'ghost trees,'" he murmured. "They bloom in the summer season. To see one in flower this late in the cycle is . . . unusual."

Beyond the dove trees was a stone wall, carmine paint faded, scratched, and peeling in some places. The music drifted over it, summoning her.

"In there," Lan said.

The gate to the courtyard presented itself in a gap between the line of dove trees standing like sentries outside the walls. This had once been a prestigious house with all the details of fortune and fēng'shuǐ carefully considered and rendered in its architectural design. Heavy vermilion doors stood beneath an arch decorated with stone carvings of the Four Demon Gods—tiger, dragon, phoenix, and tortoise—encircling a placard that read: *Yòu Quán Pài*.

Zen drew a sharp breath. "The School of Guarded Fists," he whispered. "This is where it was all along?"

She glanced at Zen. He looked pale in the moonlight, a figure cut neatly in monochrome, those black-fire eyes wide with reverence.

Lan knew that the School of the White Pines was the only of the Hundred Schools to have survived the Conquest. Even so, seeing with her own eyes what had once been a place of prestige and power fallen to such ruin hit differently.

Lan looked at the faded courtyard house. She had the impression of time flowing backward, the story of fallen grandeur reversing itself as the slashes on the doors stitched together again, the scars on the walls smoothed out, and the rubble littering the gates disappeared.

As she stepped forward, the twelve cycles she had put between her and her mother's words seemed to vanish. She might have been six cycles old again, filled with the courage to hope for a future. A destiny.

She reached for the door knockers, a pair of bronze lion heads. The gates didn't budge. "Locked," she said.

Zen lifted a hand. "Stand back." He traced a Seal in the air, fingers moving neatly and quickly; Lan caught the characters for wood, split down the center with metal. The energies around them shifted. There was the sound of something snapping inside the walls, and then, as though pulled back by ghostly attendants, the great red doors swung open.

And the music stopped.

18

In death, both body and soul rejoin the natural
course of qì in this world and the next. It is a
matter of unspeakable sorrow for a soul to remain
trapped in this world as an echo, imprisoned by
an unfinished will yet powerless to complete it.

—Lím Sù'jí, Imperial Spirit Summoner,
Classic of Death

The courtyard was a cesspool of spiritual energies. Zen sensed them, lingering in the shadows and festering in hidden corners, as soon as he stepped over the doorsill. This was the reason yīn had garnered fear amongst the common folk— and for very valid reasons. The makeup of demonic and other spiritual energies was strictly and only yīn, resulting in yīn energy's synonymity with the dark and occult side of magic over time.

There came the faintest stir of qì from somewhere before them—subtle as the brush of a finger against a string, but Zen felt it. He narrowed his eyes, willing his gaze to penetrate the lines of weeping willows bending and moaning in the evening draft.

The courtyard was empty, but there was something here.

"In there," Lan said. She pointed at the main house across the yard.

Overhead, the moon and stars were covered by clouds. He

sensed Lan suppressing a shiver behind him. Zen had the urge to reach for her.

Instead, he raised his hand and said, very quietly, "Stay behind me."

He began to walk in the direction of the main house.

A cold wind sent autumn leaves scuttling across the great yard, their dried bones rattling as they scraped against tile. Strangely enough, the place appeared pristine, as though time and conquest had left it unsullied. Zen shifted his head. He had the nagging feeling that there was something he was missing, just out of sight. Something was out of place, something odd . . .

He found it not seconds later: a single bamboo chair set out before the doors to the main house, beneath a line of dove trees. It was empty, yet the shadows pooling there seemed blacker than the rest, as though something unseen sat in it. Watching them.

It was so dark that he almost—*almost*—missed the fú.

Zen flung out an arm. "Stop," he said, but too late. Lan had been walking close to him; she stumbled, catching herself— but not before one of her toes stubbed over the faded line of blood in which the Seal had been written.

Zen grasped her shoulder and flung her back, but the damage was done. Where her foot had come into contact with the fú, a crimson glow began to wind over the strokes on the ground, catching like fire.

The air in the courtyard instantly shifted. Frost cracked over windowsills, and ice crept up their boots. A sudden gale rose, howling and plunging toward them like a pack of invisible wolves. Zen heard Lan's scream; he reached for her and drew her behind him. His other hand plunged into his black silk pouch and whipped out his own fú. The written Seal activated with a spark of his qì, paper slip shredding in a flare of dark flames. They sliced through the incoming wind, which parted with an inhuman scream before dying down.

When the flames cleared, the chair across the courtyard was no longer empty.

A silhouette was slowly forming over it: shadows gathering from the crannies and corners of the yard and seeping upward to delineate a head, a torso, arms, and legs. Within moments, a humanlike shape rose from the chair, turning to face them. It was skeletal in appearance, desiccated bluish skin draping over bones. Eye sockets sagged into darkness, in which yellowed eyeballs stared ahead without movement or expression. Strands of loose black hair hung over a gaunt face, and the long sleeves and skirts of its hàn'fú billowed about it.

This time, there was no uncertainty.

Mó. Demon. The most terrifying and rare classification of supernatural creatures. Practitioners in the days of old had hunted them down, yet Zen's training had taken place post-Conquest, when priorities for any practitioners surviving had rapidly shifted. Even more . . . Zen eyed the fú that had trapped them, the school of practitioning they stood in, and felt his gut tighten.

Mó born of common folk were already exceptionally difficult to deal with, yet this . . . this might be a mó born of a practitioner's soul. One that had held greater command over qì, that had spent a lifetime cultivating its power.

This was the second time in his life he faced a mó—and the first time he would have to fight one.

Zen drew his sword and held his right hand before him, qì pooling at the tips of his fingers. "Stay back," he commanded Lan over his shoulder.

The mó charged, and Zen sprang to meet it.

To defeat a mó, one first had to understand the principles behind its makeup: an excess of yīn energies, comprising wrath, ruin, and a will that was unfinished in life. Coupled with a powerful being already versed in wielding qì—most often a practitioner—and those energies would rot the core of the being into something dangerous, something demonic.

To destroy a mó was to undo it by meeting its yīn energies with yáng energies: an injection of qì consisting solely of yáng.

Zen drew a Dispelment Seal as he ran, pulling on the qì around him. The yáng energies of the elements woven in harmony—and sharpened to blades in the center to strike and pierce. He had studied this in the art of Seals, as well as the principles of the supernatural creatures; he knew, in theory, the step-by-step to dispelling a mó.

The Seal he'd created blazed at the tips of his fingers; this time, instead of releasing it, Zen pressed it onto his sword. Unlike the yāo he'd dispatched in the forest, mó were sentient, intelligent beings. They knew how to fight back.

Without proper placement, his Seal would be deflected.

His sword glistened, black steel carved with ancient characters that flared to life as the energies of his Seal poured in. Nightfire, one of the few family heirlooms Zen still owned, had been forged by the greatest blacksmith in the north of the Last Kingdom, imbued with the essence of fire and heat.

The demon whirled through the air, slashing with clawed hands that had turned green from rot, dark hair trailing like wisps of rope from a patchy scalp. As it opened a mouth full of blackened teeth, it let out a long, drawn-out wail. Vicious whorls of yīn energy emanated from it, invisible to the eye yet pressing toward Zen with a maelstrom of fear, of anger, of hatred, of despair, of darkness.

Two paces away from the being, Zen sent a jet of qì to his heels. He leapt, propelled higher, farther, and faster by the technique of the Light Arts. His páo fanned out as he arced his back, using momentum to flip over the mó, sword arm outstretched.

Nightfire drew blood: greenish-black, splattering onto the tiled ground. A bitter scent curdled in the air.

Zen landed. Spun.

And found himself facing an unvanquished demon.

Nightfire had left a pale slash across the demon's chest. Yet even as Zen watched, torrents of yīn energies writhed over the wound like shadows, smothering the light of his Dispelment Seal until it extinguished.

The mó slashed a hand down—and Zen felt the searing pain of its yīn energies hit his chest.

He stumbled back and coughed up warm, copper-scented liquid. It dripped down his chin as his qì churned in a maelstrom within him, jumbled from the demon's attack. His thoughts spun; he shook his head, willing it to clear.

He'd drawn the correct Seal. He'd injected it into his sword and cut the mó—so long as his Dispelment Seal came into contact with the demon, a single incision should have done the job.

So what had gone wrong?

A growl rent the air. Zen looked up as the demon crouched to leap again. This time, when Zen raised Nightfire, he was wholly unprepared.

A flash of pale silk, dark hair. A figure small and quick darted between him and the mó.

Lan lifted her arm. Time seemed to slow as she traced her fingers through the air: a stroke that called upon wood, twisting through the characters for metal and earth in a grid structure, then brushes of defense arching overhead. She was drawing the Seal for a protective shield that he'd taught her during their travels barely two weeks ago.

And she was performing it with utterly fluid strokes, as

though she'd been using it for cycles. Pulling on the different elements in the energies like an experienced lute player, weaving them together as though she held a brush in her hands.

Zen watched in utter astonishment as she finished in the blink of an eye, the beginning of the circle meeting the end to enclose the Seal.

It pulsed to life, shimmering a dull silver even in the lightless night. Cracks sounded as the ground, the trees, the metal in the structures around them rose to their defense, weaving together as the Seal called upon them and twined them into a barrier.

The mó screeched and drew to a halt.

Zen tamped down on his shock, mind hurtling forward to understand why his Dispelment Seal had not worked. He flipped through cycles of lessons and theories.

Mó: a soul trapped in a deathless death, fermenting in negative yīn energies of fury and ill will.

Yīn had to be met with yáng: tethers to the physical world around them, which he'd written into his Seal, grounded by the elements . . . also, the *sentiments* of yáng to counter the demon's wrathful hatred. *Will,* Master Gyasho had always said, *is the crux of the Seal. A Seal without the core of will is like a body without soul.*

The will to counter the mó was peace. Joy. Love. All that made this world, this life, worth living.

All that separated the living from the dead.

The mó lashed out with qì of its own. Debris exploded all around as it smashed into the barrier.

Lan cried out, That Which Cuts Stars flashing as she was flung back.

Zen moved before he could even think, slamming qì into the soles of his feet. A breath, and he was by her side. He caught her as she fell, drew her against him even as the splinters of her shield rained down all around them. There was an inexplicable ache in his throat. The look in her eyes as she'd traced the Seal—he'd seen it before, in the Teahouse when her world came crashing down around her; again in the clearing when she'd turned to face the approaching Elantian army, a slip of a girl in a torn dress, armed with nothing but a butterknife.

First time you've seen a massacre?

No.

It was the look of someone who had lost everything yet continued to fight. A look he knew so intimately, as though he'd glimpsed a reflection of his own past.

Manners, propriety, customs, codes be damned—a fire had sparked in Zen's heart, and he gave in as it spread. His arm tightened against her, wrapping over her waist. His breath caught in his chest as she responded, burying her face in the crook of his shoulder, hands coming to rest on his back.

He looked up at the mó, his mind sharpening like the blade of his sword. He understood what he'd left out of the Dispelment Seal. Though Zen didn't think he could ever know peace, joy, or love ever again, he found, in this moment, a fierce sentiment that was close.

It is the duty of those with power to protect those without.

Zen tilted his face, his cheek brushing against Lan's temple, the soft strands of her hair. He felt her heartbeat against his, the rise and fall of her chest as her breaths came quickly.

She trusted him with her life.

The knowledge was like a bolt of lightning, sparking through his veins and setting him aflame.

Zen drew the Seal, and this time, the qì flowed from his fingertips into Nightfire like a great, immutable river. The jiàn gleamed, bifurcated down its central ridge: one half split into darkness, the other shimmering with light.

The mó leapt at them, and Zen raised Nightfire.

He felt the impact as the tip struck the demon's chest. His Dispelment Seal bled across the demon and began to burn.

The effect was instant. Zen had the impression he was watching a faded painting being restored to life. Skin that had shriveled and turned bluish green from rot regained the smoothness and fullness of life, turning a pleasant fawn color; grimy and bloodied robes shifted to fabric smooth as silk; the snarling expression on the demon peeled away until they were looking at a handsome, serene-faced man. He wore pale, scholarly robes with yellow and orange clouds stitched along the hems. His hair was long and black, sleek as a fall of ink.

Zen loosed a breath as he caught sight of the sash on the apparition's waist, conferring the man's status.

Grandmaster. The core of this mó had once been the grandmaster of the School of Guarded Fists.

Zen stepped away from Lan and sheathed his sword. A knot formed in his throat as he knelt, bringing the palms of his hands to the ground before him. "Shī'zǔ," he said. "Grandmaster."

The man—the echo of his soul—inclined his head, and without a word, he began to fade, his pale light dimming until only sparks of it drifted away on a wanton wind, and then there was nothing at all but the silence of a time long gone.

Zen remained where he was, prostrated at the feet of a soul released from the fetters of this world. The sting of tears had frozen many times over in his chest. Beneath that: a chasm of anger.

The Elantians had done this.

A soft touch on his shoulder, a voice of silver bells. "Zen?"

Zen straightened. Lan was watching him, expression cautious.

"Was he . . . was he a demonic practitioner?" she asked at last.

"Yes." His voice was hoarse.

"Shàn'jūn told me that to borrow a demon's power, you have to give something in return," she said quietly. "Usually a part of your physical body. But how did . . . how did that grandmaster *become* the demon?"

It sickened him to speak, but he pushed forward anyway. "Lesser demons will typically take physical body parts as payment. But the more powerful demons will request something more valuable to them. Something that will contribute to their core of energies and grow their power, grounding them to this world." He closed his eyes. "That grandmaster must have bargained his soul to the demon, tethering them both to this place. That is how he and the demon merged into one."

"We have to keep going." Lan's voice was soft. When he opened his eyes again, he found her looking at him, gaze bright as black pebbles. "That mó—he was the grandmaster of this school. And he tethered his soul to this place, warping it into something so—so twisted . . ." She shuddered and looked away. "It must have been to guard something precious. Something he did not wish to fall into Elantian hands." A pause, and then she said, quieter still, "Perhaps it is the same thing that my mother died to protect."

Zen looked to the empty chair. Thought of the Seal written on the ground in blood, of the village fallen to ruin. The silver cuff in his pouch, engraved with the sigil of Elantian magicians.

He had the feeling there was more to it than they knew. The courtyard was thick and layered with currents of qì woven into Seals, some so ancient they had settled into the bones of the houses and the roots of the soil; some newer, pulsing gently.

Zen reached into his silk pouch and drew out three sticks

of incense. With a quick Seal, he lit them, their light and sweet smoke a welcome change from the darkness pressing in.

They walked in the opposite direction of the smoke to the western sidehouse. The door was a creaky old wooden thing with paint peeling off. Locked.

Lan stepped in front of him and pressed a finger to the wood. "There is a Seal here, made mostly of wood," she murmured, and looked at him like a student waiting for her master's approval. "Wood and metal. They're woven together in a complicated pattern. Yīn, yáng—balanced."

He tried not to let his wonder show on his face. Ordinarily, it could take moons of meditation and training for a disciple to begin to discern the elements in the qì around them, and a cycle or two before they were able to produce the most basic of Seals. For someone who had found out about the existence of practitioning just several weeks ago to perceive the traces of Seals—not to mention their makeup, and their *patterns*—was nothing short of miraculous.

"Correct. Now, watch me unlock it." Zen touched his fingers to her palm; she held very still, paying careful attention. He asked, "What combination of elements do you think would make up the Counterseal?"

"According to the cycle of destruction between the elements," she said immediately, "fire melts metal, and metal cuts down wood. So if I trace the exact opposite of this Seal using fire and metal to break the grid of metal and wood, would that work?"

"That would be one way to do it, but there are others. Performing Seals may seem like a science in its basics, but the more you learn, the more it becomes a form of art." He shifted his hand around hers, trying not to focus on the touch of her skin against his. "Channel qì. I will guide your strokes."

It was a marvel to feel the energies she summoned with

precision, each akin to pulling a single thread from a tapestry. Together, they traced the Seal, stroke by stroke, then drew the circle from beginning to end.

The Seal flashed silver briefly before dissolving into the door. Beneath the spirit screen windows, the band of fretwork brightened, the motifs of clouds and flora and fauna glowing with a metallic luster.

With a click, the door swung open.

The interior was dark and damp, a preternatural chill permeating the hallways. As soon as Zen stepped over the wooden threshold, the smoke from his incense sticks rippled suddenly.

He looked down the hallway, thick with shadows. Out of the corners of his eyes, they seemed to move.

Zen led Lan through the hallway, past shuttered doors with fretwork carved in intricate designs. It was strange, he thought, that there were no signs of pillaging or plunder. Lacquered-rosewood cabinets lined the walls, porcelain vases and sandalwood jewelry cases sitting atop them. A prayer altar remained undisturbed, statues of the myriad immortals gleaming in the dim light of the incense sticks as they passed.

Lan's voice came out in a near-whisper. "Why is the yīn so strong here?"

"Because this house is filled with ghosts," he replied. "Without a summoning, we cannot see them—but the incense can. The smoke flees from yīn." He turned to her. The red tips of the incense sticks reflected in her eyes, lined the curves of her lashes. "In a house of the dead guarded by ghosts and demons, how would we find the object most stringently protected?"

"By finding the densest concentration of yīn."

"Precisely."

They had reached the end of the corridor. A faded red door loomed in the darkness, hoary with dust and cobwebs, its copper doorknockers in the shape of swirling clouds.

Zen raised the incense sticks. The smoke plumed away from the door in a straight line.

"In there," Lan said. Her voice held a note of anticipation mixed with dread.

"In there," Zen confirmed.

She studied the door. "Another Lock Seal?"

"No." Zen trailed his hand down the wood. "I think we should just . . ." He slipped a hand over one of the copper doorknockers and released.

The knock cracked like the breaking of stone. It echoed in the air around them.

Then, slowly, of their own volition, the doors creaked open.

The chamber before them was large, the size of a classroom. It appeared utterly empty but for an elegant rosewood table in the center.

A single chair stood by it, facing them.

Zen thought of the sole chair left out in the courtyard earlier. This time, though, there was no Seal, nothing tying the souls of the dead to this room other than the faintest echoes of their living wills.

Zen had experience with finding the imprints of the dead upon this world. It was, after all, what had both saved and destroyed his life thirteen cycles ago.

He turned to Lan. "It seems the time has come for another unplanned lesson in the classifications of supernatural creatures. Watch carefully, for I am about to summon the ghosts of the dead to understand what fate befell the School of Guarded Fists."

19

Kingdom before life, honor into death.

—Grandmaster of the School of
Guarded Fists, Elantian Age, Cycle II

Zen handed Lan the three sticks of incense. Their flared tips were the only source of light, casting the chamber in an eerie red. A shiver ran up Lan's spine. She felt certain that she was on the precipice of parting a veil that had been cast onto her life since the Elantians invaded. Her mother's death, the Winter Magician's search, the half-forgotten song, the echo of her mother's imprint . . . All of it had led here.

She watched Zen steeple his fingers. "I thought Spirit Summoning was only passed down through a clan."

"You speak of the Chó clan," Zen said. "You are correct in that Spirit Summoning is their specialty—this art of practitioning is passed down through their bloodline. But they taught it to disciples from outside their clan at the School of the Peaceful Light throughout the First and Middle Kingdom periods."

"What happened after?" She had an idea, already, of the next part of the story.

"It became outlawed by the Imperial Court at the beginning of the Last Kingdom. The emperors kept a select few

Spirit Summoners from the Chó clan at court and massacred all other known summoners. Tai is the last of his clan, as far as we know." There was a hardness to Zen's tone. "The regulations are not without reason—those well versed in the arts of summoning could find powerful spirits lurking and bind their powers to them." His eyes narrowed. "I believe there is a ghost tethered to this chamber, holding a powerful Seal in place. It wants something. I will attempt to summon it."

Lan looked around the empty chamber, too dark and too still. There again, that sense of something waiting in the shadows. Watching them. "Is there a way to summon a soul . . . from the world beyond?"

Zen's gaze softened with understanding. "No," he said. "The souls that have passed on are gone, never to be called back. Common folk believe that souls pass through the River of Forgotten Death to be washed of their memories; the truth is, the qì that formed one's core simply dissipates, becoming one with the wind, the rain, the clouds, and the world all around us.

"What Tai did earlier was to gather the imprint of your mother's qì that her soul had left while in this world. Echoes, footprints, if you will, of what they once were. But unless a soul is tethered to this world as a guǐ or mó, all that we see of them are reflections of them when they were alive."

Lan looked away.

"Lan," Zen said gently, and when she met his gaze, she had the feeling he was looking straight into her heart. "Be glad the souls of those you love have passed beyond the River of Forgotten Death. For a soul to remain tethered to this world after death . . . is worse than an eternity of suffering."

With that, he began to draw. The characters for this Seal were far more complicated than any she had previously seen

Zen perform. Yet the biggest difference, she sensed, was in the qì he pulled. There was the presence of the natural elements—but for the first time, energies of yīn overpowered them. They rushed past Lan like currents of black, cold waters, weaving into the Seal. She could see the broad strokes of this Seal—the founding principles. One side of yáng, representing their world, the world of the living and the light; the other the side of yīn, representing the world of death, of souls and ghouls. In the middle: a barrier separating them.

Zen slashed a stroke through that barrier and closed the Seal. Lan saw that the characters had formed the shape of a single, giant eye wreathed in fire. It pulsed.

The chamber responded. As the black flames of Zen's Seal swept over the floors, a cold gale stirred, smelling of bones and broken things. The tips of the incense sticks—or what remained of them—flared out. And yet . . . there was light. It was soft and white, chasing after the darkness as though a layer of the world had been peeled back and this was what remained. An echo, an imprint. Figures began to move all around them, somehow sharing the space with them and yet not. Voices rose and fell like the rush of an invisible current bearing days, moons, cycles, dynasties past.

At last, the lightless light settled, all else vanishing but for a figure perched on the empty chair. It was a woman, hair pulled tight to her head in a braided bun, páo spilling like moonlit water down the length of her legs. She appeared to be asleep, an arm draped over the rosewood cabinet, cheek resting on her wrist.

She stirred, just as there came a sound of doors opening behind Lan. She spun to look, but the doors to the chamber remained as they had left them.

"Ah," Zen said quietly. "This is a memory." Glancing at him,

Lan was stricken by just how solid and full of life he looked compared to the woman. "This guǐ has chosen to communicate with us through a memory."

"Master Shēn Ài." A smooth male voice cut through space and time, reverberating slightly as though pulled from a distant dream.

The woman—the master—stood. She might have been around the age of Lan's mother. *"Is she here?"* Her voice was lovely yet faded as rust-colored roses.

"No." The word fell like the dead drop of an axe. A pause, then: *"I do not think she is coming, Ài'ér."*

Master Shēn's lips trembled. *"And my brother—"*

"The imperial government has fallen. We are left on our own."

Master Shēn's hand flew to her mouth. She closed her eyes as though to steady herself. *"Their daughter?"*

A sudden, chilling premonition struck Lan, stealing the breath from her.

"The invaders reached the Sòng dà'yuàn several days ago. Whatever reports we have received by messenger dove stated that no survivors were found."

Lan could not breathe. The room seemed to distort before her eyes, shadows curving and swaying. White snow. Blue armor. Red blood. Strings of a woodlute broken as easily as her mother's bones—

"This arrived from the Tiān'jīng Imperial Palace, addressed to you," the male speaker continued.

When Shēn Ài opened her eyes again, they were clear. Her face had set. She straightened and crossed the room.

The chamber lit up where she walked, surroundings shifting as though she held the pale light that offered a view into another world, another time. Bookshelves burgeoned, overflowing with scrolls and tomes. Paintings cascaded down the walls, bearing scenes of rivers and mountains, pagodas and pavilions, abloom in the calligraphy of poems now lost. Bamboo mats unfurled on the floors, pots of ink and rolls of rice paper stacked by each one. This had once been a classroom, flourishing with knowledge and history and culture—yet when Shēn Ài's lightless light disappeared, all else faded but for the stark walls and empty floors.

Shēn Ài stopped by the door. That, too, had shifted: peeled paint now glossy and vibrant. And beneath the doorframe—

Lan inhaled sharply. She felt Zen's hand brush her sleeve: a touch of comfort, and a question. Her heart, her mind were in freefall as she instinctively reached for him. His fingers, burning against her ice-cold ones, clasped around hers.

The male speaker was the grandmaster of the school. He stood at the door, in the same silken robes as they'd seen on his spirit in the courtyard earlier, tall and alive and wholly human. In his hands, he held a lacquerwood box inlaid with mother-of-pearl.

Lan and Zen approached, watching carefully as Shēn Ài took it from him and flipped it open.

"A xūn?" she asked, glancing up at the grandmaster as she unwrapped a red silk handkerchief to reveal what resembled a large, black egg made of glazed clay. Several columns of finger holes had been drilled into it, and on the surface, inlaid with mother-of-pearl, was the outline of a white lotus.

Lan felt her whole world snap into sharp focus. *Gods guide her to hear the song of the ocarina,* her mother had said, and Lan knew immediately that the object the ghost held was what everything—her Seal, the song, her mother's imprint—had led to.

Master Shēn held the ocarina to her lips and blew.

Nothing.

The grandmaster of the School of Guarded Fists tipped his head in bemusement. *"An ocarina that plays no music,"* he said.

Shēn Ài wrapped it carefully in the red silk handkerchief and placed it back in the box. From within, she drew out a note made on rice paper and read:

The map lies within.

When the time is right,

This ocarina will sing for the Ruin of Gods.

There was utter silence on both sides of the veil long after the echo of Shēn Ài's words faded.

"The note is from Méi'ér," the woman finished. *"She must have hidden the maps inside and sent it to us for safekeeping as a last resort."*

Blood roared in Lan's ears. Méi: plum blossoms. The flowers that bloomed against all odds in the cold of winter. The ones Māma had been named for.

"In that case," the grandmaster said quietly, *"we must hide the box and adhere to Méi'ér's final will: that none will find it until it sings. We must stake our lives on protecting it, if necessary. This is the legacy of the Order. Whomever this ocarina chooses will hold the keys to the Last Kingdom . . . to the world."*

Shēn Ài's expression steeled. *"Yes, shī'fù."*

Footsteps sounded hollowly; a third figure burst into the room, noticeably younger, face open with panic. *"Shī'zǔ,"* she gasped, *"the invaders have breached the gates of the village! Our disciples have fallen."*

The grandmaster's face was shadowed, sober as he brushed a hand to the hilt of his sword. *"Gather the remaining disciples and begin the incantation for the Boundary Seal. I am right behind you. Go."* When the disciple disappeared again, he turned to Shēn Ài. *"I can buy you one bell at most. Will you complete this last task?"*

In the face of death, his expression was one of serenity.

"Shī'zǔ. Grandmaster." Shēn Ài sank to her knees. From somewhere beyond the circle of her spirit light, the explosions

were growing louder. Distant screams rent the air. A single teardrop trickled down her cheek, yet her voice was steady as she said, *"For this, my life I vow."*

"Kingdom before life, honor into death." The grandmaster drew his sword. *"Peace be upon your soul, and may you find the Path home."*

Shēn Ài stood, cradling the box to her chest. The silence was heavy as she crossed to the back of the chamber, each breath and footstep stirring the unquiet souls resting in the room.

The master lifted a hand, touched a finger to the wall as one might hover a brush over paper, and began to trace. Within the first few characters of the Seal, Lan was lost. By her side, Zen watched with intense concentration, gaze tracking each stroke as though carving it into his mind.

At last, when Shēn Ài's hand arced in a slow, smooth circle, Zen made a sound in his throat. "The Final Art," he muttered.

The strangest thing was happening. The wall was morphing before Lan's very eyes, ridges appearing where there had been smooth stone, doorknockers sprouting. Within moments, a second set of doors appeared. Overhead, a sign read: *Chamber of Forbidden Dreams*.

Zen stepped forward. Curiosity burned in his eyes. "It is tradition for every school to have a chamber holding its most sacred art of practitioning. If the grandmasters and masters elect a disciple to enter that chamber, it is considered the highest honor."

"The Chamber of Forgotten Practices at our school," Lan supplied, thinking of the brief conversation she'd had with Chue on her first day of class.

In the memory unfurling, the doors swung open. Inside the chamber was a table with a single scroll. Master Shēn stepped forward and placed the box with the ocarina by its side. She gave the box and the note—the note from Lan's mother—one last, lingering look before shutting the latch. The click echoed.

Then she stepped back and waved a hand—and the wall began to close again.

"No!" Lan darted forward, but Zen caught her arm, pulling her back. "The chamber's going to seal itself—"

"It is but a memory," Zen replied. "And I sense it is nearing its end. Let us not disturb the message Master Shēn has painstakingly left for us."

The scene before them flickered like a candle rippling in the wind. When Lan blinked again, it had shifted, the graylight sweeping across the room in a tumultuous tide.

The doors were open, the orange light of fire catching across the chamber. Disciples lay dead across the entrance. From beyond came screams of pure, unadulterated terror, wails and sobs of pain that dug into Lan's heart.

Master Shēn stood in the center of the chamber. She seemed to have just finished a Seal; it shivered in the air, glowing pale blue for moments before disintegrating. The entire room had changed. Gone were the bamboo mats, inkpots, brushes, and rice paper. Gone were the bookcases, the centuries of tomes that had quietly held the words, poems, and stories of an entire people. The chamber had been swept bare except for the rosewood table and chair in the center.

From nearby came the sound of footsteps storming down the hall, metal striking the wood of the old western sidehouse floors. Shouts rent the air—rolling, foreign words that were all too familiar to Lan.

Master Shēn stepped forward. In the glimmer of firelight, she was a figure of grace and serenity already cast in the gilding of time. A dagger in her hand caught the light as she sat in the chair.

"*It is done,*" she whispered into the death-filled space, filled with the cries and screams of disciples she had taught and masters who had taught her. *"Kingdom before life, honor into death. Do not fail us, Ruin of Gods."* Tears shimmered in her eyes; they gathered on her lashes as she closed them. *"Peace be upon our souls, and may we find the Path home."*

The arc of her dagger cut sharp and bright across her throat.

The colorless light faded, and the ghost of Shēn Ài disappeared, leaving the chamber dark and still, just as they had discovered it. In the center, the rosewood table and chair sat, empty, draped in a patina of peace as though Shēn Ài had just woken from it minutes ago.

"There is some form of a Seal." Zen's boots scraped against the floor as he left Lan's side to prowl the chamber, hand trailing the walls. "I have sensed it since we entered, but I cannot access it." A pause. "I believe it is being held by the wills of the ghosts still tethered here. Bound, perhaps, by the souls of the very disciples who served and died here."

Lan opened her mouth to reply. Whatever words she was about to speak, however, flew from her mind as another sound filled the space.

Do-do-sol.

Three small notes, an entire world upended. She knew this song. It was the one her mother had played the morning the Elantians invaded.

And suddenly, she knew what she had to do.

Lan drew breath and hummed. *Do-do-sol.* An answer. A confirmation.

Do-sol-do, came the responding trill.

Lan replied, the notes drawn from her lips by some unknown force.

By *magic.*

When the time is right,

This ocarina will sing . . .

And sing it did. Her responses seemed to have worked as an invisible key to unlock it. Music flowed, a single, lonely tune winding through the chamber. It coursed through Lan, flooding her mind and veins and into her very soul. Something inside her stirred: something ancient, a calling that felt like home.

Lan drifted toward its source. The music pulled her to the wall—the exact spot where, twelve cycles ago, Shēn Ài had stood on the precipice of her death and opened the door to the Chamber of Forbidden Dreams. There was a Seal coiled against it; when Lan touched her palm to the smooth stone, the cold stung her fingers.

Still humming softly, Lan reached for her qì, and the exact Counterseal drifted into her mind, whole and complete and bright silver. She traced the strokes, her hands guided by the music.

The door revealed itself to her just as it had for Master Shēn. Lan pulled it open and stepped through.

Inside stood that table with the scroll and the lacquerwood box. She brushed off the thick layer of dust, and the mother-of-pearl pattern gleamed white on its lid. The music crescendoed.

Lan opened the box, and there it was: the ocarina, its glazed clay surface unmarred by the passage of time or the fall of dynasties. The box had kept dust from it so that the pale inlay of the lotus shone like captured moonlight.

A knot formed in Lan's throat; she reached forward and picked the ocarina up.

"'An ocarina that plays no music,'" Zen said quietly, repeating the words the grandmaster had spoken so many cycles ago in this very chamber. "What does your mother mean for you to do with it?"

But Lan knew. The ocarina fit perfectly in her grip, as

though it had been molded into the grooves of her palm. By some instinct, she brought it to her lips.

When the time is right, this ocarina will sing for the Ruin of Gods.

Lan blew.

The purest note rang out, a crystal snowdrop against the stale air of the chamber.

There was a sound like a ghostly sigh by Lan's side. Then, like a snipped string, the remaining Seal over the chamber broke. She heard Zen's shout as qì quivered around the chamber; felt the implosion of the net of energies Shēn Ài had woven all around them—the Seal Zen had been searching for.

He found Lan just as she'd dropped to her knees, huddling over the ocarina. Zen held her tightly against the tide of yīn energies that roared over them, bearing the screams of a hundred slain souls, the pain and sorrow of a way of life lost. The chamber shook, the illusion falling and shattering around them as the true nature of the room revealed itself. Bamboo mats had been upturned and torn, inkpots shattered and brushes snapped, scattered like broken bones across the floor. Paintings had been knocked askance from the wall, their parchment scattered about the room like ashes. Chairs and tables were overturned, and strewn across the floor were the corpses of the School of Guarded Fists' disciples, now empty skeletons.

When the chamber settled again, Lan found the truth of the School of Guarded Fists split open before her: yet another Hin landmark, fallen to the desolation of conquest.

"Lan. Lan, look at me."

She found Zen's gaze. His expression was one of ice frozen over, reminiscent of what she had seen the night he'd brought her out of Haak'gong. There had been no pity on his face, only hard-edged empathy.

Do not let them win today.

Lan thought of Master Shēn, her soul bound to this chamber to protect the ocarina for twelve cycles. Of the grandmaster, reduced to a snarling, senseless shell of a demon. Of the disciples whose spirits had remained behind in the deathless eternity of a guǐ.

Of Māma, whose last act had been to sacrifice herself to let Lan live.

And for what?

When the time is right, this ocarina will sing for the Ruin of Gods.

Ruin of Gods—she hadn't even any idea what the term meant.

All Lan knew was that the ocarina had chosen to sing for her. That twelve cycles of fruitless search over the Seal her mother had left in her wrist had led her here. That an entire school—masters, grandmaster, disciples—had given their lives for this moment.

Her grip tightened on the smooth surface of the ocarina.

She had not been able to save them—not twelve cycles ago, not even today.

She would not let that happen again.

Lan clenched her teeth and brushed away the wetness on her cheeks. She stood sharply, wrenching her arm from Zen's. "Thank you for accompanying me here, Zen," she said.

He dipped his head slightly, those ink-black lashes fluttering as he watched her. "Any idea of what that ocarina might hold?" he asked.

Lan didn't—but she was saved from her response.

A shift in the energies, the overwhelming presence of metal. Then: the faint sound of conversation, words long and rolling. The clipped fall of boots against the courtyard outside.

Elantians.

20

The Final Art is the unique craft of each school
of practitioning, unlocked as a highest honor
bestowed by the grandmaster upon his disciples.

—*The Way of the Practitioner, Addendum:*
The Hundred Schools

Zen grasped Lan's arm. "In here," he said, and pulled her to the still-open doors of the Chamber of Forbidden Dreams—the only area that appeared to have escaped the destruction of the Elantian conquest.

Lan resisted. "We'll be trapped," she whispered.

"We won't be found," Zen corrected. When Shēn Ài's illusion Seal over the entire room had broken, it had revealed the true form of this room—including the Chamber of Forbidden Dreams and the remaining network of Seals over it. "The Seals hiding this chamber of the Final Art are built into the very bricks and stones of their walls. Even the Elantians did not find it during their invasion."

She appeared to think through this reasoning before she yielded. The space was cramped, hardly bigger than a latrine stall and made to accommodate only the table with the ocarina—but Zen had not seen any other Final Art chamber to judge.

He pulled the doors closed and watched the Seals swirl into

effect, the strokes to their characters glowing softly. The designs were at a level too advanced even for him. Hand against the wood, he sensed a Seal weaving the illusion of stone onto the other side, masking the presence of the door; a few others were layered over for protection and concealment. Then, to his surprise: something resembling a Gate Seal. Studying it a moment longer, he let out a breath.

"This is ingenious," he murmured. "They created an advanced Gate Seal to transport this chamber into a different space. When the doors are opened, the Gate Seal reverses, transporting it back for access. Yet it is nearly impossible to know of the existence of the door—let alone to find it and to perform the Counterseal to open it."

He had no idea how Lan had managed to not only find but also unlock this hidden Final Art chamber, but one thing was clear. The answers to everything—the yīn in her qì, the speed of her learning, the songs only she could hear—lay in the ocarina.

The darkness in the chamber gradually eased, filled with the dim churn of the glow from the Seals as they were activated. The weaves of qì were so old, they had sunken into the foundations of the structure itself so that the bricks seemed to shimmer. Across from Zen, Lan's eyes were wide, her pupils dilated, the Seal magic brushing her cheeks like reflections of water. She stood close enough that he could feel the fabric of her páo brush against him; one of her hands was gently latched onto his sleeve.

"I thought Seals vanished once the practitioner's soul passed," she murmured.

"Correct. Yet in many cases, the weave of qì sinks in so deeply that the object retains the Seal in itself—much like the cesspools of qì that formed the bamboo yāo we met. In this case, the walls and roots of this school have retained the Seals as a part of them, becoming . . . almost sentient. Like a muscle memory."

She touched a finger to the shimmering wall, something like wonder on her face. It quickly dimmed.

"I hear them," she whispered as the footsteps and voices grew louder. "I can sense *him*." She held the ocarina to her chest, but Zen caught the brush of her thumb against her left wrist. "I think . . . I think they found me through the tracking spell."

Cold guilt trickled down Zen's back. Leaving the Boundary Seal had been a mistake. Ulara's theory had been that the spell in Lan's arm would remain active so long as it was preserved. The Seal the masters had administered to it merely hindered its power, along with the power of the Boundary Seal. Leaving Skies' End had removed one of the protective layers.

He reached out, putting a tentative hand on Lan's wrist. "The Seals on this chamber allow us a looking glass that goes only one way. We can hear them, but should they knock down this wall, they will find naught but grass and trees where we currently stand."

"Because of the Gate Seal," she replied.

He nodded, then pressed a finger to his lips. The Elantians had entered the outer chamber.

". . . magic came from here." A feminine voice, speaking with militaristic efficiency. Zen's ears pricked. *Magic*. That was what they called qì. The woman was a magician.

The sound of the Elantian language never failed to incite that old feeling of nausea and fear in him. Trapped in a small space as he was, with no way out, no way to defend himself, and most of his strength expended on the summoning Seal, the sensation was magnified. He closed his eyes and regulated his breathing, focusing his mind on the space of nothingness in the way Dé'zǐ had taught him when old memories threatened to spill into panic.

"It's empty," commented a second speaker. There was the sound of rubble being kicked. Then the same speaker said, "Well, it's not hard to tell that our army came through here in the early days."

The speaker chuckled, and Zen's blood ran cold. The way he pronounced the sentence, his intonations light and glib, yielded no uncertainty: the man was jesting about the massacre of the entire School of Guarded Fists.

Bile rose inside him, sharp, bitter, burning. It didn't have to be this way. If he let himself—if he allowed the darkest part of himself to finally resurface, he could stand a chance of taking down at least a few Elantian magicians.

"Such topics are not to be joked about," the female said sternly. "Those yellow curs practice magic with souls of their dead. We do not wish to accidentally invoke the wrath of their ghosts."

"You believe in all that Hin spiritual nonsense?" the male cackled. Zen frowned, processing the foreign language carefully in his mind. So this second man was no magician.

"*Silence.*" This word cut through their chatter like a clap of thunder. And as Lan tensed beside Zen, he suddenly realized why this third voice sounded so familiar.

It was him—the Alloy from Haak'gong. Even now, Zen could imagine the bone-white gleam of his armor, those eyes burning like blue flames in a colorless face. *The Winter Magician,* Lan had called him.

"You said you tracked the girl here, Erascius?" The female's tone was deferential when she addressed him. The other speaker had fallen quiet. The room was filled with the sharp scuffs of their boots as they prowled.

Lan made a small noise.

"I thought I did." The Winter Magician's—Erascius's—tone was cold, flat, a vast, unbroken expanse of ice that seemed to fill the chamber. "My spell grows weak with the passage of time . . . yet I believed I was . . . *close*."

As he'd spoken, his voice had drawn steadily nearer to the spot where the Seals had hidden away the Chamber of Forbidden Dreams—and Zen and Lan with it.

"Did they tamper with your spell?" the female suggested wryly. "You yourself said that you felt a period of disconnect before it flared up. What if this is a trap?"

A bitter silence followed.

"Are there spells here? Could they be hidden?"

Lan had wrapped her arms around herself, curling inward. Her eyes, though, she kept wide open.

The image struck deep in Zen's heart. He knew the feeling of helplessness in the face of violence. After all, he had stood in her place thirteen cycles ago, before a different group of soldiers bearing dragon-tailed pennants and armor of gold.

"Did you say the girl had something you wanted?" the other male speaker asked.

"I would have thought His Majesty the King would have assigned a more capable captain to work with us," the woman snarled.

"Lishabeth," Erascius said, "Captain Timosson and his company are on loan to us in a new partnership. I would counsel patience, as not all are familiar with the findings and inner workings of Royal Magicians."

"Yes, Erascius."

"Captain Timosson." There was an icy grace to the way Erascius spoke. "It takes order at every level to keep an empire as great as Elantia in power. Lishabeth and I have been assigned by the governor, at the direct order of His Majesty the King

Alessander, Angels Hold His Name, to establish the Elantian Central Outpost. These Central Plains of the Last Kingdom have gone unchecked for too long. We had once thought they held nothing but wild forest and tundra lands . . . yet our recent skirmish with the two practitioners in Haak'gong has led us to believe otherwise. Especially considering how they disappeared into the central region." A pause. "I believe there still exists an organized . . . nest of Hin practitioners that slipped through our fingers. I believe they are hiding in the Central Plains, somewhere near here . . . right under our noses."

Zen stopped breathing. The Alloy spoke of *them*—of their encounter in Haak'gong. By saving Lan, Zen had confirmed the existence of the School of the White Pines.

A pause, and then the second voice—Captain Timosson— spoke. "No, I get *that*," he said a bit gruffly. "Now that our power has stabilized on the eastern coasts, we're expanding west. More resources, better control."

"But you do not understand why this mission is so critical," Erascius said coldly. "If there still exists an order of Hin practitioners, Elantian rule could very well fall under threat one day. You have not seen their powers; you know nothing of the magic they possess, which they seem to draw from this land in a way we Royal Magicians cannot. Magic that we can learn in order to contribute to the Elantian civilization and continue our expansion across oceans. Magic as old as time, which makes them as powerful as *gods*. And while I do not expect your complete understanding as to why this mission is crucial to King Alessander's control over this land, I expect *obedience*." The last word cracked like a whip.

"Yes, my lord," Timosson said breathlessly, any traces of disgruntlement gone from his tone. "And you think we can smoke them out here?"

Erascius was so close to the hidden chamber that his voice

sounded in Zen's ear. "I wish to kill two birds with one stone: to find the secret sanctuary of Hin magicians . . . and to destroy them with the power of their Four Demon Gods."

Zen's entire body froze over.

"You can't believe those are real," Timosson said, but there was a note of uncertainty to his voice.

"I *know* they are real. I have witnessed their power first-hand, back at the Imperial Palace. They slipped through my fingers, and I have sought them ever since. The research facility I ran confirmed my suspicions that the Hin bind demons to themselves to borrow their power. I have seen the power of a regular demon. Imagine what one could do with the power of a *Demon God*."

The research facility.

It was all Zen could do to anchor his mind to the present. To clasp his arms—arms that bore scars from Elantian metalwork in the very research facility Erascius spoke of—and stop their shaking.

"I believe we came close to discovering their secrets twelve cycles ago from a Hin imperial practitioner, but she put up a stubborn resistance. I had no choice but to kill her," Erascius was saying. "I'd thought that trail cold, the secrets lost with her death. It wasn't until I felt some semblance of her magic in Haak'gong again several weeks ago that I realized: she had a daughter who had been living right under our noses all along. Therefore, we must find *her*."

A Hin imperial practitioner. Lan had told Zen this magician—Erascius—had killed her mother in order to obtain something from her.

Could *this* be what Lan's mother had died to protect? Secrets related to demonic practitioning . . . related to the Demon Gods themselves?

Impossible, Zen thought, his gaze drifting to the girl by his side. Lan, too, had gone utterly still. He could see her in the dim light of the Seals, lips parted, the box with the ocarina clasped to her chest as a child might clutch a doll for comfort.

Questions burned inside him like fire the longer he watched her. Who was her mother? How could she have come across such knowledge? The trails to the Four Demon Gods had been lost with time, become secretive as powerful practitioners across the Last Kingdom fought for their possession, and then as the Imperial Court sought to control them. And the last known of the Four, the Black Tortoise, had vanished with the death of his final binder, the Nightslayer.

"Nothing here, Erascius," Lishabeth said at last, her voice muffled as though coming from a corner of the outer chamber. "Perhaps a wanton ghoul triggered an old Seal."

The clink of boots over rubble sounded near. "I am rarely mistaken." Erascius's voice came not two steps from the hidden chamber. He seemed to have been lingering there all along. "But perhaps I will admit to error this time."

"Of course," Lishabeth said quickly. "*I* sensed it, too. Something went off here, something magical."

"They have slipped through my fingers yet again. They will not be so lucky next time." Erascius's words were a promise, laced with poison. "Let us not waste more time in these ruins. Twelve cycles, and the stench of Hin has not yet diminished."

Their footsteps faded into nothingness. Zen remained where he was, leaning against the wall, the shock of the past minutes roaring in his mind, cracking through his blood. His heart was racing as it hadn't in a long time.

"Zen?"

He blinked, his attention returning to the present. Lan stood opposite him. In the pale glow of the Seals around them, her face was white as a ghost. He stared at her, at this songgirl he'd found in a common teahouse in Haak'gong, and for the first time felt the tug of the strings of fate, moving him in a direction he could not have anticipated.

The signs had all been there. The traces of yīn qì he'd sensed back in the old hawker's shop in Haak'gong. The explosion of energies, the way she had killed an Elantian soldier without so much as batting an eyelash. The Seal-shaped scar on her wrist, her precociousness in creating advanced Seals after only weeks of practice.

And the ocarina . . . the mysterious ocarina that had sung to her.

Lan's mother might have given her clues to the location of the vanished Demon Gods.

"Zen?" Lan repeated.

He stared at her, at the ocarina case she cradled against her chest. The one that might hold the keys to immeasurable power.

The one that might change the tides of history.

Zen knew, without a doubt, Dé'zǐ's and Yeshin Noro Ulara's stances on the Demon Gods, on seeking out their power to defeat the Elantians.

The Four are gods, Zen, Dé'zǐ had said once, several cycles ago, when Zen had proposed the idea to him. *You have studied the history of our land, of the warring clans, the rise of the First Kingdom, the iron fist of the Middle Kingdom, and the blood-paved path of the Last Kingdom. You know the price men have paid to attain power. The powers of gods are meant to remain with the gods; we humans were never meant to be gods.*

Yet Zen thought of the grandmaster they had seen in the courtyard, reduced to a savage mó in a desperate bid to protect his school; to Shēn Ài and the disciples of the School of Guarded Fists, forced to bind their souls into the limbo between life and death; to the once-great symbol of civilization reduced to ruin by Elantian conquerors, unburied bodies of its defenders mocked by their murderers.

A vicious cycle he had seen across the Last Kingdom, across his people.

This was the consequence of refusing power. *This* was the damnation of rejecting the idea of becoming gods: you became ruled by newer, crueler, merciless gods.

The Hin had seen this within the eras of the First, Middle, and Last Kingdoms: the rise and fall of clans, of emperors, of dynasties. The elements were in constant flux, each vanquishing the other in a cycle of destruction and rebirth.

Perhaps this was the truth to the Way.

Perhaps this was all meant to be.

And in the darkness, a new thought came to him like a flame.

It is the duty of those with power to protect those without.

If the Hin had the power of the Demon Gods . . . if they could harness that power against the Elantians . . .

No. For his entire life, he had lived under the shadow of the Nightslayer's mistake, the one that had given the Ninety-Nine Clans their reputation and destroyed their chances of ever returning. The one that had marked demonic practitioning as a stain upon Hin history.

He knew the dangers.

Zen held out a hand. "Let me keep the ocarina safe for you," he said.

Lan's eyes darted to him; she hesitated, only a fraction of a second, but he sensed it.

Zen tapped the black silk pouch emblazoned with the emblem of red fire at his waist. "This is a practitioner's storage pouch. It can expand endlessly as needed." He forced a smile.

"I promise to take care of the ocarina for you. Have I ever broken a promise?"

For a moment, he thought she might refuse. Then Lan leaned forward, squinting at him. "Why are you smiling? I get nervous when you're all sweet talk and honeyed words."

He frowned. "You would have me brood all day, then?"

She grinned. "Exactly," she said, and just like that, she handed him the box that held the ocarina. It was no heavier than a rock, yet it seemed to hold the weight of worlds as he held it in his palms. The weight of her trust.

Carefully, Zen slipped it in his pouch. "Let us be on our way, then," he said, and pressed his fingers to the stone door. The qì of the Seals swirled against his touch, and he pulled on the threads that would form the Counterseal.

The door ground open and they stepped out.

That was when Lan screamed.

Zen's focus sharpened; he'd barely felt the shift in qì around them when fire streaked through his veins, splitting him with pain from the inside out.

Dully, Zen felt his body hit the floor. He was paralyzed, the qì in his flesh and blood unbalanced with the intrusion of cool, hard metal spliced into his bones. His mouth was filled with warmth, the sharp tang of blood mixed with the presence of metal all around them.

"Hello, my little singer." The voice drifted to him from somewhere nearby, colder than winter's ice, as the edges of his consciousness faded into darkness. "Did you truly think I would let you slip through my fingers again?"

21

Strength without restraint and power
without balance are akin to a path into
darkness without light.

—Dào'zǐ, *Book of the Way*
(Classic of Virtues), 1.7

Trapped in a wagon made of metal and darkness, Lan felt as though she'd returned to the Teahouse; to Haak'gong beneath the watchful stares of their conquerors, her every move scrutinized and her every choice made for her. The freedom of Skies' End, the days spent learning to fight with the arts of practitioning, now seemed like an illusion. As though it had never happened at all.

Her left arm throbbed, the metalwork in her flesh pulsing as it responded to the overwhelming presence of Elantian magic all around them. Metal shackled her wrists to the walls, the carriage blocking out the flow of qì from the other elements. Zen was chained to the wall across from her, locks of his hair fallen before his face. The Winter Magician had electrocuted him until he'd lost consciousness.

She couldn't tell how long the journey took; it might have been hours, or it might have been a day. At last, they pulled to a stop, the doors opened, and Lan was hauled out by a pair of Elantian Angels.

It was still night, the shadows of jagged mountains crowning the tips of the pine forest behind them. The walls rose between the trees, sudden and stark, a metal-and-stone intrusion blotting out the stars, looking so utterly foreign amidst the flow of wind and water. Lan heard the clink of chains and a thud as the guards dragged Zen between them.

A feeling of powerlessness overtook Lan as the Elantian Central Outpost loomed over them. She was awake, qì flowing around her, yet she was unable to conjure even a single Seal to save their lives.

The ground beneath their feet widened into a smoothed-out lime-mortar road, cutting a straight line through the forest toward the stronghold's walls.

Lan had never seen such walls. They had to be at least as tall as all three stories of the Teahouse: strange and stark with their rectangular gates and the flat, cylindrical watchtower as opposed to elegantly curving Hin architecture. She could sense the overwhelming press of metal woven into the foundation, fortifying the entire place like Elantian armor. Crenellations, it seemed, were one thing Hin and Elantian architecture had in common, and even from far off, she could make out the glint of white armor against flickering torches.

Heavy iron doors opened, revealing a stretch of courtyard gardens, flowers arranged clinically along a straight path to the front entrance of the castle. In Haak'gong, the Elantians had built their outpost by spreading their influence over Hin architecture; this was the first time Lan had seen a construction of purely Elantian design. Her first impression was that it was crude and unrefined compared with the exquisite details of Hin buildings. The outpost was naught more than a great gray structure of unevenly shaped stones, some even jutting out. The windows were narrow and made of glass, the torches were powered with auric light, and two towers tapered off into pointed metal spires.

The patrols stationed around the courtyard made no movement as the guards took her down the path to the entrance. On either side of the path were flower displays behind wrought-iron fences, and as Lan turned her head to look at them, she realized she recognized them all. Chrysanthemums. Azaleas. Peonies, orchids, and camellias—all flowers native to her land. All boxed neatly behind their metal prisons.

This was what the Elantians wanted of the Hin.

The doors to the castle swallowed her. They passed stone corridors lit in candlelight from glass burner lamps, decor made of gleaming metal studding the walls.

The soldiers stopped before a set of heavy metal doors, different from the other doors of refined walnut with silver handles.

As Erascius put his pale hands on the metal door handles, Lan had a sudden, sickening premonition. Whatever it was that awaited them on the other side of those doors, she did not wish to see.

Erascius pulled open the doors. A stench of yīn energies poured over Lan like a flood of river water. She clapped a hand against her heart—so strong were the sentiments of resentment, fear, and hatred that she might have drowned in them.

Behind her, she heard Zen make a choked sound.

One of the soldiers lifted a lamp to illuminate a set of steps that led them down to another stretch of tunnel. Here, the air was so thick with yīn that Lan found it difficult to breathe. Death—there had been so much death here, she thought.

It took her several moments to realize why.

There was movement to either side of them as they passed by, and as the corridor became illuminated by lamplight, Lan saw what the scurrying sounds were.

The walls of the corridor were not walls but cells. And hunched within, trapped like animals, eyes hollow when they turned to the light, were Hin. Men, women, children, sitting hunched together, arms and legs jutting like twigs. They shifted back as the soldiers' footsteps rang out, huddling in the farthest corners.

Lan's stomach turned. Her mind flashed a searing white— the color she'd seen before her mother's death, before Lan killed that Elantian Angel. Something deep inside her stirred.

A blur of blue and silver in her vision; a hand shot out, wrapping around her throat and slamming her head against the wall. Burning white faded to cold black, and Lan blinked stars from her eyes to find Erascius's winter eyes inches from her face.

"Is something wrong, little singer?" he whispered. "Will you not sing for me?"

She couldn't breathe; her head was going light, and her arms and legs were beginning to tingle. Lan summoned all the energy she had and kicked—right between his legs.

Flesh met metal as her shins connected with his armor. Erascius's mouth tightened; she felt a responding tightening of his fingers, crushing her throat.

"Hasn't your mother taught you manners?" he asked. "Ah, I forget. She's dead."

Lan spat in his face.

Slowly, the Winter Magician drew back. Took out a handkerchief and dabbed at his face until it was clean. When he looked at her again, his eyes burned like the heart of a flame.

"You'll be regretting that," he said, then gestured at the soldiers and directed, "Bring them to the interrogation chamber."

At the end of the long hallway was a chamber made wholly of metal. Inside were two steel chairs facing each other. Lan fought as the soldiers strapped her down, securing her with metal buckles; across from her, Zen was still unconscious.

Erascius leaned over Zen and, swiftly and precisely, jabbed a spot on his neck. The move reminded Lan of something she had seen the masters do: strike at certain nerves on the body that held qì to block the opponent's flow of energy—or to revitalize it.

Zen stirred. Satisfied, Erascius held out his left arm. Metal cuffs were stacked from his wrist to his elbow, gleaming in different shades of gray, gold, and copper. With his other hand, he made a gesture as though pulling on a string.

A strand of one of the silver-colored metals began to unravel from his wrist like liquid, hardening into a dozen small, thin needles that gleamed in the lamplight. They hovered in the air over Zen's chair.

Turning to Lan, Erascius said, "Well, let's see what makes you sing, shall we? With every question that I ask, should you not provide a satisfactory answer, I shall insert one of those needles into his flesh."

Lan's mind blanked. Zen was awake now. The needle drifted, aligning itself so that its tip pointed at Zen's palm.

Zen stopped moving. A terrible shadow crossed over his face; even from several paces away, Lan thought she saw his eyes widen so that the light of the silver needles sliced across them.

"First question." Erascius's voice pulled her focus back. "Who was your mother?"

Lan gritted her teeth. He knew. He knew, and he was forcing her to answer the question.

"No?" Erascius straightened slightly. He twirled his hand; the needle pointing at Zen's wrist jumped, skimming against his skin.

"Wait." If Lan gave him the answers that could do no harm—answers yielding no new information—perhaps that could buy them some time to come up with a plan. Lan licked her dry lips. "Sòng Méi." The name tasted of grief, a half-forgotten memory. "Her name was Sòng Méi."

"Very good." The needle twitched, but it remained in place. "Now, what did your mother leave you?"

Lan's heart raced. She thought of all they had just seen at Guarded Mountain, of Shēn Ài's ghost and the grandmaster's demon; of the ocarina they had protected against all odds . . . which rested in Zen's black storage pouch at this very moment.

Forcing herself to keep her eyes on Erascius, Lan replied steadily, "Whatever she meant to leave me, you destroyed."

Erascius's smile stretched. "Do you know how I so successfully interrogated the many Hin rebels who came before you? It is because I have a talent for reading people. I can tell, by the way they look at me or the subtlest shifts on their faces, whether or not they tell the truth. And you . . ." He drew closer. "You lie."

A flick of his fingers; a flash in the corner of her eyes. Zen drew a sharp, quick breath and tensed in his chair, his feet digging into the ground, his hands jerking against the buckles that strapped them down. With clinical precision, the needle burrowed into his flesh, disappearing up his wrist.

"No, stop. *Stop*," Lan gasped. "I'll tell you—I'll tell you."

Zen's jaw was clenched so hard, the veins on his neck bulged. Yet when he met Lan's eyes, he gave a nearly imperceptible shake of his head.

Lan hesitated.

A second needle drifted toward Zen's other wrist.

"An ocarina." The words tumbled from Lan's lips, hot and fast. "She left me an ocarina. She said it would play a song, but it's broken."

The needle paused. Erascius tipped his head. "An ocarina," he repeated. "Go on. Tell me more."

"Please." The desperation in her voice was so thick, she didn't even have to pretend. "That's all I know. Please, my lord—"

"*Lies,*" Erascius sang, and without hesitation, the second needle slipped into Zen's wrist. Zen's restraints jangled as they pulled taut against his arms. His face was slick with sweat as he turned to Lan, chest rising and falling with rapid breaths.

Again, he shook his head.

"I have lived by the principle that it is not the largest or most boorish of weapons that are most effective . . . but the most precise," Erascius said. The remainder of the needles gleamed in the flickering light. "Those needles are made of mercury—a poisonous metal lethal to humans. Once they enter his bloodstream, it takes sixty seconds for them to reach his heart, which they have a chance of piercing. The poison will then spread, numbing the heart until it stops." He leaned forward and swept a strand of Lan's hair behind her ears. The magician's eyes were very blue. "How many needles will it take, then, to kill him?"

Her vision blurred as she looked at Zen, warmth spilling down her face. "Please, no." Her whisper came broken. "I'll tell you. I'll tell you everything, my lord."

Erascius's smile stretched. "Very good," he said softly. "Now, tell me about what your mother left you."

"I don't know, I don't know—" Sweat trickled down her temple; she couldn't tear her eyes away from Zen. She had nothing to offer—nothing but her quick wit. She had to keep talking. "We had *just* arrived at the school when you found us. I left the ocarina there; we didn't have a chance to examine it, but if you give me time, I'll find the answers for you—whatever you need." How long had it been already? Twenty seconds? Thirty? The first needle had been in longer. "Please, ask me something else. *Please,* my lord."

Erascius studied her a moment longer. "Very well, then. Your school of practitioning. I want you to tell me exactly where it is."

She gripped the handles of her chair to stop her hands from trembling. She could sense Zen watching her; knew that if she looked at him, he would again signal silence to her even as two needles worked their way to his heart.

Kingdom before life, honor into death, the ghosts of the School of Guarded Fists whispered. There were one hundred and twenty-seven disciples and ten masters at the School of the White Pines. Giving its location away meant sentencing them all to death. Not giving its location away meant sentencing Zen to death.

She closed her eyes, a tear trickling down her cheek. So long as the Elantians ruled, the Hin would continue to contend with such choices.

"It is but five days northwest of here," Lan said quietly. "Hidden at the base of a mountain, the entrance sits behind an old, gnarled pine. I can take you there, my lord, if you spare his life."

She had long ago learned that the easiest lies to tell were those wrapped in half-truths. As she opened her eyes again to meet Erascius's gaze, she found something resembling satisfaction on his face.

"Unstrap her," he commanded the Angels standing at attention by the door. As they rushed to unchain her hands and legs, Lan couldn't shake the feeling that something worse was about to happen.

"Stand," Erascius ordered, and she did. The magician reached for something hidden in the folds of his cape—and as he brought the object forward, Lan's blood froze.

The ocarina gleamed in Erascius's hand as he lifted it to the light.

"Go on," he said. "Play me a little song."

The world shrank to the ocarina, with its sleek mother-of-pearl outline of a white lotus inlaid into black clay. The magician's pale hand twined around it, looking so out of place. And then, directly behind them, the fleet of needles hovering over Zen's wrist.

Whatever it was that Māma had died to keep safe from the Elantians . . . it all lay within the ocarina.

"In case I wasn't clear," Erascius said, his voice soft with poison, "that was an order, not a question." He lifted his hand, and before Lan could react, two more of the needles slipped into Zen's wrist.

Zen made a sound that Lan never wished to hear again.

Lan reached out. Her fingers closed over the surface of the ocarina. She pulled it from the magician with only one thought roaring in her mind: *Mine—this belongs to me*—and that she would not let the Elantians take a single thing more from her. As she lifted the ocarina to her lips, she thought of Skies' End, of Shàn'jūn, of the Teahouse and Ying and the other songgirls, of the villages burned and razed to the ground, the memories of the past twelve cycles flipping through her mind like the pages of a book until she stopped at the beginning, at the scene of Māma's death. She held on to that memory—and searched for the music within.

The song found her first. A melody pulled from her lips through the ocarina: something haunting, something that seemed to embody the passage of time, the flow of rivers into the sea, the brush of wind against bamboo leaves, the drip of rain down gray-tiled eaves. Suddenly, she was in that liminal space between reality and subconsciousness she had found whenever she'd sung back at the Teahouse, and she knew, without knowing, how to play, where to touch her fingers to coax the notes from the clay.

The song unfurled from her like a half-forgotten dream. It was one she'd found herself humming as she'd done chores back at the Teahouse, one that she had never been able to place. Yet in this moment, as she traced through her memory, she found the tune winding through the hallways of her manor house when she was a child, drifting from the window of her mother's study.

Then she was drifting upward, rising above her manor house—or, rather, the sky itself was expanding, drawing closer until she was a *part* of it, the stars glimmering like shattered crystals before her and all around her. The music flowed from her in dustings of silver, a stream winding upward until it settled between the stars. The silver glowed brightly in a snaking constellation.

Slowly, three other sets of colors settled into the stars. Nearby, a string of stars began to glow ice blue while, farther on, a set winked out and night poured into them, delineating their existence as an absence of light. Finally, in the distance, barely hovering over the curve of the western horizon, a fourth constellation flamed into crimson.

The music crescendoed, then slipped and jarred; a distant rumble sounded like thunder. The stars began to writhe, their shapes filling out, turning to her with eyes that gleamed against the dark.

Silver. Azure. Black. Crimson.

Dragon. Tiger. Tortoise. Phoenix.

She was drifting in an illusory night of her making, the song of her ocarina transposed into glowing constellations, weaving into reincarnated creatures that had existed only in legends and myths.

Lan lifted her head and looked into the eyes of the Four Demon Gods.

Shock held her in place; she had no idea how much time had passed before she tore her gaze away.

Like her, the rest of the chamber was spellbound. The light of the torches seemed to have dimmed, and above them were four quadrants of the night sky, each holding a set of stars.

Zen's face was tipped upward, and it was his expression that broke Lan from her reverie. He watched the illusion with a mixture of hope and fear so ardent that she could see it burning in his eyes.

She was suddenly aware of Erascius gazing at the constellations, the stars reflecting in those cold blue eyes. Instead of hope and fear, however, greed was carved on his face.

He reached out his hands, and those metal cuffs on his forearms began to flow out, spiraling upward to the illusion. Within the blink of an eye, they'd molded themselves into four quadrants: a perfect replica of the night skies and Demon Gods from Lan's ocarina, cast into metal. Then the metal sheets shrank and returned to encircle Erascius's arms.

The magician was *stealing* the secrets from her ocarina.

Lan's shock shifted to anger. She flexed her fingers, her mind sharpening over one lucid thought: *Mine. They are mine. And you will not have them.*

The energies spilling from her core turned.

The song changed.

Do-do-sol.

The notes stumbled from the ocarina, staccato, hesitant, broken, a memory resurfacing.

Do-sol-do.

The next chords came quicker, easier. And when she began the next line from the last memory she had of her mother, Lan felt as though the ghost of Sòng Méi had returned to play.

Qì stirred inside her, breaking through the dampness, darkness, and death pressing in around her. And somehow, her energies responded to the sound of her music, twining around the notes and flowing from the deepest parts of her.

Without warning, it surged.

Erascius shouted as qì slammed against his metal armor in a discordant clash. He flung his arms over his head just in time. Metalwork magic rippled from his cuffs, blocking the attack. When the magician looked up again, his expression was one of fury—and of something else, something indescribable. As though he was seeing the ghosts of his past.

Lan's song unfurled from her like an unstoppable tide, felling the raised swords of the Angels, whipping dents into their armor and cutting the skin of their faces. They stumbled back, running for the doors—and for several blissful moments, Lan felt as though she were in control. As though she could win.

"Stop, or he dies."

Erascius's voice cut through the whirlwind of qì, of *magic,* spilling from her. The last few notes of her song faded as she turned to the magician, who now stood by Zen. The fleet of needles had disappeared, replaced by a single sharpened blade—pointed at Zen's chest.

"Put the instrument down," Erascius said.

The qì inside Lan had built to a crescendo, pounding behind her temples. She lowered the ocarina from her lips, silence swirling in to fill the spaces where her song had rung.

Then she jammed the ocarina to her mouth and blew.

Qì exploded from her in a burst of song, ramming into the Angels who stood at the door. Erascius grunted as he crashed into the wall at the opposite end of the chamber.

A rush of triumph filled Lan. Gripping the ocarina, she turned to Zen—and her world tilted.

He was doubled over in his chair, hands straining against his bindings. A long silver blade protruded from his chest, red covering the pale skin of his hands.

Lan stumbled to him. With one riff of chords, her music broke through his cuffs; he fell forward and she caught him, careful not to touch the blade in his chest.

"Zen, *Zen,*" she whispered.

He coughed, and blood spilled crimson down his chin. He swayed against her hold, then slumped over onto the ground. With a final shudder, he went still.

Across the chamber, Erascius straightened. He drew his sword from his scabbard, the whisper of metal against leather repeated as the rest of the remaining Angels drew their weapons.

"You little—" Erascius hissed a word Lan knew to be the most demeaning of insults in his language. He stepped toward her and raised his sword. "Now that I have seen the maps to the Demon Gods with my own eyes, you have served your purpose. Here is the fate that awaited you twelve cycles ago."

His sword arced in a curve promising death.

It never made contact.

A blast of qì ripped upward, knocking the hilt from Erascius's hands and flinging the magician and his squadron of guards back once more. Lan stumbled as her knees gave way beneath her.

She found herself facing Zen.

He'd pushed himself into a crouching position, one hand on the ground and the other clutching his chest. The blood running from his wound had turned dark and was drifting upward like smoke.

"Lan," he choked out. She barely recognized his voice. His hair clung to his face, wet with sweat and blood. "Lan, *run.*"

"What? No!" She reached for him, but he jerked away. "Zen, what are you—"

"Run," he growled. The black smoke spilling from his chest grew stronger, the energies around them rippling as it flowed out. "Whatever happens next . . . I will have . . . no control over . . ."

"What are you talking about?" she cried. The qì around Zen had grown so thick, so suffused in the stench of something horribly corrupt, that she nearly gagged. Clutching her ocarina, she reached for him. Her fingers snagged on the fabric of his páo. "Zen, *look at me.*"

He tilted his head up and the curtain of his black hair parted to reveal his face. She drew back, so feral was his expression: teeth bared and lips curling. Eyes—she had seen eyes like that once back in Haak'gong, black spreading from the irises to the sclera, with only a sliver of white left.

"Because," Zen managed to gasp as the black filled his eyes, "there is a demon bound inside me, and Erascius has just cut it loose."

22

The person who follows the harmony of the
mean is on a path of duty and must never leave
it.

—*Doctrine of the Mean*, Kontenci

Thirteen cycles ago, Qīng Dynasty of the Luminous Dragon Emperor (Shuò'lóng)

The Northern Steppes

The plateaus yawned beneath an eternal blue sky, and the boy was lost. He stood knee-deep in snow, looking over a landscape of glittering white, unbroken but for silver birches stripped bare and standing like skeletons. A turn of seasons, a whole clan gone, an entire bloodline erased from the pages of history.

The snow lay thick over the grasslands he'd once called home, burying what had been left of his family. One cycle ago, there had been yurts flying black banners with red flames blazing atop; flocks of sheep dappling the lush green like clouds; lines of camels casting long shadows as merchants streamed to and from the Jade Trail. He could almost see it all, ghosts of figures weaving through the landscape, hear the phantom shouts of children as they danced on the endless feathergrasses.

They had been the last of their clan. After the fall of the Nightslayer, the remaining clans had either pledged fealty to the Imperial Court or faced mass execution. Yet there had been vestiges of clans that had gone into hiding, fleeing pursuit from the imperial army. The boy's father had led one such faction—the last of their bloodline—hiding deep within the unforgiving steppes in an attempt to disappear from the gaze of the Imperial Court.

It hadn't been enough.

The Imperial Army had been clever to attack in the midst of summer. Winter in the steppes was too cold, even for northern Hin; now the boy shivered as he staggered forward in his cotton garb, too thin this far north, his sheepskin boots a half size too small.

It had begun to snow. He used to love the snow; born in the thick of winter on the cusp of a new cycle, he'd spent each turn of age watching flakes fall like goose feathers.

Now he thought only of the father impaled by a golden sword, the mother's body used by the imperial soldiers, the cousins and aunts and uncles laid in a smoldering pile, flames licking up their bodies until they disappeared into a column of thick, choking smoke.

For some reason, the air shifted as he drew closer to their birthplace and deathbed. There was something in the atmosphere that twined around his chest, made it difficult for him to breathe, as though a stone pressed upon his heart. The closer he drew, the thicker the feeling grew, until he thought he might choke on grief and rage.

Then he saw the top of the yurt, sticking out like a grave marker, the black silk banner with the fire symbol half buried in snow. The clan leader's sigil.

His father's banner.

The winds rose into a howl, the snow flurried around him, and he sank onto the ground right where his family yurt had once sat and let out a long, anguished scream.

In the growing blizzard, something answered.

The fury in his blood froze into fear. The boy looked up. Between the plumes of his breath and the shifting curtains of snow, something moved. It was neither shape nor shadow, but something that filled the gaps of *in-between*. Something with no form but the vague edges of a presence made of the rotten aura of blood and bone and broken things.

The thing watched the boy, and the boy stared back. The initial fright gone, he was now overtaken by only curiosity— and a resigned fatalism that nothing in the world could hurt him more than what he had already been through.

He would be wrong.

"What are you?" He spoke in the language of his ancestors instead of the Standard Hin decreed by the Imperial Court. His voice scratched, rusty from disuse.

The wind crested, and a voice found him from everywhere and nowhere at once. *"I am anger. I am grief. I am born of death and destruction and an unfinished will."*

He knew. He had read the forbidden tomes of his ancestry locked in his father's birchwood chest, had heard whispers of what the ancients had once been capable of. As he spoke his next words, he found himself reaching into the side of his boot where he kept a small dagger that cut the spaces between stars. "You are a demon. Know that this dagger can slice through your core and break your energies."

"Did you not call for me?" the bodiless voice murmured. *"Did you not cast an unspoken wish for power? For revenge? For the chance to do to them what they did to your family?"* A jagged chuckle, the sound of nails scraping against bone. *"Gaze not upon me with such disgust, mortal, for I am summoned by the yīn of grief and rage and death. Like calls to like, and like it or not, you called me."*

The boy gripped his dagger tightly. "Have you a name?" he asked.

"They call me He With Eyes of Blood," came the reply. The name rang no bell of familiarity for the boy—a lesser demon, then, one not important enough to be marked down in the history books. The demon continued, its tone crooning and obsequious. *"What is it you wish for? Your deepest, darkest desire? That which has been eating away at your bright flame of a soul for the past cycle?"*

The boy knew—*knew*—better than to trust it, for he had read of demons as wicked creatures to be vanquished by only the most experienced of shamans and practitioners. But he looked to the yurt buried in the snow, to the black flame banner that had once flown high and mighty over the sprawling steppes of his homeland. And that rage and helpless despair sharpened into something else inside him.

Better to be burned by the fire of his own fury, to taste the bitterness of his wish for revenge, than to feel that devastating emptiness of *nothingness* his loss had left him.

He looked up into the formless creature. "I want power," he said. "I want enough power that I will never experience this again. I want enough power to make *them* understand what I have gone through, what my family has suffered."

The response was immediate. *"And what would you give for that power?"*

He recognized the sly edge to the demon's voice, but it did nothing to stop his answer. "Anything." A small price, he thought, for one who had nothing left.

The snow falling before him had begun to take shape—or, rather, it had begun to *flee* from something taking shape in its midst. A hulking mass the size of a camel, made only of darkness.

"I would grant you more power than any ordinary mortal holds," the demon said. *"Together, we could take down that Imperial Army in the blink of an eye; we could collapse palaces into smoke with*

naught but a thought. All I ask in return is the blood of a hundred souls."

The boy was already picturing a capital city wreathed in red and gold, pagodas and curved rooftops gleaming beneath a clear blue sky, the plated armor of its army glinting like the sun. A hundred souls—he would bring the demon a thousand if that meant taking down the Imperial Army.

"*Well, mortal child? Have we a bargain? All that I need is your word.*"

The shape in the snow grew clearer; the boy could make out a pair of black eyes limned the color of blood, bones and flesh shifting into some semblance of a warped face.

He was not frightened. He knew that the true demons in this world wore the faces of men.

"Yes," Zen said, the word falling from his lips like the cleave of a sword. "We have a bargain."

Present day
Central Plains

Black waves. Gray sand. And a sky that, just moments ago, had been in the palm of his hands.

No—something was wrong, something was terribly wrong. Just moments ago, he'd been looking into that pair of black eyes ringed red like an eclipse, set in an emaciated face, whatever semblance of flesh and bone the thing had mustered falling from its face like smoke. Its lipless mouth had peeled back, too many rows of shiny, sharp teeth bared at him in the mimicry of a smile.

The debt is paid, that voice inside him had hissed, and the teeth had begun to drip blood. *The bargain is ended.*

No, no, *no,* impossible. Because if the debt was paid, that meant—

He reached inside himself, deep into his heart, where he'd kept this secret over all these cycles.

Instead of a writhing abyss of power beneath his master's signature golden Seal, he found nothing. Just the flickers of his own qì, clean, natural, yīn and yáng in balance. Silence as deep as a slumbering mountain. And, for the first time in over twelve cycles, peace.

He stretched into his memories, and they blended into a familiar nightmare. He'd been bound to an interrogation chair, and there had been an Elantian magician. An Alloy, his arms stacked with cuffs of the different metals he could channel. The Alloy had pointed metal needles at him.

Then he'd stabbed the blade into Zen's heart, right into where the core of his demon rested. Into the center of the Seal.

He could remember Dé'zǐ Sealing the demon's power away as though it had happened just yesterday: the incense of the Chamber of a Hundred Healings, the blood red as poppies against its floorboards, Dilaya's screams faded to muffled sobs, and then silence. The golden light of Dé'zǐ's qì had revealed deep lines etched around his mouth and furrows in his brow as he weaved.

"This Seal shall command the demon to lie in slumber, yet can be broken through should your life be in danger," the grandmaster had said quietly. "But as Master Gyasho has taught you, all Seals, including this one, remain only as strong as your will to hold it in place. It is but a single layer of protection against the influence of your demon. The foundation of it, Zen, rests in the will of your heart."

The memory faded.

Zen clapped a hand to his breast and heard the pings of

metal falling into the sand next to him. He turned his head to look. Four needles and a blade, all bloodied. He dimly remembered the magician sliding those needles into his veins. That blade into his chest.

And then he saw his hand. The sky was silvering, the bleached light of a faraway dawn casting his skin in a sickly pale pallor. Skin that was now smooth. Unmarked.

He began to tremble as the pieces of a dream came back to him: Erascius pushing the blade into his chest, pain exploding through his bones like fire. Then: kneeling on the stone floor, the oppressive tang of metal crushing in from all around, the power of his demon cut loose inside him, the Seal giving way as Zen began to die. His mind had split, he'd felt the powerful qì of his demon wrap around the wound in his chest and begin to heal it. He'd gazed into the eclipse-like eyes of his demon and known no more.

". . . Zen?"

He flinched and sat up so quickly that his head spun. Huddled beneath a willow farther back on the banks of the river was Lan. Her face was drawn, her eyes large as she watched him, arms wrapped around her knees.

Relief crashed into him, and he almost lay back down on the sand. Alive—she was alive. "Lan," he croaked, and began to turn toward her.

She drew back.

He froze. She was looking at him with fear written plainly on her face—and the worst part was that he recognized it. Had seen it, more than once before.

"Lan." He struggled to keep his voice even. "What . . . happened? Please. I cannot . . . I cannot remember."

She shifted her arm, and that was when he realized that the cherry blossom patterns on her páo were actually splatters of blood. "How do you not remember?" she whispered, and the accusation in her voice hurt more than any blade. The last time someone had spoken these words to him, it was Shàn'jūn, kneeling on the floor of the Chamber of a Hundred Healings, clutching a bleeding, eleven-cycles-old Yeshin Noro Dilaya.

Dread clamped his throat shut so that he could barely breathe. His hands—his clean, unscarred hands—shook as he pressed them to his face.

Lan had been the only person in his life to not know of his past, and he had wanted to keep it that way. She'd trusted him, and he'd held on to her trust like a drowning man to air. He'd liked the way she looked at him, gaze clear of the prejudices that clouded that of others at Skies' End.

He'd liked living in a lie with her.

"They're dead," she blurted, her voice rasping, "all of them. You brought down the entire Elantian outpost."

Flashes of memories: a sky licked with orange flames, a garden of flowers with dewdrops on the leaves, clear and red.

Why is the dew red? he'd thought, and then he'd looked down at Nightfire, stained crimson. The darkness had rushed back to him, slipping into his veins like the intoxicating pull of a drug. He'd given himself back over to the demon's control again, because the realization of what it had done—what *he'd* done—was too painful to bear.

He'd slaughtered his way through the Elantian outpost. He'd killed all the soldiers.

And, along with them, the Hin they'd kept as prisoners.

"Your demon." Lan's voice grounded him to the present, the pine forest and shores and rushing river before them. He barely remembered using the last of the demon's power to conjure the Gate Seal to transport them away from the outpost. "Where is it?"

"Gone." The word scraped against his throat. A word he'd never thought he would speak for a bargain gone awry. Days after he'd bound the power of He With Eyes of Blood to him, Zen had set out for the Heavenly Capital, intending to destroy the Imperial Army that had ended the last of his clan.

Little did he know, he would arrive at the beginning of the Elantian Conquest, the collapse of the Imperial Court, and the fall of the mighty Last Kingdom. That he would be captured and studied, and his demon would lie in wait for twelve cycles, its payment unfulfilled.

Until last night.

There was the sound of sandals scraping against sand, the hiss of her páo as she stood. *Leave,* Zen wanted to beg her. *You would not wish to see me like this.*

Instead, her footsteps drew closer. He felt a brush of cold fabric against his hand.

Zen looked up. Those familiar eyes, as inquisitive as a sparrow's, searched his face. "You made a bargain with a demon," Lan said. Simple, as though she'd said, *You bought sweet potatoes at the market today.*

He closed his eyes. Nodded.

"So you ended your bargain? You made the payment?" She kept her voice soft.

Zen nodded again, reaching for that newfound emptiness inside him where the darkness of the demonic being had lain coiled for over twelve cycles.

Tonight, He With Eyes of Blood had saved Zen's life—and taken its payment by consuming one hundred souls at the Elantian outpost.

"That's good," Lan continued, and he heard movement, the slosh of water, then felt the cold press of wet cloth against his forehead. When he opened his eyes, she sat cross-legged before him, dabbing his face with the sleeve of her páo. It came away red. "We're safe now. Just rest, and—"

"Stop." His voice cracked. He reached up and shoved her arm away from his face. Her touch threatened to unmoor him; the gentleness to her tone was the furthest from anything he deserved. "Are you not afraid?"

She pressed her lips together for a moment. "I was, back there," she confessed. "But not anymore, I don't think."

"Why not? I am a demonic practitioner. I lost control over one of those creatures. I could have killed you."

She tipped her head, narrowing her eyes as she searched his face.

"But you didn't," she said. Her fingers still pressed against his face between the fabric of her páo, and he held very still, afraid one move would drive away her touch. "You're Zen. You saved my life, many times over. You taught me practitioning, you gave me the chance to fight back. I was afraid of your demon but never of you."

Her words broke something inside him. "Do you know what my bargain with that demon was?" He had no idea why he kept speaking. Perhaps it was the cycles of being told that he was a monster, of being equated with the demon bound inside him for most of his life. Perhaps it was the need to expose his sins, to prove himself unworthy of her forgiveness. "I found it one cycle after my entire family was killed, when I was seven cycles old. I swore that if it gave me power, I would give it anything in return. You know what it asked for?" He could hear that distorted voice even now, filling the blue skies with invisible clouds and making the yellow grasses tremble. "It asked me for a hundred lives. A hundred souls to feed it, the blood of a hundred bodies to quench its thirst. It carved our agreement into my hands: one scar for each soul I owed it." He looked up at her at last. "Does that not terrify you? That a child seven cycles old could make such a bargain without a second thought?"

Something flickered on her face—something like recognition, before her expression cleared. "When the Elantians killed my mother," Lan said, "I would have done anything in that moment. I would have given my soul to save her, brought down the Heavenly Capital for her life. I don't think you did anything unusual at all. You were given shit choices, and you made the best of it."

"I killed over a hundred people." The words burst from him in a choked sob. "Most of them innocent. No matter what you say, there is *no excuse* for that, Lan."

"Your *demon* killed them," she said. "That's the difference, isn't it?"

A memory surfaced. Standing at the bottom of the stone steps that led out of the dungeons, blood trailing him instead of chains. He remembered Nightfire feeling so heavy in his hands, his qì suddenly grown weak. In the darkness of the cells behind him, he could sense the yīn energies of desperation and death. His demon had stopped to drink it all in.

Light had spilled from the doors at the top of the steps, casting a figure in shadow. Erascius had turned to Zen, and he hadn't missed the glint of the magician's cold blue eyes. The man had been smiling.

"I remember you now," he'd said in his long, rolling language, the one that brought back memories of another interrogation chamber, a long table, from twelve cycles back. "You were the boy with a demonic binding we brought in during the first year of Conquest. You taught me that demons could be bound to serve."

Zen had staggered forward, but his mind had filled with flashes of hunger and bloodlust—the demon's, not his own.

With a guttural growl, He With Eyes of Blood surged forward in a swirl of black smoke. A flash of metal, and a copper light had risen to meet the darkness. Zen had watched, with a familiar feeling of horror, as the smoke of his demon was quelled by a shield bright as the sun. He felt faint spikes of pain wherever the demon's qì touched the metal magic.

Erascius's laugh rang out in the dark. "You taught me much twelve cycles ago, including how to subdue demonic power. Had I recognized you earlier, those soldiers in the chamber behind you might not have died—nor those poor innocent Hin in the cells next to you."

Zen's anger flared scorching white inside him. His demon snarled. It had condensed into a thicker mass of shadows, something four-legged and as large as a camel—the form it had taken that day in the snow when Zen had first bound it. It paced before Erascius's golden shield, eyes flashing crimson.

"You cannot control it, can you?" Erascius's voice was soft, delighted. "You are so terrified of losing control that you have let it lie dormant within you your entire life." His teeth gleamed as he smiled, leaning forward so that the shadows and light split his face in half. "If I had that much power, I wouldn't waste my time attempting to repress it. If I were you, I would *master* it. But that is where you Hin fail, is it not? My colleagues would believe it is the inferior nature of your race, but I think otherwise. I think that what destroyed the Hin civilization was the principle of *balance* that you so cherish. *Zhōng Yōng Zhī Dào*—Doctrine of the Mean. I have read your classics and learned your philosophies, and I can tell you this: if you forever adhere to the path between two extremes, then you will end up with nothing."

And then the magician had slipped into the shadows, and the shadows had found Zen's mind as his demon took over again.

"He's alive." The words were sharp, jumbled, cutting Zen's throat as he spoke now. "Erascius is alive."

Lan looked pale. "How?" she whispered.

"When the Elantians captured me and . . . studied me, he was there. He learned then how to fight and restrain a demon." Zen touched a finger to his chest, where the knife wound had been healed by his demon. "Even so, he wasn't aware of the Seal Dé'zǐ had put on the—my—demon. That its powers would remain dormant unless my life was under threat. Erascius didn't realize that trying to kill me would, instead, save my life."

But at what cost? whispered a voice in his mind. Zen thought of the Hin prisoners lying in the dungeons, their blood coloring Nightfire, their souls feeding his demon.

A new question burned into existence. If he'd had complete command over his demon, would he then have been able to destroy the Elantian outpost and save the Hin?

He could still hear the magician's wicked laugh in the dark. *If I were you, I would* master *it.*

Abruptly, he stood, aware of how much his bones ached and his qì flickered, ashes of the fire that had gone out when his bargain with his demon ended. No matter how much he wished to deny it, the qì of the demon's core had embellished Zen's own and given him strength over the cycles of their co-existence. It had been no coincidence that he'd risen quickly in the ranks of disciples at the school. The power of a demon, even one fettered by a Seal, inevitably strengthened a practitioner.

He examined their surroundings. He recognized the great river winding past them: the Coiled Dragon, or the Endless Blue, as his people had called it, beginning from the ice mountains of the Northern Steppes and winding through the Shǔ Basinlands all the way to the Central Plains. Its waters ran pale aquamarine from the minerals trapped in the melted ice. He followed its path until it became a wisp of blue that threaded into the mountain ranges in the distance.

He had brought Lan here with a Gate Seal. After He With Eyes of Blood had ravaged the outpost, it had relinquished its grip on Zen's mind and begun to fade, the bargain tethering its core to his dissolved. With the last of its power, Zen had conjured a Gate Seal to a place his instincts deemed safe. This river lay a few hours' travel from the Yuèlù Mountains, in which Skies' End hid. In the first cycles of his arrival at Skies' End, he remembered running down all nine hundred ninety-nine steps, and through the night, to this river—the one that connected him to his homeland in the north. A homeland that no longer existed.

If I were you, I would master *it.*

If his father had learned to master demonic practitioning instead of turning away from it, would his people have survived? He still remembered the army, flying banners of the Luminous Dragon Emperor, setting his home on fire. How far away they'd looked at first, a gleam of scales winding through the flat, frozen plateaus of the Northern Steppes. There had been a terrible beauty to the uniformity of this army wrought in red and gold.

Gold, for the fire and destruction they'd wrought.

Red, for the blood they'd shed.

And then, one cycle later: Tiān'jīng, the Heavenly Capital, burning. Flames devouring the pointed, gray-tiled roofs. Shot directly from the hands of pale-skinned monsters who wore metal bands around their arms and the colors silver and blue.

Silver, for the metal they wielded.

Blue, for the skies they ruled.

Zen closed his eyes, but the images remained seared into his mind. All this destruction, all this death—because he *hadn't* had power. Because he'd been trained to be afraid of it instead of to command it.

"Zen." He heard Lan's voice as though from very far away. When he opened his eyes, she stood before him, outlined against a breaking dawn. "We should move. If Erascius is still alive, doesn't that mean his tracking spell is still in my arm? He could still find us."

His focus sharpened. "May I?"

She held her arm out for him. The metal had somehow spread up to her elbow, bubbling up from her veins to the surface of her skin.

Gently, he pressed his fingers to the metalwork. She winced. His mind was already forming the Seal to cover it, yet when he reached for the strands of qì around them, he found that he could barely summon any. It swirled at his fingertips and dissipated.

He tried again, but something inside him had cracked with the slaughter and the demon's departure.

"Forgiveness." Nausea swirled in his stomach as he set her arm down. "I seem to have pushed myself too far today."

Standing amidst the rushing river and the silent, mist-filled forests, a new feeling found him. It took him a few moments to realize what it was: helplessness. It was something he hadn't tasted in twelve cycles, for even in the most life-threatening of situations, he'd known that there was a backup, a way out. That if his hand was forced, he had one last card to play.

As much as he'd tried to fight it, he'd come to rely on the power of the demon coiled inside him.

He had nothing now—no qì to perform a Seal against the tracking spell, to shield Lan from the pain of the metalwork, even to create a Gate Seal back to Skies' End.

Nothing to fight with. Nothing to defend himself with.

And no power to protect those he loved.

Worse, the Elantians were closing in on the Central Plains, on the school, on the last wisp of hope Zen had held for the Hin to take back their kingdom and regain their freedom.

You were given shit choices, Lan had said, and she was right. The choice to adhere to the path of good, to practice the Way of balance, was a luxury. Zen had devoted the past eleven cycles to following it, and it had led to this day. To this moment. A hundred dead at his hands, and still not enough to quell the terrible power of the Elantians.

The entirety of this kingdom's history had been written in the same choices.

Kill, or be killed.

Conquer, or be conquered.

His soul was already tainted—had been the moment he'd made the bargain with his demon. There was no further use in trying to be good, in pretending he could ever be a devout disciple of the Way when his history and bloodline had been anything but.

If you forever adhere to the path between two extremes, then you will end up with nothing.

"That's all right," Lan said softly, tearing him from his train of thought. "We'll go back to Skies' End. Master Nóng was supposed to have returned; he and Master Ulara will extract the metalwork. And we'll . . . we'll tell them about everything."

Back to Skies' End. He thought of the first night he'd set foot in the school all those cycles ago, of the masters' looks of revulsion when they realized what he was and what he held within him. Of how the other disciples had kept their distance from him after the incident in the Chamber of a Hundred Healings. How their stares and whispers had followed him.

His gaze drifted to his smooth, unscarred hands. What

would the masters say once they realized what he had done—that he had lost control of the demon bound to him and indiscriminately slaughtered both Elantians and Hin civilians?

"If we tell them, they will forbid us from leaving Skies' End again," he said quietly. "They will confiscate your ocarina, and they will subject me to the ferule and isolation."

Lan's fingers tightened around the smooth black surface of the ocarina. Zen realized she'd had it hidden inside her sleeves this entire time.

"My mother left me the maps to the Demon Gods for a reason," she said. "I won't let anyone take them from me. I need to understand . . . I need to understand what she wants me to do with them."

"And now the Elantians have seen the maps, too," Zen added tonelessly, careful not to give any indication of what he was thinking. It was important, right now, that she reach the conclusion herself.

"Erascius is alive. And what he has been searching for all these cycles . . . what he killed my mother for . . . it was all in here," Lan said, her eyes lifting to his with horror. "He's been looking for the Demon Gods all along, Zen."

"He told me that if he had the power of a demon, he would seek to master it, not fetter it. The Elantians wish to command the power of the Four Demon Gods. You saw what my lesser demon alone could do. Now imagine the sheer power four legendary beings might possess." His voice was low. "The Elantians would be unstoppable."

"We can't let them find the Demon Gods," she whispered.

He looked to the distant mountains, to the waking sky.

"No," Zen agreed. "Which means we must find them first."

23

A practitioner's duty is to choose to defend
rather than attack, to protect rather than harm,
and to seek peace rather than war.

—Dào'zǐ, *Book of the Way (Classic of
Virtues)*, 3.4

The first time Lan arrived at Skies' End, it emerged like a
dream: curved temple roofs threading between jagged
mountains dotted with green pines. Buildings that belonged
to the past, that had somehow defied time.

Now time was running out.

It was late afternoon, the sun sinking into the west with
red finality. They had spent the day traveling back using the
Light Arts, stopping to rest when they grew tired. Zen had
been reticent, his face pale and drawn, his eyes darting to his
hands every so often.

The Boundary Seal seemed uncharacteristically quiet
as they passed through it; even ascending the nine hundred
ninety-nine steps felt quick. They came across the Chamber of
Waterfall Thoughts first, where the Master of Texts was holding a session with the younger disciples. At the sight of Zen
and Lan, the blood drained from Master Nán's face; he stam-
mered for a disciple to supervise the class and then rushed the
two to the Chamber of a Hundred Healings.

Master Nóng had returned; Lan would now be able to undergo the operation to have the Elantian metalwork in her arm properly removed. The Master of Medicine, a serene man with a white beard and long, bushy brows, instructed her to lie down on the kàng bed and handed her a bowl of bitter broth. As the sedative began to take effect, she heard Master Nóng tell Zen that only he and his attendants could remain in the chamber. Lan wanted to reach out, to ask Zen to stay with her, but her tongue had grown heavy and her eyelids were drooping. Zen's face loomed out of the darkness until he, too, swirled into shadows, her name on his lips fading into smoke.

When she awoke again, it was deep in the night. A soft paper lamp burned on the cabinet by her kàng, casting shadows against the fretwork windows. Someone had draped a blanket over her.

Lan looked at her left arm, and that was when she registered the source of her pain. It looked as though someone had cleaved open jagged strips of her flesh, then stitched them back together. Salve glistened on her skin, mingling with blood. In the midst of it all, though, was the pale scar of her mother's Seal.

She touched her fingers to it, relieved. With the intrusive metalwork in her arm gone, she found, her head was clearer and her senses were more at peace than they had been in a long time. She closed her eyes and tuned in to the strands of qì flowing around her like the vivid colors of a brushstroke—of *music*.

That music was everywhere: in the guttering of the candle flame, the sough of wind against the pines, the gurgle of pond water outside and the sigh of air inside the chamber. It flowed past her and all around her, strings of melodies she could reach out and touch, call out to.

Light footsteps, and a familiar face appeared, its edges

softened by the flickering lamplight. She found that if she concentrated, she could almost *hear* his qì: the gentle trickle of river water, the clear chime of a bell, the clink of a spoon against a porcelain bowl.

Shàn'jūn sat by her kàng. He raised a bowl to her face. "Drink this," he said softly. "It will lessen the pain."

With his help, she sat up and took the bowl from him. It was pungently bitter, but she detected no scent of the sedative he'd given her earlier. The hot broth burned all the way down to her stomach. "Come to greet me with your worm soup again?" she said with a crooked smile.

Shàn'jūn returned it, but she could sense there was something wrong. "Always."

As the clarity to her thoughts returned, so did her memories. "Shàn'jūn," she said. "When I arrived, I had with me an instrument of sorts. An ocarina, with a carving of a lotus on it. Have you seen it?"

He set the bowl down on her bedside cabinet, then took out a roll of gauze from his hemp satchel and began to wrap her arm with the careful precision he always applied to his tasks. "Worry not, Lan'mèi. Zen entrusted it to me for safekeeping. As a disciple of Medicine, however, I must ask that you prioritize your rest—"

"I feel *completely* revitalized after your worm soup."

Shàn'jūn sighed. "Well, it seems the extraction has not cost you your wits," he muttered, then reached into the folds of his sleeves and passed Lan the ocarina.

Her fingers wrapped around its smooth clay surface as though it were a lifeline. Miraculously, the instrument had survived the battle without sustaining any damage besides a light layer of mud. Lan polished it until the inlaid mother-of-pearl lotus shone like bone.

"The masters are all wondering what happened," Shàn'jūn

said quietly, his eyes fixed on the instrument. "When you and Zen were found to be missing, they all thought . . ." He lowered his eyes. "They thought he had done something to you."

Lan's head snapped up. *Zen.* He'd been with her in this chamber right before her extraction began.

"Where is he?" she asked, and when Shàn'jūn was silent, she asked again, louder: "Where is Zen?"

"With Master Ulara," came a voice, and Tai stepped into the Chamber of a Hundred Healings, ducking slightly to fit beneath the doorframe. His gold-rimmed eyes glinted as he turned to them, his gaze pinned on the ocarina in her hands. "I heard it. I heard the souls in that thing."

"What do you mean, 'with Master Ulara'?" Lan demanded.

"Lan'mèi, please," Shàn'jūn said, reaching for her uninjured hand. "You must not upset your qì—"

"He is being interrogated," Tai said steadily, "in the Chamber of Clarity. Perhaps with the ferule."

"The ferule," she repeated numbly. Zen had mentioned the ferule, and she had no idea what it meant—yet she did know that if Ulara was involved, it did not bode well. Lan remembered the way the Master of Swords had looked at Zen with murder in her eyes. "Why is he being interrogated?"

"Lan'mèi, do you have any idea what happened?" Shàn'jūn asked quietly.

"Unless your worm soup has the effect of memory loss, I'm perfectly clear—"

"Then you would know that Zen broke the single condition of his discipleship at the School of the White Pines." Shàn'jūn's face was shadowed with sadness. "He used his demon's power, which he swore never to do. The two of you were steeped in demonic qì upon your return."

"He had no choice! We were captured by soldiers—we saw the Elantian Central Outpost—" Words tumbled from her lips, scattered and fragmented even as she pulled her thoughts together. Lan looked between Shàn'jūn and Tai, both of whose expressions were grim. "Where is the grandmaster? I'll tell him exactly what happened."

"It is not up to the grandmaster," Shàn'jūn said. "The formal process of an inquiry has been enacted. This means that after Zen has taken the ferule for breaching the Code of Conduct, it will be up to the jury of masters to vote on whether he may remain in the School of the White Pines . . . and whether he is to receive harsher punishment."

"*Harsher* punishment? He saved our *lives!*"

"It is forbidden," Tai said. "Demonic practitioning. The consequence by imperial law was death."

"And there is *reason,*" Shàn'jūn added, catching her expression. "Demonic practitioners were prone to losing control and allowing a demon to control their bodies. Oftentimes, the consequences were far worse than the benefits. Remember the Nightslayer . . ."

This had all gone horribly wrong. Zen had gone with *her* because she'd needed to go to Guarded Mountain—and now *he* was the one being punished. Worse, though, was that they had found the ocarina her mother had left her and unlocked the star maps inside it . . . star maps that led to the Four Demon Gods . . . star maps that the Winter Magician had seen and stolen.

And now Erascius planned to find the Demon Gods and invade the Central Plains. Whatever rules Zen had broken were nothing compared with what would happen if they didn't stop Erascius.

"Take me to the ferule," Lan said. "I'll tell Ulara myself—"

"No. *No,*" Tai said at the same time as Shàn'jūn said, "Your blood pressure, Lan'mèi—"

"I don't care about my blood pressure!" Lan yelled. "Zen

did this to save our lives. If anyone should be punished, it's me. We were there because *I* asked to go! And we found the ocarina my mother left me, Shàn'jūn. It holds star maps to—" She drew a breath, stopping herself short. Zen had warned her that the masters would forbid them to leave the school if they knew just what they planned.

What if, as much as she liked Shàn'jūn, her friend felt the same way?

Shàn'jūn and Tai exchanged glances. The Medicine disciple sighed. "Lan'mèi, nothing you do will help now. Yeshin Noro Ulara has long been awaiting her chance to make the case to have Zen banished from the school. She holds seniority in position at the school due to her clan bloodline, which gives her immense sway over the others. And there is not even anything you *can* do. Zen is under an inquiry, the strictest form of trial under the Code of Conduct." He hesitated. "Not to mention, they are waiting to begin yours after you awaken. I have pleaded for them to grant you a day's rest. So please, let us not stir up any more trouble, lest you are expelled from the school."

"Expelled?" Shàn'jūn raised a placating hand as Lan's voice rose again. She ignored him, gesturing wildly. "The Elantians are planning an invasion! If we wait any longer, there may not *be* a school for me to be expelled *from!*"

"Please, Lan'mèi," Shàn'jūn said. "I believe you, truly. And I overheard Zen explaining this to the masters earlier. I am certain he will present this at the inquiry." He pressed cool fingers to her hand, squeezing gently. "If we plan our moves right, we may yet save the school *and* save Zen. Ulara is hot-tempered, yet she is not without reason."

"Stay," Tai urged suddenly. "You must stay. Barging into Zen's inquiry will only add fuel to Ulara's flames."

Lan's chest was tight; she focused on steadying her rapid

breaths. They had no idea, no idea, about anything that had happened the previous night, had not seen the Elantian outpost built on the backs of Hin prisoners. They knew not what Erascius was capable of, what he planned to do—

Her head pounded with such thoughts, yet all that she could whisper was "Why does she hate him so?"

Tai folded his arms and gave Shàn'jūn a significant look. The latter nodded. When the Medicine disciple turned back to Lan, his expression was unusually grave. "When Zen first arrived at the School of the White Pines, his demon was unfettered. It controlled him more than he controlled it. The grandmaster convinced everyone to give him a chance. He believed that teaching him the Way at this school would save him. But in Zen's second year, there was an accident." He lowered his gaze and, through his long lashes, swept a look around the chamber. "It happened right here. There were three of us, playfighting, and I believe the other disciple wrestled with him too hard. Zen lost control and nearly killed the other disciple."

The story made sense of all that she had come to learn of Zen in the past few weeks. His rigid adherence to the principles of the Way. His status at the school, powerful and revered yet feared. The guilt with which he spoke of demonic practitioning.

Last night, history had repeated itself.

But he is free of the demon now, Lan thought, yet the image of his pale, unmarred hands flashed in her mind's eye. Zen had been released from his bargain with the demon—at a huge cost.

"Who was the other disciple?" she asked quietly. "The one he almost killed?"

Tai's gaze shuttered. Shàn'jūn drew a deep breath.

"Yeshin Noro Dilaya," he said. "Zen's demon took an arm and an eye from her before the grandmaster stopped it."

Dilaya. Yeshin Noro Dilaya, with her eye patch and empty right sleeve.

Lan closed her eyes. It all made sense now—the Yeshin Noros' previously unexplained hatred for Zen, their fear of demonic practitioning. Would they listen to him if he spoke the truth, of the Elantians' outpost and their plans to invade the Central Plains in search of the Demon Gods? Would they forgive him long enough to work together to stop their common enemy, or would they yield to their hatred?

She thought of the destruction Zen had wrought. An entire squadron of Elantian soldiers and so many Hin prisoners, all fallen at his hands.

At his *demon's* hands, she corrected herself.

You saw what my lesser demon alone could do. There had been a terrible emptiness in Zen's eyes as he'd spoken those words. *Now imagine the sheer power four legendary beings might possess.*

Erascius had seen the star maps; he had an idea of where the Four Demon Gods were located. If they found the Demon Gods, the Central Plains—including the School of the White Pines—would fall into their hands, whatever little hope remained for the Hin to regain their freedom destroyed.

If she could not help Zen right now, there was one other thing she could do.

Lan's knuckles were white as she gripped the ocarina and turned to Shàn'jūn. "I need your help," she said, and then looked to Tai as well. "And yours."

The Medicine disciple nodded with grim determination; the Spirit Summoner threw her a look of confusion.

"I need to know more about the Demon Gods."

Shàn'jūn almost dropped the bowl of broth he had picked up anew in an attempt to feed her. *"Pardon?"*

So Lan began at the very start, telling them of how her mother's Seal had given her a vision that led her to Guarded

Mountain and to the ocarina. Of how Erascius had pursued her, how the Elantians had caught them at the School of Guarded Fists. How she'd played the ocarina and unlocked the star maps to the Demon Gods. By the time she finished, Shàn'jūn was wide-eyed; Tai's jaw had gone completely slack.

"But half of the Demon Gods have been lost for dynasties," Shàn'jūn said. "The Black Tortoise disappeared with the Nightslayer. And"—he shot Tai a covert look—"the Imperial Court lost its hold over the Crimson Phoenix when the Elantians invaded."

Tai said nothing.

"How is it that your mother would hold the maps to them?" Shàn'jūn continued. "And even if the maps are accurate, what did your mother intend for you to do once the gods are found?"

Lan realized that she had no answers to Shàn'jūn's questions. "All that matters is that we reach them before the Elantians do," she said. "When I played this ocarina, the Elantian Royal Magician saw the star maps and preserved them. He survived Zen's demon, and now he plans to use the Demon Gods to conquer the rest of the kingdom."

"How did you know how to play that?" Tai pointed at the ocarina.

"I grew up with music," Lan replied. "I think . . . I think my mother had the ability to fight with song."

Tai's eyes never left her. The gold rings within them seemed to glimmer. "And you," he said. "Do you?"

She hesitated. "I'm not sure. I was able to hold off the magician with my mother's song. But I don't know if that was the power of this ocarina . . . or if it was me. And sometimes . . . sometimes I feel like I can hear music in qì. Like the different strands of energies are notes for me to play." She hadn't had the chance to speak to Zen about her using the ocarina to attack Erascius in the interrogation chamber, so focused had they been on the subject of the Demon Gods and Zen's demon. "Is that not an art of practitioning?" she asked.

"It is," Tai said quietly. "It *was*. It died. With the clans."

They looked at each other for a heartbeat. Gingerly, Lan held out the ocarina. "There must be imprints of my mother's soul left within this. There may be answers, if you would read it."

Before Tai could respond, the wooden doors to the Chamber of a Hundred Healings slammed open.

"Answers that'll be used as evidence in your inquiry," a new voice said.

Yeshin Noro Dilaya's mouth was set in a grim line, her steel-gray eye ablaze with triumph as she raised Wolf's Fang and pointed its curved edge at them.

"Out of my way, Herb Eater and Ghost Boy," she said with relish, and tipped her chin. "Try anything and I'll have you reported as well, for this is hardly the first time I've caught you conspiring. You were to bring her to the Chamber of Clarity as soon as she woke."

"False accusations are against Code of Conduct rule fifty-three," Lan said, "so I'd get my facts straight before I run to Mommy again. The handprint on your left cheek has barely faded since the last time she slapped you."

"Oh, I think I have my facts perfectly straight this time," Dilaya said nastily. "Seeking out the Demon Gods? I wouldn't have expected less of a power-hungry little fox spirit, but for two esteemed disciples of the school to tag along . . . well."

"Please, Dilaya shī'jiě, there has been a misunderstanding," Shàn'jūn said, raising his hands, but Dilaya only raised her dāo higher.

"I think not," she said, and her gaze landed on the ocarina.

"So. You've found the instrument your mother left you. The one her imprint said . . . what was it she said? 'To save our kingdom.' "

"It's an ocarina, you turtle-egged pig-arse," Lan snapped.

That did nothing to erase Dilaya's smirk. "Ocarina or not, I'll be taking it."

Lan switched tack. Regardless of their feelings for each other, she had to believe she and Dilaya were on the same side when it came to the Elantians. "Dilaya," she said, smoothing her voice to be placating, "please, listen to me. The Elantians are searching for the Demon Gods to use their power to invade the Central Plains and destroy the school. We must stop them."

"Oh? Curious that Zen missed this part of the tale in his inquiry," Dilaya snapped.

"You—you went? To the inquiry," Tai blurted, but Lan's mind had frozen. Zen hadn't told the masters of Erascius's plan to find the Demon Gods—the most important new discovery of their trip?

"My mother requested me as an assistant," Dilaya replied haughtily. "They are ready to adjourn for the day, but I left early to check on this little fox spirit in case she was up to something. And lo and behold."

Her words kicked Lan's brain into motion again. If Zen hadn't told the masters, there must be a reason.

She needed to see Zen. She needed to speak to him.

The ocarina seemed to pulse in her hand. She thought of the song it had seemed to play out of *her,* that had woven the illusion of the star maps and the Demon Gods shimmering in their four colors over their heads. Then she thought of the song she had played against Erascius.

Her mother's song.

Lan glanced at Tai. *Did* she have the ability to fight with song, as she suspected her mother had? There was only one way to find out.

Lan held up the ocarina. "You want this?" she called to Dilaya. "Then come get it."

With that, she raised the ocarina to her lips and blew.

Do-do-sol.

The first notes crested across the chamber like a gale, stirring sheets of paper and whipping the flames of the lamp into a frenzy. Time seemed to slow as Dilaya charged, Wolf's Fang curving through the air. As Lan played the next chords of song, the notes whipped past Dilaya like invisible throwing knives, stirring up the sleeves of her páo and splitting against her blade with audible *twangs*.

Lan closed her eyes and played the next notes—except this time, she altered them slightly. It was the subtlest shift, yet as she blew, she could sense the song shifting, the qì wrapping around it differently, comprising different components . . . almost as though she were drawing a Seal.

Do . . . sol-do.

The riff caught Dilaya: a jab on her neck, the exact spot Lan had seen Erascius hit on Zen's neck. The girl stumbled, her lips parting in shock as her body gave way to paralysis. She crumpled on the floor, her sword clanging at her side.

Shàn'jūn knelt, his face pale as he beheld the unconscious disciple of Swords. Slowly, he raised his gaze to Lan. "What was that?" he whispered, and she saw his eyes flick to the ocarina in her hands. "What did you do?"

She wished she had an explanation for him. She wished she could explain any of the events that had arisen since the night in Haak'gong. Since she'd chosen to go down this path, to follow the ghost of her mother's song.

"I don't know," Lan replied. "Forgiveness, Shàn'jūn."

She turned toward the door.

Fingers latched onto her wrist: warm and long, their grip tight. When she glanced back, she saw that it wasn't Shàn'jūn but Tai who held her. A lock of his tousled hair had fallen into his eyes; half his face was shrouded in shadows, half in the flickering light of the lamp.

"Your mother," he said quietly. "Was she a member of a clan?"

She had no idea how to answer that—no idea how the question was even relevant in this moment.

She was running out of time.

"Ask her ghost, if you so wish to know," Lan replied. "Let me go."

To her surprise, Tai stepped back, his arm falling to his side—but his eyes did not leave her.

"I know" was all he said. "I know now."

She feared that if she remained any longer, she would not leave. Lan turned and, clutching her ocarina, ran into the night.

24

A practitioner requires not only devotion of the
body but that of the mind and soul. An obedient
body with a traitorous mind is self-deception.

—Dào'zǐ, *Book of the Way (Classic of
Virtues)*, 1.6

Zen had been in the Chamber of Clarity twice before in
his life: once when he had first arrived at Skies' End, and
the second time when he had stood trial after his demon had
maimed Yeshin Noro Dilaya. Both times, the grandmaster
had saved him by appealing to the other masters, saying that
he could still be taught, his aberrant ways rectified, when he
learned the principles of the Way.

Now Dé'zǐ was silent. The chamber was dark and made
completely of stone, with carvings of the Hin pantheon of
gods and demons watching from the cornices. There were no
windows; the only light came from several paper lamps. Zen
knelt before all the masters of the School of the White Pines.
A dull pain throbbed in his back, where the ferule had left red
welts across his skin.

Dé'zǐ had long declared the ferule an antiquated method
of punishment. *Pain and cruelty can be borne by those with a will
strong enough,* he'd once said, his words ringing with finality in
this chamber. *It is the mind we must heed more.*

You were right, shī'fu, Zen thought. *Pain is only flesh-deep. My scars I bear on my soul.*

Ulara had taken pleasure in chaining his hands to the iron pole, binding him so he could barely move. Zen did not mind. He would have taken the ferule in silence either way.

It was a small price to be paid for what he had done, and what he was about to do. If the masters caught wind that he meant to hunt down the Demon Gods, banishment from Skies' End would be one of the kinder punishments.

"Well, that's it?" squawked Fēng'shí, the Master of Geomancy. He leaned back, a hemp pouch slung across his chest bearing turtle shells, bones, and a pipe he put out only in the presence of Dé'zĭ. Geomancy—the interpretation of fate according to stars and bones—had been Zen's worst subject as a disciple, and the master, though unpredictable and impartial to all but his own strange whims, bore Zen no fondness. He'd claimed to have seen the evil incarnate in Zen's soul; he'd read of Zen's deviation from the Way in the stars. "You've nothin' else to your story than how the Elantians tracked you and that girl down and you destroyed their outpost?"

"I would say that's plenty, Master Fēng," said Ip'fong, the master of Iron Fists. Large, lumbering, and essentially two hundred jīn of pure muscle, he was one for more action and fewer words. "The Elantians are preparing to launch their long-overdue invasion into the Central Plains. We have been lucky to evade their scouts throughout the cycles, but our Boundary Seal will not stand against a full army."

"Yet all this begs the question," said the Nameless Master of Assassins, his voice like smoke in a starless night, "of what these disciples were doing outside Skies' End in the first place."

"Have I not stated clearly enough?" Zen asked, his chains clinking as he raised his head to look around the chamber at the masters. "We searched for the ghost of her mother. I agreed to take the girl in hopes of giving her closure on the matter. It was affecting her studies."

"And you knew that was wrong," the Master of Texts said loudly. "You know better than to go against the Code of Conduct, Zen."

He had nothing to say to that.

"The boy lies." Ulara spoke at last. She stood a little to the side, outside the ring of lamplight. Her face was cast in shadow, but Zen could make out the gleam in her eyes. Both her dāo were strapped to her hips, the edge of light catching on the blade of Falcon's Claw. "Dilaya stumbled upon them one night. They spoke of searching for an ocarina."

"Nostalgia," Zen said coldly. Earlier that night, on the way to the Chamber of Clarity, he'd made sure to comb through every detail of his story, examining it for holes and incongruities. He had not forgotten Dilaya's intrusion at the bookhouse several nights ago—nor Shàn'jūn's and Tai's involvement. He would need to seek them out later. "The girl's mother would play the ocarina to her when she was young," he explained. "Surely Master Ulara would have higher aspirations than to make up evidence out of childish desires?"

He could not see Ulara's expression from here, but this time, another voice spoke up.

"An ocarina?" The flames steeped into Dé'zǐ's face as he leaned forward, deepening every wrinkle and sharpening the edges of his cheekbones. He suddenly looked older. Zen met his master's eyes and fought not to look away. The disappointment in Dé'zǐ's gaze was difficult to bear.

"Yes, shī'fù," Zen said, uncertain as to why his master had latched onto that small detail. "I told her we had other, more common instruments at the school she could play, yet no ocarina."

Dé'zǐ looked at Zen for several moments longer before leaning back again. Zen caught the flicker of something worse than disappointment in his master's expression. He seemed . . . *troubled.*

"The incense has burned to its end," Master Gyasho said into the silence. He gestured at the brass pot that hung from an alcove on the stone wall; nothing remained of the joss sticks but three blackened stumps. "A bell has passed, and it grows late. Let us reconvene to discuss the concerning news of an Elantian invasion, and leave Zen to physical rest and spiritual reflection."

Dé'zǐ looked to Ulara. "Dilaya will alert us as soon as Lan awakens?" he asked. Ulara nodded, and the grandmaster stood. "Very well. Let us reconvene in the Chamber of Waterfall Thoughts."

As the masters slowly filed out, Dé'zǐ approached where Zen knelt.

"There was no necessity for the ferule had you simply repented," the grandmaster said quietly.

"There was," Zen replied. "The masters would never have listened to a word I said otherwise. Their minds are already made up about me, shī'fù."

Dé'zǐ looked sad. "But the ferule will not save you either, Zen. It prompts you toward neither truth nor the Way." He raised a hand and touched it to Zen's temple. For a moment, Zen found himself leaning into his master's touch, the way he had as a child. "If the mind is made, physical pain will not deter it."

Zen jerked away.

"Tell me, Zen," the grandmaster said quietly. "Is there nothing more to the story of the ocarina?"

Zen's lips parted. Dé'zǐ's gaze was straight, clear as a blade, piercing to the very recesses of Zen's soul. Seeing, as he had when Zen was a child, the parts no one else had, the shadows and scars hidden away from the world.

Once, he might have knelt at his master's feet and begged for forgiveness. He might have told Dé'zǐ of the Demon Gods, of his plan to stop the Elantians from taking them for themselves.

Yet now, Zen realized, no matter how hard Dé'zǐ had tried to save him, Zen could not run from his fate—the one that had been written in the stars of a young child who'd lost everything on the frozen Northern Steppes of the Last Kingdom. His soul had been forsaken since the day he'd chosen to accept the demon's bargain; his story could have had only one ending, one that Dé'zǐ could not rewrite no matter how hard he tried.

"No, shī'fù." It was surprisingly easy for him to keep his tone even. "There isn't."

Dé'zǐ drew back. Shadows obscured his expression. "Very well, then," he said softly, and turned away. "I will leave you to your reflection and repentance for the evening. May you somehow find clarity and the path back to the Way."

The lamps flickered as he passed them on his way out, a slip of pale páo against the dark until the night swallowed him whole.

Zen loosed a breath, the tension flowing from his muscles. They would be sore from being bound, but that was the least of his concerns. He needed to somehow get a message to Lan so that when she woke and came for her inquiry, she would tell the same story as he had.

And the Demon Gods . . . he thought of Erascius's relentless blue eyes, of the promise within. It was only a miracle that Lan had unknowingly kept the Demon Gods' location a secret, her mother's message Sealed away within her until several weeks ago. Whoever her mother was, she had thought this through carefully.

I remember you, the magician had said. *You were the boy with the demonic binding we brought in during the First Year of Conquest.*

Zen shut his eyes as he reached back into his memories. That interrogation chamber, the long table with the metal utensils, the people with the pale faces watching as they hurt him over and over again to elicit a response from his demon. He imagined Erascius's face among them, the gleam in his winter's eyes brighter than that of the rest.

You taught me that demons could be bound to serve.

It was Zen's fault. It was Zen's fault that the Elantians had made progress into their understanding of demons and demonic practitioning; it was Zen's fault that they now suspected the existence of the School of the White Pines, of Skies' End and the disciples and masters hidden within, a last-standing Hin relic that had survived the trials of time and conquest against all odds.

If I were you, I would master it.

If the Elantians found the Demon Gods, they would be unstoppable. Any hopes the Hin harbored of taking back their freedom would be snuffed out, a candle in a gale.

His soul was forfeit, and there was only one last thing he had to do: stop the Elantians from taking the Demon Gods.

The rustle of leaves, the snap of a branch, the scuff of a sole against stone. Zen's eyes flew open just as the doors to the Chamber of Clarity shut with an insidious creak and the lamps extinguished. He could sense the other presence in the room, her qì cutting hard and sharp with the tang of steel swords.

Ulara.

She stepped in front of him, parting the darkness like a blade. The edge of her dāo pressed cold against his neck. "I have always thought the school too bureaucratic and fond of rules." Her voice was low, clinical. "My clan delivered justice with as much swiftness as we did death."

Zen held very still. Despite the cold, a trickle of sweat wound down his temple. His binds, secured by Ulara herself, held tight.

"I know you and that little fox spirit are planning something," Ulara continued. " 'Hear the song of the ocarina and follow its power?' One cannot change the nature of one's soul, nor the history written into one's blood. You may be able to fool Dé'zǐ, but I have always seen you for what you are, *Temurezen*."

It had been a long time since he'd heard his truename. The sound of it had always inflicted a combination of guilt, grief, and fury inside him, which was why he'd taken a moniker.

But now Zen found that he no longer cared.

"History has always clouded your judgment, Ulara," he replied. The blade bit into his skin; one breath drawn too deep, one slip of Ulara's finger, and his neck would be sliced open. "But in this case, perhaps you have struck wrong yet hit right about me. I care not for the state of my soul, nor do I care any longer to follow the Way. My father and my family attempted that—yet they ended up dead anyway. If I can sacrifice my soul to serve the greater good, is that not a worthwhile trade? The mistake the Nightslayer made was that he gave his soul yet never attempted to command his Demon God. Had he mastered its powers and been able to control it instead of letting it overpower him, our history would have become a different tale."

"You—" Ulara's eyes widened as the realization hit. Her hand gave a sudden tremor and Zen felt her blade split skin, felt a warm trickle down his neck. "You cannot possibly be planning to find the Demon Gods." She searched his face, and whatever she found lent horror to hers. "No. Has history taught you nothing? After all these cycles, have *we* taught you nothing?"

"You all punished me for something I did in an attempt to avenge my family; you all cared more for your petty rules and superstitious fears than for what our true focus should be: to defeat the Elantians and to reclaim our kingdom." Finally, anger that had long cooled in his heart flowed out like molten lava. "You and I are meant to be on the same side, Ulara. The enemy of my enemy is my friend—yet you have never treated me as such. All I have ever wanted was to fight with you and the other masters against our common enemy."

He could no longer see Ulara's face, but her blade caught the dredges of a lowlight as she angled it slightly. "We were never on the same side," she replied quietly. "Perhaps we could have worked to drive the Elantians out and save the Last Kingdom, but whatever world comes after that cannot hold us both. I should have done this long ago. Forgive me that I could not take a child's life all those cycles back. Now that we stand as equals, I will have no qualms about taking yours."

Cold gripped him. He tested his hands, but they were tightly bound, his fú papers out of reach. "Ulara—"

"I am sorry, Zen," she said, and she might have truly meant it. "Understand that I do this for the safety of what remains of our people. One life for the greater good—may the gods look kindly upon you. Peace be upon your soul, and may you find the Path home."

A cold wind gusted as the moon spilled out from between the clouds, Falcon's Claw glinting in the light. Sometime during their conversation, the doors behind them had slid open, shrouding the room in a dusting of white—broken by a small black shadow.

Music rang out, only it wasn't simply music. Zen felt the

notes cleave the air like a Seal, the qì gathering and sharpening around the sound in a vortex. He had seen this, just the night before, through a haze of pain.

Ulara never even had time to react. As the notes hit her, her back arched and her lips parted in a silent cry of surprise.

Without another sound, she fell, Falcon's Claw clattering to her side.

"That's an acupunctural point, but hit it hard enough and you'll cut out your opponent's qì," Lan said shakily. "Seems I did learn a few things here."

Zen exhaled. "Lan."

She was by his side in an instant. Her left arm was wrapped in gauze, but she raised the ocarina to her lips with her right hand and blew.

As two notes sounded, quick and staccato, the qì around them shifted. Something sheared through the air past both of Zen's ears, and then he felt jerks of impact on his chains. With faint _clinks_, they dropped to the ground, cut clean through at the cuffs on his wrists.

Zen fell forward, his arms searing with pain. He felt Lan's fingers on his face, cool against his feverish skin. He hadn't realized just how weak his body was until this moment. One thought pierced through the haze in his mind, and he felt the corners of his lips curl. "You came for me."

"Don't be a stupid egg," she replied. "Of course I did. I'm not hunting down those Demon Gods by myself."

His smile stretched; he couldn't help himself. Perhaps it was the pain that had made him slightly delirious. "With your current fighting abilities, you might be of some use as demon fodder."

"I changed my mind. Perhaps I'll leave you here after all."

"No." In a single motion, he wrapped an arm around Lan's

waist. Her familiar scent of lilies enveloped him as she turned to him. "I need you."

Gently, she took his other arm and slung it over her shoulders, then drew them both to their feet. He straightened, wincing as the wounds on his back burned. His páo hung over his shoulders in tatters. In the olden days, a student punished by the ferule was not issued a new outfit for several days; walking around a school or town with ragged clothing marked one as having committed a severe violation against the morals of one's school.

"You are certain," he said, his breath ragged at the exertion, "about this? Once we go . . . there is no turning back." He needed to know—he could not live with the guilt of destroying the small piece of shelter she had found. "Where we go, there will be no safety. No guarantees."

"There was never any safety or guarantee," she replied. "Not in a world like this. So long as the Elantians exist, there never will be. The masters have been in Skies' End so long, they have forgotten what life looks like for those of us on the outside." She shook her head. "Skies' End feels like a world of the past. And that's what it will become unless we can stop the Elantians. I fully intend to fight for what's left of our people and our kingdom."

The night was starless as they fled the Chamber of Clarity, their footfalls hidden by the murmur of wind through pines that had risen on the mountaintop. At this hour, disciples would have long been in bed, and Zen knew that the masters were congregated in the Chamber of Waterfall Thoughts.

As they reached the steps down the mountain, Zen paused. He glanced back at Skies' End, taking in the rugged mountains that reached for the sky, the pale temples nestled within like gems against a sleeping dragon. In several hours, the waking bell would ring clear and bright, cutting through sleepy tendrils of mist; disciples would awaken for their morning chores, Taub would begin cooking in the refectory, and the masters would emerge for their morning classes.

Zen turned his back on the place that had been his home for the past eleven cycles. When he and Lan reached the bottom of the nine hundred ninety-nine steps and crossed through the Boundary Seal, Lan turned to him.

He hesitated. They needed to perform a Gate Seal to put any form of distance between them and Skies' End . . . only he did not have the strength.

Shame, along with the hateful feeling of helplessness, wrapped a chokehold around him. Had his demon still been bound to him, he would never have become so weak from a single flogging.

But instead of waiting for him, Lan announced, "I'll do the Gate Seal."

This drove away his other thoughts. Zen frowned at her. "You cannot have learned it."

He caught the white flash of her eyes rolling. "I've watched you do it about fifty times."

Impossible. No—*improbable*. He thought of her ocarina, of the Seal on her wrist. Of how she held the star maps, the secrets to the Demon Gods. How bright her qì flowed, how she had fought Erascius with nothing but a musical instrument.

He closed the distance between them. His shoulders throbbed slightly as he reached to brush the hair back from her face, as though the answers might be written there, in her eyes.

Who are you?

"Hold on," Lan said, and lifted the ocarina to her lips. Song flowed from her, and Zen again felt the qì in each note, threading together as the melody interlaced and interweaved.

Around them, the landscape began to shimmer. As Lan closed her eyes to concentrate on wherever she was taking them, Zen cast a last glance back at Skies' End.

Then darkness swept in like a tide, washing away his home as though it had never existed.

25

And the Old Matchmaker of the Moon said
to the lovers, "This red thread I bestow upon
you. It may stretch and it may tangle, but it
will never break. Across cycles and worlds and
lifetimes, your souls are now destined."

—"The Red Threads of Fate," *Hin*
Village Folktales: A Collection

They came upon the village near the break of dawn. It emerged like a miracle in the rain, silhouettes of clay-tiled roofs curving gently upward at the ends. Ditches of muddy water formed in fields of crops carved into the mountainsides. An old wooden pái'fāng announced a rain-soaked welcome to the Village of Bright Moon Pond.

The fifth door they knocked on opened. The white-haired woman accepted a copper wén from Zen's storage pouch as payment for food and lodging and led them to an empty room across the yard. The paper on the windows was torn in some places, but the room was habitable, with a single kàng bed and a pile of old cotton blankets. The cold drafts leaking through the doors and walls stirred the candle that Lan lit, sending shadows dancing frenetically around the room.

As the landlady went to heat water for them, Zen sank against the walls with a grateful groan. Lan threw open the windows. Their room overlooked a steep cliff and an unbroken expanse of undulating mountains. Far in the distance, beyond the storm clouds, the sky had begun to catch fire with the light of the sun. The singing of village children herding water buffalo threaded through the mountains.

She breathed in deeply, savoring the *drip drip drip* of rain from gray-tiled roofs, the view of a land free of Elantians, free from conquest.

"I didn't know there were still unoccupied villages," she said softly. "In the early days of the Conquest, almost every village I ran to had signs of Elantian invasion." Metal plaques bearing their strange, horizontal language nailed to pái'fāngs; road and street names for the larger towns and cities changed to incorporate the names of the Elantian king and queen.

"Because they were along the coast, were they not?" Zen's voice was barely above a sigh. She turned and caught him looking out the window. The sunrise beyond the storm reflected in his eyes. "Much of the central Last Kingdom remains free of the Elantians' grasp. It is mostly empty and undeveloped compared with the power of the eastern coastline, but it is all that we have left."

All that we have left. It was difficult to reconcile the tranquility of a rain-drenched mountain shrouded in fog and cloud with the violence of the Elantian invasion; it felt as though she was trying to bring two utterly different worlds together.

The landlady returned with a wooden bucket, two tin kettles of hot water, and a bamboo basket of steamed mántou buns. Lan tucked into hers while she washed up as much as she could before turning to Zen.

He had fallen asleep against the wall. A sliver of his chest, pale and corded, showed through his torn páo, rising and falling gently with each breath. His jaw cut a sharp line, his brows knitted under strands of his wet hair even as he slumbered.

Lan brought the bucket and kettle over to him. Rinsing off

the rag she had been using, she dipped it in the steaming water and pressed it to his face.

His hand snapped over her wrist with startling speed; she cried out at the sudden pain. His eyes were open, and for a moment, she imagined she saw black filling the whites again. Then he blinked, and the sharpness to his expression softened. He let her go as though he'd been burned.

"Forgiveness." His voice was husky with exhaustion. "Habit."

"Well, you should have known I wasn't going to attack you," Lan said, raising the hot water kettle to pour more water into the bucket. "This isn't a teapot."

Through the steam rising gently between them, she caught his smile. Warmth rushed through her, and not only from the water.

"Your back," she said, trying to maintain nonchalance. "Let me clean it for you."

Zen's smile flickered, along with something else in his eyes. They were suddenly so close, so dark.

He seemed to realize he was staring at her. Clearing his throat, he turned and began to shrug off the tatters of his páo.

Lan drew a sharp breath. Two angry red welts cut down from his shoulder blades to his waist—yet that wasn't all. Beneath, the flesh was riddled with scar tissue, pale and shining.

Lan leaned close, dabbing at the fresh wounds as carefully as she could. She had been around plenty of men, had flirted with them boldly for a tip of one or two extra wén, yet none of that had made her this nervous. Blood rushed to her face, she hardly dared breathe, and her heart was pulsing against her rib cage so hard that she was certain Zen could hear.

"These scars," she said, and brushed the tip of her finger against a particularly long one by his spine. "Do they have a better story than the others?"

He tensed slightly beneath her touch. "No," Zen said. "Those were also from the Elantian interrogators." She regretted asking, but he went on: "They tortured me for information on demonic binding. The way it works is . . . once a demon makes a bargain with you, its interests become aligned with you. It will do anything to keep you alive in order to ensure that it receives its end of the bargain. And so . . . I couldn't die, no matter how much I wished it."

There was no emotion to his tone, yet she somehow found that more difficult to bear. Gently, she traced the towel down his wound again. She could think of nothing else to say but "Why do demons enter into bargains with practitioners?"

"In most cases, to strengthen their power," Zen answered. "As demons are formed out of malevolent pools of yīn, there is always the danger that that energy will weaken and disintegrate and return to the flow of the qì in the greater universe over time. The demons' vitality is strengthened by death, destruction, and decay—which is why most stories speak of demons' ravaging villages and killing its inhabitants. Some have realized that entering into a bargain with a human is the easier way."

The blood was gone, the wound cleaned, but Lan continued to trace gentle strokes on Zen's skin. "And did the child making the bargain with the demon at seven cycles of age have any idea of all this?"

Zen held very still. When he spoke at last, she felt his voice thrum in his chest beneath her fingertips. "Yes. But he had lost everything—his family, his home, and his world. He thought acquiring a demon's power could help him exact revenge upon those who had taken it all from him." A pause. "He was a fool."

The water sloshed as Lan wrung it from the towel. "He was a child."

"And how would a girl without any prior knowledge of practitioning be able to wield qì through a musical instrument?"

Zen had turned to face her, and his gaze was startling, arresting. *Imperial,* she thought, remembering the first impression she'd had of him. She had been accustomed to the sleazy, wine-blurred glances of the patrons of the Teahouse that were so easy to slip between. Yet when Zen looked at someone, he truly *looked,* as though nothing else existed in his world at that moment.

Lan found herself leaning forward. Heart in her mouth, she pressed the cloth to his cheek, wiping away blood from a cut. His eyes fluttered, but they did not leave her face. "My mother," she said, the confession unfurling from her in a whisper. "The day the Elantians invaded our courtyard house, she fended them off with nothing but a woodlute. I didn't understand it at the time, but I think . . . I think she was practitioning with music."

Zen drew a breath, and she watched the crease between his brows smooth as his eyes filled with some understanding she was not privy to. "You should know that practitioning through music is no regular feat."

"I know. Tai told me."

"Did he tell you anything else?"

She could not look away from his gaze. "He asked if my mother was a member of a clan. I said I did not know."

"Practitioning through song is a lost art. I have come across mentions of it in the texts I have studied, yet the historical records remain few and far between. The Imperial Court did a thorough job when they wished to bury information." The disdain in Zen's expression softened with his next words. "Most lost arts of practitioning originated from the clans. Many faded to obscurity throughout the Middle Kingdom, when clans began to hide their bloodlines in efforts to escape the court's crackdown."

She stared at him as he spoke, but her mind was far away, flipping through the same memory like the pages of a book. Her mother, snow falling, music slaying, blood spraying.

"Clans are—were—held in such high regard," Zen continued. "The arts of practitioning unique to each could be passed down only through their bloodlines. This is why they were either killed or brought to the Imperial Court to serve during the Last Kingdom."

I know, Tai had said to her right before she'd left. *I know now.* Of course—he'd recognized it because he had belonged to a clan. Because he'd been brought up in the Imperial Court.

Was that what he'd been about to tell her?

"My mother." The words forced themselves from Lan's lips. "She served the Imperial Court."

Suddenly, a memory found her: one she hadn't understood before, that she'd filed away only because it was a puzzle she could not yet figure out. She'd been in the study copying works of the famous poet Xiù Fǔ when her mother had entered, dressed in that beautiful, powerful Imperial Court hàn'fú. Lan had shot up, the horsetail brush dropping from her hands as she ran to embrace her.

When I grow up, I'll serve the Imperial Court just like you, Māma, she'd said happily.

Her mother's smile had vanished. She'd pried Lan's hands from her waist and bent, eyes quickly sweeping the empty study. *No, Lián'ér, you will not,* Sòng Méi had said quietly. *When you grow up, you must serve the people.*

"Lan," Zen said, his voice pulling her back to the present. He was still watching her, water clinging in beaded drops to his black hair, his long lashes, his corded chest. His gaze finished his question: *Do you understand now?*

She squeezed her eyes shut. The answer had lain before her all along.

Māma had been part of a clan—something Lan had believed to be the antagonistic force in all the history books she had read, all the tales she'd heard from the lips of townsfolk and villagers. In all the stories, the Dragon Emperor, Yán'lóng, had been the hero in gold-plated armor, the sun haloing his head as he slayed the rebelling clans, uniting the land and bringing peace and prosperity to the people.

But not all the people. He had sacrificed the freedom and will of the minority, made them puppets in his own court, in order to bring the illusion of harmony.

"Lan," Zen repeated, and she felt his fingers wrap around hers, firm but gentle. Heat bloomed where his skin grazed hers. "Lan, look at me."

She did, and the recognition in his eyes felt like coming home: a longing and grief for a part of her history and her identity that she had never known. The air between them had thickened, and for some reason her blood roared in her ears and her heart tumbled in her chest.

Without breaking their gaze, he reached into his black silk pouch. When he unfurled his palm, she almost stopped breathing.

He held a tassel strung with black and red beads, at the end of which rested a silver amulet carved with black flames. A red cord extended from it, meant to be tied into a necklace.

"This is one of the few relics I have left of my homeland," Zen said, "along with Nightfire and That Which Cuts Stars. It was meant to be a set of earrings, but the other was lost—so I fashioned a necklace out of it. In my clan, it is tradition for us to receive one set of silver earrings at birth, meant to be given away one day."

In my clan. Her breath caught; she remembered Taub's

words, that most Hin had clan bloodlines somewhere in their ancestries. Most had merely forgotten their own histories as the Imperial Court sought to rewrite it—but not Zen, it seemed.

"Well." Lan's lips curved, and she took on a teasing tone, meaning to break the sudden heaviness between them. "Since you have only one of the pair left, you had better choose carefully."

Zen's eyes flickered. Gently, he took her hand and turned it so that her palm faced up. Then, carefully, he slipped his other palm over hers. The amulet felt cool as his rough fingers pressed it against her skin. "I want you to have it," Zen said, "to remember that you are not alone. That you have lost so much, but I . . . I am glad to have found you."

Her heart was unsteady; she might have been drunk on plumwine. She looked into Zen's face, open with earnestness and a vulnerability she had never before seen in him, and in this moment, all the trials and tribulations she had gone through to get here might have been worth it.

Lan lowered her gaze. The red cord of the necklace had somehow gotten caught over their fingers; it draped over both of their interlocked hands, seeming to bind them together. She thought of what Ying had told her of the red threads of fate, of how each Hin was born into this world with an invisible red cord tying them to their destiny.

"Is that all?" she asked. "You wish for me to feel less alone?"

He hesitated, and she could see the conflict on his face, emotions warring with the guard he always put up. Then, without warning, all the layers of defensiveness and distance in his eyes thawed. In that moment, he spoke the words that utterly surrendered himself. "I wish for you to not go anywhere without me. In this world and the next. I wish for you to choose me." A pause, and softer: "That is, if you would wish it."

The Teahouse had taught Lan to dread the affections of men; she had listened to enough wistful stories from the older songgirls and glimpsed ample passages of novels to know that it was only an illusion. Greasy, grasping hands, leering gazes, and the exchange of girls for coin were all that her world had shown her. Being chosen had always been something to dread—and there was never a choice in return.

Lan thought of how safe she felt with Zen, how gentle he was with her. How his presence could light up her world and speed up her heart, and how she had come to gravitate toward him like the moon to the sun. Of how his touch reached through the layers of imperfection and tragedy this life had conferred upon her and reminded her of hope.

Of how she trusted him.

All the terrible stories and unwanted memories peeled away from her, and she found within herself an instinct, guiding her like a lodestone.

She pressed his hand with the necklace back to him. "Would you put it on me?" she asked.

Disbelief, followed by relief and a rush of joy, colored Zen's expression. He leaned in. She heard the hitch of his breath as she swept her hair to bare the nape of her neck. Closing her eyes, she held still and tried not to imagine the greedy touch of the patrons back at the Teahouse.

She felt the cord slide over her throat, the amulet coming to rest, cold, on her breastbone. When the tip of his finger grazed her skin, she started, yet the nausea she had dreaded did not come. Instead, she felt something new. Heat bloomed low in her belly, and desire flamed through her blood.

She dared to open her eyes and found his face inches from hers, his pupils dilated. He smelled of mountain wind and rain and smoke, the scent invoking in her a sense of belonging.

It felt natural for her to tip her head and press her lips to his.

Even the dim lighting could not hide the surprise in his expression. It gave way to something dark and heady that set her on fire as he drew her to him. Slowly, softly, with hesitation, fingers barely touching her waist as though afraid she might break. Afraid, she understood, that his kiss might conjure memories of what songgirls were made to endure at the hands of Elantians.

Lan reached up and ran a hand through the silky fall of his hair, rain-wet. The taste of him—sharp smoke and starless nights, quiet sorrow and tender hope—washed away the memories of cycles at the Teahouse. Tonight, she was but a girl, being touched by a boy for the first time in her life.

Gently, he drew back. His mouth was soft as he pressed it to her forehead, her left cheek, then her right. His hand came up to cup the back of her head as he pulled her to him. And that was all he did: he simply held her, arms wrapped over her back, their hearts beating the same rhythm in the silence broken only by the whisper of rain outside.

It was in that moment she knew—knew he understood her, more than anyone left alive in this world, and knew that she craved, more than anything, to *be* understood in a way that none had for the past twelve cycles. Not the kind aunties in the villages she'd wandered through, not the songgirls at the Teahouse, not Old Wei, not even Ying . . . she had given parts of herself and her past to them, yet she had kept hidden so much more that she herself had not even known at the time.

She was one of the last living practitioners in a conquered kingdom. Daughter of a woman who hid secrets within secrets, a family long gone. And now, the last of her clan's bloodline, with the ability to wield qì through song.

It wasn't until she felt Zen's thumb tracing her cheeks that she realized she was crying—out of the cycles of pent-up grief, the relief of knowing a part of who she was, and the joy of having found someone who *understood*. Looking into Zen's eyes felt like coming home, like gazing into a reflection of her own face.

Zen pulled her down onto the kàng. She tensed as he reached for her, but he only brushed a hand down the side of her jaw. His eyes were quiet black pools, and tonight was the first time she thought she saw through them: past the wall of ice or the raging flames. Tonight, there was tranquility in Zen's gaze, the shimmer of something that might have been joy as he beheld her, drinking her in.

They remained like that, lying side by side, gazing at each other and marveling at the small miracle of two lives having crossed, two souls having found each other in this vast world. The paper windows were thrown open to the vast sprawl of mountains and gray skies and the *pat pat pat* of rain, but in this moment, their worlds might have just held each other.

26

We divide the night sky ecliptic into four regions, each
governed by one of Four Demon Gods. Much like a
reflection of earth, the skies, too, abide by the laws of
yīn and yáng, as evidenced in the wax and wane of the
moon and the endless cycle of days and nights.

—Gautama Siddha, Introduction, *Imperial
Treatise on Astrology*

Red, blue, silver, black: the Demon Gods hovered in the illusory pieces of night sky superimposed over the real one
against the slatted ceiling of their temporary abode, the light
outlining them shifting like the glow of spirit lights up north
in the steppes during the winter moons. Zen's father had told
him those lights were the qì of warrior souls that watched over
their people.

The most curious revelation had found him upon closer
observation of the star maps, one that he hadn't spotted back
in the Elantian outpost: two of the quadrants appeared blank
but for the shapes of the Demon Gods themselves, glittering
like fragments of colored stardust. Star maps were pieces of
the night sky charted from an exact location at an exact time,
and while the other two had the shapes of the Demon Gods
superimposed against a sky with stars, the Azure Tiger and the
Silver Dragon simply existed on a canvas of black nothingness.

"Maybe Māma never found out where the other two

were," Lan had suggested when he'd mentioned this to her. "Or maybe they've been destroyed."

There was no destroying a Demon God, as far as Zen knew, but he said nothing. Instead, he had begun with the other two viable star maps.

Even with their work cut in half, mapping out just one took time. Needing the dark, they slept during the day and woke at sunset to the shouts and song of the village children coming home from tilling the fields carved into the mountainsides. There were only a handful of children, yet their winding songs in the sweet southern Hin dialect breathed life into an otherwise barren village. Conquest was strange, Zen thought. There were the realities of Haak'gong and Tiān'jīng and the other big cities, stamped all over with Elantian markings—and yet there existed Skies' End and this tiny village, little pockets of refuge that had escaped the heavy hand of invasion.

For now.

The music stopped; the star maps vanished. Lan flopped down on the kàng with a sigh, ocarina in hand. "This is the first and last time I'll ever wish that the rotten egg Master of Geomancy were here with us."

It was their third night in the Village of Bright Moon Pond, and their second working on cracking the star maps. Zen had learned some of this back at the school under the tutelage—if it could be called that—of Master Fēng. Zen had thought star maps useless back then, an outdated method of mapping, for who needed to map the night sky when he could map the earth and the solid ground beneath his feet?

He regretted that now.

Zen looked up from the parchment he crouched over, where he'd been transcribing what he saw in the illusions Lan conjured. Beyond their open window, the sun had vanished beneath the mountain; the sky breathed brilliant shades of orange and coral. The children would be home soon, singing their songs; candles would be lit, and the village would eventually fall into a slumber steeped in lonely silence.

"You must keep playing," Zen said, "or I cannot transcribe the star maps."

"Let me rest a few minutes." Lan yawned, and then her eyes took on a playful glint. "You want to try playing, and I'll draw?"

Zen sighed, but he couldn't help the smile curving his mouth. "You mock me."

"Never. I daren't."

"If I let you transcribe, our search would bring us to the other side of the world."

Lan poked her tongue out. "And if I let you play, the entire village's ears would fall off."

Zen lifted the sheet of parchment to survey his work. They'd had to beg the landlady for writing utensils, and she'd had to scour the entire village before finding a set of old tomes and yellowed parchments a traveling merchant had left behind. There was not much use for writing these days.

He was close to seeing some semblance of a location mapped out by the four shapes in the star maps. Once upon a time, with an entire library at his disposal, this would have been quick work; Hin astronomers had mapped out the changing night skies many dynasties ago, exchanging ideas and collaborating with the scholars of the neighboring Kingdom of Endhira, along the Jade Trail.

Now those records had been turned to ashes, burned by the Elantians when they seized all the great libraries of the Last Kingdom.

The thought of the Elantians closing in drove Zen's gaze back to his parchment. His head was beginning to swim. Worse than having to transcribe the star maps was the fact that they had been given no key to interpret them. Star maps were meant to have been dated and timed to note the precise hour, moon, and cycle of stars they captured; Hin astronomers had long understood that the night sky shifted with the seasons, some sections disappearing for moons before resurfacing again. This great cycle, however, reset itself every twelve moons: the same stars could be seen in the exact same location and formation at the exact hour every cycle.

Without the date and time of their maps, finding the location of the Demon Gods across a night sky strewn with pearly stars was akin to searching for a shape among the sands of the ocean.

Zen lifted his tired eyes to the window, glancing out at the true night sky, clear as a bowl of ink tonight. That was when he saw it.

Zen took the sheet of parchment he'd been staring at and flipped it. Held it up to the sky framed in the window.

His breath caught.

One of the two viable pieces of the star maps was beginning to match what he saw outside.

The Black Tortoise.

The name twisted in him like a dagger. Of all the Four they might have found first, it had to be this one: the god inextricably intertwined with the name and deeds of the Nightslayer.

He looked at the other quadrants he'd transcribed. The Azure Tiger and the Silver Dragon were still hopelessly blank, no matter how many ways Lan tried to coax stars into them with her songs. The only other readable one, the Crimson Phoenix's star map, hadn't yet matched any part of the night sky they'd been observing.

Zen returned to the Black Tortoise, driving every other thought from his mind but for the puzzle at hand. Here and there, the map curved a little, some stars more spread out than others, meaning that they saw it from a location slightly off. Slightly southwest.

This meant that the Black Tortoise lay northeast of them.

Dread clotted thick in his chest, beginning to work its way up to his throat even as he did the calculations. It would take several hours only, should he go by the Light Arts—or within reachable distance by Gate Seal.

The candle in their room flickered as a sudden cold wind blew in from the open window.

"Zen?" Lan came to crouch next to him, and he could not help but look at the way the lambent light draped soft over her outline, the shine to her eyes as she looked at the maps, then to him. His eyes trailed from her mouth to the crook of her neck where the red cord of his necklace hung, the silver amulet pressed into the curve of her chest. "What are you looking at?" she asked.

He shut his eyes briefly, hating that he could not drive the thought of her from his mind. Since when had he become so painfully aware of her presence, every move or shift or tilt of her head, the way she looped her hair behind her ears or chewed on her lip when she was thinking?

For the past eleven cycles, Zen had lived a life of austere self-discipline, following every rule and holding on to every principle he could find, convinced that doing so would pull his soul back from the abyss, would erase the demon he had hidden inside himself and the terrible bargain he had made once upon a winter sky.

Now he had broken all the Code rules, run away from school and the man who had saved him. Kissed a girl without a marriage vow—a breach of one of the most longstanding traditions of Hin society.

It is not just our bodies and flesh that must complement the Way—but our minds as well.

He finally understood what Dé'zǐ had meant by those words. For all that Zen could attempt to follow the rules of the Way and the codes outlined in the classics, there was still the part of his mind that rebelled no matter how hard he attempted to smother it. The rules had only been chains to hold him in place—a kind of self-assurance that he was working toward the good, the balance—but beneath, the person he was had never changed.

The Elantian outpost had broken something inside him, or perhaps set something inside him free. The shackles he'd put in place over himself were beginning to crumble.

He felt fingers slide over his. His eyes flew open, to see Lan looking at him, her face open and tender.

"Nothing," he said, and summoned a smile as he touched the tip of her nose. "I'm looking at you."

She broke into a smile. "You look so grave when you think," she said, and reached forward, poking her index and middle fingers to either corner of his mouth, pulling it wide. "*Smile, Zen.*"

He reached up and cupped his hand over hers, unfurling her closed fingers so that her hand splayed against his face. Closing his eyes, he sighed and pressed his mouth to her palm just as the candle burned out.

He would wish for this night to never end. For them to live in this moment infinitely, instead of the long cycles that stretched ahead of them—whatever those might bring. In all the cycles of his life he had spent fighting himself and the world, it was the little moments with Lan in which he felt as though he could breathe again. As though he'd finally walked out of that long winter night into a clear spring day.

She shifted, leaning against him, and kissed him, her familiar scent of lilies wrapping around him. Zen gave in this time, hating himself as he drew her against him, his hands remaining chaste against her back yet wanting more, always more.

He did not wish to find the Demon Gods.

He did not wish to fight the Elantians.

He did not wish to think of the school, the masters, of what might happen to them.

All he wanted in this moment was to stay in this little village in the mountains with the girl he'd fallen for and sit by a window of rain, watching her hair grow white as snow with time.

It was a desire that could be little more than a fantasy, not the reality they had been born into: the reality of Elantian rule closing its grasp tighter and tighter over the Hins' necks.

The Hin had a saying: *Speak of the demon and the demon comes.* Zen had never paid it heed—had never paid any silly superstitions any mind—but now he froze as a voice threaded through the evening.

"An army! There is an army!"

The voice was clear and bright, the same one that sang the songs of tilling fields and herding water buffalo each evening. Zen drew back, and he found his expression reflected in Lan's: the jarring realization of one waking from a dream.

They hurried out of their room, across the courtyard, their urgent steps scattering the feeding chickens. On the street, doors were being thrown open, villagers poking their heads out, faces frightened and curious at once. Their expressions mirrored those of the children, who had stopped nearby and were reporting their finds with a shine in their eyes.

"—wearing silver and blue—"

"—they looked like a *river*, Auntie!—"

"Where?" Zen grasped the nearest child, a boy about eight cycles old, his hair patchy from having been shaved off by his mother for convenience. "Where were they?"

The child gave him a frightened look. Lan smacked Zen's hand away; she turned to the child and beamed. "You saw an army of foreign devils!" she exclaimed, employing the term the Hin used to refer to the Elantians. "Are they near?"

"They were walking the mountain pass," the boy replied, pleased at her attention. He pointed to the north, where the sky had settled into a dark indigo and the mountains were no more than silhouettes. "That way."

Cold clutched Zen's stomach. *Northeast,* he thought, and the image of his star map came to him. Lan had told him Erascius had cast those star maps in metalwork magic back at the outpost; with the Elantians' superior resources, it wasn't impossible that they had already tracked down the location.

"Smart boy," he heard Lan say, pinching the child's cheek.

The boy looked up at Lan in half fascination, half fear: the expression of a child who did not yet understand the horrors this world could afford. At eight cycles old, he would have grown up post-Conquest, his life confined to this small village, knowing nothing of the outside world. Where once traveling merchants might have roamed the Last Kingdom, peddling wares and trading stories across the land, and imperial messengers might have arrived on horseback to collect taxes and bring news of the outside world, those lines of communication had long gone cold in the era of the Elantian Conquest.

"Jiě'jie," he said, "Older Sister, what will they do if they come here?"

Lan's smile widened as she brushed a smidge of dirt from the child's cheek. "Nothing, because those stupid eggs won't get here," she replied. "Jiě'jie will protect you."

"Is jiě'jie a powerful fairy?" the child asked.

Lan winked and pressed a finger to her lips, yet the smile slipped from her face as she turned and stepped back into their landlady's courtyard. The fall of night was almost complete;

the dying sun cast her face in shadows. "What do we do if they come for the villagers?" she said quietly.

They won't, Zen thought. *The village means nothing to them. They are headed northeast, to the location of the first Demon God.*

Of course Lan would think of the lives of the villagers first while Zen—Zen thought of himself and his goals.

He was saved from answering Lan by the sound of the courtyard door closing. They turned to find the old landlady of the house watching them.

"You are those, are you not?" she asked, her voice thin as a drift of smoke, and Zen did not need to hear her next words to know what she meant. *"Practitioners."*

Something in him tightened. The landlady was old—much older than the Elantian Conquest, yet still not old enough to have known the days when the warriors and heroes walked the rivers and lakes of the First and Middle Kingdoms, fighting evil and protecting the people.

"No need to say," she said. "My family was once saved by one of you from a demon. That practitioner had no wish to disclose what they were, but I knew. There is an *air* to you that is different." A shadow crossed her face. "Now, my husband and my son are dead in the war we lost to the foreigners. Only this village remains unchanged. I have long felt we have been waiting . . . for what, I did not know. Now I do."

The landlady knelt. The motion jarred Zen; he rose at the same time as Lan, both of them seizing the elbows of their elder.

"Grandmother, don't—!"

"Please, grandmother—"

"Save the children, I am begging you," the landlady whispered.

Zen looked to Lan. Where his expression would be carefully controlled and reined in as always, her face changed with her moods like a summer sky. Heartbreak glinted in her eyes, along with the sparks of a new resolve. As they helped the landlady back to her feet, he saw Lan grip her ocarina, hand fisting around it.

"Năi'nai," she said. "Grandmother. Leave it to us. Go inside."

The old woman's plea remained with Zen long after she'd slid her frail wooden door shut. He and Lan returned to their room and stood, side by side, before the open window. By now, utter darkness had fallen, and the air had quieted with a terrible stillness. The moon shone bright and clear, yet Zen could sense a shift in the qì around them pressing down like an encroaching storm cloud. And then, as he tuned his senses to the weave and weft of energies in the air, he found a dark, solid mass razing through the gentle streams of qì in the mountains and forests around.

Metal.

Elantians.

A river, the child had said, and Zen understood now as he observed the movement of the metallic mass, cutting through the qì. An army—and not just the scouting squad he'd fought off at the outpost. A real, sprawling army. Erascius had not only survived; he had returned with ten times as many forces. Zen closed his eyes, feeling the world swim around him.

He had traded an outpost for the wrath of the Elantian Empire.

And now he had no demon to fight with.

"We have to protect the village," he heard Lan say, a slight tremor to her voice. "We still have time. We can hold them off while the villagers run—"

"They will never outrun the Elantian army." Zen felt hollow as he spoke. The words seemed to be pulled from someone else's throat as he watched from far away.

"Then, what? Leave them to their deaths? We are *practitioners*, Zen. Even I know the stories—we were given this power to protect those without. Remember?" She seized him by the front of his shirt—the new one the landlady had gifted him after seeing the torn state of his páo. It was black, stitched with silk patterns of clouds and flame. He had wondered why a stranger might gift him something as precious as silk. Now he understood.

Zen closed his eyes, hating himself, hating everything. After all this time, after everything he had been through and all the cycles spent training, he was still not enough. His power had come from his demon, his prodigious practitioning abilities enhanced by its qì; without it, he was nothing. An ordinary practitioner who might be able to best a mó or a yāo, earn the veneration of common folk, yet naught but an irritation in the face of the might of the Elantian Empire.

"We are but two practitioners against the strength of the Elantian army," he said flatly. "And I no longer have my demon bound to me. There is no scenario in which we can win."

"So we run?" She released him and stepped back, incredulity twisting her face. "I won't—"

"We draw them away if they get too close." There was one single solution to both save the village and prevent the Elantians from finding the Demon Gods, and if Zen had harbored any hesitation at all in the days before, the Elantian army had given him a swift answer. He was out of choices and out of time. "They were heading north; they may yet pass by here without discovering the village. We must find out exactly where they are going."

Relief melted the tightness on Lan's face. Perhaps she was thinking he was not the monster others had made him out to be; that she had been mistaken in thinking he would run and leave people to die in his wake.

Lan nodded. "Let's go."

"No." He caught her wrist and turned her to him. This time, he could only pray that the surface of his composure did not crack. His heart was breaking, and he could not let her know. Zen swallowed and took in her face, those bright eyes and that quick mouth, the red cord of the necklace he'd gifted her. "You go round up the villagers, prepare them to flee if needed," he said. "I will scout the army's path. Do not act without my signal. If all goes well, they may yet pass by. A small, downtrodden village in the midst of the Central Plains has nothing to offer them."

She must have seen something in his expression, for she searched his face for a moment before she nodded. The trust in her eyes now felt like a curse.

Lan wrapped her fingers around his and brought their intertwined hands to her heart. A brief touch, but the gesture nearly broke his resolve. "Don't make me wait too long," she said, and then she was gone, slipped through his fingers like wind.

He had the impulse to call after her, to catch just another glimpse of her, to kneel at her feet and beg for forgiveness. Instead, Zen remained silent, trapped in his own body as he listened to her footsteps cross the yard, scattering cooing chickens. He heard the sound of doors sliding open as she entered the main room.

Then he turned to the kàng where he had left the parchment of the star maps. He folded it and tucked it into his storage pouch.

Zen faced the open window and began to pull on qì, gathering it and holding it in his core. He could already sense the overwhelming taint of metal in the natural energies, the balance of the world disturbed.

It would all be over soon.

Instead of channeling the qì to the soles of his feet in preparation for the Light Arts, Zen brought it all to his fingertips, where he began to trace a Seal. Earth and earth, on opposite ends of the circle, separated by lines of distance. Swirl, dot; departure, destination. *Northeast.* What lay northeast of here? He needed a landmark, somewhere he'd been before. Anywhere within the vicinity was fine.

The answer came to him in a twist of irony. The Coiled Dragon River ran northeast before curving into a straight line toward the Northern Steppes. Near the intersection of the Central Plains and the Shǔ Basinlands, though, was a lake. Cartographers had likened it to a pearl held by a dragon. And Zen, desperate for some reminder of his homeland in his early days at Skies' End, had gone there.

Black Pearl Lake, he thought, closing his eyes and thinking of the expanse of water that looked dark even in the daytime and served as the perfect reflection of the sky at night.

He kept the image in his mind, then traced the last strokes of his Seal.

A straight line to bridge departure and destination.

Then a circle to close.

The village, the open window, the kàng and the little room he'd shared with Lan—it all disappeared as the image in his mind swallowed him whole.

In the moments it took his eyes to adjust, he heard the crash of waves against a shore, felt the softness of sand beneath his boots. Gradually, he saw the outline of undulating mountains encircling him. The stretch of darkness before him began to take shape: the light from the stars seemed to seep into it, as though it stole from the sky itself.

He straightened, breathing in the scent of water and wind.

The mountains that rimmed the lake gave the illusion that he was in a small world of his own, the sky and sea both strewn with stars.

He swiped a fú for light, then unfolded the parchment with the star maps and held it to the glow. And there it was: the dots he had painstakingly transcribed onto the sheet nearly perfectly matched the pattern of stars overhead.

He was close.

Zen closed his eyes and combed the qì around him, searching for that tangle of anger, and hatred, and fear—the one he'd stumbled upon thirteen cycles ago at the place where his clan had been slaughtered. He found nothing but the gentle weave of wind and water, mountain and earth, all the natural elements in the qì flowing in harmony.

And yet . . . He frowned, pushing further. Beneath it all: an undercurrent of dread, of a vicious flux beneath the surface. A feeling of something older, something *off* about the place itself, something like terror that had seeped into the bones of the mountains, the roots of the trees, and the bottom of the lake.

The bottom of the lake.

Zen thought back to that winter day thirteen cycles ago, to the words He With Eyes of Blood had whispered to him. *Did you not call for me? Did you not cast an unspoken wish for power? For revenge? For the chance to do to them what they did to your family?*

He had. He had asked for all those things, and had achieved none. Instead, Zen had run in a perfect circle, coming right back to where he'd started. Except he was no longer a naive child yearning for the affection of his master, for acceptance in the world, for redemption of his soul. No, it was too late for that, and if he could achieve something with the path less taken, Zen would choose it.

He dug through his memories, calling on all that he had learned to suppress. Everything that held emotions he had tried not to feel over the past thirteen cycles: helplessness and agonizing pain at the hands of the Elantian interrogation team, terror at the sight of Yeshin Noro Dilaya's bleeding form, bitterness at the masters' cold indifference, anger at the nonsensical injustice of their decisions . . . fury at the Elantian army for what they had done to Lan, what they were about to do to the village should he fail.

Further, further back . . . to the day thirteen cycles ago when he'd smelled smoke on the high plateaus and run back to see fire tearing through the plains that had been his home, mixing with the red and gold livery and banners of the Imperial Army.

He could sense his qì building inside him, yīn energies of death and grief and fury stirring like poison through his veins. And at last, somewhere out there . . . a resounding echo. A great wave yawning, rising to meet his own tide of emotions.

Zen's eyes flew open. The lake stretched flat and black before him, broken only by the fragments of starlight from above.

He knew where the Demon God rested.

He drew qì into himself, pooling it into the soles of his feet. Then he leapt up, wind pushing against his face as he arced and fell, a streak of a comet lost to darkness.

The water was unforgivingly cold, infinitely black. Here, he was wrapped in nothing but the yīn of his own emotions and the torment of his memories. His lungs began to burn as the crushing weight of the icy water pressed him down.

Down, down . . . until he could no longer see even the speck of light that was the moon. Until the darkness was so complete that he could no longer distinguish between consciousness and not. Until his limbs froze over, holding still even as his mind screamed for them to move. Until he could no longer tell if he was sinking or floating.

And then, in the midst of that horrible silence, the emptiness of being, it came.

More of a presence, an *existence*, than anything else. A brush of a current against his body, a whisper caressing his consciousness.

Temurezen, boomed the voice that was everywhere and nowhere at once. *Long have I waited.*

Time seemed to stop. Zen was suspended in an existence in-between, one between him and the being that was older than time, more ancient than this world.

Have you come to summon me to the land of the living? The yáng of life and sun and solid ground?

Zen spoke, but his voice echoed only in his mind. *"Name yourself."*

I think you know my name, the thing replied. *I think you have searched for me long.*

"You assume incorrectly," Zen said coldly.

Oh? After your family's massacre, did you not spend many moons searching for me? Instead, you settled for the first mó that presented itself to you. The being tsked. *Pity. Such squandered time, of which only one of us is short.*

The village. The encroaching army. And Lan.

Running out of time.

"I came to bind you, demon," Zen said. *"Name your price. I am familiar with your ways of bargaining."*

Are you now? It sounded faintly amused. *You would offer me something better? Something no other mortal has?*

Zen gritted his teeth. *"Name your price."*

The qì around him swirled, suddenly growing crushing as though he held the weight of an entire mountain over him, as though the sky had pinned itself upon him. Between one blink and the next, the lake water swirled, and where he had thought there was nothing came something darker than darkness.

Zen found himself looking into the core of the Black Tortoise.

It was a shadow the size of a mountain, a faint neck with a blurred head protruding from one end. Eyes the color of blood in water, flames in the east.

Ten thousand souls, the Black Tortoise boomed. *Ten thousand souls . . . and then, you.*

Ten thousand souls. He would pay the Black Tortoise with the blood of the Elantian army.

And then . . . his own.

"My soul is forfeit," Zen replied. *"You ask nothing new."*

You, the Demon God repeated. *Not your soul. All of you. Mind . . . body . . . and at last, once you are ready, soul.*

Zen's head filled with a roaring noise. The Hin believed souls passed through the River of Forgotten Death before reaching eternal rest; his clan thought spirits were absorbed by the Great Earth and the Eternal Sky. Both, though, on the condition that they qualified for goodness in their own respects. He'd known he was far from goodness and had been prepared for his soul to be forfeit.

His soul—not his life. Not his body, his mind.

He thought of Lan, of the red cord he'd bound for her, a promise and a wish that she'd miraculously granted him. That she could hold feelings for the likes of him had seemed too good to be true . . . but it hadn't stopped him from dreaming of a future with her. A future free of persecution and war and suffering, where they could explore what this great wide world held for them. An ordinary life together, in which he could watch her skin wrinkle and her hair turn white.

But if he did not make this bargain, she would no longer even survive for them to have a chance at that.

His resolve firmed.

"Ten thousand souls first," he said, *"and then body. Then mind. And when I am ready, soul."*

Too long, hissed the Black Tortoise. *I would not wait for you to complete the delivery of ten thousand souls to savor the taste of your flesh and thought.*

They were at an impasse.

Zen waited, and at last, the Black Tortoise spoke again.

My counter: your gradual surrender. With each time that you use my power, with each soul that you deliver, I take more of your body. Then your mind. Last, your soul.

No, no, *no,* every part of him screamed against this. It was too soon; he would not have enough time.

This is my final offer, mortal, the Demon God warned, its anger sending tremors through the mountains. *Take it or leave it.*

Zen closed his eyes, blotting out the image of hellish red ones. Instead, he thought of Lan. Of the village, the old landlady who had knelt before him. Of Skies' End, his master bending to smell a sprig of snow camellia.

His life, in exchange for all theirs.

Well, Zen? The Black Tortoise's words took on a mocking tone. *Do we have a bargain?*

In another world, a different life, he might have had different choices. Better choices. But in the one Zen had been born into, this was the only path left for him. The best path.

Zen opened his eyes and looked into the burning core of the demon.

"Yes," he said. "We have a bargain."

27

There is no peace without violence, no
harmony without sacrifice, no unity without
the loss of individuality.

—Dissertations of the First Emperor,
Jīn Dynasty, Cycle I, era of the Middle
Kingdom

"Nǎi'nai. Grandmother. Please, we must leave."

The village was roused, the stars blinking to life, and still, Zen had not returned. Lan had gone to search for him after banging on every door and window in the village. There had been no trace of him in their little room. The window had been left open, overlooking the slope of mountains through which wound a trail of silver as the Elantian army continued to climb. She thought she'd felt a stir of wind, the slightest weft to the flow of qì there, almost like the trail of a Seal just extinguished.

And the parchment with the transcribed star maps, Lan realized, was gone.

She remembered his expression before she'd left him: a sad fatalism, hope stuttering out in his eyes like the last flicker of a candle. Something took root in her stomach: a seed of doubt that he'd left her here to fend for the village herself. To die by herself.

"Gū'niang," the old landlady murmured. *Young lady*. "Where would we go?"

"Anywhere," Lan said desperately. "Out of the Elantian army's way!"

The old woman sighed, and the dying candlelight carved deeper lines into her face. "Gū'niang, most of us have lived here our entire lives. Our roots are in this village, in this earth and soil itself. I was born here, I became a woman here and raised a family here, then watched them die here. When my time comes, I would wish that my old bones and soul are buried here as well."

Lan looked at where the landlady sat, on a little wooden stool by her broken wooden table, mending a scrap of cloth. The realization came like a portrait snapping into place. The Elantians might burn down their towns and cities, destroy their books, and cut off their language, but the one thing Lan had counted on the Hin to hold on to had been hope. Hope was that fickle little fellow that had tided her through the cold nights and hungry dawns when the exhaustion of another day stretched long and bleak before her. Hope, she realized, was what Māma had given her the day she had whipped out her lute and felled an army of Elantians. Hope was what Māma had entrusted to Lan, in that Seal on her left wrist: a promise that this story was not over. That she held the brush to write its ending.

Yet this village, this landlady, had survived the Elantian assault physically, but their spirits had been broken.

Lan stood. The curves of the ocarina dug into her palm. "Nǎi'nai," she said, "thank you for everything."

The village was steeped in silence as she stepped out through the creaky wooden door, the very one she'd entered with Zen just a few nights ago, a lifetime past. Overhead, the moon lent a white light to the earth, yet storm clouds had appeared in the west, sweeping over the clear skies like a curtain.

Lan walked down the dirt path to the pái'fāng that marked the entrance to the village. A single path up, a single path down. No sign of Zen. She thought again of the strange sense she'd had in their room, the missing parchment that held the star maps to the Demon Gods.

Crushing down the fear that had begun to grow in her belly, Lan focused on the qì.

She frowned. Something was wrong. Whereas she had sensed the overwhelming, suffocating stench of metal earlier, the air was now clearer, the energies of mountains and trees and water brighter. The Elantian army's presence had diminished; they seemed to be growing farther away.

Northeast, the little boy had said of the army's direction.

On impulse, she lifted the ocarina to her lips and played.

The four pieces of star maps sprang into view, the constellations of the Demon Gods glinting brightly against the true night sky beyond. Lan looked to the northeast quadrant of the star map, and her heart almost stopped.

The quadrant of the map was a near-exact match to the true night sky. And on it, marked by an absence of light, was the shape of the Black Tortoise.

The seed of doubt in her chest bloomed, squeezing so hard that she could not breathe. It made sense, if she thought back to Zen's words: *A small, downtrodden village in the midst of the Central Plains has nothing to offer them.*

Of course. She had been so singly focused on the village, on protecting the lives here. Why would the Elantians make for a poor, broken village with a scattering of children and elders? No, Erascius had made their goal clear to them: seek out the Demon Gods, and then hunt out the School of the White Pines, where the last Hin practitioners resided. With the last of Hin magic destroyed and the might of the Demon Gods in their hands, they would raze the Central Plains and all the remainder of the Last Kingdom unobstructed, sealing their power over this land once and for all.

Zen had realized this—and he had gone for the Black Tortoise . . . without her.

We are but two practitioners against the might of the Elantian army. And I no longer have my demon bound to me.

Cold spread through her. The clues had been there all along—she simply hadn't picked up on them. She'd trusted him.

He had lied to her.

If she went after him now, she might be able to reach him before it was too late. A Gate Seal wouldn't work—she had no known destination to conjure, no idea what lay several hours northeast of here.

Lan filled herself with qì until she could feel it glowing within her. Then she sent it to the soles of her feet and leapt into the night. Jagged mountains blurred around her as she picked up speed, more surefooted than she had ever been before, each leap carrying her farther than she had ever gone. Still . . . she thought of the swirl of qì left by a Seal back in their room. If Zen had gone with a Gate Seal, he would be hours ahead of her.

It was not enough. Still not enough.

Time slipped, her world comprising the rhythmic push of qì through her feet, the search for the next cliff or tree or rock to kick from. Only the stars lingered overhead, blinking as tendrils of clouds began to blot them out. *Hurry,* they seemed to whisper as she drew closer to the Elantian army, their scent of metal beginning to overpower all other threads of qì. *Hurry.*

She might have been several bells into her journey when it happened.

A whorl of energies cleaved the air. Lan stumbled, the

rhythm to her steps lost as the energies—filled with torrents of yīn, fury, and grief—crested over her. She slammed into the edge of a cliff, her nails scraping against dirt and leaves and roots as she fought for purchase. Her feet skidded against rocks, then there came a horrible lurch as she stepped onto nothingness. Her fingers wrapped around something—the root of a plant—but she was too heavy, and the plant was starting to snap. Beneath was the hungry rush of a river, and up ahead, she could just see the disappearing moon limn the rim of a great circle of mountains.

"*Zen*," she screamed, then the stalk snapped and she fell.

Pressure on her wrist; a searing pain in her shoulder as her plunge was jerked to an abrupt stop. Lan hung, suspended in the air over the cliff's edge, as her rescuer's face appeared over the edge.

"Sly little fox spirit," snarled Yeshin Noro Dilaya as the last slivers of moonlight were swallowed by clouds. "I really should have let you die."

"Dilaya," Lan panted as she lay on the ground far from the edge of the cliff, trying not to sound too grateful that the girl had just saved her life. "Is your nose so big that you can't help poking it into everyone else's business?"

"Say one more thing that rubs me the wrong way and I will fling you back off the cliff," came the response, along with the glimmer of a blade to remind Lan who was in charge. "My neck's still sore from whatever trick you used earlier."

"How did you find me?" Lan asked. The last she'd seen of Dilaya had been the girl knocked out cold on the floor of the Chamber of a Hundred Healings.

"Your friends Herb Eater and Ghost Boy told me everything," came the reply. "I tracked your qì to this place."

In the distance, the pulse of energies had stabilized, but she could still feel it washing over them like currents of a dark, suffocating river. *Yīn*, she thought, her stomach clenching against the tides of rage, grief, and suffering that pounded against her own heart. *Mó: a spirit born of wrath, ruin, rage, and an unfinished will.*

A face came to her: skin desiccated and blue-gray, clinging to a skeleton like dried vellum; yellow, unseeing eyes and a sagging mouth, patches of loose black hair falling like weeds. The worst part—how closely the thing had come to looking human, how the long sleeves and skirts of its *páo* had trailed it like a ghostly memory of who it had once been, the grandmaster's soul having been bartered over to the monster.

She recalled how Zen had stared at it in horror, and it was only now that she understood why. The mó had been a reflection of one of the fates that could befall him.

A fate he might evade if she could reach him in time.

Lan pushed herself to her feet, slapping away the hand Dilaya tried to offer her. In an extension of the same motion, she whipped out her own blade. That Which Cuts Stars glinted like a tooth. "If you're going to help me, let's go. If not, get out of my way."

Dilaya's expression was incredulous. "Little fox spirit, you think you can beat me with that toothpick?"

"Less useless words, more action, Horse-face." In one swift motion, Lan sheathed her blade. "Try to keep up."

Dilaya's angry response was lost to the roar of wind in her ears as Lan kicked off, qì propelling her into the storm-tossed night. The pulse of energies from ahead had stabilized, yet each step closer pounded dread through her bones. The image of that grandmaster who had bound his soul to a demon's pulsed before her.

The circle of mountains drew closer, and she could feel

that whatever it was she was looking for lay just beyond. In its center: a vortex of darkness and yīn qì. Its surface was dull, and as Lan descended, she had the feeling the last strands of light filtering from behind clouds were being sucked into it.

She hesitated before she took the final step forward, tipping her face to the sky. It was no use: the clouds had obscured the stars, and her memory was not good enough to memorize the star maps. Yet the throb of energies had grown stronger, like a low, eerie drum vibrating through the sternum of her ribs, rattling her teeth and bones with the yīn it carried.

This had to be the work of a Demon God.

Lan leapt, ocarina clutched in one hand and That Which Cuts Stars in the other. It wasn't until she landed on fine sand that she realized the black mass before her was a lake. Its waves roiled against the shores like the maw of a great beast, angry, violent, reaching.

A footfall sounded behind her as Dilaya landed. They stood together, watching the water claw at the land.

"You feel that, don't you?" For once, Dilaya's voice was low with something like dread. "Those yīn energies. There is a reason we speak of balance in practitioning, of using yīn and yáng in harmony. It is impossible for one's soul to defend against so much yīn for long. Over time, one will become corrupted."

Again, Lan thought of the grandmaster of the School of Guarded Fists. Something in her chest knotted.

Before them, the water quieted with a stillness that sent goosebumps up Lan's arms.

"Dilaya," she said. "You should get out of here. Go somewhere safe."

It spoke to the gravity of the situation that the other girl did not argue, only hesitated. Then there was a brush of wind and she was gone.

Lan walked up to the edge where water met earth. She

suddenly realized how unnaturally silent it was here: no chirps of cicadas, no rustling of small animals scurrying through the underbrush, no coos of birds in the branches. It was as though all life had fled from this place.

All . . . but for one.

"Zen." Her lips barely moved; she knew by some strange instinct that he would hear it.

A shadow stirred behind her, and when she turned, he was there: him, but not quite him, the boy she knew and then the shape of him lined in darkness. A blink and that darkness disappeared, as though her vision had blurred for a moment before snapping back into place.

Zen stood before her, black páo billowing in the slight breeze. The drumbeat of terrible yīn energies had vanished, the stillness gone without a trace as the lake waters rippled, the pines around them swayed, the clouds above them shifted.

"Lan," Zen said, and it was his voice, his face, her name in his mouth that she had heard over the course of the past several weeks. Relief crashed into her. "Why are you here?"

She stared at him, at that cool, unreadable face he had had the first night they'd met. The one she had found her way past little by little, like sun melting snow.

Now it felt like they were stepping backward, the distance between them growing.

"I came to find you," Lan said. "Why did you take the star maps?"

He watched her without a flicker in his eyes. "Did I? I must have by accident. I came to search for the Elantians."

Another lie. He had beaten the Elantians to this place. She could taste their approach in the air, in the steadily increasing presence of metal in the qì. There was very little time left. "There are no Elantians here." *Not yet.*

Just like that, the thread between them drew taut. Zen's gaze shuttered. "You do not trust me."

"You lied to me," she countered.

He closed his eyes briefly. "The last thing I wished was to hurt you."

"What have you done?" Lan whispered, and the walls between them finally broke.

"I have bargained the only chance we have at victory," Zen said. "My soul was forfeit from a very long time ago, Lan; it was written in the stars, as Master Fēng so loves to claim. It was a worthwhile trade: a single person for the power to save this land and this people."

"Power," she repeated. "All the masters and the classics speak of power as a double-edged sword, not to be used without balance."

His mouth thinned. "And the masters would have me relinquish my power—for what? So we can be sitting ducks to the Elantian onslaught? Just as the Imperial Court forced the clans to relinquish their powers. When the clans gave up their power, look how this kingdom repaid them."

He was right. He was right, but there was still that warning buried like a blade inside her, entrenched with memories of blood. The Hin needed power to win against the Elantians. But they also needed to be able to control that power, for power without balance, Lan realized, was destruction, no matter in whose hands.

And now, looking at the boy with darkness wrapped around him like night incarnate, she found she understood. "The masters asked you to relinquish your power because you had no *control*," Lan said. "And therefore, no way to balance it. You forget what happened at the Elantian outpost. The lessons learned from the Nightslayer."

"And you forget what the Elantians did to us. What they planned to do, had I not destroyed their foothold. You forget why the Nightslayer was forced to do what he did—*who* forced him to do what he did. There will never be a perfect balance, Lan, now of all times. As we live today, it is either everything or nothing."

She had never heard Zen speak like this, had never seen so much bitterness in his face. "And what of the innocent people whose lives were taken?" she asked, and she did not know whether she referred to Zen or to the Nightslayer. "Were they *nothing*?"

"Lan, a war cannot be won without casualties."

His words slicked up her veins in a rush of ice water. All this time, had *she* been the naive one? Of course, war came with casualties. The emperors who had ruled this land dynasty after dynasty—she could not think herself wiser than them, yet they had all bought into this notion that achieving their goals and wielding their power came with casualties.

But . . . no, Lan thought. *She* had been one of those casualties. The servants back at her courtyard house and the songgirls back at the Rose Pavilion Teahouse had been faceless, nameless casualties of *someone's* bid for power.

"Lan." Fingers wrapped around her own, and they were burning; as though beneath the familiar grooves of Zen's hands was the touch of something else. "You and I are the same. Last of our clans, last of the practitioners, last of this kingdom. Let me do this for our land, for all that we have lost and all in history that will never return." Zen's eyes were soft, and it was almost easy to let his words curl around her heart as he drew her toward him. "Let me use this Demon God's power to drive out the Elantians, then reestablish a kingdom where the clans are returned to the power they once held."

There it was again: that blade, driven hilt-deep. Fracturing his reasoning, his story. *Power*. The emperors of old had fought wars for power over the clans; the Elantians now fought to cement their power over the Hin.

But Lan thought of the words her mother had said to her: *You must serve the people*. The faceless and nameless casualties of wars fought in their name but never *for* them. The songgirls at the Teahouse, bent and broken beneath one regime; the clans who had wished only for peace, under the fist of another.

Slowly, Lan drew her hand back. "Zen," she said. "Please don't do this. You cannot control the power of a Demon God."

"I am perfectly in control, Lan."

"Not forever." Even now, she could feel it: the soft, insidious pulse of yīn from him. Dilaya had been right. It would eventually take his mind, corrupt his soul. "The Nightslayer lost his mind, and I cannot watch the same thing happen to you, Zen." She shifted her tone to become softer, pleading. "Give us some time—"

"*Us.*" He spat the word with a hiss, and for a moment, she thought she saw his eyes flicker black.

Something cut through the air with the swiftness and sharpness of a blade. Zen moved in a kiss of metal, and Nightfire sliced, catching against the other sword with a clang.

"*Conqueror,*" Dilaya growled, the word charged with a history of hatred. She straightened beneath a pine by the lake, its shadow cutting ribbons of moonlight across her. "I'll not allow you to do to this land what your ancestors did to my clan in the name of *protecting* us."

"I am not my ancestors," Zen said coldly, "but you're right. I will no longer sit by watching history repeat itself."

"Enough useless words," Dilaya snapped, leaning into Wolf's Fang with a snarl of her own. "A demonic practitioner must be eliminated before he loses his mind to the demon. And I would take that honor tonight."

Dilaya charged. She fought like a wraith, dāo flashing and cutting in perfect rhythm, limbs awhirl as though in tune to a song only she heard. For all that Lan had clashed with this girl, she couldn't help but admire her tenacity at this moment, the effortlessness with which she moved.

She was far from a match to a Demon God, though. As Zen's grip on Nightfire gave way to Wolf Fang's thrust, Zen lifted a hand—and something responded.

An explosion of qì ripped through the night, cracking through the air and heaving through the waters of the lake itself. The clouds overhead seemed to shudder, the rocks surrounding them reverberating with raw, unbridled power. Lan flung up her hands, her shield Seal wavering as the energies poured over it. Dilaya, mid-charge, was flung back ten, twenty paces. Lan heard a sickening thump, then silence.

Zen lowered his palm, closing his fingers into a fist. The qì stilled. For a moment, Lan could swear she saw a shadow of something else in his eyes—and as he turned to her, that thing lingered a moment before it vanished.

His expression, though, did not change. Cold, distant, somber, yet with a new dimension she had never seen in the Zen she had come to know: rage.

Lan glanced to Dilaya, slumped against the trunk of a pine tree. Above them and all around them, the presence of metal was so close that it pressed on every one of her nerves, overriding every other sense. A flicker of movement from the path between the mountains behind Zen; a gleam of foreign armor. The Elantians were coming.

"Lan."

She nearly flinched as she turned back to Zen. The shadows to his face had gone, and for a moment, she thought she caught the flash of something open, vulnerable to his gaze.

She could think of nothing to say other than, "Please, Zen, don't choose this."

His expression crumpled, and when he spoke, he pushed the words through gritted teeth. "Choices are for those with *privilege*, Lan. What part of that do you not understand? You said it yourself, that we're given *shit* choices and we have to make the best of them!" His voice rose into a shout, and she flinched at hearing the curse word fall from his lips. "If I could *choose* to be good, if I could *choose* the balanced path of the Way, why wouldn't I? But this was the hand the gods dealt me, the circumstances I was born into, and if I must choose the Wayward path in order to save this kingdom, then so I shall. If I must see darkness for our people to find light, then I will make that same choice, over and over and over again." He was panting slightly, his face open and pleading. His voice grew soft. "Will you stay with me on this path, Lan?"

But all Lan could think of was the Elantian outpost, the starved Hin behind bars—fathers, mothers, and children—and how there had only been blood, and bones, and broken things afterward. Unfettered, power devoured the mind of its wielder, paving the path to violence, destruction, and death without discernment. History had shown this, over and over again.

She would not fall into that trap. If she were to seek out power, she'd ensure that she be the one in control. And she would use it to serve her people. The common songgirls, the pawn shop owners and widowed landladies, the voiceless masses of her kingdom.

She shook her head. "Zen . . ."

Zen saw the answer in her eyes. He brought his hands to his face. A violent tremor passed through his body.

And then he stilled.

When he straightened, his hands slipping from his face to curl into fists at his sides, the wild, frenetic look had left his eyes. They were cold, black, and inscrutable, a night without stars.

"I have chosen my path. If you are not with me, then you are against me," he said, and she knew she had lost him.

28

The cowherd and the weaver girl were banished
to opposite ends of the skies, separated by the
River of Forgotten Death, never to hold one
another again.

—"The Cowherd and the Weaver Girl,"
Hin Folktales: A Collection

They came like a stretch of clouds, spilling over the mountain pass that curved onto the shores of the lake. Their armor was bone white beneath the trembling moon. The color of tombs. The color of death.

Zen meant to stop them here, tonight.

But he couldn't turn away, couldn't stop himself from gazing at the girl who had become his anchor to this world, the one that had stood between him and the darkness that now lingered at the edges of his mind.

Lan stepped back from him as though she'd been burned. Her eyes wavered, searching his face. Whatever she found there cast a shadow of fear and hurt across her expression.

Zen steeled his heart. He had seen that before, too many times.

Lan turned. With one burst of qì she was kneeling by Dilaya's side, wrapping her arms around the unconscious girl's waist; with the next, she was airborne, a smudge of pale páo against the cloud-covered sky as bright and as brief as a shooting star. Then she was gone, swallowed whole by the night.

Once again, Zen was alone.

It would have been so easy to take off after her. To call out to her: *Since when did you become so good at the Light Arts?* and to hear her witty response. The thought nearly brought a smile to his lips as he turned to face the army on the shore.

The incident at the Elantian outpost had changed him. Skies' End had been a flower in a vase even as the world around them turned to ashes, and now it was Erascius himself who had cracked open the porcelain for Zen.

If you forever adhere to the path between two extremes, then you will end up with nothing.

Zen opened his arms to the great core of power that had taken root inside his heart: a core that seemed to hold an entire world, from sky to sea. A core *roiling* with energies and bloodlust at the onslaught of Elantians.

The time had long passed since he was a child at Skies' End, yearning for approval, for something to hold him steady in the fresh loss of everything in his life. He had tried his master's way, and he had failed. In the end, his attempts to repress his power had resulted in a tragedy, when it should have been a victory.

Power was a blade, and the only blame was in that its wielder's hand was too weak.

This time would be different, he thought as yīn began to churn in his veins, seeping into the air and soil around him and stirring even the waters of the lake behind him.

This time, he would control it.

This time, he would *master* it.

Zen called on the power of his Demon God.

The world at once expanded and flattened. He could feel everything: the crash of waves against sand, the sigh of wind through mountains, the rattle of every leaf and the movement of every living creature, from great snow leopards prowling the icy peaks up north to the chorus of cicadas in the golden ginkgoes down south. At the same time, he felt nothing at all anymore.

He was a Demon God, and this world was his to play with, his to conquer. And all those lives across the water, his for the taking.

He surged over to them, landing at the very head of the foreign army, robes fluttering in a strong wind.

With the first clap of thunder, he began to lay waste to the humans. The storm swelled in harmony with his power as blood spilled from humans so arrogant that they thought the thin coating of metal they wore could stop him. When lightning flared across the sky, he called upon his qì of black fire, a terrible, beautiful thing that had once devoured the entire world.

Life, death, light, dark, good, evil—to him, these all existed in ephemeral and ever-changing eternity, just like the forces of yīn and yáng that had created him. This world was not meant to remain stagnant, unchanging for long. Just as the earliest clans had risen, so, too, had they fallen; dynasties cycled through time, emperors who believed themselves great and immortal wheeling past him with lifespans briefer than those of shooting stars.

Though his power was infinite, the human body that had bound him was not. The boy grew tired; he could sense grief pushing against the dam he'd set up in the boy's fragile heart.

Very well. His job here was done. He would return to his slumber until the boy brought them to their next feast.

Zen's thoughts fractured, swirling like a blend of dreams and nightmares, voices that belonged both to him and to an ancient creature coiled deep in his soul. When he came to, he stood alone on the shore. It was raining, the drops drumming against the surface of the lake, tapping on the armor of the Elantian army before him.

They lay horribly, terribly still, a mass of bodies littering the landscape. Corrupting the beauty of nature and harmony in this previously untouched land. And even as Zen gazed out at them, knowing that what they had done to the Hin was a hundred, a thousand, times worse, he could not quell the nausea rising in his throat, nor the tremor of his hands.

It was a different feeling, knowing that an entire army had done this under someone's command, whereas he—he had slaughtered these people of his own will with his bare hands. He could sense the presence of the Demon God cooling within him, a great fire in his bones simmering down to smoke.

"How many?" he panted, and the answer slithered a chokehold over his neck.

Four hundred and forty-four, the Black Tortoise whispered, its voice like fading fog. The answer was a twist of irony: four, *sì,* the unlucky number that bore such close resemblance to *sǐ,* death.

So many, yet barely a drop in the well he was meant to fill. Zen closed his eyes and imagined an hourglass he'd once seen from the Kingdom of Masyria, each fine speck of falling sand a life he had taken.

How much longer until it takes my body, my mind? Zen crushed that thought before it fully formed and said instead, sharpening his voice to cut, "You took my mind during the fight. That was not part of our bargain."

What I do cannot be comprehended by the mortal mind, came the response. *I am older than the mountains of this land, my power flowing deeper than any rivers. For your mind to attempt to rein it and channel it . . . would break you. You are* weak, *boy, not fit to wield this blade.*

"*I* control *your* power," Zen snarled. "*I* command *you*. Those were the terms."

Seals were conjured as a matter of technicality, yes, but Master Gyasho had always stated that the heart of each Seal lay in the will of the practitioner. It stood to reason, then, that the same principle might hold for controlling a demon—and by extension, a Demon God. Exert a strong enough will, and slowly, it would bend.

He sensed cunning black eyes, devoid of light yet full of fire hidden behind smoke, watching him from nowhere and everywhere at once. *Your bargain, your terms,* the Demon God replied. *But having outlived all your dynasties and eras and having been the force behind so many emperors and generals, I already see through you, all of you. You will never achieve the power of those before you should you attempt to rein in my power.* A pause, the brush of an invisible smile. *Xan Tolürigin embraced me and gave himself completely to me, and his name lives in your history, does it not? "The Nightslayer?"* A low chuckle.

Zen whipped out Nightfire and slashed, but it was useless; the shape in the darkness was only an illusion, a reflection of the thing that now lived inside him. He heard a dimming, rumbling laughter before the heavy presence retreated from his mind and vanished.

The sudden withdrawal sent him to his knees. The power of that dark fire receded through his veins with a juddering violence, and for a moment his heart gave a painful squeeze, as though his strength were not enough to keep it going. His body ached. He couldn't breathe. Black spots bloomed before his eyes.

He'd been a fool to think that he would immediately control it, *master* it. He hadn't even been able to control the power and will of a lesser demon; to hope to command a legendary being that had existed since the beginning of time was folly.

He gritted his teeth and dug his fingers into the blood-stained soil. It was still raining, yet one warm drop slid down his cheek.

Help. He needed help before his body completely gave way. He needed somewhere safe. A shelter.

He could sense the remnants of the Demon God's qì stirring, taking over and guiding his body based on instinct. Saving him—not out of kindness, of course, but out of self-preservation. It was almost always in a demon's best interest to protect its human vessel . . . until the terms of the bargain were fulfilled.

His awareness was fractured, fragments of time and scenery weaving in and out of his consciousness. When he came to again, he stood in a forest, far from the shores of the lake and the ground littered with the dead. He was utterly alone but for the pines and shadows around him. Skies' End loomed out of the thick fog, the shape of the mountain as familiar to Zen as the back of his hand. It pierced through the maelstrom of his thoughts, a place of stability, of safety.

Reality and dream blurred: a forest of pines, a waterfall's murmur, a fretwork window, bitter medicine mixed with an evening breeze. A slender face with kind eyes and lips parting gently as he blew on a bowl of broth in his hands. The scene swam in Zen's mind's eye, and he was screaming as someone carried him through a storm-tossed night, a father's voice finding him in the dark. _It will be all right, child. You are safe, with me._

His master.

Shī'fu.

His consciousness was reduced to his most primal of memories as he pushed himself to his feet, stumbling to the base of the mountain where the secret entrance lay, shrouded by the Boundary Seal. There it was, the ancient, gnarled form of the

Most Hospitable Pine, branches extended as though to welcome him back.

Zen let out a choked sob of relief as he stumbled forward. He felt the rush of cool qì against him, the whispers of the Boundary Seal as he entered.

Nine hundred ninety-nine steps to safety.

Zen was about to take the first when he was assaulted by a chorus of ghostly screams. The air around him thickened to an unimaginable density, closing over his nose and his mouth, cracking over him like hoarfrost. From the ice and fog came faces, hollowed out and twisted in their furious malevolence.

Traitor, the souls in the Boundary Seal howled. *Murderer. Demon.*

He couldn't think, couldn't breathe, couldn't do anything except back away, clutching at his face as though that would stop their onslaught. Pain crackled over his skin, lightning and fire and the stinging lash of a whip a thousand times over. Zen retreated blindly, feeling the qì surge against him.

He stumbled out into night, into silence. Fell to the ground and lay there for a moment, gasping in harried breaths and taking in the steady scent of the earth, the soil, the forest.

He was shaking as he sat up and wiped the trickle of blood from his lips.

Zen looked up just in time to see the Boundary Seal close against him.

29

The cleverest man underestimates his own
abilities and overestimates his opponent's.

—*Kontencian Analects*
(Classic of Society), 6.8

One bell earlier

Lan's Gate Seal had spat her and Dilaya out right in front of
the Most Hospitable Pine. With gritted teeth and a stream
of colorful curses, she had dragged Dilaya through the Boundary Seal.

The whispers in the Seal were urgent, frenetic, and though
she'd never been able to make out the words they spoke,
she heard something akin to fear in the spirits' voices as she
crossed it. Skies' End, as ever, lay unchanged in spite of her
harried heartbeats. The Yuèlù Mountains slumbered in silence,
draped in thick fog; storm clouds swirled over the moon.

In her exhaustion, the world around her tilted as she
set Dilaya down. "Get up, Horse-face. I'd rather curse eighteen generations of my ancestors than carry you up these
steps."

The other girl was slumped against the gnarled trunk of
a nearby pine. Her chest rose and fell with shallow breaths.
Blood had crusted on the side of her face.

"Come on, Dilaya." Lan poked the girl's nose, trying to

quell the rising fear in her chest. "I take it back, all right? I don't wish you dead anymore. Just . . . just get up."

"We all have. We all have wished her dead at least once."

Lan turned at the familiar voice. Descending the last few steps of the mountain was Tai. Crashing through the brush, he at last came to a standstill at Lan's side, shoulders slumped and hair tousled, looking extremely awkward without Shàn'jūn's effortless grace by his side.

"She is stubborn," Tai said, looking down at Dilaya. "Annoying. She will live. Shàn'jūn will see to it."

"Tai," Lan said, her voice scratching. She had so many questions, so much to say, but her last memory of him burned brighter than a flame: his hand on her wrist, his eyes lit up beneath that eternal frown. *I know,* he'd said. *I know now.*

"I did it," Tai said. "I told Dilaya you left with Zen. Do not blame Shàn'jūn. He thought you . . . were in danger." The boy's eyes were hooded as they swept the scene. They came to rest on Lan again. "Zen is gone."

She held her breath against the sudden pain the words brought. Nodded.

Tai marched over to Dilaya. He stood beneath the shadow of the jagged pine, arms hanging by his sides as he stared at the prone girl. "I will take her," he said at last. "You go. Go to the grandmaster."

Lan's feet pounded worn stone steps up the familiar path to the school. She could hear the faint murmur of conversation as she emerged from the copse of trees. The night, usually ink black and lit only by the luminescence of the moon and stars, was awash in torchlight. The boulder engraved with the characters of her school—*School of the White Pines*—was illuminated in flickering yellow light, like a warning.

The light came from the Chamber of Waterfall Thoughts.

Lan sprinted up the stone path and then over the wooden threshold of the chamber.

The masters stood in the soft light of the lotus lamps, deep in conversation. They looked up as she entered.

Lan paused. She had no idea what she should say.

The Demon Gods are back.

The Elantians are coming.

Both sounded utterly outlandish.

She was saved, unexpectedly, by Yeshin Noro Ulara.

"Where is Dilaya?" the Master of Swords asked. She wore her full armor, her hair done up in its austere middle part and two buns. Her two swords were strapped to her back, hilts gleaming in the lambent light.

Lan blinked. Given that the last time she'd seen Ulara was when she'd knocked her out, she'd been expecting murder from the elder Yeshin Noro.

"She came back with me," Lan replied. "Tai is taking her to the Chamber of a Hundred Healings."

Ulara made a move as though to leave, but at that moment, the grandmaster spoke.

"Ulara," he said. "She will be all right." Then he looked at Lan, and she felt as though he was looking into the spaces in her soul. "So you have found the first of the Demon Gods," he said at last, and the words jolted through her. "And Zen has bound it."

She stared at him, swallowing the question on the tip of her tongue. *How did you know?*

Dé'zǐ smiled. "Shàn'jūn and Chó Tài came to me with the information you had given them shortly after your departure several days ago. This has allowed us to remain one step ahead and to plan for the appropriate precautionary measures."

"The Elantians were after the Demon Gods." She had no idea why she was still defending Zen and his actions. Perhaps a part of her felt guilty. Complicit. "Zen and I only wished to find them first to stop the Elantians. But . . . he bound the Demon God to use its power to fight the Elantian army. He thinks doing so will save our lives—the lives of all Hin."

She had expected a strong reaction—for the masters to burst into conversation, perhaps. Yet there was only the exchanges of grim glances, a knowing that seemed to settle between the ten figures in the chamber.

"This buys us some time," the grandmaster said at last. "No matter the situation, I still have high expectations of Zen's abilities. We must come to an agreement on the contingency measures we have discussed, masters of the School of the White Pines."

"Are we not to discuss the situation at hand with Zen?" Ulara cut in. "Should we have a repeat of the Nightslayer, our problems may be far worse than simply dealing with the Elantians."

"The Nightslayer had yielded much of himself to the Black Tortoise and was at the end of his bargain, Ulara," Dé'zĭ replied, "whereas Zen has just bound this Demon God. Moreover, Zen believes he can save us with this newfound power; at the very least, he will buy us time before he loses all control. We must decide, right now, the course of action to take in the precious time he has given us."

"Evacuate," Ip'fong, Master of Iron Fists, suggested promptly. "The only reason we have survived the Elantians' hunt for this long was due to our location and the strength of our Boundary Seal."

"Our Boundary Seal will hold should they come searching for us," Gyasho, Master of Seals, stated. "In the thousands of cycles this school has stood, none that are unwelcome have managed to breach the Boundary Seal, nor have those with ill intentions managed to find our location."

"It will still be good to take precautions," advised Nur, Master of Light Arts.

"I, for one, will not sit here like a squatting duck, waiting to be butchered," Ulara declared. "Grandmaster, we should attack first, while we have the element of surprise. This is our land, our territory; we know the terrain. Let us use that to our advantage."

"The Elantians brought a battalion," Lan interjected. "I saw them making their way over the mountains." There had been so many. Too many. "Even you will not beat those odds, Master Ulara."

"We are doomed!" cried Fēng, Master of Geomancy. "I have read this in my oracle bones—"

"We are *not* doomed," said Cáo, Master of Archery, "not if we use clever planning and strategy. Not if we draw on our advantages. We have a wartime playbook. Let us use it."

As they deliberated in the flickering lamplight, the grandmaster's gaze remained on Lan. At last, he raised a hand, and the masters fell silent.

"We hope for the best but prepare for the worst," he said. "Master Nur and Nameless Master, evacuate the youngest through the back cliffs. Make for the west—and wait for my word." The Master of Light Arts and the Nameless Master of Assassins bowed their heads in salute. "The rest, gather those who are able and willing to fight."

"Grandmaster," Lan called, but he had walked out exceptionally quickly, and by the time she caught up to him, someone was ringing the bells to the rhythm of war. Paper lamps flared up across the mountain, small spots of yellow blinking sleepily into existence as the disciples began to wake.

Dé'zǐ turned to Lan.

"Grandmaster, you can't hope to fight the Elantian army," she said. "We have to run."

"Lan," he said, as though testing her name. "Just in time for our second session together."

Lan opened her mouth to protest. The Elantians were on their doorstep, and Zen was lost to a Demon God—truly, this was no time for a *lesson*. But the grandmaster gave her a significant look. "Please. This is important. Just a few minutes of your time."

Skies' End was beginning to wake up, disciples streaming into view from the stone steps lining the mountains. She watched as the children trembled, clutching their bundles. Watched the older disciples shore up weapons—spears, swords, and rounds and rounds of arrows. All made mostly of wood that would surely splinter against the thick metal armor of the Elantians. These disciples were barely older than children themselves. Their eyes, though, bore none of the light of youth—only the wearied, hardened looks of those who had lived lives of suffering.

The grandmaster circled the groups clustered around each master of an art of practitioning, exchanging words with each master and nodding before moving on. They would use the Thirty-Fifth Stratagem from the *Classic of War*: the Linked-Chain Attacks, which involved layering different traps to weaken the enemy in unexpected ways. It was the second-to-last of the Thirty-Six Stratagems, for use when enemy forces were overpowering.

A play of last resort, should the Elantian army breach the Boundary Seal.

"Archery as the first line of defense," Ulara called out from the very front of the congregation. "Seals, next. Swords and Iron Fists as the last."

Yet looking around at the ten masters and the disciples who had elected to stay behind, Lan realized that no stratagem from the *Classic of War* could turn the odds for a hundred or so people against an army of thousands. She looked at the faces of the children being shepherded to the back cliffs by Master Nur and the Nameless Master; saw the naked fear in the eyes of the older disciples that no weapon or armor could hide.

And suddenly, she understood, so deeply, what Zen had said to her on the shores of that black-glass lake. *It was a worthwhile trade: a single person for the power to save this land and this people.*

Because no matter what, if he hadn't sought out the power of the Demon Gods, they would lose. Power was a double-edged sword . . . but to not have it—that was to have no weapon to fight with at all.

Had she been in Zen's position, would she have declined the Demon God's offer?

"This way, Lan," the grandmaster said suddenly, turning his attention to her, and she shoved down her thoughts guiltily. She followed him back into the Chamber of Waterfall Thoughts, toward the open-air terrace. The sound of the waterfall grew louder, masking the din of wartime preparations out front.

The lotus lamps flickered, settling as Dé'zǐ came to a stop. He faced the back terrace, watching the waterfall in silence.

Lan drew a deep breath. "Grandmaster," she tried again, "we have to evacuate. The Elantian magician brought an *army*, not simply a scouting squad. Unless you plan to pull another Demon God out of your sleeves, we cannot hope to defeat them."

The last line was meant as a joke. Dé'zǐ, however, turned at this to give her a long look. It was several moments before he spoke. "There is a reason I would guard this mountain with my life, which I will explain to you." He stretched out a hand. "Might I see your ocarina?"

Her heart began to race in her chest. She'd last channeled

a lost art of practitioning through her ocarina to get past the Yeshin Noros. What if that, too, was Wayward?

"I wish nothing more than to see it," Dé'zǐ said, catching her hesitation. "It was Dilaya who first informed me that you had—what were her exact words?—'cast a curse of music on her.' Then Chó Tài recognized it for what it was. He recognized *you* . . . for who you were. For who . . . your mother was."

Mouth dry, Lan reached to her waist and pulled the instrument out from the folds of her sash. The pale mother-of-pearl lotus glinted on the smooth black surface as it exchanged hands.

Dé'zǐ looked at it a long moment, then turned heavy eyes on her. "Many great people, some of whom were very dear to me, gave their lives to protect your mother's legacy."

Lan was stunned. "You knew my mother?"

He watched her with an inscrutable expression. "I did. You must have an inkling, by now, of what she wished to achieve. What she wished to protect. But perhaps it would be most conducive for us to begin with the Demon Gods themselves. Might that help?"

Lan could only nod.

"The Four Demon Gods," Dé'zǐ began, "are beings with no goal other than to seek power. They do not distinguish between good or evil; they do not have morals. They are as old as the bones of this world. In their eyes, human beings are akin to flakes of snow, our lives ephemeral, gone in the blink of an eye. We are vessels in which they may manipulate the currents of the world and further their power and their existence."

"I thought practitioners used to bind the Demon Gods to them and channel their powers," Lan said.

"As is stated in the first principle of the Book of the Way, power is always taken from somewhere. It does not exist in a vacuum. And acquiring it always comes at a cost. Those practitioners who borrowed the power of the Demon Gods paid the price with their bodies, minds, and souls."

"Xan Tolürigin."

Dé'zǐ bowed his head. "Indeed. Your mother recognized this. We once conspired to bring down the gods together."

Her reality fractured. Breathing hard, Lan said, "All along, you have known everything? About my Seal, my past, the star maps and the ocarina?"

"Not at first. But when Dilaya told me of the ocarina and I spoke with Chó Tài, I grew certain. I simply hope it isn't too late." The grandmaster handed the ocarina back to Lan. He suddenly looked so old, so frail. "Tell me, has the ocarina sung to you of the Ruin of Gods?"

Lan started. The haunting melody from that night, from the memory of Shēn Ài's soul, came drifting back.

The map lies within.

When the time is right,

This ocarina will sing for the Ruin of Gods.

"Yes," Lan whispered.

"And how does one slay a god?"

It was a question she had never considered—never even dared imagine. She had felt the power of the Demon God back at Black Pearl Lake: suffocating, all-encompassing, as though it commanded the heavens and moved the earth at the same time.

Dé'zǐ turned to her, and his expression was mild again. "I assume you are familiar with the history of our country. How the warring clans were united into the First Kingdom." Lan nodded. "Have you ever considered how the First Emperor Jīn—once known as Zhào Jùng, a mere general, not even a clan leader—managed to win against the most powerful practitioners of the Ninety-Nine Clans? Against those who channeled the power of the Demon Gods?"

At any other time, Lan might have given a quick smile, a light answer: *He learned the lessons of the* Classic of War *better than everyone else?* But now she shook her head. She was in no mood for guessing games. They were running out of time.

"I can tell you there is a reason the history books do not cover this," Dé'zǐ continued. "You see, the clan bloodline that became the imperial family had a secret weapon. Much as each of the elements in the energies around us are caught in a cycle of creation and destruction, so, too, are the gods. And the Four Demon Gods are no exception. Like yīn to yáng, there exists a force—perhaps more than one—to surmount them. To destroy them.

"The very first shamans of our lands took this force and made it into a weapon: the Godslayer, capable of splitting the core of power and energies that made up the Demon Gods and returning them into the flow of this world."

A bell rang in her head. Lan had seen something similar, albeit on a much smaller scale. Something that lay strapped to her waist at this moment.

She could still feel Zen's hands pressed against her own, the intentness of his gaze as he spoke: *The name of this dagger is That Which Cuts Stars. This blade pierces not only human flesh but supernatural as well. Its purpose is to sever demonic qì.*

If there existed a blade that could cut through demonic qì . . . then it stood to reason there could be a much more powerful one with the ability to cut through the core of a demon—even a Demon God.

"The first shamans gifted the Godslayer to a keeper, intending for them to use it as a last resort should the power of the Demon Gods ever spiral out of control. The Godslayer was a means to maintain balance in this world, to conquer what could not be conquered.

"Yet instead of maintaining the balance, the keepers grew greedy, watching the clans grow powerful with demonic bindings. And one day, a general named Zhào Jùng marched on the clans with the Godslayer."

"But the imperial family was known to bind the Demon Gods to them, too," Lan said, thinking back to the conversation she'd eavesdropped upon in the bookhouse between Shàn'jūn and Tai. "Tai said they wielded the power of the Crimson Phoenix."

"Therein lies the problem," Dé'zi said. "The keepers were never meant to use the Godslayer for their own gain, for their pursuit of power. It was only after the Middle Kingdom was established that the imperial family began to desire possession of the Demon Gods. They hid the Godslayer and launched campaigns against the clans in a bid to consolidate power." His gaze fixed on her, steady yet heavy. "And so there arose a secret alliance: the Order of Ten Thousand Flowers, the flowers representing the peoples of this land. It began as a congregation of former clan members, then others joined the cause as well, with this very school serving as its base—unbeknownst to the Imperial Court. Our creed was to check the power of the imperial family . . . and to return balance to the kingdom. Perhaps our greatest triumph was when the Sòng clan reached an agreement to serve the imperial family as advisors in an attempt to seek out the Godslayer. Your mother included."

"My mother," Lan repeated, and her fingers drifted to the Seal on her left wrist.

Māma had left behind a trail of puzzle pieces that she hadn't been able to explain before her death. The picture was clear now: the scarred Seal on Lan's wrist that had led her to the ocarina, the star maps pinpointing the locations of the Demon Gods . . .

The only missing fragment, now, was the Godslayer.

"Your mother," Dé'zi said softly. "Sòng Méi."

There was such a weight to the way he spoke her name, like a song, a story untold. Lan's attention sharpened on the grandmaster. She knew so little of this man, of how his story . . . fit into Māma's.

Into *hers*.

The thought had barely formed in her head when a shockwave exploded through the air.

The physical world held still, yet a tsunami of energies hit her, churning with yīn. Lan doubled over, clutching her chest.

An eternity seemed to pass before she felt the tidal wave of power and darkness receding from her mind. So much grief, fury, and regret in that whorl of energies—so much yīn.

Yet there had been something familiar about the qì. Something she recognized.

Zen.

Footsteps, pounding urgently against stone toward them. As Dé'zǐ helped Lan up, Yeshin Noro Ulara strode into view. Lan had never seen her face so openly furious.

"It's him, Dé'zǐ—I've always told you that boy would be the death of us all!" Ulara snarled, her knuckles white as she gripped the hilt of her dāo. "He has completely lost control—that qì will draw the Elantians to us like a beacon! I'll kill him!"

"Ulara." Dé'zǐ's tone carried a warning. "You'll do no such thing."

More footsteps, and the remainder of the masters rushed in.

"The Boundary Seal has locked down," Gyasho said gravely. "One of our own has betrayed us."

"He *never* should have been one of our own," Ulara snapped.

"It is confirmed, then?" Even Master Ip'fong looked grim as he approached. "It is Zen?"

"I saw this coming, eleven cycles ago, when you took that boy in, Dé'zǐ!" Fēng shrieked. "I read it in the bones, divined it from the stars!"

"Silence." The grandmaster's word had the effect of a sword being drawn. Silence fell through the Chamber of Waterfall Thoughts. "We proceed as we planned. Master Ulara, it is time. Ring the bells again. Skies' End is going to war."

Whatever grief or grudges any of the masters held, they tucked it all away in this moment. Without hesitation, the remaining masters of the School of the White Pines brought their fists to their palms.

"And if our defenses should fail?" Ulara asked. She was looking straight at Dé'zǐ, and between them and the other masters, there seemed to be an exchange that Lan could not understand. A mutual understanding, a quiet pact of sorts as they turned to their grandmaster.

He replied serenely, "Should we fail, then we must release what is Sealed at the heart of this mountain."

What's Sealed at the heart of this mountain? Lan swallowed the question as Dé'zǐ lifted fist to palm, then bent into a long, deep bow.

"Masters of the School of the White Pines," he said, "and above all, my friends: it is the greatest honor of my life to fight by your side. May the Path guide us all."

The hall sprang into action, masters sprinting this way and that, the light of the lotus lamps flickering wildly in the commotion.

"Lan, with me," said Dé'zǐ, and she hurried to follow him as he strode rapidly from the hall. The night air was alight with torches and movement in the courtyard as the disciples followed their respective masters to their positions.

Dé'zǐ walked so fast that Lan struggled to keep up. He was making for the entrance, for the path down the mountain.

Pulses of qì continued to emanate from that direction. Like invisible waves, they swept over Skies' End, sending the light from candles and lamps shivering and flickering from the yīn.

Zen.

"Grandmaster." Lan sprinted to overtake him. Without thinking, she grabbed his sleeve. He slowed but did not stop. "You said there was a reason we need to guard this mountain. Is it to do with what's Sealed in it?"

"Yes."

"Well, what is it?" she blurted, unable to quell her curiosity. "Does it have to do with Zen?"

"It has to do with everything, Lan," the grandmaster replied. "In this moment, I have a request for you. Find Shàn'jūn. Brief him on what is happening with Zen, if he is not already aware; he will know what to do. Can you do that for me?"

She held on to the grandmaster's sleeve, wanting to press him further to answer her questions. But with each passing moment, she was delaying any help, any hope, for Zen.

Slowly, Lan uncurled her fingers, and Dé'zǐ's sleeve slipped from them. She met his eyes and nodded. "Yes, shī'fù. I can."

The grandmaster hesitated. He brought a hand to one side of her head, cupping it gently. For a moment, she thought he might say something to her, something that would answer all her questions, that would tilt her world back on its axis.

But then he drew back.

He left her standing on the stone path, staring after his disappearing figure until the darkness took him.

30

The greatest of walls fall with
a single misplaced brick.

—Lady Nuru Ala Šuraya of the Jorshen
Steel clan, *Classic of War*

He was adrift in a starless sea of night, of flames that burned
like black water. Here, cocooned safely within, there was
no pain, no fear, no sorrow that could reach him.

He'd come here once before, after the last of his clan had
been massacred. It had felt as though his body, mind, and soul
had fractured, no longer belonging to him—as if he watched
all that he did from behind a paper screen like a shadow puppet show.

Now, rejected by the place he'd come to know as home,
Zen felt his grief welling over, tided by a surge of fury—and
power.

It felt good to be a god.

To feel nothing at all.

You are filled with regret. The Demon God's voice rang out in
Zen's mind and all around him. *Perhaps I should show you what
happens when one begins to regret. When one grows soft and believes
power must be fettered and balance kept.*

The voice was lightening, coalescing into a single, human

timbre. The darkness in his mind, too, began to take shape. It molded itself into the silhouette of a man, tall and muscular and dressed in armor that was horribly, achingly familiar: shimmering scale and gleaming lamellar, black with red flames twisting along the seams. As his face formed, Zen tensed with the shock of it: one he had seen in paintings or sketches in ancient tomes, features twisted in cold resolution or exaggerated ire depending on the source.

But never in this expression of helplessness. Of desperation.

"*Please,*" Xan Tolürigin begged softly, his eyes fixed on a point behind Zen in the memory. "*If you spare my clan, I would agree to a truce, to rein in the power of the Black Tortoise.*"

On the same plane of memory across from Xan Tolürigin's form, tendrils of smoke began to form into another man. One who wore gold-plated armor, new and glittering and utterly unscathed by marks of war. On the pommel of his jiàn curled a golden dragon.

The sigil of the emperor.

Yán'lóng.

Zen watched in horror as the emperor tipped his head back and gave a long, booming laugh. "*What makes you think you have anything left to bargain with?*" he asked. As he spoke, great fiery wings seemed to unfurl behind him, crimson as blood. "*You forget that I, too, wield the power of a Demon God.*" He lifted a hand; it fell like an axe. "*Kill them all.*"

Smoke swept across the scene, painting the army of imperial soldiers behind him . . . and the row of Mansorian warriors kneeling beneath shackles.

Blades flashed. Blood splattered.

The emperor's laugh and Xan Tolürigin's scream rang in Zen's ears as the memory faded back into nothingness.

You see, child, crooned the voice made of darkness. *The Nightslayer's last act was an attempt at balance. Yet such is the nature of our world. An endless cycle of consumption, of the weak devoured by the strong. Now his clan lies buried in graves of winter snow, and his name is written in history as that of a villain, a madman. Remember this lesson.*

Zen's own scream was trapped in his chest, clawing into his heart and squeezing his head until he thought he might burst from the pressure. He opened his mouth—

Qì flared, bright and searing and unbearably hot, twisting quickly into a sturdy, earthen ring that churned and cast him in a cage of golden light. The Seal grew, wending its white-hot grasp around him. Clamping over each of his claws, chaining him down.

The darkness dissipated. He fell, his back against hard ground. Smells and sounds crept back to him: an evergreen forest, at night.

Someone crouched over him, hands on his shoulders. *"Zen,"* came a voice. *"Wake up."*

Zen's eyes flew open. A familiar face hovered over him. It was one he had recognized as a shelter, as belonging to someone who would protect him. "Shī'fù," he whispered.

But everything was wrong, everything was different from the day this person had saved his life. Now his head pounded and something inside him writhed as his memories came spilling back. He had betrayed the protection of the grandmaster, the man he had viewed as a father for so long. He had lost the trust of the girl he loved. And now, he realized as he turned to look at the Most Hospitable Pine, the Boundary Seal to the place he had called home for the past eleven cycles had closed itself off to him.

The grief inside him began to burn. He sat up, touching his hand to his chest. "You put another Seal over me," he said.

"To help you," Dé'zǐ replied. His voice was soft, yet it was somehow charged with authority, sincerity, and something like sadness.

He lies, came a faint voice inside Zen. A distant echo, from an abyss far away. *The Boundary Seal closed to you. Your own master views you as a danger, a threat to be subdued.*

Zen shook off his master's hands and pushed himself to his feet. "You lie," he said, though his voice shook. "You would repress the power inside me, as you have from the very beginning."

"No," Dé'zǐ said. He, too, straightened. Though the grandmaster stood nearly half a head shorter than Zen, he was effortlessly commanding in his slight frame. "I seek to help you *control* the power inside you. Right now, you are letting *it* control *you.*"

He thinks you weak. He thinks you incapable of wielding such power.

"You have never wished me to use this power," Zen said coldly. "Why? Would you rather see Skies' End, see our kingdom, fall to the Elantians?"

"You and I both know what will happen if I remove my constraint on that thing inside you. I wish not to have history repeat itself." In spite of the grandmaster's calm tone, a faint sheen of sweat had formed on his face. Zen sensed the qì to Dé'zǐ's Seal flicker.

Dé'zǐ might be able to subdue the power of a regular demon, but he was far from a match for a Demon God.

"So you're afraid of me. Of what I might do." The anger inside Zen burned brighter, resentment forged from all the years of having hated a part of his heritage, having to bow his head each time someone mentioned his clan. "You and all the other masters judged me from the very first day I set foot in your school, for my bloodline, my ancestry, and my birthright." His voice rose. "You are afraid I will establish the next clan uprising; afraid that I can change the history of this kingdom into what it was meant to be."

"I am afraid," Dé'zǐ said quietly, "that you will make your choices based on the hatred inside you instead of the love."

See what he reduces your loyalty, your filial piety, to. See how he views your sacrifice.

"*Everything* I did was out of love!" Zen's voice broke; he couldn't help it. "I loved our school. I loved our people, our land, our culture. I loved *you.*" His master drew a sharp breath, but Zen went on, words pouring from him in torrents. "But I also loved my clan. I loved my father, my family, my ancestry. I tried to deny that until now, but I will no longer. Is it so wrong of me to wish to use their legacy as a path forward for the Hin? To reestablish our kingdom as it was before, with the clans once again autonomous and free to practice their customs, their arts of practitioning?"

All along, perhaps it was the ones we loved most that we should have seen as our enemy, the Black Tortoise whispered. *In the end, their true forms show. See how they all betray you. See how they all leave you. See how they all fear you.*

"Your father and your family and your clan have passed beyond this world." There was sorrow in Dé'zǐ's eyes, but Zen knew his master's tricks. "Live not for those whose souls rest in eternal slumber in the next world . . . but for those still struggling to find that peace in this one."

There came a shift in the qì around them: a skittish curling of the passing breeze, an unease groaning through the roots of the trees all around them, echoed in the stones and the soil. The ground rumbled with the immutable march of a thousand footsteps. The air grew heavy with the presence of metal.

Impossible.

He had defeated them already, back at the shores of Black Pearl Lake. Had sensed the Demon God's shadow roving over the bodies, lapping up the yīn of their souls. There was no eternal rest and no crossing the River of Forgotten Death for those devoured by a demon.

Zen turned to view the pass between the Yuèlù Mountains and the pine forest that led to Skies' End. What he saw there chilled his blood. A pale ribbon composed of individual, gleaming parts—like a mass of silver insects or the disjointed scales of a broken creature—wound into view.

"The Elantians used one of our own stratagems against us," Dé'zǐ said quietly. " 'Openly walk the mountain pass while secretly climbing the mountain.' They used but a fraction of their own as bait and had you believe you defeated them so you let down your guard, then followed you here with the greater part of their army . . . and their Royal Magicians."

"Then I will rectify my mistake." Zen stepped forward, drawing Nightfire. His body trembled with exertion; his qì was empty, his muscles worn like a fire burnt out.

He needed strength. He needed power. He needed his Demon God. "Undo your Seal on me, shī'fù. I cannot fight like this, encumbered."

The dark fire of his new power stirred, surging against the golden cage of Dé'zǐ's Seal.

A trickle of sweat carved its way down the side of Dé'zǐ's face. "Zen, please. Do not yield to it. Do not let it influence your thoughts."

"You would die rather than let me use my power? You would sacrifice Skies' End, everyone in the School of the White Pines? With this power I can *win*, shī'fù. I can defeat the Elantians and rebuild our kingdom!"

"I am afraid that after you win, there will be nothing left of the kingdom to rebuild."

He has no faith in you, the Black Tortoise hissed. *He thinks you will make the same mistake as the Nightslayer.*

"I am not Xan Tolürigin!" Zen screamed.

Dé'zǐ's gaze was calm. "No, you are not. You are merely human, like he was."

Zen's rage grew, hardening into something cold and sharp enough to pierce. Molten metal into cool, bladed steel. "Undo your Seal on me *now*, Dé'zǐ."

His master's face closed off. "Forgiveness, Zen," he said. "I will see my own death before I let that thing inside you free."

He would have you live a half-life, a lie, rather than sacrifice his own pride. The Black Tortoise's growls crescendoed like a war drum. *He would see the end of this kingdom and his people rather than set you free. You, the true you: Xan Temurezen, descendant of Xan Tolürigin and heir to the last great demonic practitioner.*

The darkness in his mind cleared, and he saw the truth of it now, clear as a stretch of black night. The only way this could end. The only way he could be who he was meant to be—the only way he could break his master's Seal over him, defeat the Elantians, and reestablish the Last Kingdom as it was meant to be.

Zen turned and plunged his sword into his master.

Of all things, it was the fact that his master did not even resist that shocked Zen most. He'd known that his power had grown to rival that of Dé'zǐ over the past eleven cycles of his training; it was all that he'd aimed for. To become powerful, so that no one could ever hurt him again. So that no one could ever hurt those he loved again.

The sword trembled in his hands with Dé'zǐ's breathing, which already grew labored. The shadows in the corner of Zen's vision receded, the black fire in his mind cooling. He blinked and saw the same face that had rescued him from the Elantian experimental lab so long ago, after he'd been cut open and stitched back together a thousand times. A face that had smiled at him *in spite of* who he was and what he held inside him; the only one that had beheld him when all others had turned away.

Zen let go of his sword; he caught his master as he fell, hands twining around hair that had shifted from ink black to mist gray, shoulders that had once been corded with muscles that were now slimmed. Since when had his master become so fragile, so small?

Dé'zǐ coughed red down his chin. His hands, though, reached for Zen's.

There was an ache deep in Zen's throat; a pressure building in his head. "Why?" he croaked. "Why did you not resist?"

Some had described Dé'zǐ's eyes as shifting storm clouds, others as the unsettled shade of thick fog. But Zen had always thought his master's eyes were the color of steel, so sharp they could pierce with one look. And as he met his dying master's gaze, he realized that it was still Dé'zǐ who had played the winning hand.

"I could never hope to fight the power of a god and win," Dé'zǐ rasped. His grasp tightened over Zen's fingers. "I know it has not been an easy path for you to walk, Zen. One marred with the blood from your ancestors' deeds. I have tried, instead, over the past eleven cycles, to win you over . . . with love. I have loved you as much as any father can love a son. I never dared hope that you would return it in full . . . but if you have held any form of affection for me, then perhaps there is hope yet."

Zen couldn't breathe.

"I wanted to give you one last thing: the gift of my death. I hope that your choices will be guided by love, not revenge.

And I hope that, in your quest for power, you will remember this moment, this pain you are feeling. I hope you will remember what power can cost you. May it guide you going forward . . . in your darkest moments."

His voice was failing, his words grew slow and slurred, yet for all of it, he might have been slowly carving them out of Zen's flesh.

He could feel his master slipping away, his breathing growing shallow. His Seal was starting to weaken, too, the invisible cage Dé'zǐ had erected over Zen's power crumbling away. The darkness it held at bay began to seep out. A whisper stirred in the recesses of his mind, icier than the deepest winds of winter. The old man in his arms seemed to grow cold.

Gently, Zen laid his master at the entrance to Skies' End, beneath the Most Hospitable Pine. He stood, bringing his fists together in a salute. It was remarkable how steady he could hold his hands when everything inside him was on the brink of falling apart.

"Peace be upon your soul, and may you find the Path home."

He bowed, one, two, three times. His mind was fogging over, obsidian smoke curling over his thoughts, that ancient presence beginning to stir.

Zen pulled Nightfire from his master's chest and slid it back into its scabbard. Blood defiled his hands, warm and slick. When he straightened, the world looked different, as though his life was forever splintered between present and future, defined by this moment. He had been running from the person he was meant to be for so long.

It was time to face his fate.

To his clan, destiny was dictated by the stars beneath which he was born, carved into the bones of the wildhorse chosen for him at birth and written in the way the red sands of the plateaus blew in the Northern Steppes. It was something undeniable, something woven into stories that lasted beyond time. His father had known this when he'd sacrificed himself to save Zen. His great-grandfather Xan Tolürigin had known when he'd fought against the emperor of the Middle Kingdom.

And Zen knew as he walked from Skies' End, sword in hand, black flames rolling from his skin and curling over his feet, the roar of his energies cresting over as though he were screaming to the heavens.

As Dé'zǐ's golden Seal faded, something rose within him and behind him as high as the night sky itself, starless and fathomless as an abyss. A voice echoed inside him, ancient and vast, a shadow without light.

Xan Temurezen, last heir of the Mansorian clan, his Demon God whispered. *At long last, you have risen.*

31

Grief is for the living. The dead feel nothing.

—Pǔh Mín, Imperial Scholar and Spirit
Summoner, *Classic of Death*

Skies' End was a flurry of movement. People hurried to and fro, Archery disciples taking the highest vantage points, Seals disciples the very first line of defense, and Swords and Fists set up in ambush locations throughout the trees and buildings. Overhead, storm clouds surged, galloping across the sky, whipped by a rising wind. The air was charged, swollen with impending rain.

Lan fought her way through the crowd.

"Lan'mèi!"

She spun, loosing a breath of relief when she caught sight of Shàn'jūn's slim face and pale robes emerging from the direction of the Chamber of a Hundred Healings. A thousand words might not explain what had happened since the last time they saw each other, and she steeled herself against anger, sadness, or disappointment from her friend. But as they reached each other, he took her hands in his and squeezed.

"Tài'gē told me everything," he said. His hemp satchel hung by his side; inside, she heard the clinks of various bottles and vials—his emergency pack. "Dilaya is awake and already reaching for her sword—though there will be a bump to make her head even larger in the next weeks."

Lan summoned a grin for him. "Good. Dilaya fights best when she's mad, so I'll take credit for when she single-handedly cuts down the Elantian army." She grew sober. "The grandmaster asked me to fetch you. I think he is going to try to save Zen."

Shàn'jūn's lips parted. He swept a glance around them, at the disciples running about, his expression softening in the way it did only for Tai.

Lan stood on tiptoes, searching, but there was no sign of the awkwardly tall boy with his head of curls.

Shàn'jūn blushed when he saw her watching him. "We go," he said, tugging on her hand, but she hesitated.

Lan knew the pain in a goodbye left unsaid.

"Ài'ya," Shàn'jūn sighed lightly. "I will see him soon enough."

The nine hundred ninety-nine steps of the mountain had never taken so long. The energies of Skies' End had shifted. Darkness—the taste of yīn—hung thick in the air. The shadows stretched longer, twisting and morphing as they hurried down the steps. Lightning flashed in the clouds gathered overhead, followed by the rumble of thunder.

They were nearly there when Shàn'jūn suddenly grabbed her hand, drawing them to a stop. His lips parted, and for a moment, he looked at Lan, fear written plain across his face.

"I think . . . I think something has just happened." The Medicine disciple swallowed, shut his eyes briefly. "Though I lack the ability to channel much qì, I am particularly attuned to its flows. Yáng to yīn, warm to cold . . . life to death. Something has just happened, Lan, and I . . . I am afraid to find out what it is."

And then Lan felt it too: a flicker in the world of yáng, a draining of vitality as though a star had just winked out. A single, small star—but a star she knew.

Grandmaster, she thought.

It wasn't until they had reached the bottom and saw the agitated quiver of the Boundary Seal that Shàn'jūn pulled her to a sharp stop. Slowly, ever so slowly, he put a finger to his lips. Then he pointed.

Lan looked to the Most Hospitable Pine, silhouette jagged in the night.

Her gaze fell, too late, to the figure lying prone beneath it. A set of practitioner's robes, white as snow. Then: movement beyond the pine, cutting off her trail of thought. A figure rose from the body. He had held so still that she'd thought his black *páo* was part of the shadows.

The moon slid out from behind clouds at that moment, cleaving the scene into black and white, a place of silhouettes and ghosts. Zen straightened from the grandmaster's body, blood-soaked and trailing darkness as though he'd been cut from a piece of the night. Something behind him reared up, expanding until it stood taller than the highest summit and seemed to devour the moon and extinguish the stars. Lan held tightly to Shàn'jūn's hands, watching with her mouth open as the thing—the *monster*—let out a breath that shook the mountains.

Then, its great shadow seemed to wrap around Zen, and both disappeared.

Shàn'jūn's face had drained of blood. "Was that . . . ?"

Slowly, Lan nodded. "That," she said, her voice low, "was the Black Tortoise."

Somehow, she stood. Somehow, she took Shàn'jūn's hand, and pulled him down the last steps. Beyond the Boundary Seal with its ghostly chorus of warning cries. Out here, the yīn was stronger, the shadows darker.

She knelt by the grandmaster. Blood glistened against his robes, oozing across his middle and dripping onto the soil and grass of the forest. His face was pale and his hands were cold as she gathered them in her own. She thought of how formidable he'd looked in the times she had glimpsed him at Skies' End: frame slight yet powerful outlined against a brilliant, craggy horizon.

"Shī'zǔ," she whispered, and then her voice rose with uncontrolled panic. "Shàn'jūn! *Shàn'jūn—help him!*"

"I am here." Shàn'jūn knelt by the grandmaster's side, a vial of clear green liquid already in his hands. He lifted it to the grandmaster's nose and poured out a single drop.

A hiss, a burst of yáng. For a few moments, nothing happened.

Then Dé'zǐ drew a shallow breath. His eyes flew open and came to rest on Lan.

"Shī'zǔ, hold on," said Shàn'jūn. "I will save you. Hold on for me, all right?"

Lan marveled at how soothing his voice could be, how steady his hands as he took out a cloth and pressed it to the grandmaster's chest.

"Hold it there and put pressure on it," Shàn'jūn instructed Lan.

"Lan," Dé'zǐ wheezed. His fingers tightened against hers. "I am glad it is you. Listen carefully, for we have no time left."

"Please, shī'zǔ," she said. "You must conserve your strength—"

"Sòng Lián."

Her truename, spoken so gently from his lips. Lan stilled, shock icing her blood.

Her truename. He knew her truename.

She had never told him.

"You look so much like Sòng Méi," Dé'zǐ continued. If he'd spoken her name with affection, her mother's truename was a prayer on his lips. "She was the one who helped me understand things from a different perspective. That good and evil are often two sides of the same coin; it merely depends on how you see it."

"Shī'zǔ," she pleaded. "Save your strength—"

"*Listen to me.*" Dé'zǐ's eyes burned like fire. "You must remember this, Lián'ér. There was no right or wrong to the clan uprisings; the unification of the Middle Kingdom was at once the greatest and most terrible event to have befallen this piece of land. The Nightslayer was not wrong to fight for his clan—yet was it right of him to slay thousands of innocents for the same cause?" Dé'zǐ paused and gave a violent hack; dark blood bloomed on the front of his shirt. "Yīn and yáng. Good and evil. Great and terrible. Two sides of the same coin, Lián'ér, and somewhere in the center of it all lies *power*. The solution is to find the balance between them. Do you understand?"

She was shivering, shaking with the weight of his words, the vast ancient histories he spoke of, so complex that she could barely begin to understand them, let alone accept them. "Find the balance," she echoed, her teeth chattering. "Tell me how, shī'zǔ."

"The Demon Gods were never meant to be wielded without a check to their power," the grandmaster sighed. His eyes fluttered. "Let your mother's song guide you . . . bring balance to this forsaken land . . . find the Godslayer."

The words jolted up her veins like lightning. Lan seized fistfuls of the grandmaster's páo. "How?" she demanded, her patience at an end. She had tolerated enough elusive answers. "What is Sealed at the heart of the mountain, shī'zǔ?"

She was leaning forward, and at that exact moment, wind rose between the trees, nearly snatching away his whisper. Obscuring it so that only she heard.

"Of the four star maps, two are blank," Dé'zǐ rasped, "for two of the Four were already found by the Order of Ten Thousand Flowers. Sealed in the heart of Skies' End . . . is a Demon God."

The world seemed to stop, the motion of the leaves in wind and the clouds sweeping the sky slowing so that there was only Lan and the dying man before her.

"The Azure Tiger," Dé'zǐ finished, "the one that I vowed to keep Sealed until the Order found a way to destroy them all."

Two found, two missing. The Black Tortoise was now with Zen; the Crimson Phoenix had occupied a part of the night sky far west of them. The Azure Tiger had been here all along.

If so . . .

"Then where is the Silver Dragon?" she whispered.

The grandmaster's eyes fluttered.

"Shī'zǔ, do not close your eyes," she heard Shàn'jūn say, but she was still leaning over the grandmaster, searching for the truth in his face. For who he was, and how he fit into her story.

"Zen," the grandmaster panted. Sweat beaded his temples; his face was white as bone. ". . . something you must . . . know about him. His truename . . . is . . . Xan Temurezen . . ."

Xan Temurezen. The name struck like lightning. Crackled through her veins. Roared in her ears. *Xan.*

Zen's words rang in her head. *I remember the day the Hin emperor came for my clan,* he'd told her one night back at the

Village of Bright Moon Pond. *I was out herding the sheep when I heard the screams.*

Dé'zǐ nodded at her expression. "Last of the Mansorian clan . . . great-grandson and heir to Xan Tolürigin . . . the Nightslayer. Binder of the Black Tortoise."

Lan felt as though she were listening to an ancient tale spun by the poets and bards, of kingdoms and bloodlines and Demon Gods. Yet as she collected pieces of her memory, they fit between the lines, weaving together into a story that she had failed to see all along. Zen's face, drawing tight at the mention of the Nightslayer. The conflict in his eyes when she needled him about demonic practitioning; his resolution to use the Demon Gods to fight the Elantians.

His binding to the Black Tortoise, of all Demon Gods.

It all came together perfectly.

"Shī'zǔ!" Shàn'jūn said suddenly, dropping the needle and thread he had been using for sutures. "Shī'zǔ, stay with us—"

Lan looked at the dying man before her and realized that everything had come too little, too late. She had ten thousand questions left to ask him, and only seconds left.

She seized the only one that didn't matter—yet that held her entire world. "How did you know my mother?"

The pain left Dé'zǐ's face. He smiled, looking suddenly like a young man again. "I loved her," he sighed, and his gaze lingered on Lan's face. "And I will go into my next life . . . grateful . . . that I spent my last moments with you . . . my child, Lián'ér."

He spoke her name on an exhale, and his eyes shut as his lips stilled.

A great breeze swept the forest, drawing clouds over the moon and rattling the pines and ginkgos all around. The earth trembled, and then a flash of light cleaved the world into monochrome. Time seemed to stop, the clouds stifling the sky, the leaves frozen in a flurried dance, the first droplets of rain suspended in the air, shimmering like tiny, tinted glass jewels.

And then they fell.

By her side, Shàn'jūn, whose hands had not stopped moving since he'd knelt by the grandmaster, had gone utterly still. His fingers were red with blood, running in rivulets around them with the downpour and staining his practitioner's robes.

Lan felt very far away, as though she were still snared by the grandmaster's last words, trapped in those moments of truth.

My child, Lián'ér.

She had wondered, as a child, who her father might be. That curiosity had been abruptly ended with the Conquest. She'd needed to survive and to decipher what her mother had burned into the scar on her wrist. Yet now, realizing that the possibility of a father had been right in front of her for the past moon, she had the sudden urge to scream.

She looked to Dé'zǐ's face, serene even in death. To the blood that wept into the soil and drenched her páo. Since when had he known? She searched through her memories. It had to have been after she'd used her song to knock out Dilaya and rescue Zen; he'd found out from Tai, of all people.

She hadn't known him well enough to feel anything other than numb shock in this moment. That, and the possibilities of the paths that had ended with Dé'zǐ's life.

The chance to defend Skies' End.

The chance to defeat the Elantians.

The chance for her to have a father.

In the distance, there came the tremor of qì through the air: a dark, corroded energy filled with yīn and the wrath and fury of a demon.

Of a *Demon God*.

"He's let it loose," Shàn'jūn said suddenly. "I was there eleven cycles ago, when the grandmaster brought him to my master for help. He was more demon than child. Whatever was inside him had nearly taken full control of his mind." In the falling rain, Shàn'jūn's face was pale. "We must . . . we must stop him. We cannot let him lose control again."

Lan thought of Dilaya's empty sleeve, the patch over her eye. The hundreds of lives—both Elantian and Hin—back at the outpost. Those incidents had occurred with the power of a regular demon. Lan did not wish to imagine the consequences of Zen unleashing the full power of his Demon God here, so close to Skies' End. A god with no care as to who lived or who died.

The yīn around them crescendoed. The rain fell relentlessly; the wind around them shrieked.

The grandmaster was gone.

I must stop him.

Lan stood and ran. She heard Shàn'jūn calling after her, felt raindrops whipping her face. Her hands were at the sash around her waist, fingers tugging her ocarina free. It slid eagerly into place between her palms as though with a mind of its own.

Lan slowed her steps and raised it to her lips.

The melody she played flowed through her fingers, her soul. It was one she had held deep in her memory, and it came now like a dream: a bamboo forest, a warm fire, a boy whose coldness had melted like winter to spring beneath the light of her song.

She closed her eyes as she played. A single, hot tear slid

down her cheek, and if it was possible that all the desire in the world could turn back time, Lan thought she might have the strength to do so. To return to that moment in the bamboo forest.

Slowly, the yīn died down. Footsteps, padding through the rain toward her. And then a warm hand coming to cup her cheek.

She opened her eyes, and Zen knelt before her. He held one hand to his stomach, where a large gash ripped across his robes. Rain mingled with blood, dripping down his face.

She lowered her ocarina.

"Lan," he panted, and she flinched at the sound of his voice. Once, her heart might have ached at the sight of him bleeding and injured before her.

But that had been for Zen, the boy who had saved her on the walls of Haak'gong, who had patiently taught her practitioning, who had followed the tenets to the Way with rigid stubbornness.

Who had kissed away her tears and promised she would never need to be alone again.

Looking at the figure before her, dripping yīn energies, carrying shadows like black fire, she was unsure where human ended and Demon God began.

"You murdered our grandmaster," she said. He closed his eyes. His face shifted through emotions as though he wrestled with something inside himself. She continued, "And you used me to see the star maps of the Demon Gods. To find the Black Tortoise. I know what you are and who you are, Xan Temurezen."

He trembled violently. Rain carved tracks down his cheeks. "I have not been truthful with you about many things," Zen said, "but the one truth I can neither control nor deny is that you hold my heart, Lan. I have never used you for anything."

She was glad for the downpour that would obscure the wetness in her own eyes. Behind her, Dé'zǐ's body cooled. Soon, it would return to the elements of the earth, the cycle of all things natural in this world.

"None of that matters," she said quietly, "if you choose a different path to walk. Give up the Black Tortoise, Zen. We will find another way to bring balance to this land and free our people. One without the cost of innocent lives." She held out a hand.

A shadow fell across Zen's expression. He closed his eyes and clasped a palm over his face, straining as though battling an invisible force.

Dé'zǐ had said that the practitioners who channeled the power of Demon Gods lost their bodies, then minds, then souls. Zen was still inside. He was still fighting.

Lan knelt before him and took in the unfeeling, unseeing face before her. *This is Zen,* she thought. *The boy who saved your life. Who has protected you all this time.*

Leaning forward, she pressed her lips to the crook of his cheeks, kissing away the rain. It came away salty.

Zen shuddered. After what felt like an eternity, he spoke a single word.

"Lan."

His eyes opened, and they were clear.

She might have wept in relief. "Yes. I'm here."

He took her hands in his and traced a thumb over her left wrist. "You have wished for power, to protect the ones you love. There is one last thing your mother hid in your Seal that you have not yet uncovered."

She had a sudden sense of foreboding.

"I will show you what it is, right now," Zen said, and dug his fingers into her scar.

Pain seared through her arm. It splintered into her mind,

and the world fractured into black flame. She could feel her flesh burning, as though her bones had turned to molten metal and she was melting from the inside out. Darkness shrouded her mind.

Before her: a spot of white, the faintest flicker. Lan reached for it, but the tendrils of dark fire pulled her back. Even as she watched, mind blurring from the pain, the white spot drew closer. It became a dot, then a cracked circle.

No, not a circle—a character.

A *Seal*.

Her Seal.

Lan gasped as the darkness withdrew, tendrils shifting their attention to the looming Seal that glowed as bright as the moon itself. Behind it, something writhed.

The shadows shot out, latching onto the Seal, twining over its strokes and dimming its light. Cracks appeared along the Seal's surface as the black flames ate away at it.

Then it shattered.

Lan screamed as her mother's Seal dissolved into the darkness, her vision flitting between reality and illusion. The scar on her arm, once pale and puckered, had grown dark as a rotting scab. Beneath it, the pulsing glow strengthened until the scar tissue fell away altogether.

Light fractaled from her. She had the impression that she stood on the peak of an icy mountain or a frozen lake, waters aglow. Across from her, Zen's shadow cut a black arc over her light. He reached up and cupped her cheek in one hand.

"Forgiveness, Lan," he said. "I wish it didn't have to come to this. I sensed from the start that your mother's Seal was powerful, with many layers: at first to suppress your qì, then to lead you to Guarded Mountain and find the ocarina. But it was only after I met the Black Tortoise that I realized there was one final secret hidden within." His grip tightened. "Perhaps now your stance on the Demon Gods will change." His eyes darkened and his nails dug into her chin as he turned her face to look back.

Rearing up before the Boundary Seal of Skies' End, stretching higher than the summit of the mountain itself, was the white serpentine shape that had loomed over her in an illusion of a night sky.

This time, it was not an illusion.

Lan looked up at the phantom shape of the Silver Dragon of the East, towering above the Yuèlù Mountains.

Now, it looked back at her.

32

The emperor feared not the sword of his enemy
pointed at his breast, but the poison of a lover
administered in his bed.

—Grand Historian Sī'mǎ, *Records of the
Grand Historian*

Zen's demon had whispered warnings to him, of the *thing* that lay coiled at the heart of Lan's core of qì. He'd seen it: in the inexplicable way she'd killed that Elantian soldier back in the Teahouse, then again in the Chamber of Waterfall Thoughts when Dilaya had threatened her. And at last, the answer had come to him when his own Demon God spoke.

Another of us lies within that girl. Another Ancient—the one you mortals refer to as the Silver Dragon.

It had all clicked, then. Why he had sensed Lan's release of demonic qì early on. Why her regular qì contained no traces of it whatsoever.

Her mother had Sealed the Silver Dragon inside her, and one condition of that Seal was to defend Lan's life should it ever be in danger. It explained Lan's prodigious grasp of practitioning, the astonishing rate at which she had learned to manipulate qì into Seals . . . the power of a Demon God, even fettered, embellished her own abilities.

Emotions and thoughts warred within him, the lines between his thoughts and his Demon God's thoughts blurring. His hand was still wrapped around the girl's jaw, and he saw her terror as the light of the Silver Dragon reflected in her eyes. He tightened his grasp on her and her mouth fell open, gasping for air as her fingers scrabbled against his. He watched this with no more feeling than one might have toward a fish drowning on land or an insect at the end of its life.

The glow of the Silver Dragon flickered and began to dim.

He tightened his claws against the girl's flesh and felt a responding wave of nausea and fury in his stomach—directed at him. The boy, his binder. The boy was still fighting for control of his body—and he was furious.

Humans. So soft, so fragile. So sentimental.

Yet his claim to this boy's body was still tenuous, let alone to his mind and soul.

He withdrew.

Zen's thoughts drifted, shadows to light, and he found himself blinking as rain continued to wet his cheeks. His fingers were pressed so tightly against Lan's windpipe that her eyes had rolled into the back of her head. By now, the light of the Silver Dragon was no more than a speck in her left wrist, a dying ember.

With a gasp, he tore his hands from her. Lan fell forward. He caught her and held her against him, her head resting against his neck, her arms dropping to her side.

"Forgiveness," he whispered. "Please, Lan, forgiveness. I never meant to hurt you."

He sensed her shift against him. Then, without warning, pain split his chest.

Zen coughed. Black spots dotted his vision. Inside him, another voice was screaming, its shrieks tearing against his mind. The shadows of his qì flickered around him. Fading.

Lan looked up, her hand on the hilt of That Which Cuts Stars. The blade wedged between his ribs. Her hands red with blood.

"You told me not to miss," she said. "I didn't."

She twisted, then pulled the blade out.

33

Emotion must never drive war, for anger will
fade and vanity is empty, yet kingdoms lost and
lives destroyed will never come to be again.

—General Nuru Ala Šuzhan of the
Jorshen Steel clan, *Classic of War*

Zen slumped forward. Blood dripped from his mouth and from the wound in his chest, running in rivulets through the soil at the base of Skies' End. The shadows in his eyes cleared, and when he looked up at her, hair slicked to his face from rain, she knew with certainty she gazed at the boy she had fallen for back in a mist-cloaked village.

His lips curved into a slow, faint smile. "Better . . . than teacups," he whispered.

Then Zen collapsed in the mud. His eyes fluttered shut.

Lan's hands shook; the knife she clutched wept red. It was these last words that had unhinged her. A reminder of the good times, the future she had hoped for before their fates had become a tangle of star-crossed lines.

You aim for the demon's core of qì —the equivalent to our hearts. His hand, once so gentle and steady on hers. Pointing the tip at his own chest. *Then you pierce.*

The question was, had she cut the demon's core, or had she pierced Zen's heart? Or both?

What have I done? Lan thrust That Which Cuts Stars to the ground as though burned. It landed in a puddle by Zen's motionless body. *What have I done?*

"Lan'mèi!"

Shàn'jūn's voice jolted her from her reverie. The Medicine disciple emerged from the rain, hands bloody, face ashen. Behind him, Tai appeared, hair plastered to his forehead and out of breath from having come down the steps.

"Everyone felt it," the Spirit Summoner panted. "Two massive bursts of qì, exploding from the base. I came to find Shàn'jūn. What happened?"

"Please, help him," Lan whispered.

Shàn'jūn knelt by Zen. "There is a pulse," he said, and drew out his satchel. "And so there is a way. Tài'gē, light, please."

The Spirit Summoner knelt by Lan and held up a lotus lamp. With a few gestures, he drew a Seal for fire. His gaze was steady as he watched Shàn'jūn work. "Shàn'jūn," he said. "The Boundary Seal. We must get behind the Boundary Seal."

"I cannot," came the Medicine disciple's faint reply. His lips were pressed together, his brows furrowed, his hands flitting between vials and needles and packs of herbs. "The Boundary Seal has closed itself against Zen."

Lan thought again of Zen ripping open her mother's Seal, as that brilliant white light—the same she had seen at Māma's death, at the Teahouse, and then when she first met Dilaya at the Chamber of a Hundred Healings—exploded from her. This time when she reached inside herself, she could feel its presence coiled over her heart, its core of qì pulsing lightly as it sent energies through her blood and flesh.

All along, there was a final secret that Māma Sealed inside me. The fact wrapped itself around her and squeezed so tight that she could barely breathe. *The Silver Dragon.*

Looking up at the Demon God, she'd felt a sense of fear,

yet beneath it there had been a thrumming undercurrent of awe. She might have understood, then, Zen's decision. How the power and majesty of the Black Tortoise had seduced him, won him over in the end.

But Lan knew that Māma hadn't Sealed the Silver Dragon within her for her to wield its power.

She had given Lan this Demon God for Lan to *destroy* it.

"Shàn'jūn, listen. Listen to me," Tai said. "The masters have set up the lines of defense according to the Thirty-Fifth Stratagem inside the Boundary Seal. Do not ask me to watch you risk your life."

"And do not ask me to abandon my duty," Shàn'jūn replied. His tone was soft, his eyes steady as he looked at Tai. "Zen holds the Black Tortoise within him, Tài'gē. I must save him . . . I must try."

"He will heal," Tai said stubbornly. "His Demon God will heal him."

"He won't." Lan's voice cracked. She held up That Which Cuts Stars. "I used this."

Tai's expression immediately tightened. "You," he said in a hollow tone. "You have done the worst thing possible. That blade. That blade does not destroy a demon's core. It merely cuts off its demonic qì temporarily. It maims both binder and demon. Do you know—do you know what happens if Zen dies?"

Lan did not wish to know.

"When one kills the soul bound to a demon, the demon will simply find a new soul to bargain with. A new cycle of war and destruction." Tai's next words fell like the thud of a sword. "If Shàn'jūn cannot save Zen . . . we may have unleashed the Black Tortoise. Right into the waiting hands of the Elantians."

And there would be no one to stop them.

There could, came a distant voice from within her—a part of her, or a part of the thing she now knew lay within her. She thought she saw a flash of silver, a gelid eye cracking open to look at her. *You could.*

No, no, she couldn't—she *wouldn't.* Yet watching blood continue to darken the ground beneath Zen, Lan felt as though her mother had given her an impossible task. She had left Lan all the power in the world, and instead of asking her to use it, to fight with it, had commanded her to destroy it.

Her teeth began to chatter; she wrapped her arms around herself, feeling so completely lost and alone in this moment.

"Tài'gē." Shàn'jūn's sleeves were soaked with blood. The flames of Tai's lamp held steady as the yīn energies in the air—the qì of the Demon God—continued to ebb lower. With each brighter surge of the lantern, Zen's life dimmed a little more. "I need Master Nóng. My skills alone are inadequate to save Zen's life."

Tai's brows furrowed. He closed his eyes, seeming to war with himself. When he opened them again, they were sad, tender. He held out a large hand to cup Shàn'jūn's cheek. "Wait for me," he said.

Shàn'jūn's smile was painted in rain and firelight. "Always."

Tai's jaw set as he turned to Lan. "You need to fetch Master Ulara. She is closest, leading the second line of defense with the Swords disciples on the steps to Skies' End. She will help. We must keep the Elantians away from Zen."

"Ulara would leave Zen to die," Lan replied.

"Ulara would protect his Demon God," Tai retorted. "She is a member of the Order of Ten Thousand Flowers."

Lan drew a sharp breath. But, thinking back, it all made sense—how fiercely opposed Ulara had been to the Demon

Gods, how she'd tried to stop Zen before he made the decision to bind it.

Māma, Dé'zǐ, and now Yeshin Noro Ulara . . . if there were members of this Order still alive, then there was hope yet.

Lan stood and brushed a hand against Shàn'jūn's shoulders. "Wait for us," she said, and kicked off in a burst of qì. This time, the Boundary Seal was steeped in an ominous silence as she passed through. Behind, she heard Tai's footfalls following, his use of the Light Arts clumsier and louder than her own.

Slowly, the darkness lifted, yielding to the faraway light of lotus lamps. Lan thought she glimpsed the entrance stone and the eggshell walls of school temples. She was less than a dozen steps away from the top of the steps.

That was when it happened. The qì around them shifted, parting to give way to something else: the overpowering stench of metal.

The hairs on Lan's neck rose. She knew that scent, she knew that overwhelming feeling in the qì.

She spun.

The pine forest beneath the mountain was alive with movement: flashes of metal armor, everywhere, fanned out across the pass between Skies' End and the rest of the Yuèlù Mountains, completely surrounding the forest.

The Elantian army had arrived.

Several steps below her, Tai alighted in a spurt of qì. His eyes widened as he scanned the pine forest below. "No. *No.*" His voice cracked. "Shàn'jūn. *Shàn'jūn!*"

"Tai!" Lan shouted as the Spirit Summoner turned and began to retrace his steps. "Tai—"

Streaks of lightning cracked open the sky. Fire surged up the pine forests, exploding against the Boundary Seal with force that shook the ground they stood on. Lan slammed into the side of the mountain. She tasted copper in her mouth.

"SHÀN'JŪN!"

Tai had fallen to all fours. The flames in the explosion seemed to gild him in a moment that Lan would never forget: eyes so wide, the whites ringed his irises, veins bulging from his neck and temples, fingers stretching in the direction of the boy he loved. "SHÀN'JŪN!" he screamed again as he thrust himself up and launched himself forward. "SHÀN—"

The night lit up again as the second explosion came. This time, the world tilted; a bright pain seared through Lan's head, followed by a high-pitched ringing . . . and then time seemed to slow. The raindrops froze, shimmering as a shape rose through them. It was a pale, serpentine silhouette she had seen before, and its voice wrapped around her, familiar, a part of herself.

Sòng Lián, the Silver Dragon said softly. *You command the power of a Demon God within you. Use it, and you could be the salvation of your people.*

No . . . *No.* When Zen had released the power of his demon, he'd taken the lives of all the innocent Hin in the outpost. And the Nightslayer had channeled the power of the Black Tortoise and nearly destroyed everything he had been fighting for.

Would you stand aside and watch their certain death, then, her god mourned, *rather than take a chance to save their lives?*

Once, a moon ago, she had witnessed the destruction of everything she had known in her life. She'd vowed to become powerful so that she would never have to see those she loved be hurt again. Now that she had all this power, was she not even to take a chance with it?

It had never been that simple. Power always came with a price, each victory with a terrible cost. She had no idea what bargain her mother had made. What the conditions were, how easily she might lose control to the god whose power now lay coiled inside her. One wrong decision, one trick move, and Lan would be sent plunging into the abyss.

And yet . . . what if she *could* sever its power when she was at the brink of losing control? Her hands were cold, yet the hilt of That Which Cuts Stars rested slick against her palm. She had cut off the Black Tortoise's grip on Zen with it, albeit temporarily. What if she could do the same thing to herself?

If she could succeed here, she could save Skies' End. And if she could use her power to protect those she loved, she could yet save the Last Kingdom.

Several steps beneath her, Tai lay unconscious against the mountain wall that the explosion had flung him against, his chest rising and falling in shallow breaths. His hair, wet and tangled, covered his face. She thought of the way he smiled when he watched Shàn'jūn feed the carp in the moonlight.

Lan thought of Shàn'jūn, nursing her patiently beneath the fretwork window frame of the Chamber of a Hundred Healings.

Of Taub, red-faced from the heat and steam of her kitchens; Chue, chatting to her as they took their meals in the refectory; of the early-morning bells, the conversation of disciples beneath crisp winter sunlight threaded through with mist; of all the joy she had found in Skies' End that had made her life worth living again.

Of Ying, running to save her in nothing but a flimsy lotus dress.

She thought of Zen: the first time she had met him in a crowded Teahouse, then his arms wrapped around her as he whispered of a future for them, his lips brushing her cheeks to kiss away her tears.

She clenched her teeth now, the rain turning warm against

her skin. This time, though, he was not there to wipe it away. Might never be there again.

Her heart broke all over again, and with that, her will shattered.

Anger filled her.

Her Demon God reared up, its light dusting the mountains like a second moon. It watched her with eyes as blue as the heart of fire, scales shimmering like the first snowfall frozen to ice. A vision, an illusion, a part of herself.

Lan reached out a hand and dipped her finger into the stream of power that flowed from her Demon God's core.

The world breathed. She could sense it all, the brush of each raindrop against pine leaves and branches, kneading into the soil, clattering against the armor of the Elantian army that wound all the way to the next mountain.

Fear and anger swelled in her throat. Yet with it came something new: a curiosity aimed at the battle sprawled before them. A clinical study of the odds, as though she were hovering over a chessboard and each person—each *life*—were a piece to be used and discarded at will.

So this is how it feels to be a god, she thought to herself, and in that moment, Lan vowed to never give in. No matter what, she would remember, until the very end, why she did all this. Ying. Shàn'jūn. Zen. Dé'zǐ. Māma.

So long as she held on to what made her human, she would never become a god.

She gave the command.

Destroy them.

A Seal flowed from her fingertips, drawn by the god, and she suddenly understood what Zen had meant when he said performing Seals was an art in its highest form. The weave of energies was more complicated than any she had ever come across: so intricate that it might take her hours to unravel, the strokes straddling the boundary between science and art. Her hands moved together in a dance she did not know, guided by the presence of another.

Power hummed in the air around her. A glow spread from her, shrouding the mountains around her in white, reaching up into the sky itself.

The moment the Seal closed, a shockwave pulsed through the trees. She could feel it, for she was everywhere and nowhere at once, soaring through cloud and rain and plunging down the mountainside. Something deep within the ground began to shift: a tremor, reaching all the way to where the Elantian army stood.

Through the rain and darkness, all that Lan could see was a mass rising darker than the night sky, like a giant maw opening behind the army. The earth itself was bending to her will, pines and brush and soil cresting in a great tsunami to bury the Elantians. Shrieks filled the air as the soldiers, suddenly so small, began to run from Lan's Seal.

A deep-throated chuckle reverberated in Lan's head. *Fascinating, is it not, how power reduces those you once feared to naught but squirming maggots?* murmured the dragon.

Fascinating, Lan thought. She watched and tried to remember all the times the Elantians had wronged her, but in this moment, her mind was filled with their desperate screams, their lives snuffed out like candles as the earth swallowed them whole. She was drifting, swept away by the great tide of qì that coursed from her.

A blur of a silhouette barreled out of the rain, slamming her into the ground. Her concentration broke; the river of qì faltered, and her Seal dimmed.

Lan blinked. She lay on the ground, the same place on the steps she had been during the second explosion. Yeshin Noro

Ulara stood over her, outlined in the faint yellow glow from the school buildings just a dozen or so steps away.

"What have you done?" the Master of Swords cried. Her face was slicked in rain and mud—none of which masked her wide-eyed terror. This was the first time Lan had seen Yeshin Noro Ulara look afraid.

"I'm helping us win the war," Lan shouted.

"You are destroying Skies' End!" Ulara screamed. "The soil of the pine forest is the foundation to the mountain—you are digging out its roots!"

Fear cracked through Lan's bones, along with a horrible, sickening premonition. She had thought herself different, the exception to the rule; thought that she would be able to dictate the power of a god. Power always came at a cost, and victory never without loss.

"*Stop!*" she gasped, clapping a hand over her temples. "*STOP IT!*"

A soft, silky laugh echoed in her head. *Your wish is my command,* the Silver Dragon said. She saw, in the darkness of her own vision, half-lidded eyes watching her with faint amusement. *And you wished to destroy them.*

"*I wished to protect Skies' End!*" Lan yelled.

That is not what you demanded of me.

"*I command you now to stop!*" Below, the mass of earth, soil, and trees crested toward the base of the mountain like an immutable wave. It blocked out the sky, silenced even the rain—a silence wrought with screams of the dying. Of the rumbling of the earth as it continued to tear itself up by the roots.

Any closer, and Skies' End would be swallowed along with the Elantian army.

Lan clapped her hands to her waist and found two objects

strapped to her side. The smooth shell of her ocarina. And then a familiar hilt engraved with stars dancing amidst flames.

Lan slid That Which Cuts Stars from its sheath. *"STOP!"* she screamed, and plunged the dagger into her side.

There was a hiss like water meeting fire as the blade bit into the stream of power flowing from her core. In her mind's eye, the Silver Dragon's serpentine form twisted away from the pain. The destructive Seal it had conjured, which had glowed bright as a full moon before her, flickered and died.

Far below, the mass of earth collapsed with a sound akin to an explosion and the snapping of thousands of tree trunks.

Then pain whitened her mind. Lan was only aware of her legs buckling beneath her. She did not fall to the ground. A pair of arms caught her, firm with steel-plated armor. Held her.

"You did well," Yeshin Noro Ulara said.

Lan looked up at the Master of Swords. "I didn't think I'd live to hear you compliment me," she croaked.

And there it was, an image that would remain etched in her memories: the faint tug of a corner of Ulara's lips. A half smile.

Boots rang out in the night, and Dilaya alighted on the steps next to Lan, followed by Master Nóng. The Master of Medicine conjured a Seal that wound itself over Lan's and Tai's bodies, lifting them gently. It felt like being wrapped in a warm blanket.

The steps wove in and out of Lan's focus. The next time she blinked, she was lying on flat ground. Someone held a lamp over her, illuminating a familiar face.

"Master Nóng," she croaked. He was bent over her wound, applying salves and herbs—yet Lan also recognized the shimmer of a newly applied Seal. There was much earth to its composition, and it was warm with yáng. Leaning against a pillar next to her, gauze wrapped around his neck, was Tai. He sat in silence, face devoid of any emotion, hair and clothes dripping water.

"I have stanched the bleeding and the pain with a Seal," the Master of Medicine said to Lan. "Now the flesh must do its own work. You are low on your lifeblood." He held up a bowl. "Drink this."

She sat up, wincing only slightly at the dull ache of protest between her ribs. They were in the Chamber of Waterfall Thoughts, she realized, yet the lotus lamps that had always lent their light to the hall were absent. Rain fell in steady drips down the curved clay eaves outside.

Lan took the clay bowl and drank. She was back in Skies' End, yet it no longer held the same warmth for her, like a firepit with the flames gone cold, a courtyard house with no mother. Dé'zǐ, the life and soul of this school, was gone. Shàn'jūn, who should have been sitting in a corner with a bowl of his disgusting concoctions, was absent. And Zen . . .

"Zen," she blurted, her chest squeezing so tight she couldn't breathe. "The Black Tortoise—Master Ulara should have—"

"Slow down." Master Nóng raised a hand. "We have not detected any indication that the Black Tortoise has been released—yet. The masters are gathered outside, discussing the path forward from here. Come."

She pushed herself to her feet and, with Master Nóng in her wake, hobbled through the open-air hallways of the Chamber of Waterfall Thoughts. Behind, Tai got up and followed, quiet as a ghost.

Outside, Skies' End was alight with the fires of battle. At the highest vantage points, Archery disciples loosed arrows as Master Cáo directed them. Masters Ulara and Ip'fong stood in the courtyard with their disciples of Swords and Fists. Their gazes were uniformly directed upward.

High above, the invisible barrier that was the Boundary Seal glowed bright, with streaks of broken qì bleeding across it like veins. Even as Lan watched, another resounding explosion added several more fissures. She had once seen glass break at a stall in the evemarket: a vendor from one of the lands in the Near West had brought a pane of Masyrian glass, with which he'd made art. Lan had watched him bring a stone hammer to its surface, watched spiderweb cracks spread across the smooth, translucent surface until, at last, it splintered.

She thought of this as she watched the Boundary Seal take blow after blow from the Elantians.

The Seals disciples lined the edge of the terrace, their bodies and hands shifting as though in an invisible dance. Qì flowed upward, replenishing the Boundary Seal. Yet the disciples shivered in their páos from the rain, the glow of the dying Boundary Seal casting a colorless light on their pinched, exhausted faces. Their entire battle strategy—the lines of defense, the Linked-Chain Attacks—had been upheld by a group of children and was being torn apart at the seams.

She closed her eyes and reached inside herself. There was a wound where she had met her Demon God: a gash, bleeding qì profusely, from That Which Cuts Stars. She could sense some strange combination of qì clotted there—left by the knife wound—blocking her access to her Demon God. Beyond it, the Silver Dragon's pale silhouette hovered.

Even with her Demon God's attack, there were still so many Elantians. Too many.

From somewhere high up, there came a shout.

"We are out of arrows!"

In the silence that followed, another crack trembled through the ground and sky. The fissures in the Boundary Seal glowed white-hot as the Elantians' fire assaults began to seep through. Fragments of woven qì—perhaps pieces of Seals—curled up into the air like paper burning, each a flicker of light, fast fading. The night seemed suddenly filled with decaying stars, and the weave of energies that had guarded Skies' End over the timeless, relentless churn of dynasties fell like ash as, at last, the Boundary Seal shattered.

34

The Falcon's Claw, one of the twelve legendary swords
of history, took its name under the General Yeshin Noro
Fulingca, founder of the Yeshin Noro noble house of the
Jorshen Steel clan. The blade was so quick, it was said
Fulingca cut off a falcon's claw mid-flight on a hunt.

—Various scholars,
Studies of the Ninety-Nine Clans

A gale whipped through the entryway of Skies' End, bringing with it the crushing energies of metal. Below the
mountain, stretching into the white pine forests, Elantian soldiers poured up the nine hundred ninety-nine steps of Skies'
End, a metallic river of armor surging through a broken dam.

Nine hundred ninety-nine steps: all that stood between
them and the remaining Elantian army.

Lan looked around as the disciples of Swords and Fists took
their battle stances: a hundred or so practitioners—*children*—
shivering in thin, rain-soaked páos. It was suddenly almost
laughable how inadequately prepared they had been for an
Elantian invasion. Lan had seen Elantian armor up close,
plates thick and heavy compared to the fine scales of Hin mail,
and impenetrable without hefty swords. Not to mention the
sheer magnitude of how much the Elantian army outnum-
bered them.

"We must retreat."

It was Yeshin Noro Ulara who spoke. Rain clung to her hair

and eyelashes, dripped down the rigid press of her lips as she watched the encroaching army far below.

Her eyes flicked up, and this time she addressed what was left of the school. "We will not win this battle. I propose to retreat."

Uncertainty rippled through the other masters and disciples.

"Ulara-jiě, we cannot," Master Ip'fong said quietly. "We must guard that which is Sealed in the Chamber of Forgotten Practices—"

"*We* will not retreat," Ulara said, and then nodded to the clusters of disciples watching, wide-eyed. "The disciples will. They have no part in what was begun many cycles ago. I would not ask them to sacrifice themselves for the Order when it is their lives that we pledged to protect."

"I concur." Master Gyasho's soft voice rose through the rain. "The disciples should take the back way through the mountains as Master Nur and the Nameless Master did with the youngest children. We, masters of the School of the White Pines, will concentrate our defense in only one area of the mountain: the Chamber of Forgotten Practices."

"Should we come face-to-face with the Elantian army, we take out their magicians first," Master Ip'fong said slowly, nodding. "And if all fails, we release that which is Sealed rather than let the Elantians take it. They know nothing of what is hidden in the chamber; we have the element of surprise on our side."

"Then let us make haste," Master Cáo chimed in, arriving with his bow and empty arrow quiver. "The Elantians have entered our grounds: nineteen magicians and about one thousand soldiers."

Lan looked around at the masters. Even surly Master Nán and pugnacious Master Fēng appeared to be in silent agreement, nothing but grim resolve written on their faces.

She had so many questions, yet time trickled away from them like rain, the presence of Elantian metal growing ever thicker in the air.

Dilaya spoke Lan's thoughts aloud. "É'niáng, do not ask me to abandon you. I have my sword, and I have my duty."

"And what is your duty, Yeshin Noro Dilaya?" Ulara turned to her daughter. Her voice rang out through the night like thunder. "Your duty is the same as mine: it is to our heritage, and to our people, and to this land."

"It is to *you* as well, É'niáng!"

"Our ancestors have not paved the way for our present day only to watch you foolishly throw yourself into the River of Forgotten Death." Ulara's eyes burned. "Our ancestors wrote in the *Classic of War*, 'Of the Thirty-Six Stratagems, retreat is best.' Most misunderstand this to mean that the classic encourages a coward's surrender. But this stratagem tells us that when the odds are insurmountable, *surviving* is the only way forward. Living on to see another day means another chance to fight back—and another chance to win."

"The Order of Ten Thousand Flowers," Master Nán said in the sudden silence, and Lan realized all the disciples around them had turned to listen. "Why did we choose such a name? Flowers are fragile yet fierce in their tenacity to grow. This is a land of ten thousand flowers, a land of *you*, of all the cultures and clans and histories you hold. The masters here have dedicated our entire lives to planting the seeds of our culture, our heritage, the beauty of our different origins and bloodlines that make up the Last Kingdom. And you, children, carry our legacy. Live, and show them that this is the land of ten thousand flowers."

The words rang a bell. She thought of Zen in the Jade Forest on the first night they had met. *So long as we live on,* he'd said, *we carry inside us all that they have destroyed. And that is our triumph; that is our rebellion.*

Words that were suddenly more significant, now that she knew his clan origin and the depths of his history. Her throat closed; she pushed the memory from her mind. Numbly, she watched the masters issue orders, dismissing the remainder of their disciples. The disciples were silent, frozen, rain dripping down their faces and soaking through their páos.

Among them, a figure suddenly moved.

Tai.

Everyone watched in astonishment as the Spirit Summoner prostrated himself before Master Nán, the master to his discipline. Lan would never have thought Tai—proud, haughty, cold, sarcastic Tai—capable of such an act.

"Shī'fù, it has been Chó Tài's life honor to study beneath you!" Tai shouted above the sound of rain. "This disciple will carry your teachings in his mind, heart, and soul into eternity!"

From somewhere in the crowd, there came another shout. "Shī'fù! This disciple is eternally grateful for your teachings!"

"Shī'fù, this disciple swears to take your art of practitioning to the rivers and lakes of this land and beyond!"

One by one, the disciples of the School of the White Pines sank to their knees, their páos rippling like the tides of a great white river.

Lan looked around again at each master in turn. Gyasho, bald and ageless, blindfolded face raised to the skies in serenity. Fēng, scowling and hunched like a shrimp, with that mole on his nose and his satchel of oracle bones and other divination materials. Nán, looking strangely lost without his usual stack of tomes in his hands. Ip'fong, tall and staunch as a bear, metal spikes clad to his fists. Cáo, quiver empty and siyah horn bow bloodied. Nóng, unusually somber, head bowed, perhaps in remembrance of his most dedicated pupil. And Ulara, hands on the hilts of her great swords, lips pressed in a crimson line.

Seven people, against the might of the Elantian Empire.

"The honor has been ours," said Master Gyasho, bringing his fist to his palm. "The next time we meet, it will be as equals, whether in this life or the next. Carry our history, and our legacy, and live to see another day. Kingdom before life, honor into death."

The other masters brought their hands together in a salute.

Numbly, Lan watched as the disciples began to make for the back steps of the mountain. She caught sight of Chue, his arms around Taub's shoulders. The masters, too, turned to leave, fading into the rain like ghosts until they might have never been there at all.

Yet Lan found that she could not bring herself to move her feet. "Wait," she said, and caught up to the last master to leave. "Wait—Master Ulara, please."

Ulara turned to her, eyebrows raised in a question.

"Let me go with you," Lan said. "My mother gave her life for the Order of Ten Thousand Flowers. It is my duty to help."

"É'niáng, *please*," Dilaya begged. She hadn't moved either, and for the first time, she and Lan were on the same side. Tai, too, hovered nearby. "What is so precious in the Chamber of Forgotten Practices that you must defend, and why is that worth risking your life?"

One might have expected Ulara's anger at her daughter's refusal to yield. But this time, Yeshin Noro Ulara pressed her lips together. She glanced around and, seeing that the other masters were gone, turned back to her daughter. "Sealed away at the heart of the mountain," Ulara said quietly, "is the Azure Tiger."

Dilaya's mouth fell open—but this time, she seemed to find no words to say. Behind her, Tai went very still.

"Unlike the other Hundred Schools of Practitioning, the School of the White Pines never held the secret to a Final Art in its Chamber of Forgotten Practices," Ulara continued. "This school became home to the clans that came together in the Order of Ten Thousand Flowers—the underground rebel movement that sought to resolve the ageless power struggle between the Imperial Court and the clans . . . by destroying the source of the greatest power struggles in our history: the Demon Gods.

"Many in our order gave their lives for this cause, including"—Ulara's sharp eyes turned to Lan, and she thought they might have softened for a second—"her mother. We were hunting down the Demon Gods and Sealing them away while searching for the instrument with which to kill them. But before we could finish our mission, the Elantians invaded."

A flash of lightning; a gleam of silver. A sudden gale whipped up near the entrance stone of Skies' End, bringing with it the crushing energies of metal. Out of the darkness came a silhouette, tall and pale and clad in metal. His wrists flashed with varying shades of gray, gold, and bronze.

The Elantian Royal Magician Erascius stepped forward. His sharp features were curved in a cold smile. "At last," he said, the Elantian language rolling long and sinister. "The elusive home of the last practitioners of this land."

In the blink of an eye, Ulara had positioned herself between the magician and Lan, Dilaya, and Tai. Her fingers moved, and a Shield Seal erected itself before them: a wall wrought of metal, wood, and ice the height of a small hill, bordering the cliffs on either side of them.

On the other side of the shield, Erascius's face opened in a laugh. His hands gestured to summon a metal ramming pole. With a thunderous crack, it slammed into Ulara's shield.

Ulara grasped her daughter's shoulder. Her nails dug in,

her knuckles white. "Run," she said quietly. "Run, and protect Lan with your life. She holds the Silver Dragon of the East inside her. No matter what, do not let the Elantians find it." Dilaya's face blanched in shock, but her mother continued: "And take this."

The dāo gleamed as she held it out. Its handle was sleek, as though made of bone—and in the center was embedded a thick jade ring.

From the other side of the wall came thunderous booming sounds. The wall trembled, shards splintering and beginning to rain down on them.

"Falcon's Claw?" Dilaya's head snapped up. "É'niáng—"

Ulara grasped her daughter's hand and wrapped it around the hilt of the sword. Her knuckles were white as she held on to Dilaya's hand. "You will one day lead a clan, a people, and you must learn the meaning of sacrifice. *Go*," Yeshin Noro Ulara repeated, and then the fierceness to her expression yielded to a profound tenderness. "We will meet again, if not in this life, then in the next, my daughter."

Lan saw, once again, her mother standing before an insurmountable army with a lone woodlute. This time, she understood. So long as there was war, there was sacrifice. So long as there was power, there was bloodshed.

So long as there was life, there was hope.

As the matriarch to the Yeshin Noro clan moved to face the enemy, her daughter lifted her gaze to Lan.

Lan gave her a single nod. She turned, and with a burst of qì, began to make for the back steps of the mountain, followed by Dilaya and Tai.

They were now well and truly alone. Around them, Skies' End was eerily empty, its curved pavilions and halls hollow and dark. Lan couldn't help but think of the School of Guarded

Fists, how it had stood like no more than a phantasmal memory in the night, its occupants long passed into the next world.

The press of metal in the air strengthened, so much so that Lan could nearly taste it. It filled their throats, stifled the other elements in the qì around them. The rain eased. The trees, the buildings, the rocks and bones of the mountain itself seemed to go still.

They were halfway to the summit now, the Chamber of a Hundred Healings looming in the night, its windows blank and its doors open. They passed by the steps to the disciples' living quarters, and then they were at the steep set of stairs carved into the mountain, winding up toward the Peak of Heavenly Discussion. On the other side, Lan now knew, the stairs diverged, spiraling into a secret set of steps leading down the plunging cliffs.

Lan glanced down, the peak yielding a perfect view of the entryway to Skies' End. There, on the open terrace before the Chamber of Waterfall Thoughts, two figures were engaged in battle.

Erascius had broken through Ulara's shield and was advancing upon her, blow by blow. Ulara's hands were a blur as she flung written fús through the air at Erascius. They exploded around him in clouds of brimstone and fire. Before the clouds could settle, Ulara swiftly drew up a Seal.

Erascius emerged. He snapped a finger. Metal spikes shot through the air, puncturing Ulara's Seal. Ulara's sword was a blur as she defended, each *plink* of metal against metal audible from even where Lan stood.

Lan reached inside herself. Where the silhouette of the dragon had stretched sleek and silver, she found only ashes and the faintest pulse of its core, bleeding qì from the gash That Which Cuts Stars had given.

A screech of metal rent the air. Erascius drove Ulara back, his metal magic coiling about him like a whip. The Yeshin Noro matriarch was reduced to defending herself with a combination of swords and Seals.

Dilaya's knuckles were white against the hilt of Falcon's Claw; they had all stopped to watch. "Keep going," she said, but that was when they saw it.

From the darkness between trees stepped more figures, pouring through the entryway to Skies' End. *Magicians,* over a dozen of them, pale blue cloaks fluttering and metal gleaming around their wrists. They raised their arms, and the sky lit up in response.

Flashes of lightning erupted around them, exploding in fire where they hit the ground. Ulara had been engaged in a fast, deadly dance with Erascius as they sparred with both swords and magic. As explosions sounded around her, she faltered, her concentration slipping for a fraction of a second.

Erascius made a slicing motion with his hand, and one of his hovering metal blades cut through Ulara's neck like scissors through paper.

Dilaya screamed.

Lan only stared, the numbness in her heart growing. Yeshin Noro Ulara, the Master of Swords and fierce matriarch to her clan, had always stood in Lan's mind as indomitable, with a tenacity to life like a raging fire. In death, she made no sound as she fell.

Dilaya started forward. Lan lunged, latching onto one of her legs. Pain spiked in her midriff, but she clung. Through stinging eyes, she looked up.

Dilaya had never shown anything but anger or contempt in front of Lan. Thus, it frightened Lan to see the terror, heartbreak, and helplessness written on the girl's face. She clutched

Falcon's Claw in her hands, remaining terribly still as she watched more and more Elantians appear out of the night. Their boots tread over her mother's body as they advanced.

Standing at the very front, Erascius looked up.

Straight at Lan.

35

Of the Thirty-Six Stratagems, retreat is best.

—General Yeshin Noro Dorgun of the
Jorshen Steel clan, Thirty-Sixth of the
Thirty-Six Stratagems, *Classic of War*

Lan stepped back, pressing against the mountain wall, but it was too late. The magician had seen her—and she knew, by some unknown instinct, that he would come for her to finish what he hadn't been able to twelve cycles ago.

Thunder cracked across the sky. When Lan looked down again, Erascius was gone.

Dilaya stood frozen at the edge of the cliffs, staring down at the place where her mother had fallen. Shock, grief, loss, heartbreak, and anger warred on her face. The Elantian army poured into the School of the White Pines like a pale tidal wave, consuming, destroying everything in their way: the open-air terraces, the pines, the rocks, and the school temples.

Dilaya turned to Lan. She closed her eye. Swallowed. And her expression cleared. Only a steel-like determination remained in that storm-gray eye when she opened it again. She slashed Falcon's Claw in the direction of the summit; her own sword, Wolf's Fang, hung at her hip in its scabbard. "What are you waiting for?" she snapped. "Keep going!"

The steps were slippery and treacherous; Lan and Tai moved slowly, their qì spent from their wounds. At last, they stepped onto flat ground.

The Peak of Heavenly Discussion howled with the fury of the storm. Dark clouds swirled overhead, looking close enough to touch. Icy rain pelted at their faces. The fall from up here was precipitous, the steep decline of crags and pines spiraling into gray mist below. By now, the other disciples should have gotten safely down, Lan reasoned. The masters would be lying in wait near the Chamber of Forgotten Practices, ready to defend and release the Azure Tiger should the Elantians come knocking.

"Ah, my little singer. I've found you at last."

The voice, the language, the words, sent sickening shards of ice through Lan's blood.

She turned. Standing at the top of the steps she had just climbed was the Winter Magician. Even in the rain, he looked as though he held an unworldly glow: pale armor and sky-blue cloak, face and hair white, metal encircling his wrists.

He smiled. "Did you truly think your little tricks could stop me?" He chuckled. "The others might think me strange for wishing to read what your, ah, civilization might deem literature . . . but I find myself sympathetic to some points. 'Know thy enemy, and know thyself, and thou shalt not know defeat.'"

Tai moved as though to step between the magician and Lan, but Dilaya cut him off.

"Lan, *go!*" she screamed. She lifted Falcon's Claw, thumb ring flashing as she opened her stance. In the lowlight, with her hair in two buns and her mother's sword in her hand, the ghost of Yeshin Noro Ulara might have showed her face again tonight within the blood and bone of her daughter. "Don't make it so that my mother gave her life for nothing!"

"Dilaya, don't," Lan shouted. "He's too strong!"

But nothing could have stopped Dilaya. The girl let out a roar, sounding all the pent-up fury and grief of her loss.

And she charged.

All Lan saw was a flash of metal, and Dilaya went crashing backward into Tai. Falcon's Claw spun from her hand, clattering to the ground.

Lan had seen Elantian metal magic before, yet it never failed to amaze her how powerful their spells were. When she'd watched Zen or the masters of the school fight, they'd needed to take time, draw qì, to weave them into functional Seals. This she understood, for there was a science and process to Hin practitioning.

Elantian magic might as well have been a gift from the gods. From *their* gods.

Lan stepped forward, positioning herself between Erascius and her friends.

"Run," she told them over her shoulder.

Then she drew her ocarina.

"Lan, no. *No*," Tai shouted. "If he takes you, it's over." But Lan saw blood darkening Dilaya's armor as Tai supported her.

"Touching," the magician said. He watched them with a strange expression: more curiosity than hostility. "More proof that your kind bear the intricacies of emotions, and that my colleagues assume wrongly. Pity that your civilization will never advance further than its current state." He held out a hand. "Come. Resistance is futile, little singer. Your mother might have evaded my search for the power she possessed with a clever little trick, but it will not happen again."

She understood, then, that this man had hunted her for twelve cycles not solely for the Demon Gods—but also as a personal vendetta. Sòng Méi's quick thinking had stopped the Elantians from capturing the Silver Dragon, and Erascius had viewed that as a personal failure. As being bested by a people he saw as no more than vermin.

He would not relent until he corrected his failure. Until he proved that Sòng Méi's outsmarting him had been just a fluke.

There was no winning, so long as both of them lived.

"No?" Erascius lowered his hand. "Did you really think you and your band of practitioners could best the great Elantian military with some little game of hide-and-seek?"

The fear that had been a steady undercurrent thrumming in Lan's body suddenly sharpened to a knife point.

"Yes, I almost believed it when I walked in, too," Erascius said slowly, "when I entered the emptied school. I thought you'd truly fled your nest and taken everything of value within. But from the moment the magic walls hiding the presence of your school collapsed, I sensed it." His lips curled, teeth shining white in the night. "It seems we have found not one, but *two* of your proverbial Demon Gods tonight."

Lan thought of the masters protecting the Chamber of Forgotten Practices, of the Demon God that lay Sealed within. Had Erascius discovered that the Azure Tiger, too, was here on this mountain?

"What a beautiful display of power you and that boy put on against our army, with the Black Tortoise and the Silver Dragon," Erascius continued, and Lan realized he did not know about the Azure Tiger. This brought her little comfort as the magician licked his lips, eyes flitting to her left wrist. "It seems your mother was even cleverer than I anticipated, hiding her Demon God within her surviving daughter. But her little games end tonight."

Lan lifted her ocarina to her lips—but before she could play, magic curled around her body, dragging her, like a puppet on a string, into Erascius's arms. She could smell the rust of his armor, feel the callouses on his hands as his fingers closed around her throat. They stood at the edge of the summit, ground giving way to plunging cliffs.

"You and I, we'll learn everything there is about this Demon God inside you," Erascius crooned. His eyes flashed as he glanced at Dilaya and Tai, huddled at the top of the summit. "But before that . . . it seems we have a few more guests than necessary tonight. Farewell." He raised his other hand.

Lan had the sudden image of Tai and Dilaya lying on the steps, their bleeding hearts clasped in the magician's hands like some prized trophies. Twelve cycles later, history was about to repeat itself.

No.

Lan locked her arms around the magician's throat. Erascius grunted, whatever spell he had been about to cast dissipating with his surprise.

And then, beneath their feet, the mountain began to rumble. Fissures split like veins in the ground. A pulse of qì erupted from somewhere inside the mountain, filled with the yīn that Lan had come to associate with demonic energies.

Inside her, the core of her Silver Dragon stirred. She sensed a head curiously lifted in the direction of the tsunami of qì, pale eyes the size of stars, of worlds, blinking in anticipation.

A gale of energies whipped up from a gaping chasm in the mountain, blue as the heart of a flame, pouring upward into the sky. Its glow lit up the night, and from within the layers of storm clouds, Lan saw a great shape moving.

The masters had unleashed the third Demon God. This could only mean one thing: that the Elantians had broken through their defenses, that the masters had fallen back on their last resort of releasing the Demon God rather than letting it fall into Elantian hands.

Lightning flashed; the entire sky seemed to be *moving*.

For a brief moment, Lan could make out a silhouette pacing through the clouds, teeth bared and maw unhinged in a roar of triumph. Then, it leaped and vanished.

Its residual light spilled onto Erascius's face as he stared at the sky: high brows and nose, blue eyes limned with the eerie, fading glow, pale hair slicked back with rain.

Lan pulled him to her, dug her heels into the edge of the mountain, and pushed off. The ground disappeared beneath them into a spiral of fog, rain, and darkness.

They fell.

She thought she heard Dilaya scream, Tai shouting after her, but the world had shifted into a blur of gray and the roar of wind. Hands, slippery with rain, wrestling with each other. Lan hooked her leg over Erascius's, pressing her face close to his so that, in the maelstrom all around them, *she* was one thing he would not forget before his death.

Holding tightly to her ocarina, she fumbled for her dagger with her other hand. Yet in the vertigo of their fall, it was impossible to get a good grip. The tip of That Which Cuts Stars pressed against Erascius's armor, and slid off.

Elantian metal—impenetrable.

Rushing up to meet them was the cold, hard ground, the promise of swift death. He had armor on and she, nothing—but just like practitioners, even an Elantian Royal Magician could not fly.

In the end, neither of them were gods.

Lan lifted her gaze to the man who had killed her mother and destroyed her kingdom. "Look at me," she hissed in their language, "so even when we pass into the next world, you'll not forget my face."

Erascius's expression was contorted in sheer fury.

Through the fog they tumbled, toward the forest of pines and evergreens beneath Skies' End.

Kingdom before life, Lan thought, *honor into death.* She would go into her death with her eyes wide open.

That was how she saw the night itself carve open before her to swallow her whole.

Arms made of shadows encircled her, pulling her back, slowing her fall. Her limbs were pried away from Erascius's. She heard the magician shout in fury, but the wind was roaring too loudly in her ears, and the streaks of black in her vision had taken on the shape of . . . flames. The jagged pines and sharp crags beneath her drew distant as her trajectory changed.

She was no longer falling. She was flying.

Steady hands cradled her head, turning her away from the ending that awaited Erascius.

Zen's face was pale, expressionless, like a porcelain figure etched in black and white. His eyes were downcast, perhaps closed, lashes and eyebrows a curved sweep of ink. Those dark flames wreathed his body, burning him with a fire Lan could not feel.

They soared, and even the rain parted to let them through. Overhead, a shadow the size of a mountain obscured the stars. Its qì enveloped her in an ocean. All too soon, they were falling, sinking slowly and impossibly. Lan was soaked through with rain, and the wind at her back should have been freezing—yet Zen's arms around her shielded her, lending her warmth.

She closed her eyes and let her cheek rest against his shoulder. He was alive, he was *alive*. She could not be sure whether it was boy or god in control—but from the way he held her, she wanted to think there was some form of the boy who had loved her inside after all.

They landed in the shadow of a cliff, softly. Zen knelt. His practitioner's robes rippled around him in an invisible breeze, and Lan felt the qì surrounding them retreat.

Lan drew her hand back from his side. His bleeding had slowed. There was a healing Seal on the wound where she had stabbed him—and she knew its owner.

"Shàn'jūn." Her voice cracked. "Is he alive?"

Zen gave no indication he heard her.

"Zen," Lan said. No response. She raised her voice, and it broke in her desperation. "Zen. ZEN."

She grabbed his face, hard enough so that her nails dug into his skin. Tipped his chin up to look at her.

His eyes were black. Blank. His face, unmoving, might have been the most beautiful statue wrought. Rain carved a trail down his cheeks. And yet, Lan suddenly noticed, the air was dry. This was the power of a god: to stop even the spin of clouds, the nature of the earth itself.

Those practitioners who borrowed the power of the Demon Gods paid the price with their bodies, minds, and souls.

"Stop it," Lan said suddenly, and struck him squarely on his face. "Zen, *stop it*." Again. "Stop channeling its power!" And again. Over and over, until her palms stung and her blows grew weak. Zen knelt without response, taking her blows without a single blink.

The demonic qì, filled with a terrifying amount of yīn and raw power, continued to pulse from him.

Tears traced down her cheeks. She had not saved Dé'zǐ. She had not saved Skies' End. She had not saved her friends.

Now, she could not save Zen.

Lan pressed her forehead to the crook of his neck. She could feel the bulge of his amulet digging painfully into her chest. The future that had been just within their reach shrank further across a vast, impossible chasm.

"You told me you wished for me to never be alone again." The words fell from her lips in broken, jagged pieces.

Zen's chest shifted as he drew in a sudden, rattling breath. His fingers tightened against her shoulders, pushing her back.

His eyes were clear.

He held her in place for a moment more. His gaze roved her face, from her chin to her lips to her eyes, as though committing every part of her to memory.

Then he let go and stood.

Qì blazed from Zen's body again, fanning out like wings in the night, and with a single leap, he was gone, slipping through her fingers like wind.

36

Those born with the Light in their veins
must shoulder the burden of bringing Light
to those without.

—*The Holy Book of Creation,*
First Scripture: Verse Nine

In the watery light before dawn, Lishabeth watched their army lay siege to the fortress that had been the last standing Hin school of practitioning. It was satisfying to see them break through the stone and walls of buildings that had eluded them for twelve long years.

In the end, resistance was futile. Nothing could best them, and certainly not a lesser kind. The tricks the Hin had used to distract them were pathetic, child's play before the might of the Elantian Empire.

This was the inevitability of the world. Mankind born with the touch of the Creator held the burden of enlightening those born inferior. And building a new world started with destroying remnants of the old.

Their soldiers, though, did not destroy without purpose. Previously, they had laid waste to hundreds of Hin cities as a necessary means to bring about control and respect. Now they picked apart the bones of this kingdom for all that would serve them and strengthen their rule.

There was much to be gained from the wreckage.

Lishabeth laid a hand on the single boulder that stood at the top of the steps—nine hundred ninety-nine of them, with no better means to ascend than to climb them one by one, a true sign of barbarian logic. Hin characters spilled down it in an indiscernible tangled mess, bearing no resemblance to the neat, horizontal lines of Elantian lettering. Her translator had told her the boulder held the name of this place: *School of the White Pines*. Her translator had also told her the ridiculous name this mountain bore—another indication of madness, to think that rivers could flow uphill and that the sky had an end.

Still, the seven Hin practitioners had put up an impressive fight, she had to admit. Perhaps Erascius had been right to read their books, to study their magic and desire their power.

It was in the early hours of the morning that two soldiers had come to her with news of a secret passageway hidden deep in the mountain. The practitioners had been scattered around the periphery of its entrance in an ambush that—Lishabeth had to admit—had almost succeeded. Erascius's troops had been whittled down sharply with the attacks of the two demonic practitioners. Three Elantian magicians had been killed.

In the end, though, their sheer numbers had won out. Even magic could not subdue the might of metal weapons and armor.

She prowled around the cavern mouth—the Chamber of Lost Practices, her translator had informed her—and kicked at a satchel of turtle shells with disgust. They lay strewn around the body of one of the Hin practitioners, his fingers splayed near them as he'd tried in vain to reach them before her soldiers had cut his arm off.

Someone had brought the tall swordswoman here as well—the first practitioner they'd met at the gates to this place. Her curved sabers lay in a pile by her lifeless and broken body.

And then there was that large, bearish Hin, with those metal spikes strapped to his knuckles. He'd been one of the most impressive fighters of the bunch, and she almost regretted not keeping him alive to interrogate him on what the Hin called their martial arts.

The sight of him, crumpled against the cavern mouth, gave Lishabeth a sliver of satisfaction.

Two of the magicians with her were holding up the body of a slim, bald practitioner. This was the one who wielded magic in a way that had impressed even Lishabeth.

She watched the two magicians in disgust as they opened and closed the dead monk's mouth and laughed.

"Leave it," she snapped. "These are not toys. They are the valuable property of the Elantian Empire and His Majesty the King."

The two magicians—a Bronze and a Copper, the lowest-ranking, with the ability to wield only a single metal—quickly set the body back.

Two military commanders appeared with a report on progress. They had demolished every pillar of the prayer hall on the first level and were moving on to the next: a medicinal chamber.

"Remember, leave no brick unturned," she told them. "I want every item of value taken for examination. And where is the rescue squad for Erascius?"

The bite of impatience in her tone sent the two commanders scurrying off.

Lishabeth nearly rolled her eyes. Reports had come that the Alloy had plunged off a cliff from the summit of the mountain; the scouts had found him in a pine forest, bloodied and barely breathing.

Soon enough, there came a shout. "Honorable Lady Lishabeth!"

Lishabeth turned to find a squad of soldiers running her way. Between them, they carried a pallet—on which lay the bloody, broken mess of armor and limbs that was Erascius.

"Is he alive?" Lishabeth asked skeptically.

"Yes, my lady."

"Very well." She turned her attention to the cavern. There was something down there, she was almost certain. She'd felt the faintest pulses of magic from within the darkness—magic reminiscent of what she'd sensed at the lake, watching the Hin boy eradicate an entire division of their army.

Lishabeth glanced at the soldiers. She took a torch from the nearest one; with a snap of her fingers, a spark danced from the band of firesteel on her wrist. The torch roared to life.

"With me," she said to the soldiers curtly, and turned and stepped into the cavern.

She walked, hating the damp, musky air in here, the way the jagged stone walls seemed steeped in Hin magic. It made her skin crawl. Made her feel watched.

At the end of the cavern, a set of steps opened up, carved into the mountain wall. Lishabeth began her descent. The air grew thicker, the taste of Hin magic more sickening with every step. Once or twice, Lishabeth could swear she saw a shadow shift out of the corner of her eyes, heard a whisper echo in the silence around her.

Minutes passed, then abruptly, the stairs stopped. The dim light of her torch illuminated a circular chamber made of stone. She stepped inside.

The chamber was empty, yet something had once lain here: something with magic so old and powerful that it had seeped into the stone. It wasn't until she'd stalked the perimeter of the chamber that she saw it.

Imprinted into the walls and ceilings of the room, glowing faintly blue, was the outline of a great tiger.

The Azure Tiger.

Shock rendered her speechless for a moment, followed by disbelief, then fury. So *this* was what the Hin practitioners had stayed behind to guard on this mountain; they must have set it free in the final moments of battle to keep it from the Elantian magicians.

Erascius had sought these mythical beings—said to be made solely of Hin magic energy—ardently for twelve long cycles, and they had yet again let one slip through their fingers. But the Alloy had been right about one thing in his fanaticism for Hin magic. Lishabeth had seen the power of two of the Demon Gods tonight, and it was unimaginable.

One loose, Lishabeth counted, *and three others.*

The second, in that boy whose magic rippled like black fire.

The third, in that girl who cast spells with her music.

And then, a fourth and final that they had not yet managed to find.

"Medic," she called. "Send the High General Erascius to a top care facility. If he dies, you and your squad will accompany him to the grave, you understand?"

The medic's salute came quickly.

"The moment he awakens, send for me," she continued, turning to survey the empty chamber again. The imprint of magic in the shape of a blue tiger shimmered faintly against the walls. "We will begin our search for the Azure Tiger."

37

The greatest strength lies in getting
back up after one falls down.

—*Kontencian Analects*
(Classic of Society), 7.1

Dawn broke in a bleached, watery white that spread across the sky. The rains had stopped. The earth held its silence. Raindrops clung to the pines like pearls and slid off the thin leaves of dragonscale ferns. A thin shroud of mist snaked around the trees in the forest.

Dilaya knelt on the wet soil, fingers pressed to it, brows furrowed as she examined it. "They came this way" was all she said before she straightened and marched on again, hand returning to grip Falcon's Claw, as though she were afraid the sword would disappear.

Lan followed, Tai behind her.

They'd traveled in near-total silence since the night, making quick progress with long leaps and bounds of the Light Arts. Not long after Zen left, Dilaya and Tai had found Lan at the bottom of the escape steps carved into the cliffs. Together, they'd attempted to track the other disciples. There were two groups: the youngest and most vulnerable, led by Master Nur and the Nameless Master, and the group of disciples who had been ordered to flee when the Elantians had breached the Boundary Seal. Lan had the impression that Dilaya was relentlessly driving them forward to keep herself preoccupied. To stop herself—and them—from absorbing the shock of what had just happened.

Behind Lan, Tai made a sudden noise. She turned to see him standing still, head hung, swaying slightly. "I cannot sense Shàn'jūn's soul," he mumbled, shaking his head. "I am a Spirit Summoner, and yet I cannot . . ."

And then, the Spirit Summoner knelt on the ground and wept.

Lan's heart ached as she watched him, unsure of what to do or how to comfort him. Tai had never been expressive in their interactions, following like a shadow to Shàn'jūn's light. To see him without the easy smile and trailing laughter of the Medicine disciple was a lonely sight.

Lan glanced ahead. Dilaya had not stopped. Instead, the girl slammed her fist against a tree trunk and swore. "Clever," she said. "They've used evasive techniques to flee, but that means *we* cannot track them, either. They started out westward, but now there is no telling where they went."

"Dilaya," Lan said. She'd followed the girl numbly at first as they'd put as much distance as possible between them and Skies' End. Now, though, the night had gone, and with the light of day, they needed to face the horrors they had been running from. "Can we just slow down and . . . and talk?"

"Talk," the other girl growled. "About what, Lan? The fact that we are all that is left to stand against an entire empire?"

Lan fought the urge to snap back. The weight of events hung heavy in her chest, as did the final words of their masters.

The final mission of the Order of Ten Thousand Flowers bequeathed to them. To her.

Find the balance. Destroy the Demon Gods.

She had spent the entire night pondering the events that had led them to this point: pieces of a puzzle her mother had left her, and the path it pointed to. The one she still needed to follow.

Māma had been part of a rebellion—one that served neither the clans nor the Imperial Court but the people. It had aimed to destroy the Demon Gods and thus remove the source of power that the ruling parties struggled over. Together with Dé'zǐ, she had found and bound two of them: one in herself, the other in Skies' End.

That left the Black Tortoise and the Crimson Phoenix. Yet the pieces had shifted—the Black Tortoise was bound to Zen, but the Azure Tiger had been set free. The sole aspect of the equation that had remained the same was the mystery of the Crimson Phoenix. The imperial family was said to have held on to it—but the imperial family was dead.

Lan's hand rested against the smooth clay surface of the ocarina at her hip. Wherever the remaining Demon Gods were, she would find them. She would find the Godslayer.

Then she would destroy them.

"Yes," she replied to Dilaya. "That's exactly what I want to talk about. *We* survived. *We* are alive, whether we wished it or not. *We* carry the legacy and hopes of everyone who died in that battle. And so it is our duty to fulfill them." She narrowed her eyes. "Or have you forgotten the famous words of your own ancestors?"

"You—" Dilaya's face was pale, her fingers tight around the hilt of her sword. "Don't you *dare* invoke my ancestors' names."

Lan's chest churned with a storm, one that made her want to scream, to lash out, to destroy this world and herself along with it.

She met Dilaya's gaze. "Don't run from the words they and our masters left us. We've all lost people in this battle." She sensed Tai straightening to look at her. "We lived so we could fight on for them. And to do that, we need a *plan*."

Dilaya was the first to turn away, breaking eye contact. "And what *plan* would you propose?" she said, but there was less of a bite to her tone.

Lan sat. Her legs shook from exertion, and every part of her felt like lying down in the silver grass and never getting up again.

She drew a deep breath. "To win this war, we must defeat two enemies," she said. "The Elantians—and ourselves. Our Demon Gods." She was aware of Tai leaning against the gnarled roots of an old ginkgo tree, listening. The Spirit Summoner's hair was in wet tangles over his face, showing only glimmers of his gold-rimmed eyes. "The grandmaster spoke to me of the history of the Demon Gods. He spoke of balance, and the fact that the Demon Gods' power was never meant to go unchecked." Her hands went to her belt, to That Which Cuts Stars. "These instruments are only temporary checks on that power, but they cannot break the cycle of power and chaos inflicted by the Demon Gods' presence. To do so, we must cut their tethers completely."

Dilaya's eyes narrowed. "So we need that instrument my mother mentioned."

Lan nodded. "What your mother was referring to is a weapon capable of splitting the core of qì that makes up a Demon God, so that they may return to the flow of this world and the next. The first shamans devised it as a way to check the power of any one practitioner who grew too greedy under the influence of a Demon God."

"The Godslayer," Tai said quietly. Both Lan and Dilaya

turned to him in surprise. He stared straight ahead. "The imperial family kept many secrets. This was one of them. But the advisors closest to them knew."

They had not only known. They had searched for it. Quietly, at the risk of their own lives.

"The grandmaster told me about it," Lan said. "Before . . . before his death, he told me that our most important task is to bring balance to this kingdom. Our history is fraught with tensions between warring clans, the rise and fall of dynasties and imperial family lines. And all this . . . for what? For power?" She plucked up a shoot of grass and lifted it to the brightening sky. "It's time someone did what was best for the people of this kingdom, and not for the throne."

"Didn't know you actually paid attention in class," Dilaya muttered.

"Here's my plan," Lan continued. "We find the Godslayer. We use the power of the Demon Gods to fight back against the Elantians. And then"—she leveled her gaze at Dilaya and Tai—"we destroy the Demon Gods' cores with the Godslayer. No matter the cost."

"That's absurd," Dilaya said.

"It isn't," Lan returned. "By the first principle of the Book of the Way, power is meant to be borrowed. Its nature is meant to be transient. The first scholar sages and practitioners used the term 'borrowed' because it is meant to be returned, never owned. This was how the earliest shamans and practitioners were able to wield the power of the Demon Gods. Yet when the Godslayer was lost, the imperial family gained immense power through the Crimson Phoenix—*and they held on to it.* Acquiring power for power's sake was never meant to be the Way."

She hesitated, then went on: "My mother told me that those

with power were meant to protect those without. I know how dangerous it is. But I also know we cannot sit aside and watch our people suffer like . . . like this." Lan met Dilaya and Tai's eyes. "I want to find the Godslayer. I want to use the power of my Demon God against the Elantians. And I want both of you to keep me in check should I ever"—a sharp exhale, a memory of a beautiful face with fathomless black eyes—"should I ever lose control."

There was silence for several moments as her words sank in.

"Well, what happens to you?" Dilaya asked, a strange tone to her voice. "If a Demon God is destroyed, what happens to its binder?"

It was a question Lan had pondered the entire night. She glanced over to Tai, but the Spirit Summoner's head was bowed, his face obscured by locks of his hair.

"I don't know," Lan said quietly. "I guess we'll have to find out."

"Another problem is, you said the Godslayer was kept by the imperial family," Dilaya said. "They're dead. So it must be gone."

"Not," Tai said suddenly from where he crouched beneath the ginkgo tree, his tall form awkwardly folded. Lan and Dilaya turned to stare at him. "Not gone."

"What do you mean?" Lan asked. She straightened, her attention focusing.

"The imperial family was paranoid," Tai replied. "The emperor and his heir were never in the same location. And they made sure to stow precious items in a hidden place no one but the inside counsel knew of."

Lan's mouth had suddenly gone dry.

"If there is anything left for us to find," Tai said, "it rests in

Shaklahira, the Forgotten City of the West. That is where the emperor built his hidden palace, safe from the world's eyes. That is where he stored his most sacred possessions."

Lan had heard stories of the plateaus and deserts of the West, and the myths that came with them. The Hin had whispered of demons hidden in the sand dunes, of immortal monks who cast Seals of trickery in their golden temple walls. *Shaklahira* was no Hin name; it was a name given by the clans that had once ruled over the Western plateaus.

But then the Hin had told such tales of the Northern Steppes, too; of the savage Xan shaman clans to be feared, of how they'd eaten human flesh and drunk the blood of children.

Prejudice, she realized, was not a concept the Elantians had brought with them.

She rose. "Then we journey westward. We find the God-slayer. We find the Azure Tiger and the Crimson Phoenix. We rally the forces of the Demon Gods against the Elantians. Then we destroy them all and rebuild this kingdom from the ground up."

Ahead, the pine forest opened to a terrain of mountains that jutted impossibly high into the sky. A sea of clouds stirred over the peaks, and as she watched, the sun climbed the sky. Slowly, arduously, yet inevitably, it blazed, a golden core whose light spilled like fire, hot, burning, crimson.

Lan had the impression that she stood at the edge of the world as she lifted her ocarina to her lips.

Let your mother's song guide you.

Closing her eyes, she began to play. She'd found this to be the best conduit to the monster that slept within her. This time, she crafted her song to awaken its qì.

In her mind's eye, the silver core of the Demon God began to expand. Its glow brightened as its body lengthened into a rippling mass of shimmering silver scales and knife-sharp claws. A single eye cracked open, pupil large enough to swallow her body whole. Its qì was steady, healed from the wound inflicted by That Which Cuts Stars.

Lan turned to face her Demon God.

"Silver Dragon of the East," she said. "Heed my call."

The Demon God gave a slow, long blink. *You have called upon my power many times before, Sòng Lián. You simply did not know. All those times you eluded death were neither coincidence nor a testament to your ability. It was my power that brought you this far.*

"And yet you need me," Lan replied. She did not blink, did not bend or yield. "Without me, you are nothing. Without me, you can only watch the comings and goings of this world from afar when you so long to partake in them."

The Dragon watched her almost lazily. *You know the terms of our bargain,* it said, but Lan cut it off.

"No," she said slowly. "I do not. I never made *any* bargain with you."

The Silver Dragon's eyes curved in what might have been a smile.

"I did not bind you," Lan continued. "My mother did. So it is *her* bargain, not mine. You will not have access to my mind, body, or soul."

Clever mortal.

"Tell me the terms of her bargain."

Very well. The Dragon reared back, baring row upon row of shiny white teeth. *Your mother promised me her soul, for the protection of your life. That is all.*

Lan's fingers stilled. The music fell silent. Yet the Demon God remained in her vision, an illusion borne of the currents of qì. Watching her.

"Her soul," Lan whispered, ice creeping through her veins. Zen had told her that the souls devoured by a demon would never find rest, never cross the River of Forgotten Death. *For a soul to remain tethered to this world after death . . . is worse than an eternity of suffering.*

She stood, her hands suddenly trembling. "Let her soul go."

I am afraid that isn't part of the bargain, the Dragon replied. *A bargain is irreversible, young mortal.*

"There is always a way," Lan replied. "Name your condition. Name your price."

Oh, but her soul is worth so many more, the Silver Dragon crooned, and Lan had the urge to sink her nails into its face and gouge its eyes out. *I'm afraid it isn't quite replaceable. Unless . . .* It drew so close in the blink of an eye that Lan flinched. *Perhaps her daughter's soul would do. Younger in age, and with just as much power.*

"Deal," Lan replied. "When I am done with you, you may have my soul in exchange for my mother's. But only my soul— not my mind, nor my body. And only once you have fulfilled your duty of protecting my life . . . and I am ready to give it up."

The Silver Dragon narrowed its eyes. *The bargain is made,* it said, and suddenly, it lunged forward. Lan was falling, the sky and mountain and trees disappearing in a tunnel of white. In her mind's eye, she saw the white core of the Silver Dragon pulse in her chest, tendrils of its qì wrapping around her left arm so that it was aglow. Pain seared across her wrist, and when she looked down, her mother's Seal was vanishing, each stroke fading like water drying in the sun. In its place, new words wrote themselves, carving each stroke like the pale slash of a scar.

Her truename, Sòng Lián, the characters interposed upon each other. A circle drawn to surround it, to complete the Seal. The new bargain.

The glow, the fire, the pain receded. Lan blinked in the pale morning light. The sounds of the forest—the chirp of birds and hum of insects and whisper of leaves—began to return in drips and drops. Behind her, Dilaya and Tai leaned against the trunk of a pine, in soft conversation. They knew nothing of the exchange that had just taken place—one carried out in Lan's mind.

Everything and nothing had changed.

Lan turned to find the Silver Dragon still watching her, that icy gaze flickering. Its tail flicked, and it reared up suddenly, drawing to its full height in her mind's eye. Uncoiled, it towered above the tallest mountains, rising until its horned head touched the sky and its great open maw might have swallowed the sun.

Those sky-blue eyes curved in the semblance of a smile.

Well then, Sòng Lián, what will we accomplish together?

Lan turned her gaze to the rising sun, toward the mountains where Skies' End stood. Where the bodies of eight masters lay, amidst the ruins of what had once been a pinnacle of her culture, her heritage.

The Sòng clan reached an agreement to serve the imperial family as advisors in an attempt to seek out the Godslayer, Dé'zǐ had said. *Your mother included.*

"We travel west to Shaklahira, the Forgotten City," Sòng Lián said to her Silver Dragon. "We hunt down the other Demon Gods to finish what my mother started.

"Then, together, we destroy the Elantian regime."

EPILOGUE

Yīn and yáng, good and evil, great and terrible,
kings and tyrants and heroes and villains. The tropes
in the classics of old are but a matter of perspective.
Really, they are two sides of the same coin. He who
lives to tell the tale decides which side to pick.

—Collection of apocryphal and banned
texts, unknown origin

As the night receded and day spread its light over the world, the fog in his mind began to clear, too. The Black Tortoise was said to draw its energy from darkness and night; he'd noticed that daytime suited him less the more he drew on the Demon God's power.

Zen came to a stop atop the peak of a mountain. It was remarkable, the power of a Demon God. A single night's travel had achieved what he might not have in two weeks. Beneath him, the landscape was already beginning to shift. A great river snaked past the mountains, separating the Central Plains from the Shǔ Basinlands: a strip of sunken territory filled with broadleaf forests that had once been home to several clans. A few weeks' travel to the east, Zen knew, rice paddies and tea farms zigzagged like a patched cloth as far as the eye could see.

But Zen was interested only in what lay beyond the Basinlands.

Carefully, he set down the boy in his arms. Aside from several scratches on his cheeks, Shàn'jūn was mostly unmarred from the battle. Zen had managed to shield him from most of the fire and explosions.

Zen took a strip of cloth from the Medicine disciple's satchel—still damp with rain—and began to wipe down the boy's hands. Blood did not suit Shàn'jūn as dirt marred clear riverwater.

Zen's gaze lingered on the boy's face—a face that had once constituted so much of his world. They had been best friends, once. Before Zen had lost control of his first demon and hurt Dilaya. From then on, Zen had made sure to distance himself from the people he cared for most.

He simply hadn't managed to do it when it came to Lan. Even as he was now, even with her choice to stand against his goal, he could not imagine a world without her in it. He recalled, in the thick fog he'd been lost in last night, an instinct tugging on his heart. It might have been a dream, but he thought he remembered his arms around her back, breathing in the scent of lilies that clung to her, her hair tickling his cheeks. And her voice, a silver light in his world before the darkness of his Demon God had consumed him again.

A streak of pain burned in his chest when he thought of her, so intense that he stopped what he was doing for a moment to clutch a hand to his heart, gritting his teeth. Inside him, he sensed a rising anger that belonged to the other owner of his body.

Body, mind, then soul, the echo of that voice hissed.

The sun was beginning to rise. The air warmed, lush with the scents of pine and soil and rain, and Zen found himself breathing deeply as he took a water gourd out of his storage pouch. Gently, he lifted Shàn'jūn's head and tipped the gourd to his lips.

Shàn'jūn coughed. His eyes fluttered open, the warm brown Zen always remembered. When they turned to him, they widened in fear. The Medicine disciple sat up, hoisting himself out of Zen's grasp. Zen, too, drew back.

"What happened?" Shàn'jūn asked. He looked around. "Where is everyone?"

Zen knew Shàn'jūn meant one person in particular: Chó Tài, the boy who held his heart. And Zen thought, briefly, of protecting Shàn'jūn from the truth, just as Shàn'jūn had done for him when they were children. But that was a time long gone.

"Skies' End has fallen," he said tonelessly. "I do not know the fates of the others."

All but for one.

Shàn'jūn's lips were colorless. He closed his eyes. "I see."

As pain carved its faint path across Shàn'jūn's face, Zen turned his face away. Once, he might have spoken words of kindness to a friend.

But the past was the past, shifting as constantly as the sands of the Emaran Desert, burying itself day after day.

Zen needed to look to the future.

"It is a new day," he said. "A new chance to continue to fight back. You have no obligation to me, Shàn'jūn"—the boy flinched when Zen spoke his name—"but where I am going, I could use an ally."

"And where would you be going?" the Medicine disciple whispered. His face was tilted in the direction of the rising sun. Its light spilled blood-red over his delicate features. Beneath the seam of his lashes, tears pearled, shimmering in the sunlight.

Something settled in the pit of Zen's stomach, and as the red sun arced over the horizon, it might have been another moment when the path of his life again cleaved into distinct paths.

No looking back. No regrets. Whatever he had briefly

thought possible with Lan would remain in that distant village on the mountains, suspended between dream and reality.

If you are not with me, then you are against me.

Xan Temurezen stood and turned his gaze north, to the land of his ancestors.

"Home," he replied.

ACKNOWLEDGMENTS

All my stories come from my heart, but this one encompasses more: it holds the living histories I have heard from my own grandparents growing up in China and the heritage that makes up so much of my identity. I am eternally grateful to the following people for finding in this book a tale worth sharing:

Krista Marino, Master of Plot and All Things Hip & Cool, who is not only the most brilliant editor and the most supportive champion of my words, but also a uniquely amazing person. Thank you for always finding the direction of the stories I want to tell and challenging me to make them the best version they can be.

Pete Knapp, Master of Plans and Excel Spreadsheets, who said yes from day one and who continues to guide me through the publishing industry and guide my stories to grow from seeds of ideas—thank you for working tirelessly to support my books. My thanks as well to Andrea Mai and Emily Sweet and the team at Park & Fine for ensuring that my stories continue to find homes overseas in so many countries I'd love to visit one day.

The team at Delacorte Press: Lydia Gregovic, Mini-Master of Editing and the most amazing assistant editor one could ask for, whose comment of "they're like legendary Pokémon!" rings in my head to this day when I try to explain the Demon Gods; Beverly Horowitz, our very own Grandmaster and fearless leader; Mary McCue, extraordinary Master of Publicity; Colleen Fellingham and Candice Giannetti, who I'm convinced have demon god–level copyediting superpowers; April Ward and Sija Hong for the gorgeous cover, as well as the rest of the RHCB team, including Tamar Schwartz, Ken Crossland, Judith Haut, and Barbara Marcus.

Vicky Leech and the team at HarperVoyager, as well as agent extraordinaire Claire Wilson, who have championed my words from the very start and who work tirelessly to ensure that these stories find their people across the pond—I am so fortunate to work with you.

Shelley Parker-Chan, Chloe Gong, Ayana Gray, Sara Raasch, Katherine Webber, June Hur, Rebecca Ross, and Francesca Flores, whose kind early words are treasured. Thank you for taking a chance on this little (chonky) book of mine.

My friends, the people I'd pick as fellow disciples at Skies' End, whose unwavering excitement for my books is a source of support and strength. In particular, my bestie, Crystal Wong, for loyally and staunchly following all the books I publish (and so much more, but mostly for enduring the grammatical mistakes in the uncopyedited version of this manuscript); Grace Li, for reading an even earlier terrible draft and still cheering me on; Katie Zhao and Francesca Flores, for reading multiple versions of the earliest, unsold openings and providing your invaluable feedback; and of course, my earliest critique partner, Cassy Klisch, for reading countless iterations of this book in both its unsold and sold forms and still having kind words about my writing after four whole books.

Mom and Dad Sin, for your encouragement and enthusiasm as I worked through 《射雕英雄传》, for Dad's impassioned history discussions, and for supporting my Cantonese and Traditional Chinese skills. Ryan and Sherry, for helping me survive backcountry in Heavenly and being the best housemates/siblings under the stewardship of Her Majesty Olive.

Arielle (Weetzy), the best sister and companion in life, who truly understands the diaspora identity—I'm so glad we have our hours of WeChat calls and shared jokes and discussions. Thank you for being there for me. The Growlithes will soon be reunited over their empire.

Clement, for being truly the best life partner I could ask for. Thank you for taking care of all the adulting when I needed to be on deadline, for cooking and cleaning, chauffeuring and giving me the Princess Treatment. Thank you for challenging me intellectually and for the countless impassioned discussions and debates that make for a more open mind. In our next life, remember to look for a weird little Millie girl with a love for stories.

姥姥，奶奶，爷爷，姥爷：我们今天的和平以及幸福是由你们打造出的一片天地。你们是历史上的勇士和我心目中真正的英雄。

妈妈爸爸：感谢你们从小培养了我们对文化和历史的爱，一直以来耐心仔细的给我传述你们丰富的历史知识。

ABOUT THE AUTHOR

Amélie Wen Zhao (赵雯) was born in Paris and grew up in Beijing, where she spent her days reenacting tales of legendary heroes, ancient kingdoms, and lost magic at her grandmother's courtyard house. She attended college in the United States and now resides in New York City, working as a finance professional by day and fantasy author by night. In her spare time, she loves to travel with her family in China, where she's determined to walk the rivers and lakes of old just like the practitioners in her novels do.

Amélie is the *New York Times* and *Sunday Times* bestselling author of the Song of the Last Kingdom duology and the Blood Heir trilogy.

ameliezhao.com